THE ALAN GARNER OMNIBUS

ELIDOR

"Each detail, ordinary or sinister, establishes atmosphere, background or character exactly. Elidor is a remarkable book: intelligent, rich and terrifying."

The Times Literary Supplement

THE WEIRDSTONE OF BRISINGAMEN

"Marvellously exciting . . . Alan Garner is at his best writing of night and dark water . . . the story is ferocious and deeply felt."

New Statesman

THE MOON OF GOMRATH

In this saga of wild magic Alan Garner achieves really powerful effects of beauty and terror that hold a reader well beyond the close."

The Listener

Also by Alan Garner

A Bag of Moonshine
Red Shift
The Owl Service

Other omnibus editions

Lynne Reid Banks
The Indian Trilogy
containing
The Indian in the Cupboard
Return of the Indian
The Secret of the Indian

P. L. Travers
The Mary Poppins Omnibus
containing
Mary Poppins
Mary Poppins Comes Back
Mary Poppins in Cherry Tree Lane

Cynthia Voigt
The Tillerman Saga
containing
Homecoming
Dicey's Song
A Solitary Blue

Alan Garner

ELIDOR

•

THE MOON
OF GOMRATH

•

THE WEIRDSTONE
OF BRISINGAMEN

Lions

An Imprint of HarperCollins*Publishers*

For J. H.

Elidor, The Weirdstone of Brisingamen
and *The Moon of Gomrath*
first published in Great Britain in 1965, 1960 and 1963
by William Collins Sons and Co. Ltd
This edition first published in 1994
by HarperCollins Children's Books,
a division of HarperCollins Publishers Ltd,
77-85 Fulham Palace Road,
Hammersmith, London W6 8JB

3 5 7 9 10 8 6 4 2

Text copyright © Alan Garner 1965, 1960 and 1963

The author asserts the moral right to be
identified as the author of these works.

Printed and bound in Great Britain
by HarperCollins Manufacturing Ltd, Glasgow

Elidor

Alan Garner
Illustrated by Charles Keeping

Contents

"Childe Rowland to the Dark Tower came – "

KING LEAR, *act iii, sc. 4*

1. Thursday's Child

"All right," said Nicholas. "You're fed up. So am I. But we're better off here than at home."

"It wouldn't be as cold as this," said David.

"That's what you say. Remember how it was last time we moved? Newspapers on the floor, and everyone sitting on packing cases. No thanks!"

"We're spent up," said David. "There isn't even enough for a cup of tea. So what are we going to do?"

"I don't know. Think of something."

They sat on the bench behind the statue of Watt. The sculptor had given him a stern face, but the pigeons had made him look as though he was just very sick of Manchester.

"We could go and ride one of the lifts in Lewis's again," said Helen.

"I've had enough of that," said Nicholas. "And anyway, they were watching us: we'd be chucked off."

"What about the escalators?"

"They're no fun in this crowd."

"Then let's go home," said David. "Hey, Roland, have you finished driving that map?"

Roland stood a few yards away, turning the handles of a street map. It was a tall machine of squares and wheels and lighted panels.

"It's smashing," he said. "Come and look. See

this roller? It's the street index: each one has its own letter and number. You can find any street in Manchester. It's easy. Watch."

Roland spun a wheel at the side of the map, and the index whirled round, a blur under the glass.

"There must be some pretty smooth gears inside," said Nicholas.

The blur began to flicker as the revolving drum lost speed. Roland pressed his finger on the glass.

"We'll find the one I'm pointing at when it stops," he said.

The drum turned slowly, and the names ticked by: and the drum stopped.

"Thursday Street," said Helen. "Mind your finger. 'Ten, seven L'."

"Ten will be the postal district," said Roland. "You turn the map wheel until number seven is level with these squares painted red on the glass, and the Thursday Street is in square L. There."

"I can't see it," said Nicholas.

The map square was full of small roads, some too short to hold the name even when it was abbreviated. But at last the children found a "Th. S." jumbled among the letters.

"Titchy, isn't it?" said David.

"It's such a funny name," said Roland. "Thursday Street. Shall we go and see what it's like?"

"What?"

"It's not far. We're in Piccadilly here, and

8

Thursday Street's off to the right up Oldham Road. It shouldn't be hard to find."

"I might have known you'd think of something daft," said Nicholas.

"But let's do it," said Helen. "Please, Nick. You and David'll only start scrapping if we don't. And when we've found it we'll go home: then nobody's bossed about."

"OK," said David. "That's all right by me."

"It's still daft," said Nicholas.

"Can you think of anything?"

"Oh, all right. This is your idea, Roland, so you take us. Can you find the way?"

"I think so. We'll go up Oldham Road for a bit, and then cut through the back streets."

They left Watt. David and Nicholas were better tempered now that there was something positive to be done.

"This is the turning we want," said Roland after a while. "Down this next alley."

"Mm," said Nicholas. "It looks a bit niffy to me."

The children had never been in the streets behind the shops. The change was abrupt.

"Phew!" said Helen. "All those fancy windows and posh carpets at the front, and it's a rubbish dump at the back!"

They were in an alley that ran between loading bays and store-houses lit by unshaded bulbs: the kerb was low and had a metal edge, and there was the smell of boxwood and rotten fruit. Fans pumped hot, stale air into the children's faces

9

through vents that were hung with feathers of dirt.

Beyond the alley they came to a warren of grimy streets, where old women stood in the doorways, wearing sacks for aprons, and men in carpet slippers sat on the steps. Dogs nosed among crumpled paper in the gutter; a rusty bicycle wheel lay on the cobbles. A group of boys at the corner talked to a girl whose hair was rolled in brightly coloured plastic curlers.

"I don't like this, Nick," said Helen. "Should we go back up the alley?"

"No. They'll think we're scared. Look as though we know where we're going – taking a short cut; something like that."

As the children walked past, all the eyes in the street watched them, without interest or hostility, but the children felt very uncomfortable, and walked close together. The girl on the corner laughed, but it could have been at something one of the boys had said.

They went on through the streets.

"Perhaps it's not a good idea," said Roland. "Shall we go home?"

"Are you lost?" said Nicholas.

"No, but—"

"Now what's all this?" said David.

Ahead of them the streets continued, but the houses were empty, and broken.

"That's queer," said Nicholas. "Come on: it looks as though Roland has something after all."

"Let's go back," said Roland.

"What, just when it's starting to be interesting? And isn't this the way to your Thursday Street?"

"Well – sort of – yes – I think so."

"Come on, then."

It was not one or two houses that were empty, but row after row and street after street. Grass grew in the cobbles everywhere, and in the cracks of the pavement. Doors hung awry. Nearly all the windows were boarded up, or jagged with glass. Only at a few were there any curtains, and these twitched as the children approached. But they saw nobody.

"Isn't it spooky?" said David. "You feel as if you ought to whisper. What if there was no one anywhere – even when we got back to Piccadilly?"

Helen looked through a window in one of the houses.

"This room's full of old dustbins!" she said.

"What's that chalked on the door?"

"*Leave post at Number Four.*"

"Number Four's empty, too."

"I shouldn't like to be here at night, would you?" said Helen.

"I keep feeling we're being watched," said Roland.

"It's not surprising," said David, "with all these windows."

"I've felt it ever since we were at the map in Piccadilly," said Roland, "and all the way up Oldham Road."

11

"Oh, come off it, Roland," said Nicholas. "You're always imagining things."

"Look there," said David. "They've started to bash the houses down. I wonder if we'll see a demolition gang working. They do it with a big iron ball, you know. They swing it from a crane."

Something had certainly hit the street they were in now, for only the fronts of the houses were standing, and the sky showed on the inside of windows, and staircases led up a patchwork gable end of wallpaper.

At the bottom of the row the children stopped. The streets continued, with cobbles and pavements and lamp posts – but there were no houses, just fields of rubble.

"Where's your Thursday Street now?" said Nicholas.

"There," said David.

He pointed to a salvaged nameplate that was balanced on a brickheap. "Thursday Street."

"You brought us straight here, anyway, Roland," said Nicholas. "The whole place has been flattened. It makes you think, doesn't it?"

"There's a demolition gang!" said Helen.

Alone and black in the middle of the wasteland stood a church. It was a plain Victorian building, with buttresses and lancet windows, a steep roof, but no spire. And beside it were a mechanical excavator and a lorry.

"I can't see anybody," said Roland.

"They'll be inside," said Nicholas. "Let's go and ask if we can watch."

The children set off along what had been Thursday Street. But as they reached the church even Nicholas found it hard to keep up his enthusiasm, for there was neither sound nor movement anywhere.

"We'd hear them if they were working, Nick. They've gone home."

David turned the iron handle on the door, and pushed. The church clanged as he rattled the heavy latch, but the door seemed to be locked.

"They wouldn't leave all this gear lying around," said Nicholas. "They may be having a tea-break or something."

"The lorry's engine's still warm," said Roland. "And there's a jacket in the cab."

"The tailboard's down, too. They've not finished loading all this wood yet."

"What is it?"

"Smashed up bits of pew and floorboards."

"Let's wait, then," said Nicholas. "Is there anything else?"

"No – yes, there is. There's a ball behind the front wheel."

"Fetch it out, and we'll have a game."

Roland pulled a white plastic football from under the lorry, and then he stopped.

"What's the matter?"

"Listen," said Roland. "Where's the music coming from?"

"What music? You're hearing things."

"No, listen, Nick. He's right."

A fiddle was being played. The notes were thin, and pitched high in a tune of sadness. Away from the children an old man stood alone on the corner of a street, under a broken lamp post. He was poorly dressed, and wore a crumpled hat.

"Why's he playing here?"

"Perhaps he's blind," said Helen. "Hadn't we

better tell him where he is? He probably thinks there are houses all round him."

"Blind people know things like that by echoes," said David. "Leave him alone: he may be practising. Oh, hurry up, Roland! We're waiting!"

Roland let go of the ball, and kicked it as it fell.

He was about twenty yards from the others, and he punted the ball to reach them on the first bounce: but instead it soared straight from his foot, up and over their heads so quickly that they could hardly follow it. And the ball was still gaining speed, and rising, when it crashed through the middle lancet of the west window of the church.

David whistled. "Bullseye, Roland! Do it again!"

"Shh!" said Helen.

"It doesn't matter. They're pulling the place down, aren't they?"

"I didn't kick it very hard," said Roland.

"Not much!"

"Never mind," said Helen, "I'll go and see if I can climb in."

"We'll all go," said David.

"No. Stay here in case the gang comes back," said Helen, and she disappeared round the corner of the church.

"Trust you to break a window," said Nicholas.

"I'm sorry, Nick: I didn't mean to. I just kicked the ball, and it seemed to fly by itself."

15

"It flew by itself," said Nicholas. "Here we go again!"

"But it did!" said Roland. "When I kicked the ball, the – the fiddle seemed to stick on a note. Didn't you hear it? It went right through my head. And it got worse and worse, all the time the ball was in the air, until the window broke. Didn't you hear the music?"

"No. And I don't now. And I don't see your fiddler, either. He's gone."

"There's something odd, though," said David. "It was only a plastic ball, but it's snapped the leading in the window."

"Oh, it was certainly a good kick from old Roland," said Nicholas. "And listen: your fiddler's at it again."

The music was faint, but although the tune was the same as before, it was now urgent, a wild dance; faster; higher; until the notes merged into one tone that slowly rose past the range of hearing. For a while the sound could still be felt. Then there was nothing.

"What's Helen doing?" said Nicholas. "Hasn't she found it yet?"

"She may not be able to climb in," said David. "I'll go and see."

"And tell her to hurry up," said Nicholas.

"OK."

Nicholas and Roland waited.

"I never knew there were places like this, did you, Nick?"

"I think it's what they call 'slum clearance',"

said Nicholas. "A lot of the houses were bombed in the war, you know, and those that weren't are being pulled down to make room for new flats. That'll be why all those streets were empty. They're the next for the chop."

"Where do all the people live while the flats are being built?" said Roland.

"I don't know. But have you noticed? If we'd carried on right across here, the next lot of houses aren't empty. Perhaps those people will move into the flats that are built here. Then that block of streets can be knocked down."

"There's the fiddle again!" said Roland. It was distant, as before, and fierce. "But I can't see the old man. Where is he?"

"What's the matter with you today, Roland? Stop dithering: he'll be somewhere around."

"Yes, but where? He was by the lamp post a second ago, and it's miles to the houses. We couldn't hear him and not see him."

"I'd rather know where Helen and David have got to," said Nicholas. "If they don't hurry up the gang'll be back before we've found the ball."

"Do you think they're all right—?"

"Of course they are. They're trying to have us on."

"They may be stuck, or locked in," said Roland.

"They'd have shouted," said Nicholas. "No: they're up to something. You wait here, in case they try to sneak out. I'm going to surprise them."

17

Roland sat down on a broken kitchen chair that was a part of the landscape. He was cold.

Then the music came again.

Roland jumped up, but there was no fiddler in sight, and he could not make out which direction the sound was coming from.

"Nick!"

The music faded.

"Nick! – Nick!"

The wasteland was bigger in the late afternoon light; the air quiet; and the houses seemed to be painted in the dusk. They were as alien as a coastline from the sea. A long way off, a woman pushed a pram.

"Nick!"

Roland picked his way over the rubble to the other side of the church, and here he found a door which sagged open on broken hinges: two floorboards were nailed across the doorway. Roland climbed through into a passage with several small rooms leading off it. Water trickled from a fractured pipe. There were the smells of soot and cat.

The rooms were empty except for the things that are always left behind. There were some mouldering Sunday school registers; a brass-bound Bible; a faded sepia photograph of the Whitsun procession of 1909; a copy of Kirton's Standard Temperance Reciter, Presented to John Beddowes by the Pendlebury Band of Hope, February 1888. There was a broken saucer. There was a jam jar furred green with long-dried water.

18

"Nick!"

Roland went through into the body of the church.

The floorboards and joists had been taken away, leaving the bare earth: everything movable had been ripped out down to the brick. The church was a cavern. Above Roland's head the three lancets of the west window glowed like orange candles against the fading light. The middle lancet, the tallest, was shattered, and the glass lay on the earth. But there was no ball.

"Nick! Helen! David! Where are you?"

The dusk hung like mist in the church.

Roland went back to the passage. At the end was a staircase. The banisters had been pulled out, but the steps remained.

"David! Nick! Come down: please don't hide! I don't like it!"

No one answered. Roland's footsteps thumped on the stairs. Two rooms opened off a landing at the top, and both were empty.

"Nick!"

The echo filled the church.

"Nick!"

Round, and round, his voice went, and through it came a noise. It was low and vibrant, like wind in a chimney. It grew louder, more taut, and the wall blurred, and the floor shook. The noise was in the fabric of the church: it pulsed with sound. Then he heard a heavy door open; and close; and the noise faded away. It was now too still in the church, and footsteps were moving over the rubble in the passage downstairs.

"Who's that?" said Roland.

The footsteps reached the stairs, and began to climb.

"Who's there?"

"Do not be afraid," said a voice.

"Who are you? What do you want?"

The footsteps were at the top of the stairs. A shadow fell across the landing.

"No!" cried Roland. "Don't come any nearer!"

The fiddler stood in the doorway.

"I shall not harm you. Take the end of my bow, and lead me. The stairs are dangerous."

He was bent, and thin; he limped; his voice was old; there looked to be no strength in him; and he was between Roland and the stairs. He stretched out his fiddle bow.

"Help me."

"All – all right."

Roland put his hand forward to take the bow, but as he was about to touch it a shock struck his finger tips, driving light through his forehead between the eyes. It was as though a shutter had been lifted in his mind, and in the moment before it dropped again he saw something; but it went so quickly that all he could hold was the shape of its emptiness.

"What did you see?'

"See? I didn't – see. I – through my fingers – See? Towers – like flame. A candle in darkness. A black wind."

"Lead me."

"Yes."

Roland went down the stairs, a step at a time, dazed but no longer frightened. The church was somehow remote from him now, and flat, like a piece of stage scenery. The only real things were the fiddler and his bow.

"I heard your music," said Roland. "Why were you playing so far away from people?"

"I was near you. Are you not people?" They had reached the bottom of the stairs, and were standing on the earth floor of the church. "Give me my bow."

"I can't stay," said Roland. But the old man put the fiddle to his shoulder. "I'm looking for my sister, and my two brothers—" The old man began to play. " – and I must find them before dark – " It was the wild dance. " – and we've a train to catch. What's that noise? – Please! – Stop! – It's hurting! – Please!—"

The air took up the fiddle's note. It was the sound Roland had heard upstairs, but now it was louder, building waves that jarred the church, and went through Roland's body until he felt that he was threaded on the sound.

" – Please! – "

"Now! Open the door!"

"I can't! It's locked!"

"Open it! There is little time!"

"But—!"

"Now!"

Roland stumbled to the door, grasped the iron

21

handle and pulled with all his weight. The door opened, and he ran out on to the cobbles of the street, head down, driven by the noise.

But he never reached the far pavement, for the cobbles were moving under him. He turned. The outline of the church rippled in the air, and vanished. He was standing among boulders on a sea shore, and the music died into the crash of breakers, and the long fall of surf.

2.   Cloth of Gold

A cliff rose above him, and at the top were the
ruins of a castle. He was confused by the noise
that had shaken the church, but the cold thrill
and burn of the spray woke him.

Roland walked along the shore. The cliff was
an islet separated from the mainland by a channel
of foam. High over his head a drawbridge spanned the gap, and there was no other way to cross.
He would have to climb, and climb soon, for even
as he tried to find the best place to start, a wave
dragged at the rocks. The tide was coming in.

The rocks sloped on one side, and were never
more than a hard scramble: but the height was
bad. The sound of the water dropped away and
there was no wind. The cliff thrust him outwards,
and each movement felt too violent for him to be
able to keep his balance, and the tendons in his
wrists were strained by the pressure of his grip
on every hold. He knew better than to look down,
but once he looked up, and the whole mass of
the castle toppled slowly towards him. After that,
he forced himself to see only what was within
reach of his hand.

The foundations of the castle were smooth
masonry curving to the vertical wall, but between
the foundations and the bed-rock there was a

ledge which Roland worked himself along until
he reached the drawbridge.

The chains that raised the bridge had been cut,
and he was able to use one of them to pull himself
up to the level of the gatehouse. The bridge itself
was undamaged, but the gatehouse had fallen in.
Roland climbed through into the courtyard.

There were four towers to the castle, one at
each corner of the broken walls, and in the middle
of the courtyard stood a massive keep. It was
high, with few windows.

"Hello!" Roland called.

There was no reply. Roland went through the
doorway of the keep into a great hall, cold and
dim, and spanned by beams. The floor was strewn
with dead roses, and the air heavy with their
decay.

An arch in one corner led to a spiral staircase. Here the light came through slits in the wall, and was so poor that for most of the time Roland had to grope his way in darkness.

The first room was an armoury, lined with racks, which held a few swords, pikes, and shields. It took up the whole width of the keep.

Roland drew a sword from one of the racks. The blade was sharp, and well greased. And that was another strange thing about the castle. Although it was a ruin, the scars were fresh. The tumbled stone was unweathered and all the windows held traces of glass.

He replaced the sword: it was too heavy to be of use.

Roland continued up the stairs to the next door. He opened it and looked into a barren room. Shreds of tapestry hung against the walls like skeletons of leaves, and there was one high window of three lancets . . . and the glass of the middle lancet was scattered on the floor . . . and in the hearth opposite the window lay a white plastic football.

Roland took the ball between his hands, just as he had pulled it from under the lorry. The pattern of stitches: the smear of oil and brick dust: it was the same.

He stared at the ball, and as he stared he heard a man singing. He could not hear the words, but the voice was young, and the tune filled Roland with a yearning that was both pain and gladness in one.

Where's it coming from? he thought. The next room up?

If only he could hear the words. Whoever was singing, he had to hear. But as he moved, the voice stopped.

"No," whispered Roland.

The ball dropped from his fingers, and for a long time he listened to its slow bounce – bounce – bounce – down – and round – until that was lost.

"He must be up there."

Roland started to climb. He came to the room above; the last room, for ahead the curve of the stairs grew brighter as it opened on to the top of the keep.

There was no one in the room. But under the window stood a low, white, marble table, and draped from one end, as though it had been jerked off, was a tapestry of cloth of gold.

Roland went to the table. It was quite plain, except for the shape of a sword cut deep in the stone. He picked up the golden tapestry and spread it over the table. It dropped with the folds of long, untouched use, and the impression of the sword was in the cloth. And as he stepped back Roland felt the castle tremble, and the voice drifted to him through the window, far away, but so clear that he caught broken snatches of the words.

"Fair is this land for all time . . .
Beneath snowfall of flowers . . .

"O, wait for me!" cried Roland. "Don't go!"

"A magic land, and full of song . . ."

He sprang up the steps and on to the battlement of the keep.

"Green Isle of the Shadow of the Stars."

All around sea and air mingled to a grey light, and the waves were silver darts on the water. From the drawbridge a road went up towards hills and into a forest that covered the lower slopes. On the road, moving away from the castle, Roland saw the fiddler.

3. Dead Loss

By the time Roland was clear of the gatehouse the fiddler had reached the trees. Roland hurried after him.

For a while the road passed charred stumps of buildings, and fields rank with nettle. Dust, or ash, kicked up under Roland's feet, muffling his walk and coating his body so aridly that his skin rasped. Flies whined round him, and crawled in his hair, and tried to settle on his lips. The sky was dull, yet there was a brittleness in the light that hurt. It was no longer wonder that led him, but dislike of being alone.

Even the singing had lost its enchantment. For now that the old man had appeared again Roland recognised where he had heard the song before: the fiddler had played it. And so what he had imagined to be the music of his dreams was only the jingle of a half-learned tune.

Although Roland wanted to catch up with the man, he wanted less and less to reach the forest. He could make out nothing sinister at first, apart from a general atmosphere of gloom and stillness, and it was not until he was close that he knew why this forest was different from all others. The trees were dead.

Roland looked back: but he had nowhere else to go, and at that distance the castle was a tortured crag. He clutched a handful of gravel and rubbed it against his cheek. It hurt. It was real. He was there. He had only himself.

Within the forest the road dwindled to a line of mud that strayed wherever there was ground to take it: fungus glowed in the twilight, and moss trailed like hair from the branches. There was the silence of death over everything: a silence that was more powerful for the noises it contained – the far off crash of trees, and the voices of cold things hidden in the fog that moved in ribbons where there was no wind. Oaks became black water at a touch.

Roland could not tell how long he had struggled, nor how far, when the trees thinned on to moorland below a skyline of rock. The forest held neither hours nor miles, and all that he had been able to do was to wade from one bog into the next, to climb over one rotting trunk to the next, and to hope for an end to the slime.

He walked a few shambling steps clear of the trees, and collapsed in the grass. He had lost the road, and he was alone.

When he opened his eyes Roland thought that he would never move again. The chill had seeped through his body and locked him to the ground.

He turned on to his side, and dragged himself to a sitting position, his head on his knees, too cold to shiver.

However long he had slept, nothing had

changed. The light was just the same, the sky unbroken.

He began to walk uphill towards the rocks. They were higher than he had thought – packed columns of granite, splintered by frost and ribbed by wind – but he scrambled amongst them up weathered gullies to the top.

Here Roland found himself on a broad ridge shelving away to a plain which stretched into the haze. Nothing showed. No villages; no houses; no light; no smoke. He was alone. Behind him the hill dropped to the forest, and he could see no end to that. The only proof that anyone had ever lived in this land was close by him, but it gave Roland little comfort.

A circle of standing stones crowned the hill. They were unworked and top heavy; three times bigger than a man and smooth as flint. They rose from the ground like clenched fists. Roland walked into the circle which was easily four hundred yards wide, and at the middle he stopped and gazed round him.

From the circle an avenue of stones marched along the ridge, and these were sharp blades of rock, as tall as the circle, but cruel and thin. They went straight to a round hill, a mile away.

If possible, the air was quieter here: so quiet that it was as if the silence lay in Roland. He avoided making any noise, for fear that the stillness would not be broken.

But how many stones were there in the circle? Roland started to count from the left of the

avenue – eighty-eight. Or did he miss one right
at the end? Try again – eighty-five, eighty-six,
eighty-seven. It may have been that his eyes were
tired, but the flick, flick, flick, flick, flick of the
pale shapes as he counted them was making the
stones in the corner of his vision seem to move –
eighty-four, eighty-five, eighty-six, eighty-seven,
eighty-eight, eighty-nine. Just once more. One,
two three, five, six – no. One, two, three, four,
five, six, seven – the air was like a deafness about
him.

Why am I bothering to count? thought Roland.

"You must stay until you have counted them
all."

Yes, I must – who said that? Roland caught himself looking over his shoulder.

I did. I must be cracked.

The silence was so complete that his thought had sounded as loud as a voice.

I'm getting out of this.

Roland sprinted across the circle, intent only on reaching the open hill-top, and he did not notice at first that he was running into the mouth of the avenue. He swerved aside towards a gap between the stones, but as he approached, the perspective seemed to alter, to become reversed, so that instead of growing broader the gap appeared to shrink. He could not pass through.

Roland changed direction, bewildered by his misjudgment of distance – and now he was going into the avenue again. Eighty-six. Eighty-seven. Eighty-eight. Eighty-nine. Ninety. Stones don't move. There's plenty of room between them.

He fixed his eyes on one gap, and made for it.

These huge boulders were spaced many times their own width apart, yet as Roland drew near, instinct told him that the gap was not wide enough. He kept jerking back, as though from an unseen obstacle in the dark. Stones – don't – move. There's plenty – of room. He could see that there was, but even in the last yard he flinched from the stones, and the moment of passing through tore a great, wordless cry from his throat.

"I'm imagining things," said Roland.

The abruptness with which his fear had left

him was frightening in itself, for the instant Roland crossed out of the circle the stones shrank in his mind to their true size.

"You could drive a bus between them!"

But even so, the air was less stifled now, and nothing moved when he counted. – Eighty-one. Again. – Eighty-one. No trouble at all.

Roland decided to follow the avenue to the hill. He would have a better view from there, and perhaps something would give direction to his wandering: but he kept well clear of the standing stones, walking below them on the ridge.

It soon became obvious that the hill, for all its mass, was not a part of the ridge but an artificial mound, completely circular, and flat-topped.

The avenue ended at a dry moat, or ditch, that went round the hill. Roland slithered into the ditch, ran across its broad floor, and started to climb. The turf was like glass under his shoes.

From the top of the mound there was one landmark, in front of him on the plain, far off.

A heap of rocks. No, thought Roland, it's towers – and walls: all broken. Another castle. That's not much use. What else?

Roland screwed up his eyes, and after a while he thought he could make out a form that was more substantial than the shifting clouds, away to his left.

A castle. Black. Dead loss. – There's got to be something.

But the view showed only desolation. Plain, ridge, forest, sea, all were spent. Even colour had been drained from the light, and Roland saw everything, his own flesh and clothes, in shades of grey, as if in a photograph.

Three castles.

He looked to his right. Here the dark was like thunder, impenetrable. Then – It came, and went, and came again.

It's a light. On a hill. Very faint – like – a – candle – dying – Towers! Golden towers!

Roland could never remember whether he saw it, or whether it was a picture in his mind, but as he strained to pierce the haze, his vision seemed to narrow and to draw the castle towards him. It shone as if the stones had soaked in light, as if stone could be amber. People were moving on the walls: metal glinted. Then clouds drifted over.

Roland was back on the hill-top, but that spark in the mist across the plain had driven away the exhaustion, the hopelessness. It was the voice outside the keep: it was a tear of the sun.

He started for the castle at once. He crabbed down, braking with his hands. It would be all right now. It would be all right: all right now. He landed in a heap at the bottom of the mound. Close by his head four fingers of a woollen glove stuck out of the turf.

Four fingers of a woollen glove pointing out of the mound, and the turf grew smooth between each finger, without a mark on it.

Roland crept his hand forward and – the glove was empty. He dragged a penknife out of his pocket and began to hack at the turf. The root mantle lay only two inches deep on white quartz, and he cut back and peeled the turf like matting. It came in a strip, a fibrous mould of the glove below, with four neat holes. The fingers and the cuff were free, but the thumb went straight into the quartz.

Roland looked for the name tape inside the cuff. He found it: Helen R. Watson.

He stabbed the turf, but he could find no break in the quartz, nothing that he could lift. The glove was fused into the rock. There were no cracks, no lesions. The thumb went into unflawed rock, and turf had covered it.

Roland jerked the glove, but he could not move it. He threw his weight against it in all directions, and the glove twisted and swung him to his knees. He wrestled, but the glove dragged him down in exhaustion, handcuffed to the mound.

He knelt, his head on his forearm, looking at the quartz: white; cold; hard; clean. – But a stain was growing over it, his shadow, blacker and blacker. The light was changing. And from the drift of the shadow Roland knew that the cause of the brightness was moving up close behind him.

4.   Malebron

It was a man with yellow hair. He wore a golden cloak, a golden shield on his arm. In his hand was a spear, and its head was like flame.

"Is there light in Gorias?" he said.

"Help me," said Roland. "The glove."

"Is there light?" said the man.

"The glove," said Roland. "Helen."

He could think of nothing, do nothing. His head rang with heartbeats, and the hill spun. He lay on the turf. And slowly a quietness grew, like sleep, and in the quietness he could hold the glove so that it was not a grappling hand. The man stood, unmoving, and the words came back to Roland as he had heard them before the table of the cloth of gold. The table: the castle: and the man – nothing else showed the colour of life in all this wasted land.

The man's face was slender, with high cheek-bones, and the locks of his hair swept backwards as if in a wind.

"Who are you?" whispered Roland.

"Malebron of Elidor."

"What's that?" said Roland.

"Is there light in Gorias?"

"I don't understand," said Roland.

The man began to climb the hill, but he was

36

lame. One foot dragged. He did not look to see whether Roland was following.

"Are you hurt?" said Roland.

"Wounds do not heal in Elidor."

"There was a fiddler," said Roland. "He'd got a bad leg. I had to help him—"

"Now that you have come," said Malebron, "I need not skulk, in beggar's rags again. Look." They were at the top of the mound. He pointed to the distant ruined keep.

"There is Findias, Castle of the South. And the forest, Mondrum: the fairest wood in Elidor."

"It was you?" said Roland. "You? Then you must have been watching me all the time! You just dumped me by the cliff – and left me – and what have you done with Helen? And David and Nick? What's happened?" shouted Roland.

But his voice had no power in the air, and Malebron waited, ignoring him, until Roland stopped.

"And Falias, and Murias," he said. "Castles of the West and of the North. There on the plain beneath."

He spoke the names of castle and wood as if they were precious things, not three black fangs and a swamp.

"But Gorias, in the east – what did you see?"

"I – saw a castle," said Roland. "It was all golden – and alive. Then I saw the glove. She—"

"You have known Mondrum, and those ravaged walls," said Malebron. "The grey land, the dead sky. Yet what you saw in Gorias once shone

37

throughout Elidor, from the Hazel of Fordruim, to the Hill of Usna. So we lived, and no strife between us. Now only in Gorias is there light."

"But where's—?" said Roland.

"The darkness grew," said Malebron. "It is always there. We did not watch, and the power of night closed on Elidor. We had so much of ease that we did not mark the signs – a crop blighted, a spring failed, a man killed. Then it was too late – war, and siege, and betrayal, and the dying of the light."

"Where's Helen?' said Roland.

Malebron was silent, then he said quietly, "A maimed king and a mumbling boy! Is it possible?"

"I don't know what you're talking about," said Roland. "Where's Helen? That's her glove, and the thumb's stuck in the rock."

"Gloves!" cried Malebron. "Look about you! I have endured, and killed, only in the belief that you would come. And you have come. But you will not speak to me of gloves! You will save this land! You will bring back light to Elidor!"

"Me?"

"There is no hope but you."

"Me," said Roland. "I'm no use. What could I do?"

"Nothing," said Malebron, "without me. And without you, I shall not live. Alone, we are lost: together, we shall bring the morning."

"All this," said Roland, "was like the golden castle – like you sang? The whole country?"

"All," said Malebron.

" – Me?"

"You."

Findias . . . Falias . . . Murias . . . Gorias. The Hazel of Fordruim . . . the Forest of Mondrum . . . the Hill of Usna. Men who walked like sunlight. Cloth of gold. Elidor. – Elidor.

Roland thought of the gravel against his cheek. This is true: now: I'm here. And only I can do it. He says so. He says I can bring it all back. Roland Watson, Fog Lane, Manchester 20. What about that? Now what about that!

"How do you know I can?" said Roland.

"I have watched you prove your strength," said Malebron. "Without that strength you would not have lived to stand here at the heart of the darkness."

"Here?" said Roland. "It's just a hill—"

"It is the Mound of Vandwy," said Malebron. "Night's dungeon in Elidor. It has tried to destroy you. If you had not been strong you would never have left the stone circle. But you were strong, and I had to watch you prove your strength."

"I don't see how a hill can do all this," said Roland. "You can't fight a hill."

"No," said Malebron. "We fight our own people. Darkness needs no shape. It uses. It possesses. This Mound and its stones are from an age long past, yet they were built for blood, and were supple to evil."

Roland felt cold and small on the hill.

"I've got to find the others first," he said.

"It is the same thing," said Malebron.

"No, but they'll be better than me: they're older. And I've got to find them, anyway."

"It is the same thing," said Malebron. "Listen. You have seen Elidor's four castles. Now each castle was built to guard a Treasure, and each Treasure holds the light of Elidor. They are the seeds of flame from which all this land was grown. But Findias and Falias and Murias are taken, and their Treasures lost.

"You are to save these Treasures. Only you can save them."

"Where are they?" said Roland. "And you said there were four Treasures: so where's the other?"

"I hold it," said Malebron. "The Spear of Ildana from Gorias. Three castles lie wasted: three Treasures are in the Mound. Gorias stands. You will go to Vandwy, and you will bring back light to Elidor."

5.   The Mound of Vandwy

They were at the foot of the Mound.

"How do we get in?" said Roland.

"Through the door."

"What door? It's just turf."

"That is why you are here," said Malebron. "The door is hidden, but you can find it."

"How?" said Roland.

"Make the door appear: think it: force it with your mind. The power you know fleetingly in your world is here as real as swords. We have nothing like it. Now close your eyes. Can you still see the Mound in your thought?"

"Yes."

"There is a door in the Mound," said Malebron. "A door."

"What kind of door?" said Roland.

"It does not matter. Any door. The door you know best. Think of the feel of it. The sound of it. A door. The door. The only door. It must come. Make it come."

Roland thought of the door at the new house. He saw the blisters in the paint, and the brass flap with "Letters" outlined in dry metal polish. He had been cleaning it only yesterday. It was a queer door to be stuck in the side of a hill.

"I can see it."

"Is it there? Is it firm? Could you touch it?" said Malebron.

"I think so,' said Roland.

"Then open your eyes. It is still there."

"No. It's just a hill."

"It is still there!" cried Malebron. "It is real! You have made it with your mind! Your mind is real! You can see the door!"

Roland shut his eyes again. The door had a brick porch, and there was a house leek growing on the stone roof. His eyes were so tightly closed that he began to see coloured lights floating behind his lids, and they were all shaped like the porch entrance. There was no need to think of it now – he could see nothing else but these minia-ture, drifting arches: and behind them all, unmoving, the true porch, square-cut, solid.

"The Mound must break! It cannot hide the door!"

"Yes," said Roland. "It's there. The door. It's real."

"Then look! Now!"

Roland opened his eyes, and he saw the frame of the porch stamped in the turf, ghostly on the black hill. And as he looked the frame quivered, and without really changing, became another door; pale as moonlight, grey as ashwood; low; a square, stone dolmen arch made of three slabs – two upright and a lintel. Below it was a step carved with spiral patterns that seemed to revolve without moving. Light spread from the doorway to Roland's feet.

"The door will be open as long as you hold it in your memory," said Malebron.

"Aren't you coming?" said Roland.

"No. That light is death in Elidor. It will not harm you, but be ready. We have word of something merciless here, though we do not know what it is."

Beyond the dolmen arch a straight and level passage went into the hill.

"You will wait?" said Roland.

"I shall wait."

"I'm frightened."

The idea of stepping into that narrow opening in the ground choked his breath. He would be hemmed in by rock, the walls leaned, and there would be earth piled over his head, earth on top of him, pressing him down, crushing him. The walls would crush him. He tasted clay in his mouth.

"I can't do it," he said. "I can't go in. Take me back. It's nothing to do with me. It's your world, and it's all dead."

"No!" said Malebron. "Gorias lives!"

But the golden castle was shrouded in Roland's mind, and its flames were too far away to warm the pallor of the Mound.

"Find someone else! Not me! It's nothing to do with me!"

"It is," said Malebron. "Our worlds are different, but they are linked in subtle ways, and the death of Elidor would not be without its echo in your world."

"I don't care! It's nothing to do with me!"

"It is," said Malebron. His voice was hard. "Your sister and your brothers are in the Mound."

Roland saw the glove lying, free now, below the grey spirals.

"They went, each in their turn," said Malebron. "Time is different here."

"What's happened to them?" said Roland.

"They have failed. But you are stronger than any of them."

"I'm not."

"Here, in Elidor, you are stronger."

"Do you mean that?" said Roland.

"Much stronger. You will go."

"Yes," said Roland. Now that there was no choice, the panic left him.

"Take this spear," said Malebron. "The last Treasure for the last chance. It will give comfort beyond the temper of its blade."

Roland held the spear. Fires moved deep in the metal, and its edge was a rainbow.

"What are the other Treasures?" said Roland.

"A sword, a cauldron, and a stone. Except these, trust nothing. And do not think twice to use the spear: for little you may meet in Vandwy can be good."

The light in the Mound was white and soft, and appeared to come from nowhere, which made the passage indistinct, without texture or shadows. There was nothing on which Roland could focus. Sometimes he felt that he was not moving; at others that he had travelled a long way – much further than was possible if he had gone straight into the Mound. When he looked back the doorway was lost in the thick light.

And he became aware of a sound; or rather the memory of a sound. It was not loud enough for him to hear, but he kept shaking his head to break the rhythm of five or six notes, many times repeated, like drops of water. And he noticed small changes in the fabric of the light, less than the shimmering of silk, but they were keeping time with this pure, soulless beauty that he could not hear.

And still the passage continued. Roland was worried now. Something was wrong, or he had lost all his sense of bearing.

"Where's the end?" he said aloud, more to hear

his voice than to ask a question. But then he stopped. As he had spoken the words there had been a brief flaw in the light, a blemish that was gone the moment it came.

"The end of the tunnel," said Roland.

It came again; a triangle of light, within the light; an arch.

"The – end – of – the – tunnel."

Roland hung on to the thought with all his will, and again the arch appeared, more fixed now.

"Stay – there."

He could breathe without its trembling, and as he moved it drew nearer, and was rooted in stone, and he came out into a round chamber shaped like a beehive.

"Helen!"

She was sitting with David and Nicholas on the floor of the chamber, and all three were staring upwards.

"Touch it, Roland," said Nicholas. "Listen to it."

"I want to hear it again," said David.

Their voices were without tone or feeling.

Roland looked up.

It was the most delicate, the most wonderful thing he had ever seen.

A thread hung from the dome, and at the end of it was a branch of apple blossom. The branch was silver, and the blossom of crystal. The veins in the leaves and petals were like spun mercury.

"It's beautiful!" said Roland.

"Touch the flowers, Roland."

46

"They make music when you touch them."

"The loveliest music."

"It's beautiful!" said Roland.

"Touch them."

"The flowers."

"Touch."

The branch was so still that it seemed to move under Roland's gaze, and there was a fragrance of sound all about him, a music that he could not quite hear, a fading harmony of petals.

"Touch them, Roland."

If he touched them they would sing, and the music would be unlocked from the crystal, and he would hear . . .

"Touch."

If he could reach them. The branch was coming nearer. If he stood on tiptoe, and stretched upwards with his spear.

But as Roland lifted the spear flecks of yellow light crackled round its head, and he pulled back his arm, tingling with shock.

"Touch the flowers, Roland."

"You touch them!" said Roland. "Why don't you? You can't!"

He looked up again. The branch was dropping towards him on its thread like a spider.

"I'll touch them!" cried Roland, and he swung the spear.

The air burst round him as discords of sound that crashed from wall to wall, and died away, and everything went black. Helen screamed, but it was Helen, and not a mindless voice.

"Where are you?" said Nicholas.

"There's a light," said David.

"It's my spear," said Roland. "I'll hold it up. Are you hurt?"

"We're OK," said Nicholas. They all made towards the spear, and crouched together round it. "What's happening?"

"We're in the hill," said Roland. "Don't you remember?"

"Hill?" said David. "Yes – the Treasures. And Malebron. But there was light—"

"I smashed the apple branch."

"An apple branch – I looked at it. I touched it – I – can't remember."

"The Treasures," said Roland. "Did you find the Treasures?"

"No."

"What's that?" said Helen. "Over there."

"And there," said David. "And on the other side, too."

They were growing used to the spear light, and they could just make out the wall of the rock chamber. There were four arches in it. One was black, the passage mouth: but the others shone faintly.

"I'll keep a look out here," said Roland. "You go and see what they are."

"This one's a small room," said Helen.

"So's this—"

Shadows flapped in the chamber like bats as the children stooped through the arches. And for a time all was silence. Roland stood alone by the entrance to the passage, holding the spear upright on the floor. Then the shadows began to move again, and towards him from the archways, slowly and without a word, the other three came and the darkness shrank before them.

In David's hand was a naked sword. The blade was like ice, and the hilt all jewels and fire.

Nicholas held a stone, golden, that seemed to be burning inside.

And Helen was carrying a bowl – a cauldron, with pearls about the rim. And as she walked, light splashed and ran through her fingers like water.

6 The Lay of the Starved Fool

"But how did we come through from the church to the castle?" said David.

The children sat by Malebron on the ridge, clear of the hill. The dolmen arch was drab with lichen, and the stones of the avenue heeled like twisted palings. Clouds still rolled upon the plain, but there was a quickening in the air, and Findias, Falias, and Murias were etched in gold, as though they stood before the dawn.

"It is not easy to cross from your world into this," said Malebron, "but there are places where they touch. The church, and the castle. They were battered by war, and now all the land around quakes with destruction. They have been shaken loose in their worlds."

"But the fiddle: and the noise – what was that?" said Roland.

"All things have their note, and will answer to it."

"You mean, like a wine glass ringing?"

"Yes," said Malebron. "And when the church answered, it existed in both places at once – the real church, and the echo of itself. Yet more than echo, for although you opened the door here, no door opened in your world."

"Can you always do this?" said Helen.

"No. The finding is chance. Wasteland and

boundaries: places that are neither one thing nor the other, neither here nor there – these are the gates of Elidor."

"Isn't it funny how things happen?" said Roland. "You know: if we hadn't gone into Manchester today, and if we hadn't played that game with the map, and if the demolition gang hadn't had a tea-break – all these little things happening at just the right time – all ending like this."

The children looked at the four Treasures, sword, stone, spear, and cauldron, glowing in their hands.

"One each," said David.

"Yes," said Malebron. And he took the fiddle and bow from under his cloak. They were slung on a cord across his shoulder, and there was also a pouch fastened to the cord. He opened it, and took out an oblong package, and began to unwrap layer after layer of very thin oiled cloth. He smoothed each layer, and put it aside, before peeling off the next.

It was an old book, made of vellum. The leaves were hard, glossy, and crimped with age. Malebron opened the book and held it out for the children to see.

Nothing that had yet happened to Roland compared with the shock of this moment.

He was looking at a page of script written in a language that was unknown to him. And at the top of the page was a picture of himself, with Helen, Nicholas, and David by his side. The figures were stiff and puppet-like, and everything was out of scale, but there was no mistaking them. They stood close together, cradling the Treasures in their arms, their heads tilted to one side, a blank expression on their faces, their toes pointing downwards. Next to them was a round hill with a dolmen in its side, and by it another figure, smaller than the children: Malebron. His arms were spread wide, and he held the fiddle in one hand and the bow in the other.

"We've even got the right Treasures," said Roland. For in the picture he had a spear; and David, the sword: Helen, the cauldron; Nicholas, the stone.

Malebron put his finger on the script, and read:

"And they shall come from the waves.
And the Glory of Elidor shall pass with them.
And the Darkness shall not fade.
Unless there is heard the Song of Findhorn.
Who walks in the High Places."

"But who wrote it?" said David. "And how did he know?"

"This book was written so long ago," said Malebron, "that we have only legend to tell us about it.

"The legend says that there was once a ploughboy in Elidor: an idiot, given to fits. But in his fit he spoke clearly, and was thought to prophesy. And he became so famous that he was taken into the king's household, where he swore that he

52

would starve among plenty, and so it happened: for he was locked in a pantry, and died there.

"However it was, his prophecies were written in this book, which is called *The Lay of the Starved Fool.*

"Through the years it has been read only for its nonsense. But when the prophecies started to be fulfilled, when the first darkness crept into Elidor, I saw in *The Lay of the Starved Fool* not nonsense, but the confused fragments of a dream: a dream that no sane man could bear to dream: a waking memory of what was to be.

"Since then I have worked to discover the truth hidden in the Lay, because, you see, I knew nothing of what I have just told you about our two worlds. I have had to find out that for myself by trial and thought, by asking all the time: how is this true, and if it is true, how can it be?

"Do you understand, then, what it was to find the note that made the church answer, to watch Findias dissolve, to step through into your world, and to see you whom I have known for so long running towards me across the broken land?"

"It's as if everything that's ever happened was leading up to this," said Roland. "You can't say how far back it started: everything working together: like cog wheels. When I spun the street names they had to stop at that one place—"

That had been the moment when he had felt that he was being watched.

"Remember, I have said the worlds are linked," said Malebron. "And what you have done here will be reflected in some way, at some time, in your world."

"Wait a minute," said Roland. "Will you read us that bit out of the book again?"

"And they shall come from the waves.
And the Glory of Elidor shall pass with them.
And the Darkness shall not fade.
Unless there is heard the Song of Findhorn.
Who walks in the High Places."

"We've been going on as though we've saved Elidor, and now that you've found the Treasures you'll be all right," said Roland. "But doesn't the book mean that things'll be worse, not better?"

"It does," said Malebron. "We are not at the end but at the beginning. But with the Treasures we may hold Gorias, and from there win back to the other castles. Then we shall have four islands in the darkness, and some of us may yet see Mondrum green."

"But who's Findhorn?" said Roland.

"No one knows," said Malebron. "There are desolate mountains far to the north, at the edge of the world, where in the old days it was thought that demons lived. I think these are the High Places. But Findhorn and the Song are forgotten, and now that the Treasures are safe I can go to look for him there. I have proved the wisdom of the Starved Fool now, and that gives me the courage to prove it once again."

They climbed down from the ridge into Mondrum, and made their way back towards Findias
through the slime. The journey seemed much
shorter to Roland than when he had been alone,
or perhaps it was because Malebron knew where
he was going and led them straight there.

The Treasures surrounded them in a field of
colour which moved with them, so that as they
came to a tree it would change from grey, to
purple, to the livid colours of decay, and then
sink back into the dead light when they had
passed by.

They saw nothing of Findias until they reached
the open ground below the forest half a mile from
the castle, and at this distance the golden outline
did not show. But the ruins were clear in detail,
as though the children and Malebron were looking
at them through a hole in a dirty window pane.

When they were nearly at the drawbridge, Roland turned for a last sight of Elidor.

"Malebron? Something's happened – on the ridge."

They could just see the ridge above the trees, and the squat cone of Vandwy, with the avenue leading from it. The standing stones of the avenue, which they had left in disorder, were now upright, sharp, harsh, and menacing. And as they watched, a dark beam like a black searchlight leapt from the Mound.

"Run!" shouted Malebron. "I have been too proud, and Vandwy has recovered from its wound!"

The beam circled, sweeping land and sky, and before the children reached the drawbridge it caught them, and locked on to them beyond escape.

The air was as thick as water. It dragged about their limbs and clogged their lungs, and was shot through with strands of blackness which their hands could not feel or push aside, but each strand plucked at their minds like wire as they blundered through.

"Think of suns! – Meadows, and bright flowers! – Think! – Do not let night into your minds!"

Malebron walked beside the children, urging, driving them on. He moved freely, untouched by the dark.

"Your strength is your weakness now! Vandwy has sent Fear to be given shape by you! These shapes will be real, as the door was real! Keep them out!"

But the fear was in the children: a numbness that sapped the will. And soon they began to hear in the forest the pursuit that they themselves were making.

Slowly they crossed the bridge. But those few yards were longer than the whole journey. The children's vision was so blighted by the strands that they saw the bridge shoot out like a pier over the sea, and the castle was a speck where the lines of the planks converged in the distance.

The bridge became higher and narrower: and then it was tilted to the left: and then to the right: and then upwards, so that they could not walk: and then down, so that they were on a wooden precipice and dared not move: and then the bridge swung completely over, and they felt that they would drop off into the sky. And all the time Malebron fought for their minds.

"The – bridge – is – safe! You – will – not – stop! Think! Move!"

They reached the gatehouse. And as they laboured through to the courtyard there bounded from the forest something that was on two legs but was not a man, and behind it the trees ran howling.

The children fell into the courtyard, and the grip of Vandwy slackened.

"Take the Treasures!" said Malebron.

"No! You need them!"

"We are trapped. Take them to your world and

guard them there. They will be safe. And while they are free their light will not die in Elidor, and we may live."

"Come with us!" said Helen.

"I cannot. I must seal the gate. Nothing must follow you through the keep: stand well clear on the other side."

"What shall we do with the Treasures?" said Roland.

"No more than guard them. And if we fail here, the light of Elidor may live on, and kindle again in other worlds."

Malebron put the fiddle to his shoulder and began to play: faster and faster, until the notes merged and drove through the children, cutting the darkness from their minds, snapping the threads of Vandwy with the pain. The keep picked up the fiddle's note, and the surface of the stone lost its hardness, rippled like skin.

"Now go!" cried Malebron. "Go!"

The ramparts by the gatehouse bristled with silhouettes.

"Malebron!"

"Go!"

The children staggered through the doorway of the keep. The ground shook so much that they could hardly stand: their teeth burred in their heads, the walls were a fog of sound, plaster came like snow from the ceiling. A gap appeared in front of them, and they pulled and pushed each other towards it and between two floorboards that were nailed across the gap, and ran, choking, out on to the wasteland of Thursday Street.

The fiddle note held. Each brick in the derelict church was grinding against the next. Mortar dust spouted from the joints.

"Look out!" Nicholas yelled. "It's going!"

All the sounds rose together to one unbearable pitch, the wall bellied outwards, and the church fell in a groaning roar of destruction.

"Roland! The Treasures! What's happened to them?"

But Roland was gazing at the tangled ruin of the church, and could not answer.

"It's all right," he said at last. "It's all right. We'll be able to hide them now."

The children stood before the rubble as the dust cleared. It was late afternoon. A long way off, a woman pushed a pram.

In his hand Roland held a length of iron railing; Nicholas a keystone from the church. David had two splintered laths nailed together for a sword; and Helen an old, cracked cup, with a beaded pattern moulded on the rim.

7   Corporation Property

"We couldn't have looked after them as they were," said Roland.

The children became aware of voices shouting. Several men had come out of a corner shop in a street on the edge of the wasteland and were running towards the church. But no one moved: it seemed to have nothing to do with them.

"I'll have yez! I'll have yez this time!"

The men were white with fear. The first one to arrive grabbed Nicholas by the back of his collar and swung him round.

"Was there any of yez in there?" he shouted.

"Let go," said Nicholas.

"Yez'll answer me! Was there any of yez in there?"

"Righto, Paddy, that's enough," said the biggest of the men. He wore a leather belt covered with regimental badges, and appeared to be the foreman.

"Now then," he said, speaking to all the children. "I want a straight answer. Was there any of you in there when she dropped?"

"No," said Nicholas.

The foreman sagged with relief, and the colour rose in his face. Now he could afford to be angry.

"I've given you kids round here warning time and again," he said, "but you'll not learn, will you? You'll not be satisfied till one of you's killed. Well, it's going to stop. Your parents can't manage you, seemingly, so we'll see what the police can do."

"We've never been here—" said Nicholas.

"Now then," said the foreman. "We want none of your lip."

"Eh, guv'nor," said the Irishman holding Nicholas. "Do you not think a good thumpin' might be better?"

"No, Pad, you can't go on treating kids soft. Round here they think kindness is weakness. And something's got to be done. You know how it'd be the first time one of 'em was hurt, don't you? 'Gross Negligence on the Firm's Part': that's what. 'Insufficient Precautions', and the like. And no mention of all we have to contend with. No mention of 'Malicious Damage Endangering Safety of Staff': 'Damage to Tools and Plant': 'Theft'. Eh, Jack: just have a look round while we're at it."

"Righ'," said a boy wearing a tartan cap, jeans, and mud-covered, pointed shoes. He started to check the tools.

"No: it's all 'ere – wait on! Someone's pinched me football!"

"Well?" said the foreman.

"I'm sorry," said Roland. "It's – it's in there."

"Indeed," said the foreman.

"I kicked it through the window, and we went in to fetch it."

"Six bob it cost!" said Jack.

"We haven't any money on us," said David, "but we'll send you a postal order."

"Oh ay?"

"An example, that's what's going to be made of you," said the foreman. "An example. I suppose you know nothing about the lead that went missing from the roof last night, do you?"

"Of course not," said Nicholas.

" 'Of course not.' Ay, well, we'll see, shan't we? Now drop those bits of scrap you've got in your hands, and come along. It's the police station for you. Keep fast of that biggest, Pad: he'll be the ringleader."

"There's no need," said Nicholas. "We'll go with you. It's all a mistake."

"It is that," said the foreman. "Now drop that stuff."

"No," said Roland.

"You what?"

"We've not stolen them. They're ours."

"Now look: I'm not here to argue," said the foreman. "Put those things back where you found them."

"They're not yours," said Roland.

" 'Unlawful Possession of Corporation Property'," said the foreman, "as well as 'Trespass' and 'Wilful Damage'. It's not funny, me lad."

There were five men, and Jack. They were strong, but heavily built. Jack was the only one who looked capable of any speed.

"Remember what happened to the apple branch?" Roland said to Nicholas.

"Er – yes," said Nicholas.

"Are you sure?"

"Yes."

"Right!" said Roland, and he swung the length of railing up against the Irishman's elbow, down and sideways across Jack's shins, and ran.

Through the din that broke out behind him he could hear both the clump of wellingtons and much lighter footsteps, but soon the wellingtons faded.

"Keep going!" shouted Helen. "We're all here! And the Treasures!"

The children stopped when they reached the first of the streets. Only three of the men had made any effort to catch them but they had given up and were now going back to join the foreman, who was waving his arms at the Irishman and Jack.

"I hope they're all right," said Roland. "But there wasn't anything else to do, was there? I mean, we couldn't tell them, could we?"

"If you've any sense," said Nicholas, "you won't tell anybody; ever; unless you want locking up."

"Do you think they really will fetch the police?" said Helen.

"I doubt it," said Nicholas. "Not now they've lost us. But let's be moving – just in case."

It was dark when the children reached Oldham Road, and rushing crowds filled the pavement.

"It's lucky we want to go this way!" shouted Helen, and vanished behind a wedge of men all

wearing bowler hats. She reappeared, her cup held at chin height to avoid being smashed.

David and Roland had less trouble with their laths and railing, apart from a few angry grunts from people who came too near. But Nicholas was struggling with his keystone, shifting it from one hip to the other, and he was grey about the mouth.

The pressure of the crowd eased as they came to the station forecourt.

"There's a train in ten minutes," said Helen.

The crowd split at the barriers. Nicholas wobbled on one leg, balancing the stone on his knee, while he felt in his pocket for the tickets.

"Here, David," he said. "You take them."

David handed the tickets to the ticket collector, who was so busy with his punch that he never looked up – until he noticed David.

"What's all this here?" he said.

"They're our tickets," said David.

"Ay, happen they are. But you don't think you're fit to travel on a train in that state, do you?"

The children looked at themselves.

They were all coated with slime from the forest of Mondrum and on that was laid plaster, soot, and brick dust from the church.

"We'll stand," said David.

"You will not," said the ticket collector.

"But we've paid."

A restless queue was building up: people were muttering, stamping, looking at watches.

"Clear off," said the ticket collector. "And take your junk with you. I don't know how you've the cheek to try it on. There's a copper by the book stall – must I give him a shout? Eh? I thought not. Go on. Off with you."

The children slipped out of the queue and round the corner from the policeman.

"What do we do now?" said Helen.

"Move along to platform eleven," said Roland. "We can cross on to our platform over the bridge at the far end."

"But no one'll let us through," said Helen.

"No one'll see us," said Roland. "It's the platform where parcel vans go, and there's an entrance for them next to the barrier."

"We'll still be seen."

"They're too busy to be watching all that closely. Next time one of those trolleys comes along pulling mail bags walk beside it, and keep your heads down, and then once we're through, nip over into the crowd."

"There," said Roland a few minutes later. "It was easy."

"You've some nerve," said Nicholas. "Where's it come from all of a sudden?"

"You were pretty glad of it this afternoon," said David.

"Have you thought what'll be said at home?"

"Gosh, no," said Nicholas. "That's serious, isn't it? I tell you what: you and I'll wash in one lavatory on the train, and Helen and Roland in the other. There are always two in the last coach."

"OK. But we'll only have about ten minutes."

When the train arrived, the children jumped into the rear coach and locked themselves in the lavatories.

"There's no plug for the wash basin," said Helen.

"Screw up a paper towel and shove it in," said Roland.

There was very little soap. Helen and Roland washed themselves frantically, using the towels to scrape away the mud. But although the paper was harsh to the skin, it had no strength. It rolled into shreds, covering everything with pellets of sogginess.

The electric train picked up speed, and the children were thrown about between the narrow walls. They collided with each other and the wash basin, which slopped water over them at every jolt. There was hardly room to share the mirror, and they were quickly kneedeep in wet paper towels.

In the ten minutes all they managed was to accentuate their wildness. The few patches of skin threw into contrast the mud and plaster.

The children inspected each other under the lamp at the bottom of the station approach. Their house was only fifty yards up the road.

"We've made things worse," said David. "We need about six baths each."

"Do you think we could all sneak into the bathroom without being nabbed?" said Roland.

"We'll try," said Nicholas. "But there's going to be a row anyway. We can't hide our clothes."

"Let's hope the key's not been taken out of the shed yet," said David.

A spare key to the house was always kept on a ledge above the door inside the coal shed. It was still there. The children crept round to the sitting-room window and listened.

"The TV's on," said David. "One of Dad's Westerns."

"Good: plenty of noise."

"After me," said Nicholas. "And I'll murder anyone who coughs."

He slid the key into the lock, and waited until there was the cover of gunfire before opening the door. A damp, carbolic air met them in the hall. Nicholas felt for the light switch and eased it on.

The hall floor and the stairs were carpeted with newspapers. All the furniture was gone, and the shade from the light.

Nicholas closed the door, and led the way. They were just on the stairs when they heard their mother call, "Is that you, Nick?"

"It was the switch!" said David. "It always makes the picture jump."

"Keep moving," said Nicholas: then, louder, "Yes: we're back!"

But it was hopeless. The sitting-room door opened, and there stood Mrs Watson, and behind her a thousand redskins bit the dust.

8   The Deep End

Nicholas ought to have had more sense at his age. What was he thinking of to let everyone get into this state? Didn't he realise that all the clothes were packed? Their mother had quite enough to do without this. Couldn't they be trusted to behave properly when they were out by themselves? And surely there were better ways of spending the time than acting like hooligans in the slums.

The television set was in a bare room among the packing cases. Its own cardboard box was waiting open next to it on the floor. The sound had been turned down at the beginning of the row, which was accompanied as a result by a silent counterpoint of gun battle and cavalry charge. And although the picture was badly distorted, even in the worst moments of the telling off everybody's eyes kept sliding round to the screen.

"And what's that rubbish?" said Mrs Watson.

"Some – things we found," said Roland.

"And you brought them back? Good heavens, child, what will you do next? Take them outside at once: you don't know where they've been."

The children escaped to the bathroom while their mother unpacked the cases to find them a change of clothes.

Cleaning was a lot easier than it had been on
the train, but the lime in the plaster set hard
when they tried to wash their hair.

"Where've you put the Treasures?" said
Helen.

"In the shed," said Roland.

"How are we going to stow them in the furniture van tomorrow?"

"We're not."

"But we can't leave them!"

"Of course not," said Roland. "But the house

70

is going to be empty for at least a month, so we'll hide the Treasures here, and when we've found somewhere safe for them at the new house we'll come back and collect them."

"Where'll we hide them, though?" said Helen.

"Through the hatch in our room," said Nicholas.

"Yes," said David. "No one'll look there."

In the wall of the boys' attic there was a door about a foot square, leading into the space between the ceiling joists and the roof. It was too small for an adult to climb through without having a good reason.

"And when Mum's cooled down, perhaps we can tell her about it: or at least ask her to let us keep the Treasures in the house," said Roland. "They'll be all right if we clean them up a bit."

"I've not much hope of that," said Nicholas. "You can't blame Mum for going off at the deep end tonight, and she won't forget it in a hurry. And what are you going to tell her? And who's going to try? If we say, 'Mum, we went into an old church and came out in a different place on the other side and these are really four valuable Treasures,' what'll happen? You know how hot she is on the truth."

"But it is the truth," said Roland.

"And would you believe it if it hadn't happened to you?"

"Yes – if it was somebody I trusted," said Roland.

71

"Well, perhaps you would," said Nicholas. "But normal people wouldn't."

"Could we say they're for something one of us is doing at school?" said Helen.

"But it wouldn't be the truth."

"Oh, Nick!"

"Have you ever tried lying to Mum?" said Nicholas.

"Then what can we do?"

"I don't know," said Nicholas. "We've got to manage it by ourselves. No one can help us."

Among the confusion of the next morning it was easy for the children to hide the Treasures behind the bedroom wall. Roland squeezed through the hatch and laid them out of sight between two joists.

At last the tailboard of the furniture van was fastened, and the children went on ahead in the car with their parents.

The new house was only about six miles away. Mrs Watson spoke of it as a country cottage, which it may have been a hundred years earlier, but now it stood in a suburban road, and its front door, with the porch, opened on to the footpath.

It was a brick cottage with four rooms and a lean-to kitchen, but Mr Watson had had a bathroom and an extra bedroom built over the kitchen. The old blackleaded grates had been scraped and replaced with yellow tiles, except for the one in the sitting room, which Mr Watson had made himself in rustic brick.

Mrs Watson had searched antique shops for

horse brasses to hang on the walls, and she had also found three samplers, two coach lamps, and a framed map of the county, hand coloured, and dated 1622.

The cottage was convenient for the station, so that Mr Watson could travel to work in Manchester, yet being in an outer suburb there were fields half a mile away. It was a much smaller house than the one they were leaving, but Mrs Watson said that it was worth the sacrifice for the children to be able to grow up in the country.

The first thing Roland saw when the car turned into the road was the porch.

For an instant he felt that something would happen. The porch was out of place here now: it belonged to Elidor. His vision of it against the Mound had been so clear that the actual porch was a faded likeness by comparison. But suppose when they opened the door there was a passage beyond it, lit by a dead light . . .

"Here we are," said Mr Watson. "Welcome home, everybody."

There were newspapers on the floor, but the carbolic smell was going.

They set up base next to the kitchen – in the dining room, according to Mrs Watson, but the children called it the middle room. The stairs went up one wall, and under them was the larder.

The furniture was unloaded into the sitting room, which opened by way of the porch straight on to the footpath, without any hall.

By evening it was possible to eat off a table, to watch television, and to sleep.

The children went to bed early. The stairs came through the floor of the boys' room, so they all sat in Helen's, which, being newly built, had a well-fitting door.

"We'd better decide what we can do to keep the Treasures safe," said Roland.

"Drop them in a lead box and bury them," said Nicholas.

"We must be able to put our hands on them quickly," said David, "in case Malebron wants them back at any time."

"I don't think he will," said Nicholas. "We may as well face it at the start. You saw what came out of the forest, and what were climbing over the battlements. He didn't stand a chance."

"I thought that at first," said Roland. "But I think there was one chance. Didn't you notice something about Malebron right at the end? He wasn't really frightened: he was more excited – as if the important thing was to send us through the door."

"That's just it," said Helen. "He didn't care what happened to him as long as the Treasures were safe."

"I don't know," said Roland. "He said that it was Fear coming out of the Mound, and we were making all those things out of it with our imaginations. Well, he was right, because I'd seen some of them before."

"You would have!" said Nicholas.

"That bird with arms," said Roland, "and that thing with its face in the middle of its chest – they're in those pictures in the art hall at my school. You know: where everybody's being shovelled into Hell."

"And did you see that tall thin thing covered in hair, with a long nose?" said Helen. "I can remember dreaming about it when I was little, after I'd been frightened by Mum's fox fur."

"What are you driving at?" said David. "Do you mean that those things were real only as long as we were there, or scared of them?"

"So once we'd left Elidor they'd all disappear?" said Helen.

"I think so," said Roland.

"I hope so," said Nicholas. "But we'll probably never know."

"What are we going to do about the Treasures?" said David. "Should we make a special place for them which we can keep a secret?"

"Better not," said Roland. "If we don't have them with us we can't be sure they're safe."

"It'd be easier to talk Mum round if we had the real sword to show her," said David, "and not two bits of stick."

"But haven't you noticed?" said Roland. "The Treasures still feel their own shapes when you hold them. They only look like scrap."

"Oh, I don't know anything about that," said Nicholas. "Yours may feel different, but a stone's just a stone when you're humping it around."

9   Stat

Roland decided to fetch the Treasures at the end of the first week in the cottage. Every Friday he brought his games clothes home from school in a rucksack, and there would be plenty of room for the cup and the stone, while he could manage the other Treasures easily.

It was left to Roland because he was the only one to go to school by train. He would get off at the station for the old house, collect the Treasures, and catch the next train home.

It felt strange to walk down from the platform with the usual travellers – other schoolchildren, and businessmen old and rich enough to leave their offices at half past three – to walk down the steps, and then to see not the hall light shining through the stained glass of the front door, but a 'For Sale' board behind the hedge, and the windows blank.

When Roland unlatched the gate he realized how much of his life had not moved with him to the cottage. The unique sounds of a house: the noise of that gate, of his feet on that path. Wherever he went he would never take those with him. And yet already there was something different about the house, even after a week. Roland felt it as a kind of awkwardness, almost uneasiness, in his being there, and as he reached the door

this suddenly became so strong that the hair on
the back of his neck tingled, and his palms were
cramped with pins and needles.

It was a sensation so close to fear, and yet
Roland was not afraid – then the door opened in
front of him as he put the key in the lock.

There was a man standing in the shadowy hall.

"What are you on, son?" said the man in a
hard, flat, Manchester voice.

"Noth – nothing," said Roland.

The man was wearing overalls and carried some
electrical equipment. Once Roland saw this he
was reassured.

"I used to live here. We moved last week, and
I've come back to pick up a few things."

"Such as?"

"Oh, just some bits and pieces."

"You're not one of these here radio enthusiasts,
by any chance?" said the man. "A little knowledge is a dangerous thing, you know. You could
do yourself a mischief."

"Oh, no," said Roland. "My brother's keen, and I've another brother with a transistor set, but I'm no good at that sort of thing."

"Ay," said the man. "There's summat peculiar going on here: there is that."

"What do you mean?" said Roland.

"Well," said the man, "all this week we've had nowt but complaints at the post office from the streets round here about radio and TV interference, and a lot more besides – a proper deluge. So me and me mate comes out in our detector van this afternoon, and there's no two chances about the signal we're getting from this house. There's summat here jamming every frequency we've got and a few more on top, I'd reckon."

"But the electricity's switched off at the meter," said Roland.

"I know it is," said the engineer. "I had to go to the house agent's for a key, and I've checked mains and wiring. No, it's summat like a generator going full belt – and then some."

"Can't you tell which room it's in?" said Roland.

"Not a chance. It's too strong. Every needle's peaking high enough to kench itself as soon as we switch on. We'll have to come in the morning and try again. It may just be a freak, though I doubt it."

He looked back up the stairs.

"And I'll tell you another thing. This house is full of stat."

"What?"

"Stat – static electricity. And I'll tell you summat else. I can't earth it! What do you say to that?"

"Er – oh, yes?" said Roland.

"Eh? I can't earth it!" said the engineer. "What?"

"Gosh," said Roland, since the man persisted in demanding an answer.

"I've not seen owt like it: I have not. It's a right bobby-dazzler."

The GPO van drove off into the dusk, leaving Roland in the hall. The engineer had warned him not to switch the electricity on, just in case there was a fault that he had not been able to find. But Roland had never intended to make the visit obvious, and he had brought a torch with him.

The air inside the house was so dry that it rustled as he moved. A blue spark cracked between his hand and the banisters when he climbed the stairs, and it felt as though all his hair was on end. Every time he touched anything, sparks flashed.

It must be the electricity he was talking about, thought Roland.

He went up to the attic. Roland's lips and mouth pricked with the metallic sweetness of the air. But he reasoned that perhaps this was because he was at the top of the house. He knelt down to open the hatch.

There was a strong smell of ozone in the space under the roof. The Treasures were as he had left them. Roland squirmed through the hatch and went sideways over the joists to avoid the ceiling plaster in between.

The fine dust that lay over everything did not rise when he disturbed it. It was so charged with the static electricity that it clung like fur. Roland felt that he was crawling on an animal.

He worked the Treasures from joist to joist, put them through into the room, and dragged himself after them. He wrapped the stone in his football shirt, and the cup in a towel: then he turned to close the hatch. But there were the shadows of two men in the torchlight on the attic wall.

After the first pulse of horror Roland did not move. He saw every detail of plaster on the wall: he heard every sound in the house and in the road outside. He did not breathe: his mind raced so that every second was ten.

The shadows were not anybody in the room. It was too small and bare for anybody to be in it unseen. And they would have to be between the torch and the wall to make shadows.

This was my bedroom. There's nothing to be frightened of here. They're marks on the wall. Damp patches because the house is empty.

He went closer. They remained the same size. Flat shadows on the wall: motionless, sharp, and black.

It's an optical illusion. I'll shut my eyes and count ten. Or it's all that static electricity. It's a freak, like the man said.

Roland shut his eyes, but he could still see the

80

two figures, reversed like a negative image, yellow against the black screen of his eyelids. He opened his eyes: black on yellow. Closed them: yellow on black: but just as clear. He shook his head, and the men vanished, and then appeared. He turned his head slowly to one side: and back.

He could see the shadows with his eyes closed only when he was facing the wall.

Roland opened his eyes and switched off the torch. In the darkness of the attic the yellow shadows were full size. The air was alive with tiny sparks, and they were thickest round the outline of the shadows, like iron filings clustering about a magnet.

Now the force in the room seemed to hold Roland's head locked in one position so that he could not look away. A numbness was spreading into his limbs, and in his mind and all around him he felt or heard a noise, high, whining, powerful, and the sparks merged into blue flame along the edges of the two shapes.

He willed his hands to switch on the torch, but the flame still showed even in the light, and the blackness of the shadows was more solid than the wall itself. The shadows were becoming independent of the wall, cut loose by the blue flame. They stood both in front of the wall and behind it. They were becoming not shadows, but black holes in the air: holes in space.

Roland felt that if he watched a moment longer something irrevocable would happen, and that by watching he would be the cause.

He threw himself backwards from the attic and leapt down the stairs. Cold fire blazed around him from the air. He cleared the last six steps to the hall, sensing the whole weight of the house poised over his head. He opened the front door and ran on to the path without looking back. Behind him the door slammed shut on the silent, empty rooms.

10   Choke

Of course it seemed different once he was on the train.

In the brightly lit compartment, and among other people, he realized that there could be a normal explanation for everything. He knew that static electricity could produce strange effects, and the engineer had said there was a lot of it in the house. He had frightened himself before by staring at something quite ordinary in a poor light. "Come off it, Roland. You're always imagining things." That was a family joke.

When he reached home Roland put the Treasures on a high shelf in the garage, where they would be unnoticed until they could be hidden in the loft over the bathroom.

By now most of his fright had dropped away. He left the garage, crossed to the house, and shut the kitchen door behind him, all rather quickly, but already the impression of what he had seen was becoming very confused. The shadows were not so clearly shadows; they could have been faults in the wall plaster shown up by the torchlight, or an effect of the dust and the static electricity: somehow.

Friday was the best day of the week. After tea, homework could wait: the first cloud would not appear before Sunday morning, A whole evening lay ahead to be enjoyed.

The children washed up while their mother arranged sandwiches and cake on a trolley for supper. Mr Watson went out in the car to buy a box of chocolates to celebrate their first week in the cottage, and then he brought in coal and stoked the fire.

"Did you get them?" said David to Roland.

"Yes, they're in the garage."

"What is it on TV tonight, Frank?" said Mrs Watson from the sitting room.

"I'm just looking, dear," Mr Watson answered.

"Do you know anything about static electricity?" said Roland.

"A bit," said David.

"There was an engineer from the post office at the house. He said there'd been complaints. He said the house was full of static electricity, and—"

"It's the circus; then a play; and then ice skating," said Mr Watson.

"Oh, good! Hurry up, children! The circus is on in a few minutes. And there's a play, and ice skating."

"—and he said there must be a generator—"

"Right, Mum!" said David. "Coming! A generator wouldn't give static."

"But there were sparks everywhere: little blue ones."

"Never mind," said Nicholas. "Leave it. Dad's just switched on."

The family settled down by the fire. The box of chocolates was passed round; Mrs Watson sited her footstool; Mr Watson polished his glasses with a special cloth impregnated with silicones; they all sat in expectation.

The first thing that happened was that as the television set warmed up it gave out an electronic howl, which climbed the scale until it was like a knife driven through the teeth, and then sank to a scream.

"It's a tuning note," said Mrs Watson.

"Doesn't sound like it to me," said David.

"Turn it down a bit, Frank, till it's warmed up," said Mrs Watson. "It'll be all right."

The scream died, and broke into a staccato cough.

"That's not a tuning note," said David.

The television set blinked, and for a second they glimpsed the head and shoulders of an announcer, and then it looked as if a motor cycle had ridden over his face, leaving the tread marks on the screen and dragging his nose and ears sideways out of the picture.

"It's the Contrast, Frank."

Mr Watson heaved himself from his chair and began to turn the controls. He was too near to see if he was doing any good. It seemed to be raining in the studio.

"That's better," said Mrs Watson. "No! You've

gone too far. Back. Oh, that's no good. Try the
other way."

The screen became alternately a dazzling silver
and a blackness shot through with meteorites.

"Let me have a go, Dad," said David.

"Don't interfere," said Mrs Watson. "Your
father knows what he's doing. Now. There.
There, that's better."

It was still raining, but they could tell that
some horses were galloping round a circus ring.

Mr Watson went back to his chair. At that
moment the picture began to float upwards. It
was followed by another. A leisured string of
pictures: plop; plop; plop.

"Your Vertical Hold's gone," said David.

Mr Watson tramped across the room, and turned another knob with gentle fury. The pictures slowed. Mr Watson was breathing through his moustache. The picture stopped – half out of frame: a black band through the middle of the screen: above, were galloping hoofs, below, horses' heads and nodding plumes.

"Ease it up," said Mrs Watson. "It's coming – it's coming. Too much!"

The pictures shot into a fuzz. Mr Watson spun the knob in both directions, but it had no effect. He turned all the controls separately and together. He switched the set off and on again several times. He tried other channels. Nothing worked.

"Oh, leave it off," said Mrs. Watson. "It would happen on a Friday."

"Never mind," said Mr Watson. "I'll phone the shop first thing in the morning."

"That's not now, is it? What are we going to do?"

"There's tonight's paper, dear, if you'd like to look at that—"

"Oh, very well – thank you."

Mrs Watson took the evening paper, and made a point of reading it. Every minute or so she would turn the pages fretfully, and hit them into shape, as if they were responsible for the television breakdown.

Mr Watson sat in his chair, gazing at the fire.

David and Roland brought themselves books from upstairs.

Nicholas started to glance through a pile of magazines.

Helen doodled on the cover of one of the magazines, giving a film star a moustache, beard, and glasses.

"Isn't it quiet?" she said.

"I'm going to listen to my transistor," said Nicholas.

"That's a good idea," said Mrs Watson. "Fetch it down, Nick. It'll be nice to have some music if we're reading."

"I think I'll just try the TV again," said Mr Watson. "You never know."

"Don't," said Mrs Watson. "It'll only make you bad tempered. We'll listen to the wireless, and then I'll bring the supper. I shan't be sorry to have an early bed tonight. It's been a tiring week."

"Have you messed up my transistor?" said Nicholas from the doorway. He was looking at David, and his face was hot.

"Why should I want to touch your puny transistor when I've built a real wireless of my own?" said David.

"Someone has," said Nicholas. "Is it either of you two?"

"Not me," said Roland. "What's wrong with it?"

"You listen," said Nicholas, and he pushed the button of his portable radio. A whooping noise rose and fell against a background of atmospheric crackle that drowned any broadcast. "It's the same on all stations. It was OK this morning, so who's wrecked it?"

"Wait a minute," said David. He put down his book and ran upstairs.

"I promise we've not touched your wireless," said Helen.

"No one's been in your room all day, Nick," said Mrs Watson.

"That's another wash-out, then," said Nicholas. He flopped into the chair and snatched open a magazine.

"My radio's conked, too!" David called. "It must be a magnetic storm."

"Would it stop the TV?" said Mrs Watson.

"No," said David. "That doesn't work the same way."

Nobody could sit still for long. It was so unnatural for the room to be quiet; there was a tension in the silence, as if a clock had stopped.

Mr Watson thumbed the pages of a gardening catalogue. He whistled a tune to himself, but it wasted away.

Every small movement made someone look up, and every sound was an irritation. Then into this silence there broke the noise of a car engine. It hiccupped on one cylinder, hesitated, and the remaining cylinders fired. Mr Watson dropped his catalogue.

"That's our car," he said.

"Nonsense, Frank."

"I tell you, it's our car!"

He pulled back the curtain that stopped the

draught from the front door, slid the catch, and ran out on to the footpath in his carpet slippers.

"Frank! You'll catch your death!"

They all chased after Mr Watson, and came upon him standing outside the padlocked garage door. Inside the garage the car engine throbbed, about to stall.

"Go and bring a torch and the key, Nick," said Mr Watson.

The engine picked up again.

"Who can it be? How's he broken in?" said Mrs Watson.

"I don't know, dear," said Mr Watson. "It's very funny."

"Perhaps it's a ghost," said David.

"David!" said Mrs Watson.

"Oh, no! Do you think it is?" said Helen.

"Of course not. You see what happens when you say stupid things?"

"Sorry, Mum," said David. "Only a joke."

Even so, when Nicholas had brought the key and Mr Watson unlocked the door, everyone felt a creeping of the scalp as the door swung open.

The car stood in a haze of exhaust smoke. Nobody was in the garage. The ignition was switched off, and the key was in Mr Watson's pocket. He sat in the driving seat and frowned at the dashboard.

"Aha," he said, with an attempt at understanding. "Ah."

"What is it, Dad?" said Nicholas.

"I'd not put the choke right back in."

Mr Watson stuck his finger against one of the knobs. The engine died.

"There'd be just enough petrol seeping through to fire the engine," he said. "Now then, all inside out of the cold! The mystery's solved! Come along!"

"But, Dad," Roland heard David say as he helped Mr Watson shut the door, "you'd still need the ignition on to start the motor. Wouldn't you?"

If Mr Watson replied, Roland did not hear him.

The diversion made half an hour pass. It was good to come to the fire from the dark, and they gathered round the hearth, warming their hands, and talking away the uneasiness they had all felt in front of the locked garage.

But the heat of the fire drove them apart to their own little islands in the room. Mr and Mrs Watson faced each other in armchairs. David and Roland, with their shoes off, were competing from behind their books for an unfair share of the sofa. Nicholas sat on a leather pouffe, reading the advice columns in all the magazines. Helen was drawing heads in profile looking to the left. She could never draw them looking to the right.

The evening dribbled by.

"Hark," said Mrs Watson. "What's that?"

"I can't hear anything," said Mr Watson.

"It's upstairs."

The whole family listened.

"Oh, yes," said Helen. "It's a – a sort of buzzing."

"Shut up a minute, then," said David. "I can't – oh, yes—"

"Go and see what it is, Frank," said Mrs Watson. "The immersion heater may not be plugged in properly."

"Then shall we have supper?" said Mr Watson. "I could do with a bite." His soft, heavy tread creaked on the stairs.

"Now what's your father up to, I wonder," said Mrs Watson after several minutes. "Has he gone to bed? It'd be just like him."

"No," said Roland. "He's coming. That noise is louder, too."

Mr Watson came downstairs as slowly as he had climbed. He halted in the doorway of the room: his face was blank with unbelief. In one hand he held his electric razor. The razor was working, although in his other hand Mr Watson held the loose end of the flex.

"It's my razor," he said.

"Well, can't you stop it?" said Mrs Watson. "Can't you switch it off?"

"There's nothing to switch off. You plug it into the light."

"But that's ridiculous, Frank! It's not plugged into anything. You must be able to switch it off."

"I can't, dear. It works from the mains."

"Then what's it doing now?"

"I don't know, dear."

Mr Watson put the razor on the table. Its vibrations made it turn like the head of a tortoise.

"It was in its case on top of the medicine cupboard. It'd nearly shaken itself off. I had a job to catch it."

"Dead weird, isn't it?" said Nicholas. "The power must be coming from somewhere, unless there's a fault."

"There's no fault in the razor," said David. "It's going perfectly!"

"I don't like it," said Helen. "It's almost – alive."

"It's spooky."

"David!" said Mrs Watson. "I will not have you putting such thoughts into other people's heads! You know there must always be a perfectly simple explanation for everything that happens. There's obviously something wrong with the razor, and we'll take it back to the shop tomorrow and let a qualified electrician see it."

"I'll wrap it in a towel and put it away," said Mr Watson, "or else it'll get on our nerves. I must say, I wouldn't have thought it."

"Now we're all up, let's have supper," said Mrs Watson. "Will you bring the trolley through, please, Roland, for the cups and saucers? I'll go and put the kettle on."

"It's still pretty spooky, whatever Mum says," David muttered.

"Now, David," said his father.

"Well it is, Dad. You can't run away from it.

Things don't start by themselves. You must have something to—"

Mrs Watson's scream interrupted him. They rushed through into the kitchen, and found her staring at the electric food mixer, which was spinning at top speed.

"Switch it off!" cried Mrs Watson.

"It is switched off, Mum," said Nicholas, and he took the plug out of the socket, to be certain. The mixer did not falter.

"It – started," said Mrs Watson. "I was nowhere near it."

"Now will you believe me?" said David.

As if to back him up, the drum of the washing machine slowly began to turn behind its glass door.

"It's all right, dear," said Mr Watson. "There'll be a fault in the supply. David, go and switch off the mains, and we'll see."

David pressed a lever on the electricity meter and all the lights in the house went out. But the mixer and the washing machine threshed away in the darkness.

"Very well," said Mr Watson. "Put the lights on."

They ate a poor supper. Mrs Watson was upset, but Mr Watson said that nothing could be done at the moment, and that they should try to have a good night's sleep. It would all be put right in the morning. It was not a fault at the mains, so there was no danger. Nevertheless, he gave himself away by setting up a camp bed for Helen in his room. Now no one would be alone.

At first the boys tried to talk when they were in bed, but their father called to them to go to sleep. So they lay awake through that night, listening to the machinery. At two o'clock in the morning the food mixer burned itself out. But the washing machine rumbled on. The children and their parents stared clear-eyed at the dark.

11.　The Last Spadeful

"What was that you were chuntering about last night, Roland, before Dad told you to shut up?" said Nicholas.

"I know what's causing all this," said Roland. "It's the Treasures."

Mrs Watson was in bed suffering from a headache. She had put cotton wool in her ears to keep out the noise of the washing machine. Mr Watson was having trouble over finding an electrician: either the numbers were engaged, or he became involved in long arguments.

"I don't know how they're doing it," said Roland, "but they are. Malebron said they'd still give light in Elidor even when they're here, so they must be generating something."

"Generators!" said David. "Yes! They could! Roland, you've hit it! If Malebron said that, the Treasures must be giving off energy. And if it's generated over a wide enough range of frequencies it'll spoil TV and radio reception – and it'll turn electric motors!"

"Does that mean that as long as I'm looking after a stone I'll not be able to use my transistor?" said Nicholas.

"It depends what the range is," said David. "But probably you won't."

"It fits what happened when I went to collect

them," said Roland. "The GPO van, and all that static."

"The van makes sense," said David. "But generators don't generate static electricity. And if the Treasures are generators—"

"There's a lot of 'if' in this," said Nicholas.

"But we'll have to do something quickly," said Roland. "We can't hide the Treasures for long. They'll be found and taken away from us. There'll be another van looking for them this morning, I bet, unless we can stop the interference they're causing."

"The only thing to do is to try and screen them," said David. "If we put them in a metal box and bury them it should block out most of the interference, if the energy is anything like electricity – and it must be, even in Elidor."

"That's what I said we should do at the start," said Nicholas. "Dig a hole and bury 'em. Well, it's a bit thick if I can't listen to the radio. And anyway, we look so daft carting these things round – you and Roland playing soldiers with bits of iron and wood, and Helen at a doll's tea party, and me – well, what am I doing looking after a lump of stone as if it was the crown jewels?"

"But Malebron trusted us to look after them," said Roland. "We can't let him down. And Elidor—"

"You give me the pip sometimes," said Nicholas. "You really do. All right: I was as excited as you when it happened. But what is it once you've got used to the idea? Is it any better than our world? It's all mud and dust and rock. It's dead, finished. Malebron said so. And you should think about him a bit more, too. Did he care how we made out as long as he found his Treasures? He sent us trotting off into that Mound one after the other, but he didn't go in himself. What right has he to expect us to spend the rest of our lives like – like broody hens?"

"But you saw him," said Roland. "How can you forget him if you've seen him?"

Nicholas shrugged his shoulders. "Oh, well," he said. "Well. Well, I didn't say anything was wrong with him: he was just self-centred."

"Do stop arguing," said Helen. "Honest, Roland, if David's right, then what Nick wants to do is best even if you don't like why he's doing it."

"Now what's all this noise?" said Mr Watson. The washing machine had covered his approach. "You know your mother's got a bad head."

"Sorry, Dad," said David. "Any luck?"

"It's very strange," said Mr Watson, "but every single electrician says he's been having calls all night, and no one can promise to come before this afternoon."

"So it wasn't just us," said David.

"It's intolerable," said Mr Watson. "Your poor mother didn't sleep a wink. I'm going round to the electricity office now to insist that they do something immediately. It can't go on."

"Can we dig in the garden, please?" said Helen.

"Yes: yes: anything you like," said Mr Watson, "as long as you don't disturb your mother. She's dropped off."

"We'll have to bury the Treasures," said David as soon as their father had gone. "If they've been causing all this trouble, the electricity people or the post office will find them. It's the only way, Roland."

"David and I'll take first go at the digging,' said Nicholas. "We'll have to make it deep, and Dad won't think much of it if he comes back before we've finished."

Helen and Roland went upstairs and brought down four polythene bags to hold the Treasures. It was hard to squash all the air out of the bags so that they would take up as little space as possible. Helen fastened the necks with rubber bands, and covered this seal with a lashing of twine. Roland found an old dustbin among the rubbish that had been cleared out of the cottage and was waiting to be removed from the bottom of the garden.

The Treasures looked no different: a stone, a piece of railing, two laths, and a cup. Roland put them into the dustbin and tied the lid down with a length of flex from David's radio spares.

When Helen and Roland climbed into the hole it was up to their chests. The sides were mottled layers of earth, darkest at the top, growing lighter and sandier towards the bottom, and veined brown with dead roots. Shards of pottery winked blue and white in the soil.

"Have you noticed?" said Helen. "Wherever you dig there's always millions of broken plates. It was the same at the other house. People must have been throwing them away for years."

They were head-deep in almost pure sand, and they could barely lift the spade loads to clear the pile at the edge of the hole.

"You'll do at that," said David. "It's the best we can manage in the time. Give us your hand and I'll pull you out."

"Right," said Helen. "Last spadeful coming up – oh!"

She drove the spade into the sand, and it hit something which cracked. Helen knelt and picked out several fragments of earthenware.

"Oh, I think it was a whole jug!" she said. "And I've smashed it. Look, Roland. Oh, isn't it lovely!"

She wiped a piece with her hand. It was a creamy brown colour, with a blue tinge of lead in the glaze, and there were the head and forelegs of a unicorn lined in dark red.

"Gosh, it must be centuries old," said Roland.

"I'm going to mend it," said Helen. "Oh, what a pity! If only I hadn't broken it! I'd give anything not to have broken it!"

"We'll be copped if you don't hurry up," said Nicholas.

Helen and Roland were pulled out of the hole, and the dustbin was lowered in. They kicked and shovelled the earth back, and stamped it down.

"There," said Nicholas.

When they went into the kitchen to clean their hands the washing machine had stopped.

12.   The Letterbox

Electricians checked the house, and went away again. Mr Watson made a flower bed on the heap of soil where the Treasures were buried. A year passed.

And all this time Roland avoided using the front door. He felt that he could never trust the door to be the way out of and into the cottage. It became a compulsion, like walking on kerbstones.

Helen mended the jug she had found in the hole. It was a large pitcher, and it had broken into five pieces. She spent hours glueing them together, almost in tears when she thought of what she had done. The pitcher had lain in the ground such a long time, and such a little care would have saved it. Now she was too late, and nothing could make it whole again.

The unicorn reared below the lip, poised at the height and stillness of movement. An instant later, Helen thought, and it would have been gone.

There was no other decoration except for two lines of thick black lettering under the unicorn,

Save mayde that is makeles
Noe man with me mell.

"What does it mean, Dad?" said Nicholas.

"I'm not sure," said Mr Watson. "It's some sort of verse – perhaps it's a family motto, something like, you know, that Scottish one, 'He gets hurt who meddles with me'."

"What's a makeless maid?" said Roland.

"Well, it's hard to say exactly. I suppose you could find it in the dictionary."

"You've made a very good job of mending that, Helen," said Mrs Watson. "You can't really see the cracks."

"But I know they're there," said Helen.

The year passed. It was a dark Sunday afternoon. Helen and Nicholas had gone for a ride on their bicycles: David and Roland were sitting at the table in the middle room, revising the work they had done at school that term. Through the window they could see their mother and father in the garden. Mr Watson was planting some rose bushes.

Roland tried to concentrate on his history book. He had to read twenty pages, and he found that he was more aware of the number of a page than of what was printed on it. Eventually the words became a procession, and his mind drifted from them, first to the tablecloth, and then to the window. He saw that David was drawing patterns in the margin of his notebook.

"Revision's the worst part of the term, isn't it?" said Roland. "You think you know the stuff,

but you don't: and you can't take it in because
you've heard it all before and it's gone stale."

"I can't get used to not having a front garden,"
said David. "Every time someone goes past the
house I think they're coming here. And that front
door's driving me round the bend."

"Oh?" said Roland. "Why?"

"It keeps buzzing," said David. "Haven't you
noticed? It must be traffic that makes it vibrate.
Anyway, what with that, and the footpath right
next to the house, you can't think straight, even
in here."

"I've never liked the porch," said Roland. "I
used it to open the Mound, and ever since it's
felt wrong."

"What?" said David. "Open what?"

"The Mound," said Roland. "In Elidor."

"Oh, that," said David.

"What do you mean, 'Oh, that'?" said Roland.
"Elidor! Elidor! Elidor! Have you forgotten?"

"OK," said David. "We don't want the whole road to hear."

"Elidor," said Roland. "So why can't we talk about it? You and Nick always change the subject."

"I think you ought to cool down a bit on this Elidor business," said David.

"You're mad!" said Roland.

"All right," said David, "we have been talking about it."

"I don't remember," said Roland.

"Nick said you'd only start getting worked up and we'd have a row, so we didn't tell you."

"Good old Nick!" said Roland. "He would! Thanks very much!"

"You see?" said David. "You're shouting already."

"But you're pretending it doesn't matter," said Roland. "Didn't it mean anything to you – Malebron and the Treasures, and that golden castle, and, and – everything?"

"Listen," said David, "Nick's not all that dim, although you think he is. A lot of what he says makes sense, even if I don't agree with everything myself."

"What does he say, then? That there's no such place as Elidor, and we dreamed it?"

"In a way," said David.

"He's off his head."

"No, he's gone into it more than any of us," said David. "And he's been reading books. He says it could all have been what he calls 'mass hallucination', perhaps something to do with shock after the church nearly fell on us. He says it does happen."

"And I suppose the mud we scraped off was a mass hallucination," said Roland.

"Yes, I know," said David. "But I think he may be right about the Treasures. Try to remember. When the church was shaking all round us we couldn't see what we were doing, and we were falling all over the place, and everything jarred so much we didn't know where we were. That's true, isn't it?"

"I suppose so."

"Well," said David, "even if we were holding the real Treasures they could have been knocked out of our hands and we could have grabbed hold of the other things without noticing."

"I didn't," said Roland.

"But it is possible," said David.

"If you can believe that, you can believe in the Treasures," said Roland. "And what about the things that happened next? The television, and Dad's razor, and your theory about generators?"

"Yes, it was a bit rum," said David. "But it could have been a coincidence. And anyway it was a long time ago. And nothing's happened since."

"That's the whole point!" said Roland. "That's why we buried them! If we dug them up it'd start all over again."

"There's not much chance of that," said David. "Now that Dad's made his prize flower

106

bed there, it'd be more than anyone's life's worth
to touch it."

David and Roland looked out of the window
into the garden. Roland was about to go on with
the argument, but what he saw stopped him.

Mr Watson was crouching a few feet away from
a rose bush that he had just planted. Others lay
nearby, their roots in bags. Very gingerly, and
rather like a boxer, Mr Watson sidled towards the
flower bed. He stretched out his hand, flinching:
nearer: and nearer; then he jumped back as if the
bush had bitten him. The children watched him
do this twice before they left their work and ran
into the garden.

"What's up, Dad?" said David.

By this time Mrs Watson had joined her husband and was peering at the bush.

"It's this Mrs A. R. Barraclough," said Mr
Watson. "I keep getting a shock from it."

"A shock?"

"No, not quite, but there's a distinct sound
when I try to touch it, and I can feel a tingling
in my hand."

"Your hair's all frizzy, too, Frank," said Mrs
Watson. "How very interesting: look, David and
Roland. There must be thunder about somewhere." She put her hand near the bush, and
they all heard a sharp crack.

"Be careful, dear," said Mr Watson.

"It's all right, Dad," said David. "That's static
electricity."

Roland hurried to different parts of the garden, touching shrubs, trees, walls, fences.

"There's nothing here," he called. He came back to the flower bed and put out his hand. Crack. "It's only this place." He looked hard at David.

"Run and see if the glass is dropping, Roland," said Mrs Watson. "I do hope Helen and Nick aren't going to be caught in a storm."

Roland went into the house. His face was flushed, and he was breathing quickly.

The barometer hung on the sitting room wall. The needle was slightly higher than it had been the previous day.

"Coincidence!" said Roland. "Huh!"

While he was reading the barometer the front door vibrated – a short, resonant buzz, not very loud, but noticeable. He had heard it before on several occasions, but it was only now since David had complained about it that the sound grated on him.

The door buzzed again, a longer note. Roland turned from the barometer, and as he passed the door he heard someone step into the porch. There was no mistaking this. The footpath had its own sound, and so had the porch. The flagstone gave a hard echo between the brick walls. Someone had stepped into the porch.

Without waiting for the knock, Roland drew back the curtain. The upright letterbox in the top of the door was open, and pressed close against it Roland saw an eye.

He snatched the curtain across and held it tightly in place. He heard a slight movement, and the door knob was turned both ways, and the door shifted against the Yale lock. He could hear breathing, too.

"Who is it?" said Roland.

No one answered. The door still buzzed.

Roland dashed out into the garden. "There's someone trying to get in through the front door!" he shouted.

It was so obvious that Roland was frightened that Mr Watson dropped his spade and hurried round the side of the house to the footpath. Helen and Nicholas were wheeling their bicycles on to the kerb.

"Who's in the porch?" said Mr Watson.

"I didn't notice anybody," said Nicholas.

The porch was empty, and so was the road.

"Why? What's the matter?"

"Someone looked through the letterbox and tried to open the door," said Roland. "Now: about half a minute ago."

"But they couldn't have," said Helen. "We were free-wheeling to see who could get nearest to home without touching the pedals. We were ages coming down the road."

"Nobody went anywhere near the house," said Nicholas.

"Yes, they did!" cried Roland. "I heard them, and when I pulled the curtain there was this eye – staring!"

"Who'd want to do that?" said Nicholas. "There'd be nothing to see but curtain."

"Was it you frightening Roland, Nick?" said Mr Watson.

"Me? No!"

"Because if it was, I've told you before I won't stand for it. You're old enough to know better than to play stupid tricks like that."

"But it wasn't me, Dad!"

"Very well," said Mr Watson. "But I don't want it to happen again, that's all."

"I did see somebody!" said Roland. "I did!"

"Now come along inside, Roland," said Mrs Watson. "You know, you're your own worst enemy."

"But Mum, I did see somebody!"

"I don't doubt it," said Mrs Watson. "But you mustn't let your imagination run away with you. You're too highly strung, that's your trouble. You'll make yourself ill if you're not careful."

Roland was found to have a temperature of a hundred and one. Mrs Watson gave him aspirin and sent him to bed, cooked him a light tea, and sat with him until he appeared to be calmer.

When the other children went to bed they were told to go quietly so as not to wake Roland. They tiptoed upstairs without switching the light on.

"Come in here, you lot," said Roland.

13.   "Silent Night"

Next morning the static electricity had dispersed. The rose bed was normal.

At this time of the year it was dark when the children came home, and so the only chance Roland had of inspecting the garden was after breakfast. Monday, Tuesday, Wednesday passed, and nothing happened. He tried to vary his approach so that no one would see what he was doing. He brought in coal, or carried cinders out, or threw scraps for the birds. He noticed that food landing near the bed was always the last to be taken, and the sparrows and starlings never gathered there to fight over a crust as they did in the rest of the garden. A single bird would dart in and snatch the food, and the quarrelling would not begin until the bird was clear of the rose bed.

On Thursday morning Roland was having his breakfast when Mrs Watson threw a piece of burned toast out of the window. The toast fell on the path, and lay untouched. Roland saw one bird fly down from a chimney, but when it was over the garden it braked in the air, shot sideways, and flew back to the chimney, where it sat, ruffling its feathers and wagging its head. A few minutes later it tried again, with the same result. No other birds came near.

As soon as he could Roland went into the

garden. There were plenty of birds in the orchard over the fence next door, but they were all silent. Roland crossed the path, and as he came near to the rose bed his hair started to move on his neck, and the palms of his hands tingled.

By smuggling his mackintosh into the last lesson Roland was able to leave school as soon as the bell rang. He cut through the playing field and ran a mile to the station, and so caught the early train, which went half an hour before his usual one. Roland sprawled in the carriage. His shirt was out of his trousers, rumpled in sticky folds on his back. He felt as if he was bursting in the carriage heat: but he would reach home before dark.

The street lamps were on when he walked up the road from the station. He plucked leaves off the hedges as he passed. Ivanhoe, Fern Bank, Strathdene, Rowena, Trelawney: respectable houses bounded by privet, each with its square of grass. Two days ago the first Christmas tree had appeared in a front room window, and now every house had one displayed, and they were all bigger than the first tree.

Whinfield, Eastholme, Glenroy, Orchard Main. What could happen here? thought Roland. Even the toadstools are made of concrete. But it's our house that has the porch . . .

He stopped in front of the porch, smelling the bitter privet leaves rolled between his fingers. The name of the house, carved on a varnished section of log, hung from two chains, by the arch.

Screwed into the door was a plaque which said, "Here live Gwen and Frank Watson", then came a knot of flowers, and underneath, "with Nicholas, David, Helen, and Roland". But the porch still did not belong. It makes it worse, thought Roland. They'll know they've found us.

He went into the garden. There was nothing to be felt. Roland put his school books away before going back to the rose bed. He touched the bushes, prodded the soil, walked round the bed. What makes it come? Is it the Treasures? If it is, why isn't it there all the time?

There was hardly any light except for the afterglow of the sun in the clear sky. The ground was freezing already. And then, in the middle of Roland's casting about, he felt the static electricity as suddenly as if a switch had been pressed.

And when he looked at the rose bed he saw the shadows of two men standing there.

They were motionless, as they had appeared in the attic wall. Flat shadows. But they were not thrown on anything solid, they were shadows on the air.

Roland backed away to the path, and the shadows stayed where they were. He edged round to the side. They narrowed with perspective until he was at right angles to them, and then they disappeared until he moved past them. They were visible from in front and behind, and Roland could not see through them. And yet they were two-dimensional: they had no depth: looked at from the side, there was not a hairline of darkness.

Roland went closer to the rose bed. He was both frightened and excited by the shadows.

"Just stay there," he said. "Just stay there. They'll have to listen after this. Just stay there till the others come."

His throat ached, and the ache moved into the neck muscles, sending a sharp pain through his forehead. The air pricked with light: the shadows gleamed like ink. Roland's neck was cramped fast. He remembered how it had been in the attic, how he had watched until it was nearly too late. He was doing something by looking at the shadows, and the whining noise was coming now. He forgot about proving himself right. It was too dangerous. He had to move, while he could.

Roland floundered across the garden towards the house. His knees and the small of his back felt as though they were bubbles of air, and the ground was never where he thought it was.

"Your tea's ready," Mrs Watson called when she heard Roland in the kitchen.

"Thanks, Mum," he said.

It was eight o'clock before all the family was ready to watch the television. Mr Watson had settled down about ten minutes earlier, and so when Mrs Watson and the children joined him they were surprised to find that he had not switched the television on.

"Is something wrong, Frank?" said Mrs Watson.

"No. I'm listening to the carol singers. They're the first this year."

In the distance they could hear uncertain treble voices.

"*Silent Night,*' said Mr Watson. "My favourite."

"I heard them three weeks ago," said Mrs Watson. "They start earlier every year."

"I suppose, before long," said Mr Watson, "they'll run it in with Guy Fawkes and get all the collecting done at one go."

"Are we having the telly on, Dad?" said Nicholas.

"In a minute," said Mr Watson, "in a minute. Let's be seasonable. It's not every night of the year we can hear carols, and we'll have to pay for them, so let's have our money's worth. They sound as though they're outside Mrs Spilsbury's. We should get them at the next move."

But as he said this, they heard the scuffle of feet in the porch.

"Oh, really," said Mr Watson. "Already? It's a bit much to expect to be paid for something we can't hear. Go away! We want *Silent Night* outside the window before you have a penny!" He winked at the others. "I'll complain to your union!"

There was a further scuffle, and the doorknob rattled.

"Young scamps," said Mr Watson. "They might have the decency to knock. Go away! Off with you!"

A pause. Then they heard footsteps on the

pavement, and a whispered muttering, and then, still whispered, "Ready? One, two, three," and several voices in different keys began to sing *Away in a Manger*. Before they reached the end of the first line there was a polite knock at the door. "That's more like it," said Mr Watson, and opened the door.

"Merry Christmas," said the small boy in the porch. He brandished a money box. "And a Happy New Year."

"Now why couldn't you do it properly the first time?" said Mr Watson. "There was no need to rattle the door like that. And I did ask for *Silent Night*."

The boy gaped at him.

"What d'you mean, mister? We've been up the road. No one rattled your door."

"Come now, come," said Mr Watson. "I distinctly heard you larking about in my porch."

"We never—"

"Thank you!" said Mr Watson.

"We didn't—"

"I said thank you. Now listen: all I'm asking is that you sing what I requested – *Silent Night* – and that you refrain from rattling my door. That's reasonable, isn't it?"

"No one rattled your door, mister," said the boy. "We weren't anywhere near your door."

14   The High Places

Roland said nothing about the shadows. When the other children had come home he had not had the courage to go outside again. He realized, too, that nothing less than the shadows themselves would convince Nicholas, and next morning and all Saturday there was no static charge in the garden.

"I wish you'd have a look at that front door, Frank," said Mrs Watson at tea on Saturday. "It judders every time a car goes past. It's the kind of noise that sets my teeth on edge: I could hardly sew for it this afternoon. It's become much worse lately."

"Very good, dear," said Mr Watson. "I'll see what can be done in the morning. It may need a touch of the screwdriver."

"And I wish you had paid those boys the other night, instead of preaching at them. They've been in and out of that porch all day. It's their way of getting their own back, I suppose."

"I explained at the time that it was a matter of principle," said Mr Watson. "But what have they done now?"

"Oh, they've been dragging their feet, turning the doorknob, flapping the letterbox – that sort of thing."

"Didn't you stop them?" said Mr Watson.

"They're much too quick. They're off and out of sight the moment they hear the curtain rings move. I gave it up after the second time. They'll soon tire of it when they see we're not to be drawn."

"Or they'll be provoked to worse mischief," said Mr Watson. "My mother was once nearly frightened to death when some louts dropped a rip-rap through her letterbox. It could have set the house on fire, too. Oh, no: we must put a firm stop to it."

"Listen," said Nicholas. "They're at it again. Shall David and I nip out and clobber them?"

"Certainly not," said Mr Watson. "I mean to deal with this once and for all. I'm going to catch them from behind. You just go on talking normally."

"Don't do anything silly, Frank," said Mrs Watson.

Mr Watson let himself out by the back door. The children and their mother listened to the shuffling that was going on in the porch.

"Sounds as though there's quite a few of them," said David. "I wonder if Dad will be all right."

"Don't be daft," said Nicholas. "That kid who was collecting was only eight or nine. I still think we should clobber them. Dad'll lay the law down, but he won't do anything else, except ask their names and addresses. And who'd be mug enough to give him real ones?"

The back door opened, and Mr Watson stamped in.

"Too late!" he said. "Not a soul in sight."

"We heard them all the time you were out, Frank," said Mrs Watson. "They've never stopped. Are you sure you went?"

"My dear Gwen," said Mr Watson, "the street lamp across the road shines right into the porch. They're hiding in gateways, but I'm not playing their game for them."

"They are not hiding, Frank. You didn't listen to what I said. They were in the porch all the time, and they are there now."

"Eh? What? Good heavens!"

The letterbox snapped shut.

"But this is preposterous!"

Mr Watson was pale with indignation.

"We'll soon deal with that, though! If I open the door when they're not expecting it, I'll trap them against the porch. Then we'll see who's being so funny."

"No, Dad!" said Roland. "Don't. Please don't."

Mr Watson frowned Roland to silence, and put his hand on the catch, taking care not to move the brass rings on the curtain. The doorknob turned. Mr Watson threw the door open.

"Got you!"

"Dad! No!"

Roland tried to reach his father to pull him away, but he became entangled in the curtain.

119

Mr Watson was thrusting the door hard against the inside wall of the porch.

"Now then," he said. "Now then."

But as he eased the pressure, the heavy oak door scooped him off his feet and slammed him back into the room. The door crashed shut, and Mr Watson fell over Roland, tearing the curtain down on top of them both.

Nicholas pushed forward. "No. Don't go," said Mrs Watson. There had been something brutal in the speed with which the door had moved. "Nick."

They dragged the curtain from Mr Watson. He was sitting dazed on the floor, and one eye was beginning to close. His nose was bleeding.

"Hooligans!" he said. "Arrant hooligans!"

"You go looking for trouble," said Mrs Watson when she bathed his eye. "For all you know it could be one of those teenage gangs off the overspill."

"You said it was the carol singers."

"I know I did, but it wasn't, was it? Eight-year-olds wouldn't have done this, would they? Roland, come away from that window. You'll egg them on to something else if they're still hanging around. Ignore them, and they soon lose interest."

Roland watched the poplar branches curling like tentacles round the street lamp. The road glistened. But he knew that when he had stood next to his father at the door, all beyond the

porch had been in darkness, except for the glow of a log fire burning nearby.

It was three in the morning when Roland went downstairs. Coals tinkled in the grate, and the clock raced with the double note that Roland never heard in daylight. The front door vibrated, although the only traffic was the long-distance lorries on the main road a quarter of a mile away.

He knew that it was up to him to do something. After this there would be more than curiosity.

He listened at the curtain. He had switched off the pencil torch and clipped it in his pyjama pocket. There was no sound of movement or

121

breathing in the porch, and so Roland eased himself into the space between the curtain and the door. Still no sound, apart from the quiet jarring of the wood. The air smelled of curtain, and a thin draught slipped round him: the coconut matting needled his feet. Roland braced himself on to his toes and looked with one eye through a gap between the letterbox frame and its hinge.

Now that the room was dark Roland could see quite well in the shadow-light of Elidor.

It was nowhere that he recognized. In his narrow angle of vision there was nothing but mountains; peaks, crags, ice, and black rock stabbed upwards. The porch seemed to be at the top of a cliff, or a knife-backed ridge. Roland had the sensation of a sheer drop behind him in the room. Down the mountainside in front lay a camp of tents, and there was a hunting party winding from it up a track that passed the door. The men rode stags and carried lances, and some had bows across their backs. Wolfhounds ran before them. Close to the porch there was a bivouac in the shelter of a rock. Here the fire Roland had glimpsed burned pale and colourless, and next to it squatted a man holding a spear.

A hound sniffed at the porch, but was called off sharply. The riders looked at the door as they went by. One of them spoke to the man at the fire, who was now standing. He shook his head and pointed with the spear down to the camp.

At this moment the door stopped vibrating, and the scene vanished, and Roland was squinting out at his own night, and all he could hear was the lorries.

He lowered his heels. The man had been a sentry, guarding the porch. They had found it. They knew it was a way through. They would come when they were ready. It's my fault, thought Roland. I made it. What can I do?

The door buzzed again. He lifted himself up.

Although only a few seconds had passed, it must have been longer in Elidor. The fire was bigger, and there was a different sentry. The new man was walking up and down to keep warm.

It must be freezing, thought Roland. And why do they need such a huge camp? They can't live up here all the time: there's nothing but rock and ice, thousands of feet high. – High. – A high place. – High places. – "Who walks in the High Places". Findhorn. That's it: the Song of Findhorn. Malebron was going to look. He said there were mountains. Then they're looking, too!

It was impossible that this could be Malebron's camp. These men had his nobility, his bearing, his dress, but only Malebron had had the golden light about him. Their beauty was the beauty of steel, every line of them cut hard as an engraving.

Oh, what can I do? thought Roland.

The sentry halted, and stared at the letterbox, as if he had heard Roland speak. Then he came towards the door.

Roland slid down as far as he could. He heard the familiar footsteps in the porch, and a hand pushed the letterbox open: the knob was turned;

the door moved against the lock: scuffle: and silence. When Roland dared to look the sentry was bending over the fire and stirring food in a pot.

It's my fault. I made it. I made it. The answer stopped him.

I must unmake it.

Roland fixed his eye on the porch. Go away. Disappear. Scram. Go on. The porch did not hear. Roland tried to will it away, to think of nothing, but he could not imagine "nothing": it had no shape to build in his mind. He felt as weak as if he was pushing the bricks with his hands.

The sentry was restless and kept walking over to the door.

Think, Roland told himself. Think. How does a house fall? You don't just shove it over. The church. What happened first? It was the mortar between the bricks: running out. That's it. Bricks can't stay up without mortar.

He closed his eyes and pictured the arch in his mind. When it was fixed there he concentrated on the joints of the brickwork. Grey mortar. Loose. Dry. Crumbling. Oh, come on. Come on.

Roland heard a sound, a whisper like rain on leaves. He heard it again. A thin dust was settling in the porch. Come on, you porch! You're not all real. You're an echo: not all solid. Come on, you echo!

The mortar grew to a trickle. He dared to open his eyes, and although the dust-fall slackened it did not stop. He forced his mind like a drill between the bricks of the porch in Elidor.

The sentry yelled, but Roland broke his concentration only long enough to see that the man had noticed what was happening, and was running to the camp.

Come on! Break! Come on! More! A brick fell, and another, and a crack went up to the roof. That's it! He picked at the gap, heaving, tearing. It was easier. The bricks dropped. If he could undermine the roof, the weight of the stone tiles would pull the whole thing down. But he was labouring now with the cutting edge of his mind dulled, and every stroke was taking more energy to drive home. Men were hurrying from the camp. He sobbed and groaned and hit unaimed blows at the porch with all his will.

The men carried two-handed axes, and the first to reach the door swung his axe down into the wood. The house boomed like a drum. The axe was wrenched out, and up, and down it smashed again. Roland gathered his energy and made one blind lunge. Everything of him poured out, and after that there was nothing: and into this nothing the porch began to fall.

A third time the axe struck, but the blade was muffled, and the fourth made no sound at all. The men shouted in silence, and the porch grew dim. Beyond the peaks of the mountains two beams of yellow light flashed in the sky, and behind the sky was a bloom of darkness. The shadow of another porch covered the bricks, close as a skin, but whole where the arch was broken. The man with the axe hewed the door, yet could not touch it, and he jumped clear as the roof and walls crashed towards him, and Elidor drowned in the headlights of a car that was turning off the main road. The twin yellow beams flickered through the poplar trees, and glanced from the wall of the porch. Roland sagged against the door. The wood was like ice on his brow.

15   Planchette

The telephone rang while Mr Watson was having breakfast.

"That was the Brodies," he said when he came back to the table. "They're giving a party for their two on the twenty-ninth, and ours are invited. There'll be a card in the post, but John Brodie wanted to know now so that the date can be fixed. It'll be your night out," he said to the children, "to make up for when your mother and I go to the Greenwoods' New Year dance."

"I'm still not sure about that," said Mrs Watson. "They're young to be left."

"They're plenty old enough to look after themselves," said Mr Watson. "Aren't you?"

"But do we have to go to this party?" said Nicholas.

"Of course," said Mrs Watson. "It'll be great fun. And the Brodies are such nice people. We ought to see more of them."

"But we don't know the kids," said Nicholas. "It sounds deadly. I can't stand pass-the-parcel."

"We've accepted now," said Mr Watson. "And it lasts till eleven-thirty, so I think you'll find it's quite a grown-up party."

"Oh, heck," said Nicholas.

"I must remember to put them on the Christmas card list," said Mrs Watson.

127

David came in from outside.

"Dad! Have you seen the front door? It isn't half a mess!"

There were three gashes in the door. Two of them were cut an inch into the oak, but the third was more of a dent, as if it had been made with less force than the others.

"I thought I heard banging in the night," said Mrs Watson, "but I must have turned over again."

"But this is vandalism!" said Mr Watson. "We're being persecuted. It's – it's intolerable. Really, the lengths they'll go to just to vent their spite. Why, this must have been done with an axe!"

"That's what you must expect when you have overspill in a decent area," said Mrs Watson. "They shouldn't be allowed to build out in the country. People aren't going to change when they move from the city. And goodness knows what it will do to property values."

"It's sheer vandalism," said Mr Watson.

But later in the day he filled the gashes with a wood compound, and tightened the hinges and the door catch, which seemed to cure the vibrations.

"I thought a touch of the screwdriver would do the trick," he said..

The party loomed. The Brodies lived in a big house that had stood by itself among fields but was now surrounded by the local council's new estate. Both the children went to boarding school.

"It's going to be wet," said Nicholas as they set out on the night.

"Oh, I don't think so," said Mr Watson. "Hard frost. Clear sky. It'll stay like this for a couple of days at least. The glass is very steady."

"I meant the party," said Nicholas.

Jennifer and Robert Brodie met the Watsons formally on the doorstep. There were about a dozen other guests, and they drank fruit cup. They played games, "to break the ice". These involved pushing a matchbox from nose to nose, and mixing the girls' shoes up and then having to find the owners.

Then they danced to gramophone records. But Helen was the only one of the four who could dance. Nicholas had had two lessons, which made him more wretched than anybody. There were Excuse-me Dances, and Novelty Dances, and Forfeit Dances. Those without a partner had to dance with a mop.

At nine o'clock they went in to supper. There was a game with name-cards to decide who sat where, but Nicholas cheated so that the Watsons were together and at the far end of the table.

"Isn't it smashing!" said Helen.

"Two and a half hours more," said David.

"Can't we go now?" said Roland.

But the food was good. The Brodie children called their father Jo-jo, and he told funny stories all the time. Then everybody started to pull crackers. Roland pulled his with Helen. He unrolled the paper hat, and read the motto, and shook the cracker to see if it was empty. Something dropped on the table.

"What's up, Roland?" said David. "Are you feeling sick?"

"What have you got?" said Roland.

"A hat; and a motto; same as you."

"What else?"

"Only one of those useless bits of junk you always have in crackers."

"What is it?"

"A tie clip, or something: a kind of sword made of pink plastic. It says 'Hong Kong' on the back."

"I've got a spear," said Roland.

"Mine's a little plastic goblet," said Helen.

"What have you got, Nick?" said Roland.

"Please, Roland!" said Helen. "Please don't go on!"

"What's inside your cracker?" said Roland.

"Calm down," said Nicholas. "You'll have them thinking you've gone barmy."

"Tell me what's in that cracker besides the hat and the motto!"

"Oh, that," said Nicholas. "A pink brick. Do you want it?"

"A brick? You mean a stone!"

"Oh, good grief, Roland! Not again! Anyway, it's a dice. And it's a pretty poor one, too. The spots aren't coloured."

"It's shaped like a stone; it could be made of stone even if it is a dice," said Roland.

"Well it isn't, it's made of plastic, and so's everything else."

"It's pushing things a bit," said David. "Or are you saying Malebron's sending us souvenirs from Hong Kong?"

"I don't know what I'm saying—"

"That's true," said Nicholas.

"—but it's not a coincidence."

"Of course it's a coincidence," said Nicholas.

"Then if it is," said Roland, "it coincides with something. You don't have a coincidence on its own. And what it coincides with is the Treasures. It makes them more real."

David crossed and uncrossed his eyes.

"You can't laugh them off now!" said Roland. "Everything's linked. Malebron said so. Even if these are bits of a cracker, they're part of something else, and you can't get away from it."

"Oh, do belt up," said Nicholas.

"Are we all happy down this end of the table?" said Mr Brodie, appearing behind David's shoulder. "Plenty of what you want? More pudding? Fruit cup?"

"Thanks: we're fine," said Nicholas.

Roland went through the rest of the evening in a daze, which insulated him from the round of games and dances that followed. By about eleven o'clock everyone was tired of dancing, and nobody could think of any fresh games. They all sat round the room, and it looked as though the last thirty minutes were going to drag into exhaustion.

"I know," said Jennifer Brodie. "Let's have a séance! Like we had last Christmas! Please, Jo-jo!"

"Oh, yes! Let's!" several others said.

"Right you are," said Mr Brodie. "But don't go scaring yourselves. It's only a parlour game, remember. There's nothing in it."

"What's a séance?" said Helen.

"Talking to ghosts – table-rapping, and that sort of thing," said Nicholas.

"I don't want to do it," said Roland. "It sounds too creepy."

"Come on," said David. "It's Christmas. And you heard him say it's only a game."

"Please may we use Grannie's planchette?" Jennifer asked her mother. "It's more fun with that, and you had it out for your party last night."

"If you take care of it, darling," said Mrs Brodie.

"Yes, Mummy."

There was a conversation between Mr and Mrs Brodie at the door, but all Roland heard was, "—not as if they're old enough – scribble – nothing frightening—"

"Our grannie was a Spiritualist," said Robert Brodie. "And she had this planchette for getting messages from Grandpa. All he ever said was, 'Bury me under the river'."

"And did you?" said Nicholas.

"You try it," said Robert.

Mrs Brodie came back into the room holding a small, heart-shaped board with a pencil sticking through a hole at the pointed end. The board stood on castors so that it could move in any direction.

"The thing is," said Jennifer, "that we all sit round the table, and whoever works the planchette lays their right hand on it very gently, and the board travels across the paper on these wheels. The pencil's touching the paper, and so you get what's called Automatic Writing. Only you mustn't watch what you're doing, because it's not you writing. It's the Other Side."

"Sounds corny to me," said Nicholas.

"No, it isn't," said Jennifer. "If you try to write deliberately the board skids about. Now who's going to do it?"

"I think it's time young Roland here did his stuff," said Mr Brodie. "He's been very quiet all evening."

"I'd rather not," said Roland.

"It's only fun," said Robert.

Roland was hustled to the table, where the planchette was laid on the back of a roll of wallpaper. "The writing's big," said Jennifer, "so you need plenty of room.

"Put your finger tips on the planchette very lightly: that's it. Now, everyone sit still. You mustn't speak. Think of nothing. And if the board moves, Roland, don't look at it. It's best if you keep your eyes closed all the time. I'll do the talking bit. Right. Off we go."

They all sat round the table. Complete silence

was impossible. Some of the girls started giggling almost at once.

"Sh!" said Jennifer every few seconds.

"My arm's going numb," said Roland. "Can I have a rest?"

"No," said Jennifer, "Sh!"

Two minutes went by, and Jennifer cleared her throat.

"Is anyone there?" she said to the ceiling. "Is anyone there?"

The planchette jerked as if Roland had cramp in his arm, and the pencil made a formless scribble on the wallpaper.

"Is anyone there?" said Jennifer, and she nodded excitedly and stuck her thumb up.

The planchette scribbled again.

"Who is it?"

The planchette moved along the paper in loops like someone's first attempt at writing.

"Not bad, Roland," said Nicholas.

"I'm not doing anything."

"Sh!" said Jennifer. "Who is it?"

"My arm's gone cold," said Roland. "I can't feel anything."

"If you talk you'll spoil it," said Jennifer. "Look!"

"What's happening?" said Roland.

"Helen squeaked.
"Har, har," said Nicholas.

"What do you want?" said Jennifer.
The pencil moved.

"What is that?" said Jennifer, speaking pre-
cisely.
"An amœba," said David.

135

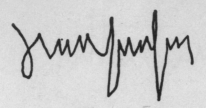

"I do not understand," said Jennifer.
The pencil scribbled again.

And then,

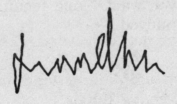

"I still cannot understand," said Jennifer.
"Please tell me more."
The pencil swept across the paper.

And then it wrote,

findhorn

"Findhorn!" cried Helen.

"What?" said Roland. "What?" The planchette immediately slid away.

"Did it write that? Findhorn? Malebron? This unicorn?"

"Oh, you shouldn't have stopped!" said Jennifer. "It was coming so well."

"Enough's enough," said Mr Brodie.

"He's trying to tell us about Findhorn!" said Roland. "The Song of Findhorn, remember! Findhorn's a unicorn! He had to keep trying . . ."

"All right, you did it nicely," said Nicholas. The other guests were staring. "Your writing's crummy, but you always could draw. You'd be even better with practice."

"It wasn't me! Try it yourself!"

"OK," said Nicholas. "I will."

He put his fingers on the board as Roland had done.

"Go on, write your name!"

"OK, OK; cool off."

But no matter how he tried Nicholas could not manage the planchette. It rolled in all directions. One of the boys laughed.

"Here, give it to me again," said Roland. "He may be wanting to tell us something else. Quick!"

"Er – I think that about wraps things up for tonight, don't you, people?" said Mr Brodie. "Carriages at eleven-thirty, you know."

He became brisk and Mrs Brodie removed the planchette. Everyone started to pick up coats in the hall, and to say thank you. Some were waiting for their parents, and others were being taken home by Mr Brodie. He switched on the outside light, and opened the door to go and bring his car round to the front of the house. A white mist coiled through the doorway into the hall.

"Oh dear, what a bore," said Mrs Brodie. "It won't be much fun driving in this. Those who aren't going with John had better take your coats off: your parents may be some time. Put the gramophone on, Jen, and we'll have another dance."

"I think we'd be quicker walking, don't you?" said Nicholas. "It's not far."

"Yes," said David. "Really, we mustn't stay, thanks all the same."

"Can we ring up home to stop Dad from turning out, please?" said Nicholas.

"Certainly," said Mrs Brodie. "If you're sure that's what you want to do."

Nicholas rushed to the telephone. "Hello, Dad," he said. "It's Nick. Look, don't bother to fetch us: we'll walk. No, honest, we'll be home by the time you could get here in this. We'll cut through the new estate and up Boundary Lane – you know, that cinder path by the allotments. Yes, of course I know the way. Yes, we'll borrow a torch. Right. See you in about half an hour."

They borrowed a torch, but found that there was no need to use it. The mist was a ground mist, and they could clearly see the tops of trees and houses, and the bright moon.

"Anything rather than another dance," said Nicholas as they went down the drive from the house. "Well done, Roland. You broke it up nicely. Old Jo-jo thought you were going to throw a fit."

Roland did not answer.

"How did you pick up the knack of that board so quickly?" said Nicholas.

"Shut up," said Roland.

"You what?"

"I said shut up."

"Oh, all right."

They walked in silence. The concrete road of the new estate was easy to follow, except where

139

it branched, or produced a roundabout. Near the Brodies' house the estate was almost finished. The upstairs windows were dabbed with whitewash. And then further in, the windows were raw holes, and the moon shone through the roofs. After that there was nothing but the mist, and they followed the kerbstone across what was still a field.

"It – it was a lovely unicorn you drew," said Helen at last. "Just like the one on my jug."

"I didn't draw it," said Roland.

"Oh, lay off," said Nicholas.

"Malebron drew it," said Roland. "He was trying to tell us something, and you stopped him."

"Now listen," said Nicholas. "It's about time you grew up. Shall I tell you what all that was about? You've got this Malebron thing on the brain. OK, so you didn't fake it on purpose: you wrote it unconsciously, and you drew the unicorn because Helen found the jug when you were digging that hole in the garden. That's how people's minds work. If you'd read the books about it you'd see for yourself you're up the creek."

"Oh, shut up," said Roland.

The road ended near a stile that led into the cinder path by the allotments. The path had chestnut palings on one side and a hedge on the other. It ran through a no-man's-land between two built-up areas and came out on the road where the Watsons lived. At one point it crossed a stream over a bridge of railway sleepers.

The path was so narrow that the children had to walk in twos. The night was absolutely still.

"Careful at the bridge," said David. "There aren't any hand-rails. We're nearly—"

The sound of air being torn like cloth burst on them, a dreadful sound that cracked with the force of lightning, as if the sky had split, and out of it came the noise of galloping hoofs. There was no warning, no approach: the hoofs were there, in the mist, close to the children, just ahead of them, on top of them, furious.

"Look out!"

They fell sideways against paling and hedge as

a white horse charged between them out of the moonlight, pulling the mist to shreds. All about them was hoof and mane and foam, and they heard the horse gallop away along the path and leap the stile into the field.

The children clung to each other.

"Is everyone OK?" said Nicholas.

"Yes."

"I've ripped my coat."

"That was a near do," said David. "I didn't hear it till it clattered on the bridge, did you?"

"It's probably bolted from the riding school," said Nicholas.

"It didn't have a saddle on," said David.

"It's broken out of its stable," said Helen. "They wouldn't have left it outside in the winter."

"Yes," said Nicholas. "Did you see the mess it was in? It must have fouled some barbed wire."

"But wasn't it a beauty?" said David. "That mane!"

The children crossed the bridge and walked on towards the road.

"I was scared," said Helen. "But the poor thing must have been more frightened than I was."

"It couldn't have stopped," said Nicholas. "If we hadn't got out of the way it'd have trampled us to bits. Don't say anything to Mum or Dad: they'd have a heart attack."

"Gosh, that put the wind up me," said David.

"Its tail hit me in the face," said Helen.

"Funny how the moonlight made it look so big, too," said Nicholas. "That, and being on a narrow path."

"I hope it's not in any pain," said Helen. "It may do more damage if it's still frightened."

"It could have killed us," said David.

"Yes, but not a word," said Nicholas. They were on the road now. "Tidy yourself a bit, Roland. We don't want to look as though we've been beaten up."

But Roland hung back in the middle of the road.

"Come along, Roland, keep together."

"Why are you talking like this?" shouted Roland. "You all saw it! Why are you pretending? You saw the horn on its head!"

"Come for a walk," said David.

It was the first time any of the children had spoken to Roland all day. Nicholas had gone off on his bicycle. Helen was careful to stay near her mother about the house, and David had been involved with his wireless textbooks.

"If you like," said Roland.

They went down the road into Boundary Lane. They crossed the bridge, and then David went back over; stopped; and crossed again.

"OK, Roland," he said. "You win."

"Oh?" said Roland. "Do I?"

"I know how you feel," said David, "but there's no point in sulking. Things are too serious now."

"What do you mean, 'now'?"

"All right, they always have been."

"Then what's made you change your mind today instead of last night?" said Roland.

"Well, for one thing," said David, "the cinders are all cut up by hoof marks on this side of the bridge, but not on the other. Even Nick would have to call that evidence. The unicorn broke through right here."

"So it was a unicorn?" said Roland.

"Of course it was," said David. "And we'll have to do something about it. I'm dead scared."

"I thought you agreed with Nick."

"I'd like to," said David. "But there was something that didn't fit: it's been bothering me for weeks. It's that static electricity. You see, even if you believe the Treasures are real and are generators, the static shouldn't be there. And it comes and goes."

"How do you know?" said Roland.

"Oh, I've been experimenting ever since Dad was on about his roses. It's there most days, early morning or dusk."

"You didn't tell me!"

"I didn't want to," said David. "Anyway, I think I know what's causing it. They're looking for the Treasures in Elidor, and they've found them."

"Found them!"

"Yes: it's quite simple. It's like getting a radio fix on a transmitter. You have two receivers some distance apart, and they pick up the direction the signal's coming from. Then you draw the two lines on a map, and where they cross is the transmitter."

"So what?"

"Well, if the Treasures are generating energy, that's going through to Elidor, you should be able to get a fix on them in Elidor. Can't you see what happens next? They lay this fix, and when they go to the place where the lines cross there's nothing there! They can point to a spot in the air, or on the ground, or anywhere, and say, 'That's where the Treasures are', but they can't touch them!"

"You mean, they can find the place in Elidor which coincides with our garden, but they can't get through?" said Roland.

"Exactly. So what do they do? They keep trying to find the Treasures, and they keep pouring energy into the same spot, like cracking a safe, but it's not going anywhere. There's this terrific charge keeps building up – and some of it leaks through to here as static electricity!"

"If you say so," said Roland. "But would they have the equipment to do it with? It didn't feel as if it's that kind of place, really."

"I don't know," said David. "But they're managing somehow."

"Could they do it with their minds?" said Roland. "That's how most things seemed to work there."

"A sort of telepathy?" said David. "Yes, why

not? All you'd need would be two people to lay the fix, and—"

"Two people?" cried Roland. "Have you ever seen anything by the roses?"

"No," said David. "There's been this static."

"Listen," said Roland. "We've got to prove it to the others once and for all: now, while they're still jittery about last night. If I show you you're right, will you explain to Nick and Helen how it works?"

"Yes: sure. It's only an idea, though. The details may be wrong."

"Come on."

They ran back home.

"What are you going to do?" said David.

"Never mind," said Roland. "I'll show you. If nobody knows beforehand then Nick won't be able to talk so much about hallucinations."

Nicholas was oiling his bicycle when they reached the cottage. David went inside for Helen. She came out looking apprehensive. The afternoon light was fading.

"Now then," said Roland. "Last night."

"I don't want to talk about it," said Nicholas.

"Why not?"

"I don't, that's all."

"Why is it so important for you to think Elidor isn't real?" said Roland.

"I'll give you a thick ear in a minute," said Nicholas.

"What about you, Helen? Do you think we all imagined Elidor?"

147

"Oh, please, Roland. Let's not row about it: please."

"Yes, it's stupid to argue," said Nicholas. "We can think what we like, but we're here now, and the Treasures, even if they are Treasures, are under the rose bed, and Elidor's finished. It's all over."

"That's where you're wrong, Nick," said David. "You may have finished with Elidor, but Elidor's not finished with us."

"Whose side are you on?" said Nicholas.

"There aren't any sides," said David. "Not after last night."

"I can explain that," said Nicholas.

"And can you explain this?" Roland had gone to the rose bed and was holding his hand near one of the bushes. They all heard the crack, and saw the spark jump.

"This once, Nick," said David. "Listen to Roland this once. If you're not convinced, I promise we'll not talk about it again."

"Oh," said Nicholas, "anything for a quiet life. What's he going to do?"

"I don't know."

Again Roland had felt the charge as abruptly as if it had been switched on, and he arranged everybody in a tight group on the lawn facing the spot where the shadows had appeared.

"Can you feel the static electricity?" he said.

"I don't like it," said Helen. "It's giving me gooseflesh."

148

"Watch the rose bed. And keep watching," said Roland.

"Are you sure you know what you're doing?" said David.

"My neck's aching," said Helen.

"Don't move. Keep watching," said Roland. Oh, where are they? They must come. Nick's got to see them—"

"So it's static electricity," said Nicholas. "It's happened before."

"You're telling me!" said David. "But it's getting stronger. I'm all pins and needles. We must be in some kind of energy field."

Just once more, and never again. It was as strong as this last time. They must come. They must, they must – That's it! "There! Look!"

The two shadows stood on the rose bed.

"You fool!" groaned David. "You've done it now. It's the fix!"

"But that's what I've always seen," said Roland. "What about it, Nick? Go on, have a good look. You can walk round them."

Nicholas made a strangled noise in his throat.

"Is this one of your hallucinations, eh?" said Roland, and tried to turn his head to see how Nicholas was reacting. But his neck muscles were locked. The shadows darkened.

"I can't move!" said Helen. "I can't move! Oh, my neck!"

"It's all right," said Roland. "They go away if you leave them."

"You cretin!" said David. "They're using us! Shut your eyes! Don't look!"

"I can still see them! In my head!" cried Helen.

The air whined. The shadows were pools fringed with light, no longer in the garden, no longer anywhere: free of space, they had no depth and no end.

"I didn't mean it," said Roland. "I only wanted to show you – so you'd know."

He could hardly speak for the numbness that welled through him. His strength was being sucked out.

"Can't you stop them?" whimpered Helen. "Oh, look! – Look!"

A white spot had appeared in the middle of each shadow, quivering like a focused beam of light. The spots grew, lessened their intensity, changed, congealed, and became the expanding forms of two men, rigid as dolls, hurtling towards the children. They matched the outlines of the shadows, and were rising like bubbles to the surface. As they came nearer their speed increased: they rushed upon the children, and filled the shadows, and eclipsed them – and at that instant they lost their woodenness and stepped, two men of Elidor, into the garden.

They were dressed in tunics and cloaks and carried spears. Shields hung on their backs. They were bewildered, and stood as if they had woken in the middle of a dream. Then they both looked at the soil between them where the Treasures were buried.

150

There was no static electricity in the air, and the hold on the children disappeared.

The men lifted their eyes, stared round at the garden, and then ran across the lawn and swung themselves over the fence into the orchard next door. Helen, David, and Roland did not move, but Nicholas broke forward after the men. He snatched up stones and threw them wildly into the trees. He was sobbing.

"You're not safe loose," said David. "You need locking up."

"I didn't know what it was," said Roland. "And you wouldn't listen to me. I had to show you. It's Nick's fault as much as mine."

"You're so mad keen to be proved right, you'd do anything, wouldn't you?" said David.

"Save your breath," said Nicholas. "We've got to decide what to do."

"There's nothing we can do," said David. "This raving nit has seen to that. We might as well hand over the Treasures before one of us gets a spear in his back."

"Look: all I've ever wanted is to be left alone," said Nicholas. "I thought if we dropped this Elidor business we'd be all right. So fair enough, I'm to blame as much as Roland. My way hasn't worked. Have you got a better one?"

Nobody said anything.

"Then how about this?" said Nicholas. "We can't fool ourselves any longer, so let's do the opposite. Let's go out and bash them first, before they bash us."

"But they've got spears," said Roland.

"I didn't mean it that way," said Nicholas. "It's the Treasures they're after: right? They're not really interested in us."

"You can't give them the Treasures!" said Roland. "You can't let Elidor die like that! You can't! It's the most important thing there is!"

"If I thought it'd help," said Nicholas, "I'd hand the Treasures over. But those two would still be here, and so would the Treasures. When they came out of their shadows they'd no more idea of where they were than we had when we landed in Elidor. If they can't find a way back with the Treasures there'll be more coming after them. But if the Treasures are in Elidor, we'll be left in peace."

"Fine," said David. "But how do you get the Treasures into Elidor?"

"Search me," said Nicholas.

"Malebron won't have a hope," said Roland.

"That's his problem," said Nicholas. "We didn't volunteer for this."

"Nick's right," said David. "We can't hide them, and we can't fight for them."

"What about the unicorn?" said Helen.

"That's what I mean," said Nicholas. "When you start messing around with these things, you don't know where it'll end. We'll have half of Elidor in our back garden if we're not quick."

"But that was Findhorn," said Roland. "He was being hunted. You saw those gashes all down his side. He had to break into our world to escape. They want to kill him before Malebron can find him. Malebron was trying to tell us. There's something he wants us to do."

"Then he can want," said Nicholas.

153

It was clear the following morning that there was not much time. During the night, slates had been taken from the coalhouse roof, and their fragments littered the rose bed. They had been used as spades, but the frozen ground had broken them.

Mrs Watson was too busy to notice anything all day. She had an appointment with the hairdresser's in the afternoon, and then she was going into Manchester to meet Mr Watson. They were having dinner with some friends before the New Year dance, which was being held at a large hotel in the middle of the city.

"What'll be the next move?" said David.

"They'll come back tonight with something to dig up the Treasures," said Nicholas. "It'll be easy enough. There are plenty of garden sheds round here. I think we're pretty safe in daylight, though. They'll be lying up till it's dark."

"So we lift the Treasures first, is that it?" said David.

"Yes: we'll have about an hour after Mum leaves before it starts to freeze."

"What's Dad going to say when he sees the mess?"

"It needn't be a mess," said Nicholas. "We can stick the bushes in again, and we'll throw the earth on to a couple of ground sheets."

Helen drew a sketch plan of the rose bed and labelled the bushes so that they could be replanted. Tools and ground sheets were made ready.

"Now, are you sure you can look after your-selves?" said Mrs Watson. "There's cold meat and pickles, and be sensible about going to bed, won't you? Don't sit up all night in front of the television, and fetch the coal in before dark, and put the fire guard up. The hotel's phone number is on the pad."

"Stop flapping, Mum," said David. "We'll be all right."

"You'll miss the train," said Nicholas.

"Oh, heavens! Is that the time? Oh, I some-times wonder if it's worth the fuss. I wouldn't go if your father wasn't so set on it."

"Goodbye, Mum," said Helen. "Have a lovely time."

The children watched their mother until she was out of sight round the corner of the road.

"Phew," said Nicholas.

They dug in relays without a pause.

The knots in the flex tying the lid to the dustbin had swollen, and they had to wait while David rummaged upstairs for his wire cutters. The poly-thene bags were milky with condensation when the children pulled them out of the bin, but the Treasures seemed to be no different for their year underground.

The children dropped the dustbin back, and trod the soil down as it was shovelled into the hole. The rose bushes were more or less straight.

"I think we ought to put the Treasures under our beds for tonight, said David after tea, "and try and get rid of them tomorrow."

"Yes, but how?" said Nicholas.

"That's it," said David. 'We're lumbered. Have you any brilliant schemes, Roland?"

Roland shook his head.

David switched on the television set. "And it must be tomorrow," he said. "Remember this?" As the set warmed up, the screeching and whistling began, and the picture, when it came, was a herringbone of black and white. "It won't be long before Dad's razor starts, either. There'll be fun tonight."

"They look so harmless, don't they?" said Helen. "This cup: it's ugly: nothing like that bowl with pearls all round it, and full of light."

"But can't you feel that they're still the Treasures?" said Roland. "They're still the same."

"Yes, I suppose you're right," said David. "The real sword and these two bits of wood have the same kind of 'swordness' about them. That's not changed."

"Let's try it," said Helen. "I'll go and bring an ordinary cup from the kitchen, and we'll see if there's any difference."

"For crying out loud!" said Nicholas. "Are you all off your rockers? – There! And I bet it's Mum's best china!"

They had heard a cup smash on the floor in the kitchen. Helen came running through the middle room and slammed the door behind her.

"I was – I was taking a cup," she said, "off the – the shelf. And someone – lifted the latch

156

on the back door. It went up – and down. I'd never have heard it: it was so quiet."

"Is the door bolted?" said Nicholas.

"Yes."

"But you'd hear anyone coming round the side of the house."

"I didn't. Nothing. Somebody tried the latch. I couldn't hear it."

"They know we've got 'em," said David. "Obviously. They'd know straight away."

"Wait a minute," said Nicholas. "Keep calm."

"Dial 999," said David.

But before he could say any more there was the sound of falling glass in the middle room.

"Out of the way!" shouted Nicholas.

He pushed Helen aside and threw open the door. A window pane had been broken, and a thin arm was feeling for the latch inside. The telephone was on the window-sill.

Nicholas grabbed the poker from the hearth and crashed it down on the arm. There was a howl, and the arm jerked out of sight.

"Everybody here, quick!" said Nicholas. "Shove the dresser across! And the other window! Stack the chairs on the table in front of it!"

"What about the kitchen?" said David.

"Leave that. Only the fanlight opens. Now bring your coats and the rucksack into the other room. Hurry! I'll put the light off in here."

"Nick: what'll we do?" said Helen, when they were together in the sitting room.

"Quiet a minute," said Nicholas.

157

He went to the front door and listened at the curtain.

"There's one of them in the porch. We can't keep them out. The dresser and the chairs will hold them up a bit, but that's all. We've got to move. We'll be safe in a crowd, or where there's plenty of light. They won't risk being caught."

"Where'll we go?"

"Anywhere. It doesn't matter."

Nicholas packed the stone in the rucksack. "Here, give me your cup," he said to Helen. "There's room for it."

"No," said Helen. "I'll carry it. I'd rather."

"Please yourself. Now listen. Have we any money?"

"I've some from Christmas," said Roland.

"So have I," said Helen.

"How do we get out, first?" said David.

"We'll crunch him behind the door," said Nicholas. "Like Dad, only better. We wait till we hear the other one climb through, and when he's sorting himself out from the furniture we'll flatten this one against the porch and run for it. Mind you don't trip over the curtain."

"Here he comes," said David.

The dresser pitched forward on to the floor.

"Ready?"

"Mum's Willow Pattern," said Helen.

There was a sound of scuffling, and more glass tinkled, and then someone fell heavily over the dresser.

"Now!"

Nicholas slipped the catch. They thrust their shoulders against the door and lashed it open. They felt the resilience of a body trapped between the door and the wall. A man cried out. And the children were running down the middle of the road, their legs hammering the smooth surface till their thighs burned.

Roland glanced over his shoulder and saw a figure lope from the porch and cross the lamplight to the darkness of the hedge along the footpath.

"They're coming!"

"Make a row! Fetch people out!"

"Help!"

"Help!"

Helen screamed.

"Help! Help!"

Lights were switched off all down the road.

"Help! Help!"

Visitors were leaving one house, but they stepped back, and shut the door. On the other side of the dimpled glass a broken pattern of a man reached up to slide the bolt.

"Please! Help!"

Christmas trees in front windows disappeared as the curtains swirled across.

"You lousy rotten devils!" yelled David.

"Keep moving!"

The children ran from pool to pool of the street lamps and sometimes they glimpsed a shadow, and sometimes there was a tall silhouette: and there was always too much darkness. When they turned the corner the white fluorescence of the railway station at the end of the road was like a sanctuary. They drove themselves towards its glass and concrete, as if the danger behind, the danger of spear-edge and shield-rim, would be powerless in the neon glare.

They jostled through the barrier on to the platform. A train was idling its motor: the porter was waving to the guard, and when he saw the children he opened a door.

"Come on, come on, if you want it."

They were carried forward by the impetus of their running, and almost all the porter had to do was to deflect them by the arm into the compartment, one after the other, like dominoes falling.

"Right away!"

The train glided out of the station, and quickly gathered speed.

" 'Right away'," said David. " 'Right away'! As easy as that!"

"Too easy," said Roland.

"How do you mean?"

Roland pulled a face. "Too easy: I dunno."

"I thought we'd had it then," said Helen. "I could feel those spears. Any second, I thought."

"We were lucky," said Nicholas.

"Yes, we were," said Roland, "weren't we?"

"How far shall we go?" said David.

"All the way," said Nicholas. "Into Manchester. It's safest."

"We'd better tell Mum and Dad," said Helen.

"I'd like to see you try," said Nicholas. "We'll say there was someone breaking in, so we cleared out. There'll be enough of a shambles to prove we weren't kidding."

"And then what?" said David. "There's the rest of the night left for the Treasures to be pinched. What time does the dance end?"

"One o'clock."

"Right. We shan't do anything now. We'll meet Mum and Dad out of the dance, and then it'll be three o'clock at least before all the fuss is over. With luck, we'll not go to bed at all."

They paid their fare at the terminus, and walked down the long slope from the station into the city. The streets were brilliant with lights and decorations. People hurried along in groups, making a lot of noise, and very cheerful.

"We want the cheapest place to keep warm in while we're waiting," said Nicholas. "Let's try a coffee bar."

The children sat at wrought-iron tables in a room that was all bamboo and rubber plant. Non-stop South American music came from a loud-speaker and was killed by the gush of the coffee machine. The children sat there for an hour, ordering more coffee when the waitress glared hard enough.

"It's not going to be cheap, at this rate," said Nicholas.

"I'm still jumpy," said Helen. "I feel as though everybody's watching us, though I know they're not."

"Me too," said David. "And we ought to move. We're not all that safe. It's about a three-hour walk into Manchester from our house: give them another hour to allow for dodging people: so they'll be arriving about two hours from now. They'll home on to the Treasures wherever we are. The only thing to do is to stay on the move, then they won't be able to lay a fix so easily."

"I know!" said Roland. "Let's ride on buses. If we keep changing, they'll never track us down."

"That's it," said David.

They drank their coffee and went out into the street.

"Which one?" said Helen. "There are dozens."

"Any bus'll do," said Roland. "The first that stops. There! That Number 76!"

They ran along the pavement to the bus stop.

"Inside," said the conductor, a West Indian. "Plenty of room inside."

The children took the front two seats behind the driver. Nicholas put the rucksack on his lap.

"Where do you go?" said David.

"Brookdale Park," said the conductor.

"One and three halves all the way, please," said Nicholas.

The bus crawled round the city centre. The traffic was dense, and people were using the streets as footpaths, but in a short while the Christmas glitter dropped behind. The bus was passing through an area of garages, public houses, and government-surplus stores.

"It's a bit grim up this end, isn't it?" said David.

"Don't you know where we are?" said Roland. "We've just turned off Oldham Road. We're near Thursday Street."

The bus stopped. "Hurry along, please," said the conductor. "Both sides."

"Shoor, a little bit of Heaven – fell-l-l – from out the sky one day – !"

The voice sang, blurred and loud, on the platform. The children looked round, and saw the conductor help a big Irishman up the step. He caught at the overhead rail, missed, and slumped heavily on to the back seat. He wore an army greatcoat, and he was very drunk.

"Man, you started your New Year early," said the conductor.

"Good luck," said the Irishman.

"Where you for?"

"Home."

"I don't know where that is. You tell me."

"Ballymartin, County Down." He was staring straight ahead of him. "There's a rocky old road I would follow," he sang, "to a place that is Heaven to me. Though it's never so grand, still it's my fairyland—"

"We don't go there, man. Brookdale Park any good?"

The Irishman held a coin between his fingers. The conductor took the money, and put a ticket and the change in the Irishman's coat pocket.

The other passengers were trying to ignore him. They became interested in their newspapers, or the advertisements in the bus, or the view from the window.

The Irishman hung over the back of the next seat. "Eh, missus," he said to the woman sitting there. "Missus." She froze. "Good luck," said the Irishman, and appeared to go to sleep.

The woman moved, and went upstairs. At once the Irishman lurched round and sat on the edge of the empty seat. His shoulder filled the gangway. He leaned forward to tap the arm of the man in front.

"Eh, guv'nor."

David gasped. "Don't look!" he whispered to

the others. "Don't let him see your faces! It's him! Paddy, from the demolition gang!"

"And we've still got the Treasures!" said Helen. "He'll murder us!"

"Would he remember?" said David. "It's more than a year ago, and he's properly sloshed."

"If someone had swiped me with an iron railing, I'd not forget 'em ," said Nicholas. "Stick your head down, Roland."

Paddy tried again. "Eh, guv'nor. Have yez a piece of paper I could be writin' on?" The man twitched his arm away. "Oh, it may be for yeeeears – " sang Paddy, "and it may be for ever – !" The man stood up, and pushed past him.

"Ruddy Micks!" he said.

"Good luck," said Paddy, and moved forward another seat.

"Here, you wanting paper?" said the conductor. "I got some you can have." He tore a couple of sheets out of a notebook and gave them to Paddy.

"That's dacent," said Paddy. He felt in his pockets and fished out a stump of pencil, and became absorbed in trying to write on his knee in the swaying bus.

"Brookdale Park!" shouted the conductor. The bus stopped, and the engine was switched off. The conductor went round to talk to the driver. The children and Paddy were the only people left.

"Shall we run for it?" said David.

"Not a hope," said Nicholas. "We couldn't get past him."

"Eh?" said Paddy. "Are yez there, then?" He strained to focus on the children, hauled himself upright, and crashed down again on the seat opposite Nicholas.

"Eh, a-vic," he said. "Would yez be helpin' me with this letter?"

"Er – yes: sure," said Nicholas.

"I'm not the illiterate, yez'll understand. I can put a letter together with the best of them. Oh, yes. But it's a terrible night I've had. A terrible night."

There was no recognition.

"Yes, of course. What do you want me to do?" Nicholas relaxed his grip on the rucksack.

"I'm resignin'," said Paddy. "Oh, they don't see me again. It's me letter of resignation. If I tell yez what to say, will yez be puttin' it down? Ah – eh – 'To the foreman. Dear Sir. – Dear Sir'. Eh – have yez written that?"

"Yes," said Nicholas.

"Ah, well then. 'Dear Sir.' Oh, it's a terrible night."

"Is that in the letter?" said Nicholas.

"Eh? Oh, no. No. 'Dear Sir, Herewith me resignation' – That's good: that's good – 'me resignation I won't be comin' no more it's no place for a good Catholic yours truly Mr Patrick Mehigan'."

"Do you want to sign it?" said Nicholas.

"No. Eh, no. No. Leave it, a-vic."

Paddy took the letter, folded it, and stared at it in silence. Nicholas was about to give a signal for them to creep away, when Paddy spoke.

"Am I drunk?"

"I beg your pardon?" said Nicholas.

"I said, am I drunk?"

"Er – perhaps: a little."

"And no wonder," said Paddy. "But is horses with horns any sight for a workin' man?"

"What?" cried Roland. "Where? Where did you see it?"

"Hello there," said Paddy. "It's a terrible night."

Roland bobbed on the seat. "When? Was it today? Here?"

"Lay off him," said David. "He can't follow you. Hey, Paddy: tell us about it. We're listening."

"Arragh: yez'll not believe me."

"We shall. I promise. Please, Paddy."

"Well then," said Paddy, "yez'll understand it's not a livin' wage on this job if yez can't make a bit extra on the side, like. So I'm goin' back after dark to pick up the odd scrap or two of lead I'd seen lyin' about the place. So there's this yard where I've put a few pieces by under an old bath, see? So I goes in – and there's this horse, all white, and this horn on its head yez could hardly stand up for the sight of. Well, as soon as it has wind of me it's away out of it, and divil a care whether I shifts or no, right past me, and there's me on my back. There now. Yez'll not believe that."

"Don't worry," said Nicholas. "We believe you."

"Yez'll not believe it," said Paddy. "I didn't meself." He reached inside his coat and pulled out a wallet. "But when I'm in the pub afterwards recoverin' like, I find these caught in me buttons." He opened the wallet, and lying between two ragged envelopes were a few wisps of hair.

The children had never seen anything like them. They were neither white nor silver. They were strands of pure light.

Roland caught his breath. "Let me hold them," he said.

"Oh, no," said Paddy, drawing back. "I'll not let no one touch them. There's no luck in it. I has a drink to see if they'll go away, but they won't. I takes a peep after every drink, but they're still there. Oh, it's a terrible night."

"Hi, you waiting for something?" said the conductor. "It's the end of the road, man."

"The same again, please," said Roland.

"It's a free country," said the conductor. "But where's he going?"

"Home to Ballymartin," said Paddy. "I'll not be stayin' here."

"We want the stop where he got on," said Roland, holding out the money.

"Wait a minute—" said David.

"OK," said the conductor. He took Paddy's fare out of his coat pocket and put another ticket in.

"Good luck," said Paddy, and began to read his letter. It was upside down, but he admired it.

The bus left them at the corner of a gaslit street. Paddy seemed to be feeling better for the ride.

"Will you show us where you saw this horse?" said Roland.

169

"I will not," said Paddy.

"Hold on, Roland," said David.

"Please," said Roland.

"I'll show yez the way, but I'll not go."

"Me neither," said Helen.

They walked to the next corner, and Paddy stopped by instinct outside the frosted glass door of a public house.

"If yez goes on down the next street," he said, "yez'll be near enough." His attention was wandering, drawn to the sound of a piano and laughter from the other side of the door. "Eh – I think I'll be havin' a drop to keep out the cold," he said. "It's been a terrible night."

He pushed open the door. Noise swamped the pavement and he disappeared among the faces, smoke, heat, and din of the public house. The door swung shut.

The children stayed on the corner. Ahead of them the street was a tunnel: no lamps were lit: the houses were empty.

19   The Wasteland

" 'Coincidence'!" said Roland. "That's all you can say. 'Coincidence.' You make me sick!"

"Well, if you think we're trapesing round in that hole," said David, "you can think again."

"But if we find him everything will be all right," said Roland.

"I'm too scared," said Helen.

"You landed us in enough trouble yesterday with your hen-brained ideas," said David. "We're not going. And that's flat."

"Oh yes we are!" said Roland – and sprinted for the blacked-out street.

"Roland! You great steaming chudd! Come back!"

The voices died behind him.

They'll have to come now! They daren't leave me!

He ran along the wider streets until his eyes were used to the dark. The moon had risen, and the glow of the city lightened the sky. He twisted down alleyways, running blindly, through crossroads, over bombed sites, and along the streets again.

I'll find 'em when they're right in. It'll be easy. They'll be calling after me.

The iron railing was heavy. He carried it hanging at arm's length, and it was beginning to pull

his shoulder down. Roland stopped, and listened. There was only the noise of the city, a low, constant rumble that was like silence.

He was in the demolition area. Roof skeletons made broken patterns against the sky.

Now that he was tired Roland felt less sure of himself. But at the time it had seemed the only thing to do. He had looked at the three stubborn faces, and had known that he could not argue with them any more. It was not a matter of disbelief. They believed him: but they were frightened. And Roland was frightened too.

The streets were so quiet. His footsteps echoed on the cobbles. The ruins hemmed him in. Doors and windows stared at him: abandoned furniture crouched among the rubble. A tin can rattled down a pile of bricks in the shadow of a building.

"Here!" Roland called. "I'm here!"

No answer.

Roland went on. The difficulty was that he could never see far in any direction because of the streets. The whole place was a maze of right angles. The other children might be near, but he would miss them, and he was not going to shout again.

Roland searched for a place that would be safe to climb, and found a staircase on the exposed inner wall of a house. The top step was the highest part of the house: everything above it, including the bedroom floor, had been knocked down.

Roland tested his weight, but the wood was firm, so he went up.

He could see little more of the streets from the top than from the ground. Behind him was a double row of back yards. The entry between them showed as a cleft.

They're bound to come sooner or later, thought Roland. The best thing is to stay put.

He sat on the top of the stairs in the moonlight. It was freezing hard. Roofs and cobbles sparkled. Roland felt better. The menace left the streets, and instead he was aware of the quietness of something poised, as if he could always sit here under the moon.

But the cold began to ache into him. He wondered if the others had decided to stay in one place and wait until he came.

This thought bothered him, and he was still trying to make up his mind when the unicorn appeared at the end of the street.

He was moving at a fast trot, and he wheeled about at the crossroad, unsure of the way. Then he came on towards Roland.

Roland sat there above the street and watched the unicorn pass below him, and he dared not even breathe.

The unicorn turned aside to pause at entries and gaps in the walls. He would stand at the threshold of a house, one hoof raised, but always he swung away, and on down the street.

His mane flowed like a river in the moon: the point of the horn drew fire from the stars. Roland shivered with the effort of looking. He wanted to fix every detail in his mind for ever, so that no matter what else happened there would always be this.

The unicorn turned into the next street, and Roland lost him until he heard the clatter of rubble in the entry, and there was the high neck moving between the walls.

He hurried down the stairs as quietly as he could, and groped his way through the house to the yard. He climbed over the entry wall as the unicorn reached the far end. Roland went after him.

The entry finished in a square of earth and cinders completely enclosed by walls. The unicorn had heard Roland and was waiting, alert, in the middle of the square. They both stood motionless, watching each other.

"Findhorn. Sing – Findhorn."

He was within twenty feet of the unicorn. The nostrils flared.

"Sing, Findhorn."

The unicorn stamped his hoof and his ears dropped flat to his skull. Roland halted.

"You must sing! You've got to!"

He took a step forward, and the horn plunged towards him. Roland dodged aside, and the unicorn went by at a canter, heading for the entry.

"No!" shouted Roland, and ran after the unicorn. "Wait! You mustn't go!" He caught up with him and tried to turn him. "Hey! Hey! Hey!" He waved his arm. The unicorn stopped. "Whoa back!" He recognized the lowering of the neck, and moved in time. Still the unicorn did not follow up the thrust, but carried on towards the entry.

"Wait!" Roland blocked the way. "Findhorn! Sing!" And he flourished the iron railing, the spear, in the unicorn's face.

The silver body grew black against the sky as the unicorn reared and brought his hoofs thrashing down. Roland flung himself sideways, and the hoofs showered him with frozen grit. He scrambled on all fours. "No, Findhorn!" But the unicorn was on him, cruel and merciless. Round and round, spraying cinders: only Roland's agility saved him: hoofs and horn and teeth: round and round.

There could be no end to it, no escape. Roland's nerve failed. He ran for the wall.

"Jump!"

He heard the voice, and through sweat he saw a hunchbacked shape kneeling on the broad coping stone of the wall. "Catch hold!" An arm reached, and he leapt, grabbed, and half swung, half clawed himself up the wall.

"You never learn, do you?" said Nicholas. The stone in the rucksack on his shoulders had nearly overbalanced him when he took Roland's weight. They lay together, not daring to move, while the horn flashed below them.

"Where've you come from?" gasped Roland.

"I was in the street on the other side, and I heard you beefing."

"We've got to make him sing," said Roland. "It's the way to save Elidor. That's what we're here for."

"What?" said Nicholas. "That? Sing? Don't make me laugh!"

"He must. He's got to. He's frightened: you can't blame him."

The unicorn was pacing backwards and forwards under the wall.

"He doesn't seem frightened to me," said Nicholas. "I'd say he wanted to finish us off."

"That's because he saw the spear. He thinks he's being hunted again. Look at those scars all along his flank."

"He doesn't give up, does he?" said Nicholas. "I'm glad we don't have to go down there."

"But we do," said Roland. "I dropped the spear when I jumped."

"That's that, then," said Nicholas. "We'll have to get by on three Treasures. But why is the unicorn here in the first place?"

"Trying to go back, I think," said Roland. "He knows this is one of the gates through. I was watching him in the street."

"Have you seen David and Helen?"

"No," said Roland. "Aren't they with you?"

"We lost each other crossing a bombed site."

"Oh."

"Yes, you've made a right mess of things one way or another," said Nicholas.

"We must find them," said Roland.

"You don't say! Well, where are they?"

Nicholas swept his arm to include the whole city. The row of houses they were on was at the edge of the demolition area. On the other side from where the unicorn was waiting lay the open wasteland.

Roland looked across the frozen landscape. He started, nearly falling off the wall.

"There!" he said. "There they are!"

Two figures were running together towards the houses.

"Thank goodness for that,' said Nicholas. "Ahoy! David! Helen! Here!"

"Hello!" shouted a voice.

"That's David!" said Roland. "He's in the street!"

"Then who are those two?" said Nicholas.

But by now the figures were near enough for Roland and Nicholas to see the cloaks, and the moon gleamed on the spears in the wasteland.

David's head poked through the back window of a house.

"So you've collared the little twerp," he said. "Where was he?"

"Up here, quick," said Nicholas.

"I'll wring your neck for you one of these days, Roland," said David. "Is Helen with you?"

"No. Stop waffling, and get up here quick!" said Nicholas. David stepped over the window-sill into the yard, and climbed the bank of rubbish that was piled against the wall. Roland and Nicholas gave him a hand up on to the coping stone.

"What are you doing here?" said David. "Oh, crumbs!" He found himself looking straight down at the unicorn.

"That's not the only thing," said Nicholas. "Have you seen what's coming?"

The two men were near the edge of the waste-land, heading straight for the children.

"Happy New Year," said David. "Let's nip along the wall to the other side of this square."

"I can't leave the spear," said Roland.

"You'll have one all to yourself soon enough if we don't shift," said Nicholas.

They began to move along the wall. Findhorn kept pace with them below.

"Roland wants him to sing," said Nicholas. "Then we can all go home."

"You're stark raving bonkers," said David.

"But he must sing," said Roland. "It was in that book. 'And the Darkness shall not fade unless there is heard the Song of Findhorn.' It's prophecy. He has to sing!"

"No, he hasn't," said David. " 'Unless' doesn't mean he's going to. It doesn't even mean that he can. Sing? You go down there and we'll see who does the singing!"

"Watch out," said Nicholas. "They're here."

The men were on the wall across the corner of the square.

David brandished the lath sword. "Treasures! Stinking bits of wood!"

"Into this house and through the yard," said Nicholas.

"What if the door's blocked?" said David. "Some are."

"Wait," said Roland. "They've seen Findhorn."

And the unicorn had seen the men. He veered from the wall towards the centre of the square, snorting, tearing the earth, levelling his horn, showing fury.

The men unslung their shields before dropping into the square.

"They're going to kill him to stop him from singing!" cried Roland.

The men separated. They threw their spears from a distance, and then advanced with swords.

The men came on. Findhorn swung his head, uncertain which to kill. The men crouched. And Findhorn launched himself at them. The man he attacked did not fight, but jumped aside, and the other sprang in and struck at Findhorn, tearing a gash down the shoulder, and when Findhorn whipped round, the first man thrust in to the side. And this way they played the unicorn so that he could never follow up his charge. The men were round him like dogs. From the wall, it looked as if they juggled with lightning.

"Where are you off to?" said Nicholas.

Roland was walking back along the coping. "It's all right."

"I bet it is. You come here."

Roland began to run, his arms outstretched for balance. He heard Nicholas start after him but he did not look. He was trying to find the place where he had jumped on to the wall.

The men were working Findhorn to a corner. Out in the dirt lay the railing. Roland sat on the edge. One of the men saw the railing, and shouted. He left the unicorn and ran for the Treasure. Roland twisted on to his stomach, lowered himself, and dropped.

He landed in the dark of the wall, close to the fighting. The man picked up the railing and came for him. Nicholas was above, but the height was too much, and Roland went out to meet the man.

Nicholas slithered down into the yard on the other side of the wall. He heaved at the flat iron

181

bar that bolted the door. It moved. Nicholas opened the door and dodged between the unicorn and the sword and out to Roland. The man was closing on him with the Treasure, but Roland did not pause. He screamed and his arms were stretched as he ran on to it, not caring, not

thinking, trying only to grasp, and the man was
firm and steady for the lunge.

Nicholas caught Roland round the throat with
one arm and took hold of his hair with the other
hand. He yanked him backwards, and used the
weight of his tumbling to start to drag him to the

door. The man came on, but Nicholas did not look, did not take his eyes from the door in the wall. Roland's heels dug black furrows in the dirt, but he could not stop him. They fell together. Nicholas kicked the door, and rammed the bar back into its socket. A warning shout was lost in pounding hoofs, there was one cry beyond and the wood was split by horn. It stood out above Roland's head.

The horn jerked back, and the wood groaned, and a weight slumped against the door on the other side.

David was on the coping stone, looking into the square.

"He didn't have a chance. Right through his back, and everything."

Roland and Nicholas climbed up to David. While Findhorn had pulled himself clear, the other man had taken the railing and fled for the entry. He could not face the unicorn longer alone.

Findhorn charged.

"Helen!" said David. "He's whipped the spear!"

"Remember that, Roland," said Nicholas. "Just in case, remember that. Just in case."

The unicorn had been so far ahead that they rushed out of the entry into the street, thinking they would catch no more than a glimpse at a corner. But they nearly ran into him.

They scattered for cover.

The unicorn was careering up and down the street, silver and dark with wounds.

"He's gone berserk!" shouted David.

"He can still smell the man," said Nicholas. "He could be anywhere."

"It's hardly real!" said David. "All fire and air!"

Findhorn spun on his hind legs and his nostrils smoked in the frost. And Helen walked round the corner of the street. She stopped in the middle of the cobbles when she saw the unicorn. She was holding the cup in both hands.

"Helen! Look out! Get behind a wall or something!"

Findhorn went down the street like a wind of flame. Helen seemed unable to move.

And then Findhorn checked, and shied, and halted. He raised his head and walked delicately towards Helen, and when he reached her he left all his fierceness and knelt before her, and lay down. Helen knelt, too, and he put his great head in her lap.

"It's all right," Roland called softly. "He won't hurt you."

"I know," said Helen.

Roland climbed down, and walked up the street. Nicholas shouted something after him, but he did not hear.

"What is it, Roland?" said Helen. "Oh, what is it?"

She was looking into Findhorn's eyes.

" 'Save maid that is makeless, no man with me mell'," whispered Roland.

Helen began to cry silently.

"I've broken it," she said.

"Sing, Findhorn," said Roland. "Please sing."

The unicorn stared up at Helen, and for the first time Roland looked into his eyes. What he saw he could not speak. It was too strong to bear.

"Findhorn. Findhorn. You must sing. It'll be all right if you sing. No one will hurt you. No one can. You'll be safe. Please. Sing."

He heard David and Nicholas come and stand behind him. Findhorn did not move. All his strength slept.

"You can save Elidor. I know you can. I know now. Sing, Findhorn."

A brick crashed into the street. Down one side, only the front of the terrace remained, and the man was coming along the top of the wall, the railing, the spear, raised. Behind him the city glowed.

David and Nicholas closed round the unicorn, but there was nothing they could do.

"Sing! It'll be too late!"

Findhorn strove almost as if to speak, but he could not, and he could not.

The man paused: balanced himself to throw.

"Sing: oh, sing."

Helen cradled his head, and stroked the curls of light.

"Up!" shouted Roland. "Up! Findhorn! Run! Oh, Findhorn! Findhorn! No!"

The spear hissed down, the railing sank between the unicorn's ribs to the heart. The white neck arched, and the head lifted to the stars and gave tongue of fire that rang beyond the streets, the city, the cold hills and the sky. The worlds shook at the song.

A brightness grew on the windows of the terrace, and in the brightness was Elidor, and the four golden castles. Behind Gorias a sunburst swept the land with colour. Streams danced, and rivers were set free, and all the shining air was new. But a mist was covering Findhorn's eyes.

Roland took hold of the railing, and pulled. He felt it grate against bone. He pulled.

"Now!" said Nicholas. "Now's our chance! Give them back now!"

He broke the straps on the rucksack to get at the stone.

Roland pulled on the railing. It was clear of the bone, and slid in flesh.

The song went on, a note of beauty and terror.

He looked through the windows out over Elidor. He saw the tall figure on the battlements of Gorias, with the golden cloak about him. He saw the life spring in the land from Mondrum to the mountains of the north. He saw the morning.

It was not enough.

"Yes! Take them!"

He cried his pain, and snatching the cup from Helen, he threw it and the railing at the windows. Nicholas and David threw their Treasures. They struck together, and the windows blazed outward, and, for an instant, the glories of stone, sword, spear and cauldron hung in their true shapes, almost a trick of the splintering glass, the golden light.

The song faded.

They were alone with the windows of a slum.

THE WEIRDSTONE OF BRISINGAMEN

Alan Garner
A Tale of Alderley

CONTENTS

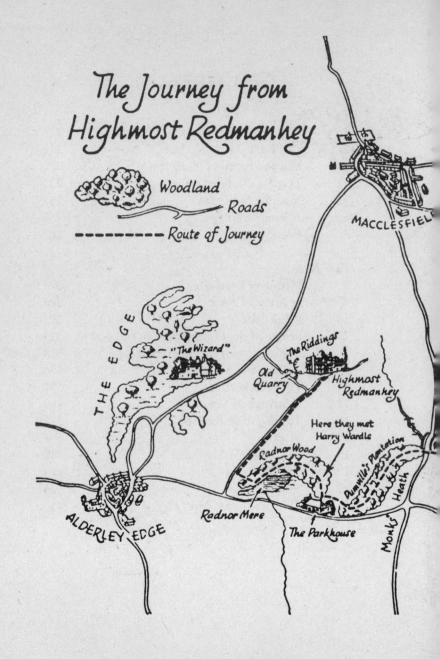

The Journey from
Highmost Redmanhey

Woodland
Roads
------------ Route of Journey

MACCLESFIELD

THE EDGE

"The Wizard"

The Riddings

Old Quarry

Highmost Redmanhey

Here they met
Harry Wardle

Radnor Wood

Dumville's Plantation

Monks' Heath

ALDERLEY EDGE

Radnor Mere

The Parkhouse

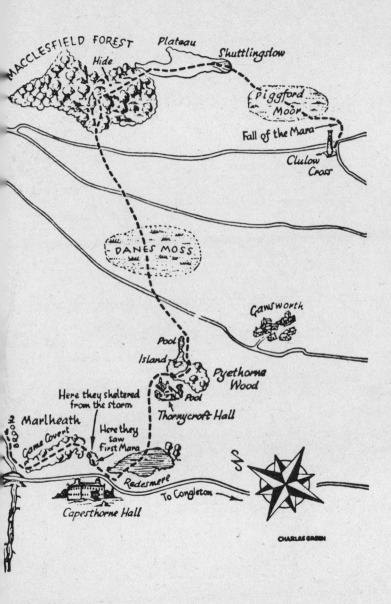

MACCLESFIELD FOREST   Plateau   Shuttlingslow

Hide

Piggford Moor

Fall of the Mara

Clulow Cross

DANES MOSS

Gawsworth

Pool

Island

Pyethorne Wood

Pool

Here they sheltered from the storm

Thornycroft Hall

Marlheath

Game Covert

Here they saw first Mara

Redesmere

To Congleton

Capesthorne Hall

CHARLES GREEN

The Legend of Alderley

*In every prayer I offer up, Alderley,
and all belonging to it, will be ever a
living thought in my heart.*

REV. EDWARD STANLEY: 1837

At dawn one still October day in the long ago of
the world, across the hill of Alderley, a farmer
from Moberley was riding to Macclesfield fair.

The morning was dull, but mild; light mists
bedimmed his way; the woods were hushed; the
day promised fine. The farmer was in good spirits, and he let his horse, a milk-white mare, set
her own pace, for he wanted her to arrive fresh
for the market. A rich man would walk back to
Mobberley that night.

So, his mind in the town while he was yet on
the hill, the farmer drew near to the place known
as Thieves' Hole. And there the horse stood still
and would answer to neither spur nor rein. The
spur and rein she understood, and her master's
stern command, but the eyes that held her were
stronger than all these.

In the middle of the path, where surely there
had been no one, was an old man, tall, with long
hair and beard. "You go to sell this mare," he
said. "I come here to buy. What is your price?"

But the farmer wished to sell only at the

201

market, where he would have a choice of many offers, so he rudely bade the stranger quit the path and let him through, for if he stayed longer he would be late to the fair.

"Then go your way," said the old man. "None will buy. And I shall await you here at sunset."

The next moment he was gone, and the farmer could not tell how or where.

The day was warm, and the tavern cool, and all who saw the mare agreed that she was a splendid animal, the pride of Cheshire, a queen among horses; and everyone said that there was no finer beast in the town. But no one offered to buy. A sour-eyed farmer rode out of Macclesfield at the end of the day.

Near Thieves' Hole the mare stopped: the stranger was there.

Thinking any price was now better than none, the farmer agreed to sell. "How much will you give?" he said.

"Enough. Now come with me."

By Seven Firs and Goldenstone they went, to Stormy Point and Saddlebole. And they halted before a great rock embedded in the hillside. The old man lifted his staff and lightly touched the rock, and it split with the noise of thunder.

At this, the farmer toppled from his plunging horse and, on his knees, begged the other to have mercy on him and let him go his way unharmed. The horse should stay; he did not want her. Only spare his life, that was enough.

The wizard, for such he was, commanded the

farmer to rise. "I promise you safe conduct," he said. "Do not be afraid: for living wonders you shall see here."

Beyond the rock stood a pair of iron gates. These the wizard opened, and took the farmer and the horse down a narrow tunnel deep into the hill. A light, subdued but beautiful, marked their way. The passage ended, and they stepped into a cave, and there a wondrous sight met the farmer's eyes – a hundred and forty knights in silver armour, and by the side of all but one a milk-white marc.

"Here they lie in enchanted sleep," said the wizard, "until the day will come – and come it will – when England shall be in direst peril, and England's mothers weep. Then out from the hill these must ride and, in a battle thrice lost, thrice won, upon the plain, drive the enemy into the sea."

The farmer, dumb with awe, turned with the wizard into a further cavern, and here mounds of gold and silver and precious stones lay strewn along the ground.

"Take what you can carry in payment for the horse."

And when the farmer had crammed his pockets (ample as his lands!), his shirt, and his fists with jewels, the wizard hurried him up the long tunnel and thrust him out of the gates. The farmer stumbled, the thunder rolled, he looked, and there was only the rock above him. He was alone on the hill, near Stormy Point. The broad full moon was up, and it was night.

And although in later years he tried to find the place, neither he nor any after him ever saw the iron gates again. Nell Beck swore she saw them once, but she was said to be mad, and when she died they buried her under a hollow bank near Brindlow wood in the field that bears her name to this day.

PART ONE

CHAPTER 1

Highmost Redmanhey

The guard knocked on the door of the compartment as he went past. "Wilmslow fifteen minutes!"

"Thank you!" shouted Colin.

Susan began to clear away the debris of the journey – apple cores, orange peel, food wrappings, magazines, while Colin pulled down their luggage from the rack. And within three minutes they were both poised on the edge of their seats, case in hand and mackintosh over one arm, caught, like every traveller before or since, in that limbo of journey's end, when there is nothing to do and no time to relax. Those last miles were the longest of all.

The platform of Wilmslow station was thick with people, and more spilled off the train, but Colin and Susan had no difficulty in recognizing Gowther Mossock among those waiting. As the tide of passengers broke round him and surged through the gates, leaving the children lonely at the far end of the platform, he waved his hand and came striding towards them. He was an oak of a man: not over tall, but solid as a crag, and barrelled with flesh, bone, and muscle. His face was round and polished; blue eyes crinkled to the humour of his mouth. A tweed jacket strained across his back, and his legs, curved like the timbers of an old house, were clad in breeches, which tucked into thick woollen stockings just above the swelling calves. A felt hat, old and formless, was on his head, and hob-nailed boots struck sparks from the platform as he walked.

"Hallo! I'm thinking you mun be Colin and Susan." His voice was gusty and high-pitched, yet mellow, like an autumn gale.

"That's right," said Colin. "And are you Mr Mossock?"

"I am – but we'll have none of your 'Mr Mossock', if you please. Gowther's my name. Now come on, let's be having you. Bess is getting us some supper, and we're not home yet."

He picked up their cases, and they made their way down the steps to the station yard, where there stood a green farm-cart with high red wheels, and between the shafts was a white horse, with shaggy mane and fetlock.

"Eh up, Scamp!" said Gowther as he heaved the cases into the back of the cart. A brindled lurcher, which had been asleep on a rug, stood and eyed the children warily while they climbed to the seat. Gowther took his place between them, and away they drove under the station bridge on the last stage of their travels.

They soon left the village behind and were riding down a tree-bordered lane between fields. They talked of this and that, and the children were gradually accepted by Scamp, who came and thrust his head on to the seat between Susan and Gowther. Then, "What on earth's *that?*" said Colin.

They had just rounded a corner: before them, rising abruptly out of the fields a mile away, was a long-backed hill. It was high, and sombre, and black. On the extreme right-hand flank, outlined against the sky, were the towers and spires of big houses showing above the trees, which covered much of the hill like a blanket.

"Yon's th'Edge," said Gowther. "Six hundred feet high and three mile long. You'll have some grand times theer, I con tell you. Folks think as how Cheshire's flat as a poncake, and so it is for the most part, but not wheer we live!"

Nearer they came to the Edge, until it towered above them, then they turned to the right along a road which kept to the foot of the hill. On one side lay the fields, and on the other the steep slopes. The trees came right down to the road, tall beeches which seemed to be whispering to each other in the breeze.

"It's a bit creepy, isn't it?" said Susan.

"Ay, theer's some as reckons it is, but you munner always listen to what folks say.

"We're getting close to Alderley village now, sithee: we've not come the shortest way, but I dunner care much for the main road, with its clatter and smoke, nor does Prince here. We shanner be going reet into the village; you'll see more of yon when we do our shopping of a Friday. Now here's wheer we come to a bit of steep."

They were at a crossroad. Gowther swung the cart round to the left, and they began to climb. On either side were the walled gardens of the houses that covered the western slope of the Edge. It was very steep, but the horse plodded along until, quite suddenly, the road levelled out, and Prince snorted and quickened his pace.

"He knows his supper's waiting on him, dunner thee, lad?"

They were on top of the Edge now, and through gaps in the trees they caught occasional glimpses of lights twinkling on the plain far below. Then they turned down a narrow lane which ran over hills and hollows and brought them, at the last light of day, to a small farmhouse lodged in a fold of the Edge. It was built round a framework of black oak, with white plaster showing between the gnarled beams: there were diamond-patterned, lamp-yellow windows and a stone flagged roof: the whole building seemed to be a natural part of the hillside, as if it had grown there. This was the end of the children's journey: Highmost Redmanhey, where a Mossock had farmed for three centuries and more.

"Hurry on in," said Gowther. "Bess'll be waiting supper for us. I'm just going to give Prince his oats."

Bess Mossock, before her marriage, had been nurse to the children's mother; and although it was all of twelve years since their last meeting they still wrote to each other from time to time and sent gifts at Christmas. So it was to Bess that their mother had turned when she had been called to join her husband abroad for six months, and Bess, ever the nurse, had been happy to offer what help she could. "And it'll do this owd farmhouse a world of good to have a couple of childer brighten it up for a few months."

She greeted the children warmly, and after asking how their parents were, she took them upstairs and showed them their rooms.

When Gowther came in they all sat round the table in the broad, low-ceilinged kitchen where Bess served up a monstrous Cheshire pie. The heavy meal, on top of the strain of travelling, could have only one effect, and before long Colin and Susan were falling asleep on their chairs. So they said good night and went upstairs to bed, each carrying a candle, for there was no electricity at Highmost Redmanhey.

"Gosh, I'm tired!"

"Oh, me too!"

"This looks all right, doesn't it?"

"Mm."

"Glad we came now, aren't you?"

"Ye-es . . ."

CHAPTER 2

The Edge

"If you like," said Gowther at breakfast, "we've time for a stroll round before Sam comes, then we'll have to get in that last load of hay while the weather holds, for we could have thunder today as easy as not."

Sam Harlbutt, a lean young man of twenty-four, was Gowther's labourer, and a craftsman with a pitchfork. That morning he lifted three times as much as Colin and Susan combined, and with a quarter of the effort. By eleven o'clock the stack was complete, and they lay in its shade and drank rough cider out of an earthenware jar.

Later, at the end of the midday meal, Gowther asked the children if they had any plans for the afternoon.

"Well," said Colin, "if it's all right with you, we thought we'd like to go in the wood and see what there is there."

"Good idea! Sam and I are going to mend the pig-cote wall, and it inner a big job. You go and enjoy yourselves. But when you're up th'Edge sees as you dunner venture down ony caves you might find, and keep an eye open for holes in the ground. Yon place is riddled with tunnels and shafts from the owd copper mines. If you went down theer and got lost that'd be the end of you, for even if you missed falling down a hole you'd wander about in the dark until you upped and died."

"Thanks for telling us," said Colin. "We'll be careful."

"Tea's at five o'clock," said Bess.

"And think on you keep away from them mineholes!" Gowther called after them as they went out of the gate.

It was strange to find an inn there on that road. Its white walls and stone roof had nestled into the woods for centuries, isolated, with no other house in sight: a village inn, without a village. Colin and Susan came to it after a mile and a half of dust and wet tar in the heat of the day. It was named The Wizard, and above the door was fixed a painted sign which held the children's attention. The painting showed a man, dressed like a monk, with long white hair and beard: behind him a figure in old-fashioned peasant garb struggled with the reins of a white horse which was rearing on its hind legs. In the background were trees.

"I wonder what all that means," said Susan. "Remember to ask Gowther – he's bound to know."

They left the shimmering road for the green wood, and The Wizard was soon lost behind them as they walked among fir and pine, oak, ash, and silver birch, along tracks through bracken, and across sleek hummocks of grass. There was no end to the peace and beauty. And then, abruptly, they came upon a stretch of rock and sand from which the heat vibrated as if from an oven. To the north, the Cheshire plain spread before them like a green and yellow patchwork quilt dotted with toy farms and houses. Here the Edge dropped steeply for several hundred feet, while away to their right the country rose in folds and wrinkles until it joined the bulk of the Pennines, which loomed eight miles away through the haze.

The children stood for some minutes, held by the splendour of the view. Then Susan, noticing something closer to hand, said, "Look here! This must be one of the mines."

Almost at their feet a narrow trench sloped into the rock.

"Come on," said Colin, "there's no harm in going down a little way – just as far as the daylight reaches."

Gingerly they walked down the trench, and were rather disappointed to find that it ended in a small cave, shaped roughly like a discus, and full of cold, damp air. There were no tunnels or shafts: the only thing of note was a round hole in the roof, about a yard across, which was blocked by an oblong stone.

"Huh!" said Colin. "There's nothing dangerous about *this*, anyway."

All through the afternoon Colin and Susan roamed up and down the wooded hillside and along the valleys of the Edge, sometimes going where only the tall beech stood, and in such places all was still. On the ground lay dead leaves, nothing more: no grass or bracken grew; winter seemed to linger there among the grey, green beeches. When the children came out of such a wood it was like coming into a garden from a musty cellar.

In their wanderings they saw many caves and openings in the hill, but they never explored further than the limits of daylight.

Just as they were about to turn for home after a climb from the foot of the Edge, the children came upon a stone trough into which water was dripping from an overhanging cliff, and high in the rock was carved the face of a bearded man, and underneath was engraved:

DRINK OF THIS
AND TAKE THY FILL
FOR THE WATER FALLS
BY THE WIZHARDS WILL

"The wizard again!" said Susan. "We really must find out from Gowther what all this is about. Let's go straight home now and ask him. It's probably nearly tea-time anyway."

They were within a hundred yards of the farm when a car overtook them and pulled up sharply. The driver, a woman, got out and stood waiting for the children. She looked about forty-five years old, was powerfully built ("fat" was the word Susan used to describe her), and her head rested firmly on her shoulders without appearing to have much of a neck at all. Two lines ran from either side of her nose to the corners of her wide, thin-lipped mouth, and her eyes were rather too small for her broad head. Strangely enough, her legs were thin and spindly, so that in outline she resembled a well-fed sparrow, but again that was Susan's description.

All this Colin and Susan took in as they approached the car, while the driver eyed them up and down more obviously.

"Is this the road to Macclesfield?" she said when the children came up to her.

"I'm afraid I don't know," said Colin. "We've only just come to stay here."

"Oh? Then you'll want a lift. Jump in!"

"Thanks," said Colin, "but we're living at this next farm."

"Get into the back."

"No, really. It's only a few yards."

"*Get in!*"

"But we . . ."

The woman's eyes glinted and the colour rose in her cheeks.

"You – will – get – into – the back!"

"Honestly, it's not worth the bother! We'd only hold you up."

The woman drew breath through her teeth. Her eyes rolled upwards and the lids came down until only an unpleasant white line showed; and then she began to whisper to herself.

Colin felt most uncomfortable. They could not just walk off and leave this peculiar woman in the middle of the road, yet her manner was so embarrassing that he wanted to hurry away, to disassociate himself from her strangeness.

"*Omptator*," said the woman.

"I . . . beg your pardon."

"*Lapidator.*"

"I'm sorry . . .'

"*Somniator.*"

"Are you . . . ?"

"*Qui libertar opera facitis* . . ."

"I'm not much good at Latin . . ."

Colin wanted to run now. She must be mad. He could not cope. His brow was damp with sweat, and pins and needles were taking all awareness out of his body.

Then, close at hand, a dog barked loudly. The woman gave a suppressed cry of rage and spun round. The tension broke; and Colin saw that his fingers were round the handle of the car door, and the door was half-open.

"Howd thy noise, Scamp," said Gowther sharply.

He was crossing the road opposite the farm gate, and Scamp stood a little way up the hill nearer the car, snarling nastily.

"Come on! Heel!"

Scamp slunk unwillingly back towards Gowther, who waved to the children and pointed to the house to show that tea was ready.

"Th – that's Mr Mossock," said Colin. "He'll be able to tell you the way to Macclesfield."

"No doubt!" snapped the woman. And, without another word, she threw herself into the car, and drove away.

"Well!" said Colin. "What was all that about? She must be off her head! I thought she was having a fit! What do you think was up with her?"

Susan made no comment. She gave a wan smile and shrugged her shoulders, but it was not until Colin and she were at the farm gate that she spoke.

"I don't know," she said. "It may be the heat, or because we've walked so far, but all the time you were talking to her I thought I was going to faint. But what's so strange is that my Tear has gone all misty."

Susan was fond of her Tear. It was a small piece of crystal, shaped like a raindrop, and had been given to her by her mother, who had had it mounted in a socket fastened to a silver chain bracelet which Susan always wore. It was a flawless stone, but, when she was very young, Susan had discovered that if she held it in a certain way, so that it caught the light just . . . so, she could see, deep in the heart of the crystal, miles away, or so it seemed, a twisting column of blue fire, always moving, never ending, alive, and very beautiful.

Bess Mossock clapped her hands in delight when she saw the Tear on Susan's wrist. "Oh, if it inner the Bridestone! And after all these years!"

Susan was mystified, but Bess went on to explain that "yon pretty dewdrop" had been given to her by her mother, who had had it from *her* mother, and so on, till its origin and the meaning of the name had become lost among the distant generations. She had given it to the children's mother because "it always used to catch the children's eyes, and thy mother were no exception!"

At this, Susan's face fell. "Well then," she said, "it must go back to you now, because it's obviously a family heirloom and . . ."

"Nay, nay, lass! Thee keep it. I've no childer of my own, and thy mother was the same as a daughter to me. I con see as how it's in good hands."

So Susan's Tear had continued to sparkle at her wrist until that moment at the car, when it had suddenly clouded over, the colour of whey.

"Oh, hurry up, Sue!" said Colin over his shoulder. "You'll feel better after a meal. Let's go and find Gowther."

"But Colin!" cried Susan, holding up her wrist. She was about to say, "Do look!" but the words died in her throat, for the crystal now winked at her as pure as it had ever been.

CHAPTER 3

Maggot-breed of Ymir

"And what did owd Selina Place want with you?" said Gowther at tea.

"Selina Place?" said Colin. "Who's she?"

"You were talking to her just before you came in, and it's not often you see her bothering with folks."

"But how do you know her? She seemed to be a stranger round here, because she stopped to ask the way to Macclesfield."

"She did *what*? But that's daft! Selina Place has lived in Alderley for as long as I con remember."

"She *has*?"

"Ay, hers is one of the big houses on the back hill – a rambling barn of a place it is, stuck on the edge of a cliff. She lives alone theer with what are supposed to be three dogs, but they're more like wolves, to my way of thinking, though I conner rightly say as I've ever seen them. She never takes them out with her. But I've heard them howling of a winter's night, and it's a noise I shanner forget in a hurry!

"And was that all she wanted? Just to know how to get to Macclesfield?"

"Yes. Oh, and she seemed to think that because we'd only recently come to live here we'd want a lift. But as soon as she saw you she jumped into the car and drove away. I think she's not quite all there."

"Happens you'd best have a word with yon," said Bess. "It all sounds a bit rum to me. I think she's up to summat."

"Get away with your bother! Dick Thornicroft's always said as she's a bit cracked, and it looks as though he's reet. Still, it's as well to keep clear of the likes of her, and I shouldner accept ony lifts, if I were you.

"Now then, from what you tell me, I con see as how you've been a tidy step this afternoon, so let's start near the beginning and then we shanner get ourselves lost. Well, yon place wheer you say theer was such a grand view is Stormy Point, and the cave with the hole in the roof is the Devil's Grave. If you run round theer three times widdershins Owd Nick's supposed to come up and fetch you."

And so, all through their meal, Gowther entertained Colin and Susan with stories and explanations of the things they had seen in their wanderings, and at last, after frequent badgering, he turned to the subject of the wizard.

"I've been saving the wizard till the end. Yon's quite a long story, and now tea's finished I con talk and you con listen and we needner bother about owt else."

And Gowther told Colin and Susan the legend of Alderley.

"Well, it seems as how theer was once a farmer from Mobberley as had a milk-white mare . . .

". . . and from that day to this no one has ever seen the gates of the wizard again."

"Is that a *true* story?" said Colin.

"Theer's some as reckons it is. But if it did happen it was so long ago that even the place wheer the iron gates are supposed to be has been forgotten. I say yon's nobbut a legend; but it makes fair telling after a good meal."

"Yes," said Susan, "but you know, our father has always said that there's no smoke without a fire."

"Ay, happen he's getten summat theer!" laughed Gowther.

The meal over, Colin and Susan went with Gowther to take some eggs to an old widow who lived in a tiny cottage a little beyond the farm boundary. And when they were returning across the Riddings, which was the name of the steep hill-field above Highmost Redmanhey, Gowther pointed to a large black bird that was circling above the farmyard.

"Hey! Sithee yon carrion crow! I wonder what he's after. If he dunner shift himself soon I'll take my shotgun to him. We dunner want ony of his sort round here, for they're a reet menace in the lambing season."

Early in the evening Colin, who had been very taken with the legend of the wizard, suggested another walk on the Edge, this time to find the iron gates.

"Ay, well, I wish you luck! You're not the first to try, and I dunner suppose you'll be the last."

"Take your coats with you," said Bess. "It gets chilly on the top at this time o'day."

Colin and Susan roamed all over Stormy Point, and beyond, but there were so many rocks and boulders, any of which could have hidden the gates, that they soon tired of shouting "Abracadabra!" and "Open Sesame!" and instead lay down to rest upon a grassy bank just beneath the crest of a spur of the Edge, and watched the sun drop towards the rim of the plain.

"I think it's time we were going, Colin," said Susan when the sun had almost disappeared. "If we don't reach the road before dark we could easily lose our way."

"All right: but let's go back to Stormy Point along the other side of this ridge, just for a change. We've not been over there yet."

He turned, and Susan followed him over the crest of the hill into the trees.

Once over the ridge, they found themselves in a dell, bracken and boulder filled, and edged with rocks, in which were cracks, and fissures, and small caves; and before them a high-vaulted beech wood marched steeply down into the dusk. The air was still and heavy, as though waiting for thunder; the only sound the concentrated whine of mosquitoes; and the thick sweet smell of bracken and flies was everywhere.

"I . . . I don't like this place, Colin,' said Susan: "I feel that we're being watched."

Colin did not laugh at her as he might normally have done. He, too, had that feeling between the shoulder blades; and he could easily have imagined that something was moving among the shadows of the rocks: something that managed to keep out of sight. So he gladly turned to climb back to the path.

They had moved barely a yard up the dell when Colin stopped and laughed.

"Look! Somebody *is* watching us!"

Perched on a rock in front of them was a bird. Its head was thrust forward, and it stared unwinkingly at the two children.

"It's the carrion crow that was round the farm after tea!" cried Susan.

"Talk sense! How can you tell it's the same one? There are probably dozens of them about here."

All the same, Colin did not like the way the bird sat hunched there so tensely, almost eagerly; and they had to pass it if they wanted to regain the path. He took a step forward, waved his arms in the air, and cried "Shoo!" in a voice that sounded woefully thin and unfrightening.

The crow did not move.

Colin and Susan moved forward, longing to run, but held by the crow's eye. And as they reached the centre of the dell the bird gave a loud, sharp croak. Immediately a cry answered from among the rocks, and out of the shadows on either side of the children rose a score of outlandish figures.

They stood about three feet high and were manshaped, with thin, wiry bodies and limbs, and broad, flat feet and hands. Their heads were large, having pointed ears, round saucer eyes, and gaping mouths which showed teeth. Some had pug-noses, others thin snouts reaching to their chins. Their hides were generally of a fish-white colour, though some were black, and all were practically hairless. Some held coils of black rope, while out of one of the caves advanced a group carrying a net woven in the shape of a spider's web.

For a second the children were rooted; but only for a second. Instinct took control of their wits. They raced back along the dell and flung themselves through the gap into the beech wood. Fingers clawed, and ropes hissed like snakes, but they were through and plunging down the slope in a flurry of dead leaves.

"Stop, Sue!" yelled Colin.

He realized that their only hope of escape lay in reaching open ground and the path that led from Stormy Point to the road, where their longer legs might outdistance their pursuers', and even that seemed a slim chance.

"Stop, Sue! We must . . . not go . . . down . . . any further! Find . . . Stormy Point . . . somehow!"

All the while he was looking for a recognizable landmark, since in the fear and dusk he had lost his bearings, and all he knew was that their way lay uphill and not down.

Then, through the trees, he saw what he needed. About a hundred feet above them and to their right a tooth-shaped boulder stood against the sky: its distinctive shape had caught his eye when they had walked past it *along a track coming from Stormy Point!*

"That boulder! Make for that boulder!"

Susan looked where he was pointing, and nodded.

They began to flounder up the hill, groping for firm ground with hands and feet beneath the knee-high sea of dead leaves. Their plunge had taken them diagonally across the slope, and their upward path led away from the dell, otherwise they would not have survived.

The others had come skimming lightly down over the surface of the leaves, and had found it difficult to check their speed when they saw the quick change of direction. Now they scurried across to intercept the children, bending low over the ground as they ran.

Slowly Colin and Susan gained height until they were at the same level as the pursuit, then above it, and the danger of being cut off from the path was no longer with them. But their lead was a bare ten yards, and shortening rapidly, until Colin's fingers, scrabbling beneath the leaves closed round something firm. It was a fallen branch, still bushy with twigs, and he tore it from the soil and swung it straight into the leaders, who went clamouring, head over heels, into those behind in a tangle of ropes and nets.

This gained Colin and Susan precious yards and seconds, though their flight was still nightmare: for unseen twigs rolled beneath their feet, and leaves dragged leadenly about their knees. But at last they pulled themselves on to the path.

"Come on, Sue!" Colin gasped. "Run for it! They're . . . not far . . . behind . . . now!"

The children drew energy from their fear. Above their heads a bird cried harshly three times, and at once the air was filled with the beating of a gong. The sound seemed to come from a distance, yet it was all about them, in the air and under the ground.

Then they ran clear of the trees and on to Stormy Point. But their relief was short-lived; for whereas till that moment they had been fleeing from twenty or so, they were now confronted with several hundred of the creatures as they came out of the Devil's Grave like ants from a nest.

Colin and Susan halted: gone was their last hope of reaching the road: the way was blocked to front and rear: on their left was the grim beech wood: to the right an almost sheer slope dropped between pines into a valley. But at least there was no known danger there, so the children turned their faces that way and fled, stumbling and slithering down a sandy path, till at last they landed at the bottom – only to splash knee-deep in the mud and leaf-mould of the swamp that sprawled unseen down the opposite wall of the valley and out across the floor.

They lurched forward a few paces, spurred on by the sound of what was following all too close behind, but then Susan staggered and collapsed against a fallen tree.

"I can't go on!" she sobbed. "My legs won't move."

"Oh yes you *can*! Only a few more yards!"

Colin had spotted a huge boulder sticking out of the swamp a little way up the hill from where they were, and, if only they could reach it, it would offer more protection than their present position, which could hardly be worse. He grabbed his sister's arm and dragged her through the mud to the base of the rock.

"Now climb!"

And, while Susan hauled herself up to the flat summit, Colin put his back to the rock, like a fox at bay turning to face the hunt.

The edge of the swamp was a mass of bodies. The rising moon shone on their leather hides and was reflected in their eyes. Colin could see white shapes spreading out on either side to encircle the rock; they were in no hurry now, for they knew that escape was impossible.

Colin climbed after his sister. He ached in every muscle and was trembling with fatigue.

When the circle was complete the creatures began to advance across the swamp, moving easily over the mire on their splayed feet. Ever closer they came, till the rock was surrounded.

From all sides at once the ropes came snaking through the air, as soft as silk, as strong as iron, and clung to the children as though coated with glue; so that in no time at all Colin and Susan fell helpless beneath the sticky coils, and over them swarmed the mob, pinching and poking, and binding and trussing, until the children lay with only their heads exposed, like two cocoons upon the rock.

But as they were being hoisted on to bony shoulders it seemed as though a miracle happened. There was a flash, and the whole rock was lapped about by a lake of blue fire. The children could feel no heat, but their captors fell, hissing and spitting, into the swamp, and the ropes charred and crumbled into ash, while pandemonium broke loose through all the assembly.

Then, from the darkness above, a voice rang out.

"Since when have men-children grown so mighty that you must needs meet two with hundreds? Run, maggot-breed of Ymir, ere I lose my patience!"

The crowd had fallen silent at the first sound of that voice, and now it drew back slowly, snarling and blinking in the blue light, wavered, turned, and fled. The dazed children listened to the rushing feet as though in a dream; soon there was only the rattle of stones on the opposite slope; then nothing. The cold flames about the rock flickered and died. The moon shone peacefully upon the quiet valley.

And as their eyes grew accustomed to this paler light the children saw standing on a path beneath a cliff some way above them an old man, taller than any they had ever known, and thin. He was clad in a white robe, his hair and beard were white, and in his hand was a white staff. He was looking at Colin and Susan, and, as they sat upright, he spoke again, but this time there was no anger in his voice.

"Come quickly, children, lest there be worse than svarts abroad; for indeed I smell much evil in the night. Come, you need not fear me."

He smiled and stretched out his hand. Colin and Susan climbed down from the rock and squelched their way up to join him. They were shivering in spite of their coats and recent exertions.

"Stay close to me. Your troubles are over, though I fear it may be only for this night, but we must take no risks."

And he touched the cliff with his staff. There was a hollow rumble, and a crack appeared in the rock, through which a slender ray of light shone. The crack widened to reveal a tunnel leading down into the earth: it was lit by a soft light, much the same as that which had scattered the mob in the swamp.

The old man herded Colin and Susan into the tunnel, and, as soon as they were past the threshold, the opening closed behind them, shutting out the night and its fears.

The tunnel was quite short, and soon they came to a door. The children stood aside while the old man fumbled with the lock.

"Where High Magic fails, oak and iron may yet prevail," he said. "Ah! That has it! Now enter, and be refreshed."

CHAPTER 4

The Fundindelve

They were in a cave, sparsely but comfortably furnished. There was a long wooden table in the centre, and a few carved chairs, and in one corner lay a pile of animal skins. Through the middle of the cave a stream of water babbled in the channel it had cut in the sandstone floor, and as it disappeared under the cave wall it formed a pool, into which the old man dipped two bronze cups, and offered them to Colin and Susan.

"Rest," he said, pointing to the heap of skins, "and drink of this."

The children sank down upon the bed and sipped the ice-cold water. And at the first draught their tiredness vanished, and a warmth spread through their limbs; their befuddled shock-numbed brains cleared, their spirits soared.

"Oh," cried Susan, as she gazed at their surroundings as though seeing them for the first time, "this can't be real! We *must* be dreaming. Colin, how do we wake up?"

But Colin was staring at the old man, and seemed not to have heard. He saw an old man, true, but one whose body was as firm and upright as a youth's; whose keen, grey eyes were full of the sadness of the wise; whose mouth, though stern, was kind and capable of laughter.

"Then the legend *is* true,' said Colin.

"It is," said the wizard. "And I would it were not; for that was a luckless day for me.

"But enough of my troubles. We must discover now what is in you to draw the attentions of the svart-alfar, since it is indeed strange that men-children should cause them such concern."

"Oh please," interrupted Susan, "this is so bewildering! Can't you tell us first what's been happening and what these things were in the marsh? We don't even know who you are, though I suppose you must be the wizard."

The old man smiled. "Forgive me. In my disquiet I had forgotten that you have seen much that has been unknown to you.

"Who am I? I have had many names among many peoples through the long ages of the earth, and of those names some may not now be spoken, or would be foreign to your tongue; but you shall call me Cadellin, after the fashion of the men of Elthan, in the days to come, for I believe our paths will run together for a while.

"The creatures you encountered are of the goblin race – the svart-alfar, in their own tongue. They are a cowardly people, night-loving, and sun-loathing, much given to throttlings in dark places, and seldom venturing above ground unless they have good cause. They have no magic, and so, alone, are no danger to me; but it would have fared ill with you had I not known their alarm echoing through the hollow hill.

"And now you must tell me who *you* are, and

what it is that has brought you into such danger this night."

Colin and Susan gave an account of the events leading to their arrival in Alderley, and of their movements since.

"And this afternoon," said Colin finally, "we explored the Edge, and spent the rest of the day on the farm until we came here again about half past seven, so I don't see that we can have done anything to attract *any*body's attention."

"Hm," said Cadellin thoughtfully. "Now tell me what happened this evening, for at present I can find no reason in this."

The children told the story of their flight and capture, and when they had finished the wizard was silent for some time.

"This is indeed puzzling," he said at last. "The crow was sent to arrange your taking, and I do not have to guess by whom it was sent. But *why* the morthbrood should be concerned with you defeats me utterly; yet I must discover this reason, both for your safety and my own, for my destruction is their aim, and somehow I fear you could advance them in their work. Still, perhaps the next move will tell us more, for they will soon hear of what took place this night, and will be much alarmed. But I shall give you what protection I can, and you will find friends as well as enemies in these woods."

"But why are *you* in danger?" said Susan. "And who are the – what was it? – morthbrood?"

"Ah, that is a long story for this hour, and one

of which I am ashamed. But it is also, I suppose, one that you must hear. So, if you are rested, let us go together, and I shall show you part of the answer to your question."

Cadellin led the children out of the cave and down a long winding tunnel into the very heart of the hill. And as they went the air grew colder and the strange light fiercer, turning from blue to white, until at last they came into a long, low cavern. An echoing sigh, like waves slowly rippling on a summer shore, rose and fell upon the air; and before the children's eyes were the sleeping knights in their silver armour, each beside his milk-white mare, just as Gowther had described them in the legend, their gentle breathing filling the cave with its sweet sound. And all around and over the motionless figures the cold, white flames played silently.

In the middle of the cave the floor rose in the shape of a natural, tomb-like couch of stone; and here lay a knight comelier than all his fellows. His head rested upon a helmet enriched with jewels and circlets of gold, and its crest was a dragon. By his side was placed a naked sword, and on the blade was the image of two serpents in gold, and so brightly did the blade gleam that it was as if two flames of fire started from the serpents' heads.

"Long years ago," said Cadellin, "beyond the memory or books of men, Nastrond, the Great Spirit of Darkness, rode forth in war upon the plain. But there came against him a mighty king, and Nastrond fell. He cast off his earth-shape and fled into the Abyss of Ragnarok, and all men rejoiced, thinking that evil had vanished from the world for ever; yet the king knew in his heart that this could never be.

"So he called together a great assembly of wizards and wise men and asked what should be done to guard against the enemy's return. And it was prophesied that, when the day should come, Nastrond must be victorious, for there would be none pure enough to withstand him since, by that time, he would have put a little of himself into the hearts of all men. Even now, it was said, he was pouring black thoughts from his lair in Ragnarok, and these would flow unceasingly about mankind until the strongest were tainted and he had a foothold in every mind.

"Yet there was hope. For the world might still be saved if a band of warriors, pure in heart, and brave, could defy him in his hour and compel him to sink once more into the Abyss. Their strength would not be in numbers, but in purity and valour. And so was devised the following plan.

"The king chose the worthiest of his knights, and went with them to Fundindelve, the ancient dwarf-halls, where they were put into enchanted sleep. This done, the most powerful magicians of the age began to weave a spell. Day and night they worked together, pausing for neither food nor sleep, and, at the end, Fundindelve was guarded by the strongest magic the world has known, magic that would stay the sleeping warriors from growing old or weak, and that no evil could ever break.

"The heart of the magic was sealed with Firefrost, the weirdstone of Brisingamen, and it and the warriors became my charge. Here I must stay, for ever keeping watch, until the time shall come for me to rouse the Sleepers and send them forth against the malice of Nastrond."

"But, Cadellin," asked Susan, "in these days how can you hope to win a fight with only a hundred and forty men on horseback?"

"Ah," said the wizard, "you must remember that the hour of Nastrond is not yet at hand. It was prophesied that these few could prove his desolation, and I have faith: the wheel may turn full circle ere that day will come."

This cryptic reply was hardly satisfying, but by the time Susan had tried to make sense of it and found that she could not, the wizard had resumed his tale.

"Now it happened that, at the Sealing of Fundindelve, there were not more than one hundred and thirty-nine pure white mares in the prime of life, to be found anywhere. Therefore I was forced to wait for that one horse to complete my company, and when at last such a horse came my way, I little knew that it would be so dearly bought.

"But now I must leave this matter and speak of Nastrond. Word of what we had done at Fundindelve soon reached him, and he was both angry and afraid; yet his black art was of no avail against our stronghold. So he too devised a plan.

"In the next chamber to that of the Sleepers had been stored jewels and precious metals for the use of the king to help put right the ills of the world, if he should conquer Nastrond. This treasure, since it lay in Fundindelve, was safe as long as the spell remained unbroken; and although Nastrond had no thought for the treasure, he did desire most furiously to break the spell, for, if this were achieved, the Sleepers would wake and become normal men, who would grow old, and die, and pass away centuries before his return, since there would no longer be magic left upon the earth powerful to hold them once more ageless in Fundindelve.

"To this end he summoned the witches and warlocks of the morthbrood, and the lord of the svart-alfar, together with many of his own ministers, and put greed and craving for riches in their hearts by telling them of the treasure that would be theirs if they could only reach it. And from that hour they have striven to find a way to break the spell. At first I had no need to fear, for the sorcery of the morthbrood, though powerful, and the hammers and shovels of svarts could have no effect where the art of Nastrond had failed. But then, on the day that I found the last white mare, disaster fell upon me.

"This light around us is the magic that guards all here, and its flames are torment to the followers of Nastrond; and the source of the magic, as I have said, rests in the stone Firefrost. While Firefrost remains, and there is light in Fundindelve, the Sleepers lie here in safety. Yet each day I dread that I shall see the flames tremble and give way to shadows, and hear the murmur of men roused from sleep, and the neigh of horses. For I have lost the weirdstone of Brisingamen!"

Cadellin's voice trembled with rage and shame as he spoke, and he crashed the butt of his staff against the rock floor.

"Lost it?" cried Susan. "You can't have done! I mean, if it's a special stone it should be easy to find if it's lying around somewhere in here . . . shouldn't it?"

The wizard smiled grimly. "But it is *not* here. Of that, at least, I am certain. Come, and I shall show you proof of what I saw."

He beckoned the children towards an opening in the wall and into a short tunnel not more than thirty feet in length, and halfway down Cadellin stopped before a bowl-shaped recess about six inches high and a yard above the level of the floor.

"There is the throne of Firefrost," he said, "and you will see that it is now vacant."

They passed through into a cavern similar to the last, and Colin and Susan halted in awe.

Here lay the treasure, piled in banks of jewels, and gold, and silver, which stretched away into the distance like sand dunes in a desert.

"Oh," gasped Susan, "how beautiful! Look at those colours!"

"You would not think them so beautiful," said

Cadellin, "if you had run through your fingers every diamond, pearl, sapphire, amethyst, opal, carbuncle, garnet, topaz, emerald, and ruby in the whole of this all too spacious cave, in search of a stone that is not there!

"I spent five years labouring in this cave, and as many weeks scouring every gallery and path in Fundindelve, but without success. I can only think that that knave of a farmer was a greedier and more cunning rogue than he appeared, and that, as he followed me from here, laden as he was with wealth, his eyes fell upon the stone, and he slyly took it without a word. Perhaps he thought it was merely a pretty bauble, or he may even have seen me replace it after I had tethered his horse with sleep while he crammed his pockets here.

"Seldom have I need to visit these quarters, and it was a hundred years before I next came this way and found that the stone had gone. First I searched here; then I went into the world to seek the farmer or his family. But, of course, by this time he was dead, and I could not trace his descendants; and although my quest was discreet the morthbrood came to hear of it, and they were not long in guessing the truth. Throughout the region of the plain they coursed, and even to the bleak uplands of the east, towards Ragnarok, but neither they nor the ferreting svarts found what they sought. Nor, for that matter, did I.

"Should Firefrost come into Nastrond's hand my danger would be great indeed; for although he is powerless against the magic it contains, if he could destroy the stone then the magic, too, would die away.

"Firefrost was an ancient spellstone of great strength before the present magic was sealed within, and it would not readily suffer destruction; so while the light shines here I know that somewhere the stone still lives, and there is hope.

"There you have the story of my troubles, and, I trust, the answer to your questions. Now you must return to your home, for the hour is late and your friends will be anxious – and they may have ample cause for worry if we cannot solve this evening's problems soon!"

They went back into the Cave of the sleepers, and from there climbed upwards by vast caverns till the way was blocked by a pair of iron gates, behind which the tunnel ended in a sheer rock wall. The wizard touched the gates with his staff, and slowly they swung open.

"These were wrought by dwarfs to guard their treasures from the thievish burrowings of svarts, but without magic they would be of little use against what seeks to enter now."

So saying, Cadellin laid his hand upon the wall, and a dark gap appeared in the blue rock, through which the night air flowed, cold and dew-laden.

It looked very black outside, and the memory of their recent fear made Colin and Susan unwilling to leave the light and safety of Fundindelve; but, keeping close to the wizard, they stepped through the gap, and stood once more beneath the trees on the hillside.

The gates and the opening closed behind them with a sound that made the earth shake, and as they grew used to the moonlight the children saw that they were standing before the tooth of rock that they had striven to reach as they floundered in the depths of the beech wood, with svart-claws grasping at their heels.

Away to the left they could make out the shape of the ridge above the dell.

"That's where the svarts attacked us," said Colin, pointing.

"You do not surprise me!" laughed the wizard. "Saddle-bole was ever a svart-warren; a good place to watch the sun set, indeed!"

They walked up the path to Stormy Point. All was quiet: just the grey rocks, and the moonlight. When they passed the dark slit of the Devil's Grave Colin and Susan instinctively huddled closer to the wizard, but nothing stirred within the blackness of the cave.

"Do svarts live in all the mines?" asked Susan.

"They do. They have their own warrens, but when men dug here they followed, hoping that Fundindelve would be revealed; and when the men departed they swarmed freely. Therefore you must keep away from the mines now, at all costs."

Cadellin took the children from Stormy Point along a broad track that cut straight through the wood as far as the open fields, where it turned sharply to twist along the meadow border skirting the woodland. This, the wizard said, was once an elf-road, and some of the old magic still lingered. Svarts would not set foot on it, and the morthbrood would do so only if hard pressed, and then they could not bear to walk there for long. He told the children to use this road if they had need to visit him, and not to stray from it: for parts of the wood were evil, and very dangerous. "But then," he said, "you have already found that to be true!" It would be wiser, he thought, to stay away from the wood altogether, and on no account must they go out of doors once the sun had set.

The track came to an end by the side of The Wizard Inn, and they had gone barely a hundred yards from there when they heard the sound of hoofs, and round the corner ahead of them came the shape of a horse and cart, oil lamps flickering on either side.

"It's Gowther!"

"Do not speak of me!" said Cadellin.

"Oh, but . . ." began Susan. "But . . ."

But they were alone.

"Wey back!" called Gowther to Prince. "Hallo theer! Dunner you think it's a bit late to be looking for wizards? It's gone eleven o'clock, tha knows."

"Oh, we're sorry, Gowther," said Colin. "We didn't mean to be late, but we were lost, and stuck in a bog, and it took us a long time to find the road again."

He thought that this half-lie would be more readily accepted than the truth, and Cadellin obviously wanted to keep his existence a secret.

"Eh well, we'll say no more about it then; but think on you're more careful in future, for with all them mine holes lying around, Bess was for having police and fire brigade out to look for you.

"Now up you come: if you've been traipsing round in Holywell bog you'll be wanting a bath, I reckon."

On reaching the farm Colin and Susan wasted no time in dragging off their muddy clothes and climbing into a steaming bath-tub. From there they went straight to bed, and Bess, who had been fussing and clucking round like a hen with chicks, brought them bowls of hot, salted bread and milk.

The children were too tired to think, let alone talk, much about their experience, and as they drowsily snuggled down between the sheets all seemed to grow confused and vague: it was impossible to keep awake. Colin slid into a muddled world of express trains, and black birds, and bracken, and tunnels, and dead leaves, and horses.

"Oh gosh," he yawned, "which is which? Are there wizards and goblins? Or are we still at home? Must ask Sue about . . . about . . . oh . . . knights . . . ask Mum . . . don't believe in farmers . . . farm – no . . . witches . . . and . . . things . . . oh . . ."

He began, very quietly, to snore.

On the crest of the Riddings, staring down upon the farmhouse as it lay bathed in gossamer moonlight, was a dark figure, tall and gaunt; and on its shoulder crouched an ugly bird.

CHAPTER 5

Miching Mallecho

The next day was cool and showery. The children slept late, and it was turned nine o'clock when they came down for breakfast.

"I thought it best to let you have a lie in this morning," said Bess. "You looked dead beat last neet; ay, and you're a bit pale now. Happen you'd do better to take things easy today, and not go gallivanting over the Edge."

"Oh, I think we've seen enough of the Edge for a day or two," said Susan. "It *was* rather tiring."

Breakfast was hardly over when a lorry arrived from Alderley station with the children's bicycles and trunks, and Colin and Susan immediately set about the task of unpacking their belongings.

"What do you make of last night?" asked Susan when they were alone. "It doesn't seem possible, does it?"

"That's what I was wondering in bed; but we can't both have imagined it. The wizard *is* in a mess, isn't he? I shouldn't like to live by myself all the time and be on guard against things like those svarts."

"He said things *worse* than svarts, remember! I shouldn't have thought anything could be worse than those clammy hands and bulging eyes, and their flat feet splashing in the mud. If it's so, then I'm glad I'm not a wizard!"

They did not discuss their pursuit and rescue. It was too recent for them to think about it without trembling and feeling sick. So they talked mainly about the wizard and his story, and it was late afternoon before they had finished unpacking and had found a place for everything.

Colin and Susan went down to tea. Gowther was already at the table, talking to Bess.

"And a couple of rum things happened after dinner, too. First, I go into the barn for some sacks, and, bless me, if the place inner full of owls! I counted nigh on two dozen snoozing among the rafters – big uns, too. They mun be thinking we're sneyed out with mice, or summat. *I've* never seen owt like it.

"And then again, about an hour later, a feller comes up to me in Front Baguley, and he asks if I've a job for him. I didner like his looks at all. He was a midget, with long black hair and a beard, and skin like owd leather. He didner talk as if he came from round here, either – he was more Romany than owt else, to my way of thinking; and his clothes looked as though they'd been borrowed and slept in.

"Well, when I tell him I dunner need a mon, he looks fair put out, and he starts to tell me his hard luck story, and asks me to give him a break, but I give him his marching orders instead. He dunner argue: he just turns on his heels and stalks off, saying as I might regret treating him like this before long. He seemed in a fair owd paddy! All the same, I think Scamp had best have the run of the hen-pen for a neet or two, just in case."

The wizard had told Colin and Susan to keep their windows closed, no matter how hot and stuffy their bedrooms might become, so the colder weather was not unwelcome, and they slept soundly enough that night.

Not so Gowther. The furious barking of Scamp woke him at three o'clock. It was the tone used for strangers, high-pitched and continuous, not the gruff outbursts that answered other dogs, birds, or the wind. Gowther scrambled into his clothes, seized his shot-gun and lantern, which he had put ready to hand, and made for the door.

"I knew it! I knew it! The little blighter's after my chickens. I'll give him chickens!"

"Watch thy step, lad," said Bess. "You're bigger than he is, and that's all the more of thee for him to hit."

"I'll be all reet; but he wunner," said Gowther, and he clumped down the stairs and out into the farm-yard.

Thick clouds hid the moon, there was little wind. The only sounds were the frantic clamour of the dog and the bumping of frightened, sleep-ridden hens.

Gowther shone his light into the pen. The wire netting was undamaged, and the gate locked. In the centre of the lamp's beam stood Scamp. His hackles were up, in fact every hair along his spine seemed to be on end; his ears lay flat against his skull, and his eyes blazed yellow in the light. He was barking and snarling, almost screaming at times, and tearing the earth with stiff jerky movements of his legs. Gowther unfastened the gate.

"Wheer is he, boy? Go fetch him!"

Scamp came haltingly out of the pen, his lips curled hideously. Gowther was puzzled: he had expected him to come out like a rocket.

"Come on, lad! He'll be gone else!"

The dog ran backwards and forwards nervously, still barking, then he set off towards the field gate in a snarling glide, keeping his belly close to the ground, and disappeared into the darkness. A second later the snarl rose to a yelp, and he shot back into the light to stand at Gowther's feet in a further welter of noise. He was trembling all over. His fury had been obvious all along, but now Gowther realized that, more than anything else, the dog was terrified.

'What's up, lad? What's frit thee, eh?" said Gowther gently as he knelt to calm the shivering animal. Then he stood up and went over towards the gate, his gun cocked, and shone the light into the field.

There was nothing wrong as far as he could see, but Scamp, though calmer, still foamed at his heels. Nothing wrong, yet there was something . . . wait! . . . he sniffed . . . was there? . . . yes!!! A cold, clammy air drifted against Gowther's face, and with it a smell so strange, so unwholesome and unexpected that a knot of instinctive fear tightened in his stomach. It was the smell of stagnant water and damp decay. It filled his nostrils and choked his lungs, and, for a moment, Gowther imagined that he was being sucked down into the depths of a black swamp, old and wicked in time. He swung round, gasping, wide-eyed, the hairs of his neck prickling erect. But on the instant the stench passed and was gone: he breathed pure night air once more.

"By gow, lad, theer's summat rum afoot toneet! That was from nowt local, choose how the wind blows. Come on, let's be having a scrat around."

He went first to the stable, where he found Prince stamping nervously and covered with sweat.

"Wey, lad," said Gowther softly, and he ran his hands over the horse's quivering flanks. "Theer's no need to fret. Hush while I give thee a rub."

Prince gradually quietened down as Gowther rubbed him with a piece of dry sacking, and Scamp, too, was in a happier frame of mind. He carried his head high, and his din was reduced to a growl, threatening rather than nervous – as though trying to prove that he had never felt anything but aggressive rage all night.

Ay, thought Gowther, and yon's a dog as fears neither mon nor beast most days; I dunner like it one bit!

In the shippons he found the cows restless, but not as excited as Prince had been, for all their rolling eyes and snuffling nostrils.

"Well, theer's nowt here, Scamp; let's take a look at the barn."

They went into the outhouses, and nowhere was there any hint of disturbance, nor did anything appear to have been tampered with.

"Ay, well everywheer seems reet enough now, onyroad," said Gowther, "so we'll have a quick peek round the house and mash a pot of tea, and then it'll be time to start milking. Eh dear, theer's no rest for the wicked!"

The sky was showing the first pale light of day as he crossed the farmyard: soon another morning would be here to drive away the fears of the night. Already Gowther was feeling a little ashamed of his moment of fear, and he was thankful that there had been no one else there to witness it. "Eh, it's funny how your imagination plays . . ." He stopped dead in his tracks, while Scamp pressed, whining, close to his legs.

Out of the blackness, far above Gowther's head, had come a single shriek, too harsh for human voice, yet more than animal.

For the second time that night Gowther's blood froze. Then, taking a deep breath, he strode quickly and purposefully towards the house, looking neither to the right nor to the left, neither up nor down, with Scamp not an inch from his heels. In one movement, he lifted the latch, stepped across the threshold, closed the door, and shot the bolt home. Slowly he turned and looked down at Scamp.

"I dunner know about thee, lad, but I'm going to have a strong cup of tea."

He lit the paraffin lamp and put the kettle on the stove, and while he waited for the water to boil he went from room to room to see that nothing was amiss here at least. All was quiet; though when he looked into Susan's room a sleepy voice asked what the time was and why Scamp had been making such a noise. Gowther said that a fox had been after the hens, or so he thought, but Scamp had frightened him off. He told a similar story to Bess.

". . . and he started barking at his own shadder, he was that excited."

"Ay? Then what is it as has made *thee* sweat like a cheese?" said Bess suspiciously.

"Well," said Gowther, confused, "I reckon it's a bit early in the day to be running round, at my age. But I'm not past mashing a pot of tea – er – I'll bring you one: kettle's boiling!"

Gowther sought the kitchen. It was never easy to keep anything from Bess, she knew him too well. But what could he say? That he, a countryman, had been frightened by a smell and a night bird? He almost blushed to think of it.

By the time he had made the tea, washed, and finished dressing, it was light outside and near milking time. The sun was breaking through the cloud. Gowther felt much better now.

He was halfway across the yard when he noticed the long, black feathers that lay scattered upon the cobblestones.

CHAPTER 6

A Ring of Stones

Thursday at Highmost Redmanhey was always busy, for on top of the normal round of work Gowther had to make ready for the following day, when he would drive down to Alderley village to do the weekly shopping, and also to call on certain old friends and acquaintances whom he supplied with vegetables and eggs. So much of Thursday was taken up with selecting and cleaning the produce for Friday's marketing.

When all was done, Colin and Susan rode with Gowther to the wheelwright in the nearby township of Mottram St Andrew to have a new spoke fitted to the cart. This occupied them until teatime, and afterwards Gowther asked the children if they would like to go with him down to Nether Alderley to see whether they could find their next meal in Radnor mere.

They set off across the fields, and shortly came to a wood. Here the undergrowth was denser than on most of the Edge, and contained quite a lot of bramble. High rhododendron bushes grew wild everywhere. The wood seemed full of birds. They sang in the trees, rustled in the thicket, and swam in the many quiet pools.

"I've just realized something," said Colin: "I

felt the Edge was unusual, and now I know why. It's the . . ."

"Birds," said Gowther. "There is none. Not worth speaking of, onyroad. Flies, yes; but birds, no. It's always been like that, to my knowledge, and I conner think why it should be. You'd think, with all them trees and such-like, you'd have as mony as you find here, but, considering the size of the place, theer's hardly a throstle to be found from Squirrel's Jump to Daniel Hill. Time's been when I've wandered round theer half the day, and seen nobbut a pair of jays, and that was in Clockhouse wood. No, it's very strange, when you come to weigh it up."

Their way took them through a jungle of rhododendron. The ground was boggy and choked with dead wood, and they had to duck under low branches and climb over fallen trees: but, somehow, Gowther managed to carry his rod and line through it all without a snag, and he even seemed to know where he was going.

Susan thought how unpleasant it would be to have to move quickly through such country.

"Gowther," she said, "are there any mines near here?"

"No, none at all, we're almost on the plain now, and the mines are over the other side of the hill, behind us. Why do you ask?"

"Oh, I just wondered."

The rhododendrons came to an end at the border of a mere, about half a mile long and a quarter wide.

"This is it," said Gowther, sitting down on a fallen trunk which stretched out over the water. "It's a trifle marshy, but we're not easy to reach here, as theer's some as might term this poaching. Now if you'll open the basket and pass the tin with the bait in it, we can settle down and make ourselves comfortable."

After going out as far as he could along the tree to cast his rod, Gowther sat with his back against the roots and lit his pipe. Colin and Susan lay full length on the wrinkled bark and gazed into the mere.

Within two hours they had three perch between them, so they gathered in their tackle and headed for home, arriving well before dusk.

The following morning in Alderley village Susan went with Bess to the shops while Colin stayed to help Gowther with the vegetables. They all met again for a meal at noon, and afterwards climbed into the cart and went with Gowther on his round.

It was a hot day, and by four o'clock Colin and Susan were very thirsty, so Bess said that they ought to drop off for an ice-cream and a lemonade.

"We've to go down Moss Lane," she said, "and we shanner be above half an hour; you stay and cool down a bit."

The children were soon in the village café, with their drinks before them. Susan was toying with her bracelet, and idly trying to catch the light so that she could see the blue heart of her Tear.

"It's always difficult to find," she said. "I never know when it's going to come right . . . ah . . . wait a minute . . . yes . . . got it! You know, it reminds me of the light in Fundin . . ."

She looked at Colin. He was staring at her, open mouthed. They both dropped their eyes to Susan's wrist where the Tear gleamed so innocently.

"But it *couldn't* be!" whispered Colin. "Could it?"

"I don't . . . know. But how?"

But how?

"No, of course not!" said Colin. "The wizard would have recognized it as soon as he saw it, wouldn't he?"

Susan flopped back in her chair, releasing her pent-up breath in a long sigh. But a second later she was bolt upright, inarticulate with excitement.

"He couldn't have seen it! I – I was wearing my mackintosh! Oh, *Colin* . . . !!"

Though just as shaken as his sister, Colin was not content to sit and gape. Obviously they had to find out, and quickly, whether Susan was wearing Firefrost, or just a piece of crystal. If it *should* be Firefrost, and had been recognized by the wrong people, their brush with the svarts would at last make sense. How the stone came to be on Susan's wrist was another matter.

"We must find Cadellin at once," he said.

"Because if this *is* Firefrost, the sooner he has it the better it will be for us all."

At that moment the cart drew up outside, and Gowther called that it was time to be going home.

The children tried hard to conceal their agitation, yet the leisurely pace Prince seemed to adopt on the "front" hill, as it was called locally, had them almost bursting with impatience.

"Bess," said Susan, "are you sure you can't remember anything else about the Bridestone? I want to find out as much as I can about it."

"Nay, lass, I've told you all as I know. My mother had it from her mother, and she always said it had been passed down like that for I dunner know how mony years. And I believe theer was some story about how it should never be known to onybody outside the family for fear of bringing seven years' bad luck, but my mother didner go in much for superstition and that sort of claptrap."

"Have you always lived in Alderley?"

"Bless you, yes! I was born and bred in th'Hough" (she pronounced it "thuff") "but my mother was a Goostrey woman, and I believe before that her family had connections Mobberley way."

"Oh?"

Colin and Susan could hardly contain themselves.

"Gowther," said Colin, "before we come home, Sue and I want to go to Stormy Point; which is the nearest way?"

"What! Before you've had your teas?" exclaimed Bess.

"Yes, I'm afraid so. You see, it's something very important and secret, and we *must* go."

"You're not up to owt daft down the mines, are you?" said Gowther.

"Oh no," said Colin; "but, please, we must go. We'll be back early, and it doesn't matter about tea."

"Er well, it'll be your stomachs as'll be empty! But think on, we dunner want to come looking for you at midneet.

"Your best way'll be to get off at the gamekeeper's lodge, and follow the main path till it forks by the owd quarry; then take the left hond path, and it'll bring you straight to Stormy Point."

They reached the top of the Edge, and after about quarter of a mile Gowther halted Prince before a cottage built of red sandstone and tucked in the fringe of the wood. Along the side of the cottage, at right angles to the road, a track disappeared among the trees in what Gowther said was the direction of Stormy Point.

The children jumped from the cart, and ran off along the track, while Gowther and Bess continued on their way, dwelling sentimentally on what it was to be young.

"Don't you think we'd better go by the path Cadellin told us to use? He said it was the only safe one, remember."

"We haven't time to go all that way round,"

said Colin; "we must show him your Tear as soon as we can. And anyway, Gowther says this is the path to Stormy Point, and it's broad daylight, so I don't see that we can come to any harm."

"Well, how are we going to find Cadellin when we're there?"

"We'll go straight to the iron gates and call him: being a wizard he's bound to hear . . . I hope. Still, we must try!"

They pressed deeper and deeper into the wood, and came to a level stretch of ground where the bracken thinned and gave place to rich turf, dappled with sunlight. And here, in the midst of so much beauty, they learnt too late that wizards' words are seldom idle, and traps well sprung hold hard their prey.

Out of the ground on all sides swirled tongues of thick white mist, which merged into a rolling fog about the children's knees; it paused, gathered itself, and leapt upwards, blotting out the sun and the world of life and light.

It was too much for Susan. Her nerve failed her. All that mattered was to escape from this chill cloud and what it must contain. She ran blindly, stumbled a score of paces, then tripped, and fell full length upon the grass.

She was not hurt, but the jolt brought her to her senses: the jolt – and something else.

In falling, she had thrown her arms out to protect herself, and as her head cleared she realized that there was no earth beneath her fingers, only emptiness. She lay there, not caring to move.

"Sue, where are you?" It was Colin's voice, calling softly. "Are you all right?"

"I'm here. Be careful. I think I'm on the edge of a cliff, but I can't see."

"Keep still, then; I'll feel my way to you."

He crawled in the direction of Susan's voice, but even in that short distance he partly lost his bearing, and it was several minutes before he found his sister, and having done so, he wriggled cautiously alongside her.

The turf ended under his nose, and all beyond was a sea of grey. Colin felt around for a pebble, and dropped it over the edge. Three seconds passed before he heard it land.

"Good job you tripped, Sue! It's a long way down. This must be the old quarry. Now keep quiet a minute, and listen."

They strained their ears to catch the slightest sound, but there was nothing to be heard. They might have been the only living creatures on earth.

"We must go back to the path, Sue. And we've got to make as little noise as possible, because whatever it is that made this fog will be listening for us. If we don't find the path we may easily walk round in circles until nightfall, even supposing we're left alone as long as that.

"Let's get away from this quarry, for a start: there's no point in asking for trouble."

They stood up, and holding each other's hand, walked slowly back towards the path.

As the minutes went by, Susan grew more and more uneasy.

"Colin," she said at last, "I hadn't run more than a dozen steps, I'm sure, when I tripped, and we've been walking for a good five minutes. Do you think we're going the right way?"

"No, I don't. And I don't know which *is* the right way, so we'll have to hope for the best. We'll try to walk in a straight line, and perhaps we'll leave this fog behind."

But they did not. Either the mist had spread out over a wide area, or, as the children began to suspect, it was moving with them. They made very slow progress; every few paces they would stop and listen, but there was only the silence of the mist, and that was as unnerving as the sound of something moving would have been. Also, it was impossible to see for more than a couple of yards in any direction, and they were frightened of falling into a hidden shaft, or even the quarry, for they had lost all sense of direction by now.

The path seemed to have vanished; but, in fact, they had crossed it some minutes earlier without knowing. As they approached, the mist had gathered thickly about their feet, hiding the ground until the path was behind them.

After a quarter of an hour Colin and Susan were shivering uncontrollably as the dampness ate into their bones. Every so often the trunk of a pine tree would loom out of the mist, so that it seemed as though they were walking through a pillared hall that had no beginning, and no end.

"We must be moving in circles, Colin. Let's change direction instead of trying to keep in a straight line."

"We couldn't be more lost than we are at present, so we may as well try it."

They could not believe their luck. Within half a minute they came upon an oak, and beyond that another. The fog was as dense as ever, but they knew that they were breaking fresh ground, and that was encouraging.

"Oh, I wish Cadellin would come," said Susan.

"That's an idea! Let's shout for help: he may hear us."

"But we'll give our position away."

"I don't think that matters any more. Let's try, anyway."

"All right."

"One, two, three. Ca-dell-in! Help! Ca-dell-in!!"

It was like shouting in a padded cell. Their voices, flat and dead, soaked into the grey blanket.

"That can't have carried far," said Colin disgustedly. "Try again. One, two, three. Help! Ca-dell-in! Help!!!"

"It's no use," said Susan; "he'll never hear us. We'll have to find our own way out."

"And we'll do that if we keep going at our own pace," said Colin. "If whatever caused this had intended to attack us it would have done so by now, wouldn't it? No, it wants to frighten us into rushing over a precipice or something like that. As long as we carry on slowly we'll be safe enough."

He was wrong, but they had no other plan.

For the next few minutes the children made their way in silence, Susan concentrating on the ground immediately in front, Colin alert for any sight or sound of danger.

All at once Susan halted.

"Hallo, what's this?"

At their feet lay two rough-hewn boulders and beyond them, on either side, could be seen the faint outline of others of a like size.

"What can they be? They look as though they've been put there deliberately, don't they?"

"Never mind," said Colin; "we mustn't waste time in standing around."

And they passed between the stones, only to stop short a couple of paces later, with despair in their hearts, cold as the east wind.

Susan's question was answered. They were in the middle of a ring of stones, and the surrounding low, dim shapes rose on the limit of vision as though marking the boundary of the world.

Facing the children were two stones, far bigger than the rest, and on one of the stones sat a figure, and the sight of it would have daunted a brave man.

For three fatal seconds the children stared, unable to think or move. And as they faltered, the jaws of the trap closed about them; for, like a myriad snakes, the grass within the circle, alive with the magic of the place, writhed about their feet, shackling them in a net of blade and root, tight as a vice.

As if in some dark dream, Colin and Susan strained to tear themselves free, but they were held like wasps in honey.

Slowly the figure rose from its seat and came towards them. Of human shape it was, though like no mortal man, for it stood near eight feet high, and was covered from head to foot in a loose habit, dank and green, and ill concealing the terrible thinness and spider strength of the body beneath. A deep cowl hid the face, skin mittens were on the wasted hands, and the air was laden with the reek of foul waters.

The creature stopped in front of Susan and held out a hand; not a word was spoken.

"No!" gasped Susan. "You shan't have it!" and she put her arm behind her back.

"Leave her alone!" yelled Colin. "If you touch her Cadellin will *kill* you!"

The shrouded head turned slowly towards him, and he gazed into the cavern of the hood; courage melted from him, and his knees were water.

Then, suddenly, the figure stretched out its arms and seized both the children by the shoulder.

They had no chance to struggle or to defend themselves. With a speed that choked the cry of anguish in their throats, an icy numbness swept down from the grip of those hands into their bodies, and the children stood paralysed, unable to move a finger.

In a moment the bracelet was unfastened from Susan's wrist, and the grim shape turned on its heel and strode into the mist. And the mist gathered round it and formed a swirling cloud that moved swiftly away among the trees, and was lost to sight.

The sun shone upon the stone circle, and upon the figures standing motionless in the centre. The warm rays poured life and feeling into those wooden bodies, and they began to move. First an arm stirred jerkily, doll-like, then a head turned, a leg moved, and slowly the numbness drained from their limbs, the grass released its hold, and the children crumpled forward on to their hands and knees, shivering and gasping, the blood in their heads pounding like trip-hammers.

"Out – circle!" wheezed Colin.

They staggered sideways and almost fell down a small bank on to a path.

"Find Cadellin: perhaps . . . he . . . can stop it. I think that may be . . . Stormy Point ahead."

Their legs were stiff, and every bone ached, but they hurried along as best they could, and a few minutes later they cried out with relief, for the path did indeed come out on Stormy Point.

Across the waste of stones they ran, and down to the iron gates; and when they came to the rock they flung themselves against it, beating with their fists, and calling the wizard's name. But bruised knuckles were all they achieved: no gates appeared, no cavern opened.

Colin was in a frenzy of desperation. He prised a stone out of the ground, almost as big as his head, and, using both hands, began to pound the silent wall, shouting, "Open up! Open up! Open up!! Open up!! Open up!!!"

"Now that is no way to come a-visiting wizards," said a voice above them.

CHAPTER 7

Fenodyree

Colin and Susan looked up, not knowing what to expect: the voice sounded friendly, but was that any guide now?

Over the top of the rock dangled a pair of feet, and between these were two eyes, black as sloes, set in a leathery face, bearded and bushy-browed.

"Rocks are old, stubborn souls; they were here before we came, and they will be here when we are gone. They have all the time there is, and will not be hurried."

With this, the face disappeared, the legs swung out of sight, there was a slithering noise, a bump, and from behind the rock stepped a man four feet high. He wore a belted tunic of grey, patterned with green spirals along the hem, pointed boots, and breeches bound tight with leather thongs. His black hair reached to his shoulders, and on his brow was a circlet of gold.

"Are – are you a dwarf?" said Susan.

"That am I." He bowed low. "By name, Fenodyree; Wineskin, or Squabnose, to disrespectful friends. Take your pick."

He straightened up and looked keenly from one to the other of the children. His face had the same qualities of wisdom, of age without weakness, that they had seen in Cadellin, but here there was more of merriment, and a lighter heart.

"Oh please," said Susan, "take us to the wizard, if you can. Something dreadful has happened, and he must be told at once, in case it's not too late."

"In case what is not too late?" said Fenodyree. "Oh, but there I go, wanting gossip, when all around is turmoil and urgent deeds! Let us find Cadellin."

He ran his hands down the rough stone, like a man stroking the flanks of a favourite horse. The rock stirred ponderously and clove in two, and there were the iron gates, and the blue light of Fundindelve.

"Now the gates," said Fenodyree briskly. "My father made them, and so they hear me, though I have not the power of wizards."

He laid his hand upon the metal, and the gates opened.

"Stay close, lest you lose the way," called Fenodyree over his shoulder.

He set off at a jog-trot down the swift-sloping tunnel. Colin and Susan hurried after him, the rock and iron closed behind them, and they were again far from the world of men.

Down they went into the Edge, and came at last, by many zigzag paths, to the cave where they had rested after their meeting with Cadellin. And there they found him; he had been reading at the table, but had risen at the sound of their approach.

"The day's greeting to you, Cadellin Silver-brow," said Fenodyree.

"And to you, Wineskin. Now what bad news do you bring me, children? I have been expecting it, though I know not what it may be."

"Cadellin," cried Susan, "my Tear must be Firefrost, and it's just been stolen!"

"What – tear is this?"

"*My* Tear! The one my mother gave me. She had it from Bess Mossock."

And out poured the whole story in a tumble of words.

The wizard grew older before their eyes. He sank down upon his chair, his face lined and grey.

"It is the stone. It is the stone. No other has that heart of fire. And it was by me, and I did not hear it call."

He sat, his eyes clouded, a tired, world-weary, old man.

Then wrath kindled in him, and spread like flame. He sprang from his chair with all the vigour of youth, and he seemed to grow in stature, and his presence filled the cave.

"Grimnir!" he cried. "Are you to be my ruin at the end? Quick! We must take him in the open before he gains the lake! I shall slay him, if I must."

"Nay, Cadellin," said Fenodyree. "Hot blood has banished cool thought! It is near an hour since the hooded one strode swampwards; he will be far from the light by now, and even you dare not follow there. He would sit and mock you. Would you want that, old friend?"

"Mock me! Why did he leave these children unharmed, if not for that? It is not his way to show mercy for mercy's sake! And how else could despair have been brought to me so quickly? I am savouring his triumph now, as he meant me to.

"But what you say is reason: for good or ill the stone is with him. All we can do is guard, and wait, though I fear it will be to no good purpose."

He looked at the children, who were standing dejectedly in the middle of the cave.

"Colin, Susan; you have witnessed the writing of a dark chapter in the book of the world, and what deeds it will bring no man can tell; but you must in no way blame yourselves for what has happened. The elf-road would have been but short refuge from him who came against you this day – Grimnir the hooded one."

"But *what* is he?" said Susan, pale with the memory of their meeting.

"He is, or was a man. Once he studied under the wisest of the wise, and became a great lore-master; but in his lust for knowledge he practised the forbidden arts, and the black magic ravaged his heart, and made a monster of him. He left the paths of day, and went to live, like Grendel of old, beneath the waters of Llyn-dhu, the Black Lake, growing mighty in evil, second only to the ancient creatures of night that attend their lord in Ragnarok. And it is he, arch-enemy of mine, who came against you this day."

"No one in memory has seen his face or heard his voice," added Fenodyree. "Dwarf-legend speaks of a great shame that he bears therein: a gadfly of remorse, reminding him of what he is, and of what he might have been. But then that is only an old tale we learnt at our mother's knee, and not one for this sad hour."

"Nor have we time for folk-talk," said Cadellin. "We must do what we can, and that quickly. Now tell me, who can have seen the stone and recognized it?'

"Well, nobody . . ." said Colin.

"Selina Place!" cried Susan. "Selina Place! My Tear went all misty! Don't you remember, Colin? She must have seen my Tear and stopped to make certain."

"Ha," laughed Fenodyree bitterly. "Old Shape-shifter up to her tricks! We might have guessed the weight of the matter had we but known *she* was behind it!"

"Oh, why did you not tell us this when we first met?" the wizard shouted.

"I forgot all about it," said Colin: "it didn't seem important. I thought she was queer in the head."

"Important? Queer? Hear him! Why, Selina Place, as she is known to you, is the chief witch of the morthbrood! Worse, she is the Morrigan, the Third Bane of Logris!"

For a moment it seemed as though he would

erupt in anger, but instead, he sighed, and shook his head.

"No matter. It is done."

Susan was almost in tears. She could not bear to see the old man so distraught, especially when she felt responsible for his plight.

"Is there nothing we can do?"

The wizard looked up at her, and a tired smile came to his lips.

"Do? My dear, I think there is little any of us can do now. Certainly, there will be no place for children in the struggle to come. It will be hard for you, I know, but you must go from here and forget all you have seen and done. Now that the stone is out of your care you will be safe."

"But," cried Colin, "but you can't mean that! We want to help you!"

"I know you do. But you have no further part in this. High Magic and low cunning will be the weapons of the fray, and the valour of children would be lost in the struggle. You can help me best by freeing me from worry on your behalf."

And, without giving the children further chance to argue, he took them by the hand, and out of the cave. They went in misery, and shortly stood above the swamp on the spot where they had first met the wizard, three nights ago.

"Must we *really* not see you again?" said Colin. He had never felt so wretched.

"Believe me, it must be so. It hurts me, too, to part from friends, and I can guess what it is to have the door of wonder and enchantment closed to you when you have glimpsed what lies beyond. But it is also a world of danger and shadows, as you have seen, and ere long I fear I must pass into these shadows. I will not take you with me.

"Go back to your own world: you will be safer there. If we should fail, you will suffer no harm, for not in your time will Nastrond come.

"Now go. Fenodyree will keep with you to the road."

So saying, he entered the tunnel. The rock echoed: he was gone.

Colin and Susan stared at the wall. They were very near to tears, and Fenodyree, weighed down with his own troubles, felt pity for them in their despondency.

"Do not think him curt or cruel," he said gently. "He has suffered a defeat that would have crushed a lesser man. He is going now to prepare himself to face death, and worse than death, for the stone's sake; and I and others shall stand by him, though I think we are for the dark. He has said farewell because he knows there may be no more meetings for him this side of Ragnarok."

"But it was all our fault!" said Colin desperately. "We *must* help him!"

"You will help him best by keeping out of danger, as he said; and that means staying well away from us and all we do."

"Is that really the best way?" said Susan.

"It is."

"Then I suppose we'll have to do it. But it will be very hard."

"Is his task easier?" said Fenodyree.

They walked along a path that curved round the hillside, gradually rising till it ran along the crest of the Edge.

"You will be safe now," said Fenodyree, "but if you should have need of me, tell the owls in farmer Mussock's barn: they understand your speech, and will come to me, but remember that they are guardians for the night and fly like drunken elves by day."

"Do you mean to say all those owls were sent by you?" said Colin.

"Ay, my people have ever been masters of bird lore. We treat them as brothers, and they help us where they can. Two nights since they brought word that evil things were closing on you. A bird that seemed no true bird (and scarce made off with its life) brought to the farm a strange presence that filled them with dread, though they could not see its form. I can guess now that it was the hooded one – and here is Castle Rock, from which we can see his lair."

They had come to a flat outcrop that jutted starkly from the crest, so that it seemed almost a straight drop to the plain far below. There was a rough bench resting on stumps of rock, and here they sat. Behind them was a field, and beyond that the road, and the beginning of the steep "front" hill.

"It is as I thought," said Fenodyree. "The black master is in his den. See, yonder is Llyn-dhu, garlanded with mosses and mean dwellings."

Colin and Susan looked where Fenodyree was pointing, and some two or three miles out on the plain they could see the glint of grey water through trees.

"Men thought to drain that land and live there, but the spirit of the place entered them, and their houses were built drab and desolate, and without cheer; and all around the bog still sprawls, from out the drear lake come soulless thoughts and drift into the hearts of the people, and they are one with their surroundings.

"Ah! But there goes he who can tell us more about the stone."

He pointed to a speck floating high over the plain, and whistled shrilly.

"Hi, Windhover! To me!"

The speck paused, then came swooping through the air like a black falling star, growing larger every second, and, with a hollow beating of wings, landed on Fenodyree's outstretched arm – a magnificent kestrel, fierce and proud, whose bright eyes glared at the children.

"Strange company for dwarfs, I know," said Fenodyree, "but they have been prey of the morthbrood, and so are older than their years.

"It is of Grimnir that we want news. He went by here: did he seek the lake?"

The kestrel switched his gaze to Fenodyree, and gave a series of sharp cries, which obviously meant more to the dwarf than they did to the children.

"Ay, it is as I thought," he said when the bird fell silent. "A mist crossed the plain a while since, as fast as a horse can gallop, and sank into Llyndhu.

"Ah well, so be it. Now I must away back to Cadellin, for we shall have much to talk over and plans to make. Farewell now, my friends. Yonder is the road: take it. Remember us, though Cadellin forbade you, and wish us well."

"Goodbye."

Colin and Susan were too full to say more; it was an effort to speak, for their throats were tight and dry with anguish. They knew that Cadellin and Fenodyree were not being deliberately unkind in their anxiety to be rid of them, but the feeling of responsibility for what had happened was as much as they could bear.

So it was with heavy hearts that the children turned to the road: nor did they speak or look back until they had reached it. Fenodyree, standing on the seat, legs braced apart, with Windhover at his wrist, was outlined against the sky. His voice came to them through the still air.

"Farewell, my friends!"

They waved to him in return, but could find no words.

He stood there a moment longer before he jumped down and vanished along the path to Fundindelve. And it was as though a veil had been drawn across the children's eyes.

PART TWO

CHAPTER 8

Mist over Llyn-dhu

Autumn came, and in September Colin and Susan started school. Work on the farm kept them busy outside school hours, and it was not often they visited the Edge. Sometimes at the weekend they could go there, but then the woods were peopled with townsfolk who, shouting and crashing through the undergrowth, and littering the ground with food wrappings and empty bottles, completely destroyed the atmosphere of the place. Once, indeed, Colin and Susan came upon a family sprawled in front of the iron gates. Father, his back propped against the rock itself, strained, redder than his braces, to lift his voice above the blare of a portable radio to summon his children to tea. They were playing at soldiers in the Devil's Grave.

Nothing remained. This place, where beauty and terror had been as opposite sides of the same coin, was now a playground of noise. Its spirit was dead – or hidden. There was nothing to show that svart or wizard had ever existed: nothing, except a barn full of owls at Highmost Redmanhey, and an empty wrist where once a bracelet had been.

The loss of the bracelet was the cause of slight friction between the Mossocks and the children.

Bess was the first to notice that the stone had gone, and Susan, not knowing what to do for the best, poured out the whole story. It was really too much for anyone to digest at once, and Bess could not think what to make of it at all. She was upset over the loss of the Bridestone, naturally, but what troubled her more was the fact that Susan should be so fearful of the consequences that she would invent such a desperate pack of nonsense to explain it all away. Gowther, on the other hand, was by no means so certain that it was all fantasy. He kept his thoughts to himself, but in places the story touched on his recent experiences far too accurately for comfort. However, the affair blew over and no one mentioned it again, though that does not mean to say it was forgotten.

Shortly before Christmas Colin discovered that the owls had left the barn, and for days after, the children were in a fretful state of anxiety over what the disappearance could mean.

"Either Cadellin's got the stone back again," said Colin, "or he's lost the fight."

"Or perhaps it's only that he's sure we're out of danger; or perhaps . . . no, that wouldn't make sense . . . oh, I wish we *knew*!"

And although they spent two whole days ranging the woods from end to end, they found no clue to help them. If there had been a struggle as fierce as Cadellin had predicted, then it had left no trace that they could see.

★

It was a young winter of cloudless skies. The stars flashed silver in the velvet, frozen nights, and all the short day long the sun betrayed the earth into thinking it was spring. And late one Sunday afternoon at the end of the first week in January, Colin and Susan climbed out of Alderley village, pushing their bicycles before them. They walked slowly, for it was not a hill to be rushed, and the last stretch was the worst – straight and steep, without any respite. But once they were at the top, the going was comparatively good.

They did not ride more than a hundred yards, however, for Colin, who was leading, jammed on his brakes so violently that he half-fell from the bicycle and Susan nearly piled on top of him.

"Look!" he gasped. "Look over there!"

It could be only Cadellin. He stood against the skyline of Castle Rock, staff in hand, facing the plain.

At once all promises were forgotten: the children dropped their bicycles and ran.

"Cadellin! Cadellin!"

The wizard spun round at the sound of their voices, and made as if to leave the rock. But after three strides he checked his pace, stood for a moment, and then walked to the bench and sat down.

"Oh, Cadellin, we thought something must have happened to you!" cried Susan, sobbing with relief.

"Many things have happened to me, but I do not feel the worse for that!"

There was displeasure in his face, tempered with understanding.

"But we were so worried," said Colin. 'When the owls disappeared we wondered if you'd . . . you'd . . ."

"I see!" said Cadellin, breaking into laughter. "No, no, no, you must not look on life so fearfully. We called the birds away because we knew that you were no longer in danger from the morthbrood."

"Well, we thought of that," said Colin, "but we couldn't help thinking of other things, too."

"But what *about* the morthbrood?" said Susan. "Have they still got my Tear?"

"Yes, and no," said the wizard. "And in their greed and deceit lies all our present hope.

"Grimnir has the stone. He should have delivered it to Nastrond, but the morthbrood and he intend to master it alone. Perhaps they believe Firefrost holds power for them. If so, they are mistaken!

"And here we have wheels within wheels; for Grimnir and Shape-shifter, as rumour has it, are planning to reap all benefits for themselves, and leave the brood and the svarts to whistle for their measure. So says rumour; and I can guess more. I know Grimnir too well to imagine that he would willingly share power with anyone, and the Morrigan, for all her guile, is no match for him. And it may be among all this treachery that we shall find our chance; but for the present we watch, and wait. Firefrost is not in Nastrond's hand, and for that we must be thankful.

"There! You have it all, and now we go our ways once more."

Colin and Susan were so relieved to find the wizard unharmed that parting from him did not seem anything like so bleak an experience as it had been before.

"Is there still nothing we can do?" asked Susan.

"No more than you have been doing all these months. You have played your part well (if we forget this afternoon!), and you must continue to do so, for we do not want you to fall foul of *that* one again."

He pointed with his staff. About the trees through which the Black Lake could normally be seen hung a blanket of fog. Elsewhere, as far as the eye could see, the sunset plain was free of haze or mist, but Llyn-dhu brooded under a fallen cloud.

"It has been there for over a week," said the wizard. "I do not know what he is about, but my guess is that he is trying to seal Firefrost within a circle of magic to prevent its power from reaching Fundindelve. He will not succeed, and he has not the strength to destroy the stone. But then, I have not the power to take it by force, so the matter rests, though we do not."

Cadellin walked with the children as far as the road, and they left him, lighter at heart than they had been for many a day.

The mist was still there the following morning. Colin and Susan had set out on their bicycles soon after dawn to spend the day exploring the countryside, and when they had reached the top of the "front" hill Colin had suggested taking another look at Llyn-dhu. So there they now were, sitting on Castle Rock, and gazing at the mist.

For a long time they were silent, and when next Colin spoke he did no more than put his sister's thoughts into words.

"I wonder," he said, "what it's like . . . close to."

"Do you think we'd be breaking a promise if we went just to look?"

"Well, we're *looking* now, and we'd be doing the same thing, only from a lot nearer, wouldn't we?"

That decided it; but then they realized that they had not the least idea of how to reach the lake. However, by picking out what few landmarks they knew, it seemed that if they made for Wilmslow, and there turned left, they would be heading in something like the right direction. So, without further delay, Colin and Susan rode to Alderley, bought a bottle of lemonade to go with their sandwiches, posted a view of Stormy Point to their father and mother, and within thirty minutes of making their decision were in the centre of Wilmslow, and wondering which road to take next.

"There's the man to ask," said Colin.

He had seen a small beetle of a car, from which was emerging a police sergeant of such vast proportions that he hid the car almost completely from view. It was incredible that he could ever have fitted into it, even curled up.

The children cycled over to him, and Colin said:

"Excuse me, can you tell us the way to Llyn-dhu, please?"

"Where?" said the sergeant in obvious surprise.

"Llyn-dhu, the Black Lake. It's not far from here."

The sergeant grinned.

"You're not pulling my leg, are you?"

"No," said Susan, "we're not – promise!"

"Then somebody must be pulling yours, because there's no such place of that name round here that *I* know of, and I've been at Wilmslow all of nine years. Sounds more Welsh than anything."

Colin and Susan were so taken aback that, for a moment, they could not speak.

"But we saw it from Castle Rock less than an hour ago!" said Susan, and tears of exasperation pricked her eyes. "Well, we didn't really see it, because it was covered in mist, but we *know* it's there."

"Mist, did you say? Ah. now perhaps we're getting somewhere. There's been fog on Lindow Common for days, and the only lake in the district is there. Do you think that's what you want?"

Llyn-dhu, Lindow: it could be: it *had* to be!

"Ye-es; yes, that's it," said Colin. "We must have got the name wrong. Is it far?"

They followed the sergeant's directions, and after a mile came upon an expanse of damp ground, covered with scrub, and heather, and puddles. A little way off the road was a notice board which stated that this was Lindow Common, and that cycling was prohibited. And in the middle of the common was a long lake of black peat-stained water.

The children stood on the slimy shore. The air was dank and the scenery depressing. The common was encircled by a broken rash of houses, such as may be seen, like a ring of pink scum, on the outskirts of most of our towns and villages today.

"Garlanded with mosses and mean dwellings." Fenodyree's words came back to the children as they looked at the brick-pocked landscape. But what was most obviously wrong was that they could see all this. For it they were indeed at Llyndhu, then, within the space of an hour, it had rid itself of every trace of the mist that had shrouded it for the last ten days.

"Do you think this is it?" said Colin.

"Ugh, yes! There couldn't be *two* like this, and it's a black lake all right! I wonder what's happened."

"Oh, let's go," said Colin: "this place gives me the willies. We've done what we set out to do; now let's enjoy the rest of the day."

After a cup of coffee in Wilmslow to dispel the Lindow gloom, the children pedalled back towards Alderley. They had no plans, but the sun was warm, and there were a good six hours of daylight left to them.

They were crossing the station bridge at Alderley when they saw it. A light breeze, blowing from the north-east, trailed the village smoke along the sky, but halfway up the nearer slope of the Edge a ball of mist hung as though moored to the trees. And out of the mist rose the chimneys and gaunt gables of St Mary's Clyffe, the home of Selina Place.

CHAPTER 9

St Mary's Clyffe

The room was long, with a high ceiling, painted black. Round the walls and about the windows were draped black velvet tapestries. The bare wooden floor was stained a deep red. There was a table on which lay a rod, forked at the end, and a silver plate containing a mound of red powder. On one side of the table was a reading-stand, which supported an old vellum book of great size, and on the other stood a brazier of glowing coals. There was no other furniture of any kind.

Grimnir looked on with much bad grace as Shape-shifter moved through the ritual of preparation. He did not like witch-magic: it relied too much on clumsy nature spirits and the slow brewing of hate. He preferred the lightning stroke of fear and the dark powers of the mind.

But certainly this crude magic had weight. It piled force on force, like a mounting wave, and overwhelmed its prey with the slow violence of an avalanche. If only it were a quick magic! There could be very little time left now before Nastrond acted on his rising suspicions, and then . . . Grimnir's heart quailed at the thought. Oh, let him but bend this stone's power to his will, and Nastrond should see a true Spirit of Darkness arise; one to whom Ragnarok, and all it contained, would be no more than a ditch of noisome creatures to be bestridden and ignored. But how to master the stone? It had parried all his rapier thrusts, and, at one moment, had come near to destroying him. The sole chance now lay in this morthwoman's witchcraft, and she must be watched; it would not do for the stone to become *her* slave. She trusted him no more than could be expected, but the problem of how to rid himself of her when she had played out her part in his schemes was not of immediate importance. The shadow of Nastrond was growing large in his mind, and in swift success alone could he hope to endure.

With black sand, which she poured from a leather bottle, Shape-shifter traced an intricately patterned circle on the floor. Often she would halt, make a sign in the air with her hand, mutter to herself, curtsy, and resume her pouring. She was dressed in a black robe, tied round with scarlet cord, and on her feet were pointed shoes.

So intent on her work was the Morrigan, and so wrapped in his thoughts was Grimnir, that neither of them saw the two pairs of eyes that inched round the side of the window.

The circle was complete. Shape-shifter went to the table and picked up the rod.

"It is not the hour proper for summoning the aid we need," she said, "but if what you have heard contains even a grain of the truth, then we see that we must act at once, though we could have wished for a more discreet approach on your part." She indicated the grey cloud that pressed against the glass, now empty of watching eyes. "You may well attract unwanted attention."

At that moment, as if in answer to her fears, a distant clamour arose on the far side of the house. It was the eerie baying of hounds.

"Ah, you see! They are restless: there *is* something on the wind. Perhaps it would be wise to let them seek it out; they will soon let us know if it is aught beyond their powers – as well it may be! For if we do not have Ragnarok and Fundindelve upon our heads before the day is out, it will be no thanks to you."

She stumped round the corner of the house to the outbuilding from which the noise came. Selina Place was uneasy, and out of temper. For all his art, what a fool Grimnir could be! And what risks he took! Who, in their senses, would come so obviously on such an errand? Like his magic, he was no match for the weirdstone of Brisingamen. She smiled; yes, it would take the old sorcery to tame *that* one, *and* he knew it, for all his fussing in Llyn-dhu. "All right, all right! We're coming! Don't tear the door down!"

Behind her, two shadows moved out of the mist, slid along the wall, and through the open door.

"Which way now?" whispered Susan.

They were standing in a cramped hall, and there was a choice of three doors leading from it. One of these was ajar, and seemed to be a cloakroom.

"In here, then we'll see which door she goes through."

Nor did they delay, for the masculine tread of Selina Place came to them out of the mist.

"Now let us do what we can in haste," she said as she rejoined Grimnir. "There may be nothing threatening, but we shall not feel safe until we are master of the stone. Give it to us now."

Grimnir unfastened a pouch at his waist, and from it drew Susan's bracelet. Firefrost hung there, its bright depths hidden beneath a milky veil.

The Morrigan took the bracelet and placed it in the middle of the circle on the floor. She pulled the curtains over the windows and doors, and went to stand by the brazier, whose faint glow could hardly push back the darkness. She took a handful of powder from the silver plate and, sprinkling it over the coals, cried in a loud voice:

"*Demoriel, Carnefiel, Caspiel, Amenadiel!!*"

A flame hissed upwards, filling the room with ruby light. Shape-shifter opened the book and began to read.

"*Vos onmes it ministri odey et destructiones et seratores discorde . . .*"

"What's she up to?" said Susan.

"I don't know, but it's giving me gooseflesh."

"*. . . eo quod est noce vose coniurase ideo vos conniro et deprecur . . .*"

"Colin, I . . ."

"Sh! Keep still!"

"*. . . et odid fiat mier alve . . .*"

Shadows began to gather about the folds of velvet tapestries in the farthest corners of the room.

For thirty minutes Colin and Susan were forced to stand in their awkward hiding-place, and it took less than half that time for the last trace of enthusiasm to evaporate. They were where they were as the result of an impulse, an inner urge that had driven them on without thought of danger. But now there was time to think, and inaction is never an aid to courage. They would probably have crept away and tried to find Cadellin, had not a dreadful sound of snuffling, which passed frequently beneath the cloakroom window, made them most unwilling to open the outer door.

And all the while Shape-shifter's chant droned on, rising at intervals to harsh cries of command.

"Come, Haborym! Come, Haborym! Come, Haborym!"

Then it was that the children began to feel the dry heat that was soon to become all but intolerable. It bore down upon them until the blood thumped in their ears, and the room spun sickeningly about their heads.

"Come, Orobas! Come, Orabas! Come, Orabas!"

Was it possible? For the space of three seconds the children heard the clatter of hoofs upon bare boards, and a wild neighing rang high in the roof.

"Come, Nambroth! Come, Nambroth! Come, Nambroth!"

A wind gripped the house by the eaves, and tried to pluck it from its sandstone roots. Something rushed by on booming winds. The lost voices of the air called to each other in the empty rooms, and the mist clung fast and did not stir.

"*Coniuro et confirmo super vos potentes in nomi fortis, metuendissimi, infandi . . .* "

Just at the moment when Susan thought she must faint, the stifling heat diminished enough to allow them to breathe in comfort; the wind died, and a heavy silence settled on the house.

After minutes of brooding quiet a door opened, and the voice of Selina Place came to the children from outside the cloakroom. She was very much out of breath.

"And . . . *we* say the stone . . . will . . . be safe. Nothing . . . can reach it . . . from . . . outside. Come away . . . this is a dangerous . . . brew. Should it boil over . . . and we . . . near, that . . . would be the end . . . of us. Hurry. The force is growing . . . it is not safe to watch."

Mistrustfully, and with many a backward glance, Grimnir joined her, and they went together through the doorway on the opposite side of the hall, and their footsteps died away.

"Well, how do we get out of *this* mess?" said Colin. "It looks as though we're stuck here until she calls these animals off, and if she's going to do any more of the stuff we've been listening to, I don't think I want to wait that long."

"Colin, we can't go yet! My Tear's in that room, and we'll never have another chance!"

The air was much cooler now, and no sounds, strange or otherwise, could be heard. And Susan felt that insistent tugging at her inmost heart that had brushed aside all promises and prudence when she stared at the mist from the bridge by the station.

"But Sue, didn't you hear old Place say that it wasn't safe to be in there? And if *she's* afraid to stay it must be dangerous."

"I don't care; I've got to try. Are you coming? Because if not, I'm going by myself."

"Oh . . . all right! But we'll wish we'd stayed in here."

They stepped out of the cloakroom and cautiously opened the left-hand door.

The dull light prevented them from seeing much at first, but they could make out the table and the reading desk, and the black pillar in the centre of the floor.

"All clear!" whispered Susan.

They tiptoed into the room, closed the door, and stood quite still while their eyes grew accustomed to the light: and then they saw.

The pillar was alive. It climbed from out the circle that Selina Place had so laboriously made, a column of oily smoke; and in the smoke strange shapes moved. Their forms were indistinct, but the children could see enough to wish themselves elsewhere.

Even as they watched the climax came. Faster and faster the pillar whirled, and thicker and thicker the dense fumes grew, and the floor began to tremble, and the children's heads were of a sudden full of mournful voices that reached them out of a great and terrible distance. Flecks of shadow, buzzing like flies, danced out of the tapestries and were sucked into the reeking spiral. And then, without warning, the base of the column turned blue. The buzzing rose to a demented whine – and stopped. The whole swirling mass shuddered as though a brake had been savagely applied, lost momentum, died, and drooped like the ruin of a mighty tree. Silver lightnings ran upwards through the smoke: the column wavered, broke, and collapsed into the ball of fire that rose to engulf it. A voice whimpered close by the children and passed through the doorway behind them. The blue light waned, and in its place lay Firefrost, surrounded by the scattered remnants of Shape-shifter's magic circle.

Colin and Susan stood transfixed. Then slowly, as if afraid that the stone would vanish if she breathed or took her eyes off it, Susan moved forward and picked it up.

In the silence she unclasped the bracelet and fastened it about her wrist. She could not believe what she was doing. This moment had haunted her dreams for so many months, and there had been so many bitter awakenings.

In a small room crammed under the eaves Selina Place and Grimnir waited. Both were keyed to an almost unendurable pitch. They knew well the price of failure. Not once in a thousand years had any of their kind disobeyed the charge of Nastrond, but all at some time had stood in the outer halls of Ragnarok and looked on the Abyss. Thus did Nastrond bind evil to his will.

"It cannot be long now," said the Morrigan. "Within five minutes the stone must . . ."

A trail of smoke drifted under the door and floated across the room, and a bubbling sound of tears accompanied it. The Morrigan jumped from her chair: her eyes were wild, and there was sweat on her brow.

"*Non licet abire!*" She threw her arms wide to bar the way. "*Coniuro et confirmo super . . .*" But the smoke curled round her towards the hearth, and leapt into the chimney mouth. A wind sighed mournfully past the windows, and was still.

"No! No," she mumbled, groping for the door; but Grimnir had already flung it open and was rushing along the corridors to the stairs. He was halfway down the first flight when there was the sound of breaking glass, and the staircase was momentarily in shadow as a dark figure blocked the window at its head. The Morrigan's harsh voice cried out in fear, and Grimnir turned with the speed and menace of a hungry spider.

The noise roused Colin and Susan from their trance. Again the Morrigan shrieked.

"Here, let's get out of this!" said Colin, and he pulled his sister into the hall. "As soon as we're outside run like mad: I'll be right behind you!"

Quite a hullabaloo was breaking out upstairs, and most of the sounds were by no means pleasant; at least they made the other hazard seem less formidable – until Colin opened the door. There was a rasping growl, and out of the mist came a shape that sent the children stumbling backwards into the house, and before they could close the door the hound of the Morrigan crossed the threshold and was revealed in all its malignity.

It was like a bull terrier; except that it stood four feet high at the shoulder, and its ears, unlike the rest of the white body, were covered with coarse red hair. But what set it apart from all others was the fact that, from pointed ears to curling lip, its head and muzzle were blank. There were no eyes.

The beast paused, swinging its wedge-shaped head from side to side, and snuffling wetly with flared nostrils, and when it caught the children's scent it moved towards them as surely as if it had eyes. Colin and Susan dived for the nearest door, and into what was obviously a kitchen, which had nothing to offer them but another door.

"We'll have to risk it," said Susan: "that thing'll be through in a second." She put no trust in the flimsy latch, which was rattling furiously beneath the scrabbling of claws. But as she spoke they heard another sound; footsteps rapidly drawing near to the other door! And then the latch did give way, and the hound was in the room.

Colin seized a kitchen chair. "Get behind me," he whispered.

At the sound of his voice the brute froze, but only for an instant: it had found its bearings.

"Can we reach a window?" Colin dared not take his eyes off the hound as it advanced upon them.

"No."

"Is there another way out?"

"No."

He was parrying the lunges and snappings with the chair, but it was heavy, and his arms ached.

"There's a broom cupboard, or something, behind us, and the door's ajar."

"What good will that do?"

"I don't know: but Grimnir may not notice us, or the dog may attack him, or . . . oh, anything's better than this!"

"Is it big enough?"

"It goes up to the ceiling."

"Right. Get in."

Susan stepped inside and held the door open for Colin as he backed towards it. The hound was biting at the chair legs and trying to paw them down. Wood crunched and splinters flew, and the chair drooped in Colin's hands, but he was there. He hurled the chair at the snarling head, and fell backwards into the cupboard. Susan had a vision of a red tongue lolling out of a gaping mouth, and of fangs flashing white, inches from her face, before she slammed the door; and at the same moment, she heard the kitchen door being flung open. Then she fainted.

Or, at least, she *thought* she had fainted. Her stomach turned over, her head reeled, and she seemed to be falling into the bottomless dark. But *had* she fainted? Colin bumped against her in struggling to right himself: she could feel that. And the back of the cupboard was pressing into her. She pinched herself. No, she had not fainted.

Colin and Susan stood rigidly side by side, nerving themselves for the moment when the door would be opened. But the room seemed unnaturally still: not a sound could they hear.

"What's up?" whispered Colin. "It's too quiet out there."

"Shh!"

"I can't see a keyhole anywhere, can you? There should be one somewhere." He bent forward to feel.

"Ouch!!"

Colin let out a yell of surprise and pain, and this time Susan nearly *did* faint.

"Sue! There's no door!"

"Wh-what?"

"No door! It's something that feels like smooth rock going past very quickly, and I've skinned my hand on it. That's why my ears have been popping! We're in a lift!"

Even as he spoke, the floor seemed to press against their feet, and a chill, damp air blew upon their faces, and they were aware of a silence so profound that they could hear their hearts beating.

"Where on earth are we?" said Colin.

"It's probably more like where *in* earth are we!"

Susan knelt on the floor of the cupboard and stretched out her hand to where the door had been. Nothing. She reached down, and touched wet rock.

"Well, there's a floor. Let's have our bike lamps out and see what sort of place this is."

They took off their knapsacks and rummaged around among the lemonade and sandwiches.

By the light of the lamps they saw that they were at the mouth of a tunnel that stretched away into the darkness.

"Now what do we do?"

"We can't go back, can we, even if we wanted to?"

"No," said Susan, "but I don't like the look of this."

"Neither do I, but we haven't really much choice; come on."

They shouldered their packs and started off along the tunnel, but seconds later a slight noise brought them whirling round, their hearts in their mouths.

"That's torn it!" said Colin gazing up at the shaft, into which the cupboard was disappearing. "They'll be on to us in no time now."

CHAPTER 10

Plankshaft

The children went as fast as they could, stumbling over the uneven floor, and bruising themselves against the walls. The air was musty, and within a minute they were gasping as though they had run a mile, but on they sped, with two thoughts in their heads – to escape from whatever was following them, and to find Cadellin or Fenodyree. If only this were Fundindelve!

The passage twisted bewilderingly, and when Susan pulled up without notice or warning, Colin could not avoid running into her, and down they sprawled, though they managed to keep hold of their lamps. There was no need to ask questions. The tunnel ended in a shaft that dropped beyond the range of their light. And hanging from a spike driven into the rock was a rope-ladder. It was wet, and covered with patches of white mould that glistened pallidly, but it looked as though it would bear the children's weight. The urgency of their plight killed all fear: they dared not hesitate. Both hands were needed for the climb, so they tucked the lamps inside their windcheaters, and went down in darkness.

The rope was slippery, and it took all their willpower to descend at an even pace. They did this by moving down rung by rung together,

Colin setting the pace by counting. "One – two – three – four – five – six – seven." He was ten rungs higher than his sister, and the urge to increase the rate was very strong; he tried not to think of what might happen if Grimnir reached the top of the ladder while they were still on it. "A hundred and forty – and one – two – three – four – five."

"I'm at the bottom!" called Susan. "And it's wet!"

The end of the ladder dangled a few inches above an island of sand that lay at the foot of the shaft, and from here four ways led off, none very inviting. Two were silted up, and two were flooded. Colin chose the shallower of the flooded tunnels, along which stray lumps of rock served as unreliable stepping-stones, and for a few yards the children made dry, if cumbersome, progress. Then Colin, in helping Susan over a particularly wide stretch of water, saw the end of the ladder begin to dance wildly about in the air. Someone obviously had started to descend.

The brown water splashed roof-high as Colin and Susan took to their heels, skidding over slimy, unseen rocks. But the tunnel sloped upwards, and to their relief, they left the water behind and were running on dry sand. This, however, was not long an asset: for soon it lay so thickly that the children were compelled to run bent double, and, finally, to scramble on hands and knees.

What if the roof and floor meet, thought Susan, and we have to go back . . . or wait?

Sweat was blinding her, her hair and clothes were full of sand, stones added to her bruises, and her lungs ached with the strain of drawing air out of the saturated atmosphere: but she had her Tear, and this time Susan was going to keep it, even if all the witches and warlocks that ever were came after her.

Suppose we can't go on, though . . .

But almost at once her fears were allayed: the lamp's beam outlined the end of the tunnel against a blackness beyond.

"Oh, glory be!" she spluttered, and they crawled out on to a soft mound of sand. At first, they could only droop on all fours, heads sagging like winded dogs, and gulp in the cold air, which was a little more wholesome than that of the tunnel; and, from the sudden lack of resonance, they guessed that they must be in a cavern. Every movement in the tunnel had produced a magnified, hollow echo, which made their breathing now appear dry, and remote. The children staggered to their feet, and looked about them.

In shape and size it was just such another cave as the Cave of the Sleepers in Fundindelve, but instead of the light, darkness pressed in from every side. The yellow walls were streaked with browns, blacks, reds, blues, and greens – veins of mineral that traced the turn of wind and wave upon a shore, twenty million years ago.

Colin bent down and listened at the tunnel mouth.

"I can't hear anything," he said, "but we'd better move on, if we can."

Losing their pursuer was an easy task. It seemed that they were in an intricate system of caverns, connected by innumerable tunnels and shafts. These caverns were remarkable. The walls curved upwards to form roofs high as a cathedral, and the distance between the walls was often so great that, at the centre of a cave, the children could imagine themselves to be trudging along a sandy beach on a windless and starless night. The loose sand killed all noise of movement, and helped the silence to prey on their nerves: moreover, it made walking hot, laborious work, and the air was still not good; ten minutes under these conditions sapped their energy as much as an hour of normal tramping would have done.

Tunnels entered and left the caves at all angles and levels. They turned, twisted, branched, forked, climbed, dropped, and frequently led nowhere. They would run into a cave at any point between roof and floor, and wind out on to dizzy ledges, which in turn dwindled to random footholds, or nothing at all. And the square-mouthed shafts were a continual hazard. Through some, the distant floors of lower galleries could be glimpsed, while others disappeared into unknowable depths. It was no place for panic. Every corner, every bend, every opening, had to be approached with the greatest caution, for fear of an unwanted meeting; and the caves were the worst of all. After crossing through half a dozen or so, and peering round at the holes which stared sightless from all quarters. Colin and Susan took to scuttling over the floor and diving into the first tunnel they saw, trusting blindly that that particular one would not be tenanted. In the tunnels they were close to wall and ceiling, lamps held their own with shadows; but in the caves the children felt truly lost, for their puny light only accentuated their insignificance, and the feeling of being exposed to unseen eyes grew ever stronger. Somewhere within this labyrinth someone was hunting them down, and Colin and Susan were never more aware of this than when they broke cover beneath a soaring dome of rock and ran through the nightmare sand.

How far they travelled, and for how long before they had to rest, was impossible to judge: time and distance mean little underground. But at last they could go no further, and, chancing upon a tunnel with a partially blocked entrance, they wriggled inside and lay stretched on the floor. They were consumed by heat and thirst, and fumbled impatiently in Colin's pack for the lemonade. For minutes afterwards the tunnel sounded with gulpings, and gaspings, and sighs of indulgence.

"Better save some for later," said Colin.

"Oh, all right: but I could drink the sea dry!"

The children relaxed their aching limbs and talked in whispers. But first they switched off the lamps; there was no point in adding to their troubles by hastening the moment when the batteries would be exhausted.

"Listen," said Colin, "the main thing right now is to find a way out of here without being caught. I don't think there's much doubt about where we are; it must be the copper mines. And if that's so, then there are several ways out. But how do we find them?"

They thought for some time in silence: there seemed to be no answer to this problem.

"There must be some . . . wait a minute!" said Susan. "Yes! Look: if we're in the mines the way out must be above us, mustn't it? Nearly all the entrances are on top of the Edge."

"Yes . . ."

"Well, if we follow only the tunnels that lead upwards, we're bound to be moving in the right direction, aren't we? I know it's not much of an idea, but it's better than wandering aimlessly until Grimnir and Selina find us."

"It's not only those two I'm worried about," said Colin. "Have you noticed how the sand is churned up everywhere? It's too soft to give clear impressions, but it shows that these mines aren't as empty as they look. And remember what Cadellin said about avoiding them at all costs because of the svarts."

Susan had not thought of that. But the added danger could not alter the situation, and although they talked for some time, they could think of no better plan. Still, it took courage to switch on their lamps and leave their safe retreat for the perils of the open tunnel.

So they journeyed into despair. For no way led upwards for long. Sooner or later the floor would level and begin to drop, and after an hour of this heartbreak Colin and Susan had less than no idea of their whereabouts. Then, imperceptibly, they began to feel that they were gaining ground. They had wormed along the crest of a sand-bank that rested on the edge of a cliff, high under the roof of a boulder-strewn cave. Sand rolled continually from under them and slid into the emptiness below: the whole bank seemed to be on the move. At the end of the ridge was a tunnel mouth, and the rock beneath their feet, when finally they made contact with it, was almost as welcome as green fields and the open sky. This tunnel was different: it was longer than most, and less tortuous.

"Colin, this time I think we're on the right track!" said Susan, who was in the lead.

"I think perhaps we are!"

"Oh!"

"What's the matter? Is it a dead-end?"

"No, but it's . . ."

Colin peered over his sister's shoulder. "Oh."

The widest shaft they had yet come upon lay before them, and stretched across its gaping mouth was a narrow plank. This was wet, and partly rotten, and no more than three inches rested on the lip of the shaft at either end.

"We'll have to go back," said Colin.

"No: we must cross. The tunnel leads somewhere, or the plank wouldn't be here."

And Susan stepped on to the plank.

Colin watched his sister walk over the pit: he had never known her to be like this before. She had always been content to follow his lead, seldom inclined to take a risk, no matter how slight. Yet now, for the third time in one day, she was deliberately facing great danger, and with a composure that claimed his respect even while it nettled his pride.

Susan was two-thirds of the way across when the plank tilted sideways an inch. Colin felt the sweat cold sweat on his spine: but Susan merely paused to correct her balance, and then she was across.

"There! It's easy – a bit rocky near the middle, but it's quite safe. Walk normally, and don't look down."

"All right! I know how to do it as well as you!"

Colin started out. It was not too bad: the plank was firm, and he was prepared for a slight movement just over halfway. But even so, when it came it caught him unawares. He felt the plank shift: he teetered sideways, his arms flailing. Two swift shambling steps, the plank seemed to swing away from him, the lamplight whirled in an arch, he saw that his next step would miss the plank, the shaft yawned beneath him, and he leapt for his life.

"Are you hurt?"

Colin pulled himself into a sitting position, and rubbed his head.

"No. Thanks, Sue."

He felt sick. For a second, which had seemed an age, he had crouched on one foot, poised over the drop, with his other leg hanging straight down the shaft, unable to produce the momentum to roll forward. And Susan had reached out and grabbed him by the hair, and brought him pitching on to his face in the tunnel.

"Do you mind if we have a rest?"

"We may as well, before we go back over the plank."

"*What?*"

"Look for yourself."

Colin shone his lamp along the tunnel and groaned. From where they were sitting, the floor plunged down, and, for as far as they could see, there was no change in its course.

"Down, down, always down!" cried Susan bitterly. "Are we never going to see daylight again?"

"Let's carry on, now that we're here," said Colin. "You never know, this may be the way out." He did not want to face the plank again, if it could possibly be avoided.

The passage dropped at an alarming rate. The floor was of smooth, red clay, and once Susan, going too fast, lost control and slid for several yards before she could stop herself. They learnt the lesson and went cautiously from them on.

Down, down, down, further than they had ever been before. And then the tunnel veered to the left, zigzagged violently, and came to an end on a ledge overlooking a great void. Colin lay on his stomach and peered over the edge.

"Well, we tried."

Seven or eight feet below was a lake of chocolate-coloured water, capped with scuds of yellow foam. Some yards away a bar of sand showed above the surface, but beyond that there was nothing.

"Oh, let's get back to the plank!" said Colin.

All the way up he was wondering how he could bring himself to cross the plank; and there it was before him, and Susan was saying, "Do you think you can manage?"

"'Course I can!"

Colin willed himself forward. His ears sang, his legs were rubber, his breath hissed through his teeth, his heart pounded, there was rock under him.

"Nothing to it!"

He shone the light on the plank for Susan to cross.

"Yes, it is easier. It slopes up coming this way." Susan was in the middle now. "I wonder how deep the shaft is." She stopped.

"No, Sue! Don't look down, it'll make you giddy! Come across: don't stop!"

'I'm all right! I want to see how far down it goes."

And she turned the beam of her lamp into the shaft.

She saw the wet rock, ribbed and gleaming like

a gigantic windpipe, fall away beneath her and vanish into darkness far below, and . . . Susan screamed. The lamp dropped from her hand and crashed from wall to wall into the shaft's throat. It was a terrible depth. She swayed, and fell forward, clutching the plank so violently that it began to quiver and grate against its anchorage. Susan knelt, staring into the hole and whimpering with fear.

"Sue! Sue, get up! What's the matter? *Sue!*"

"Eyes! Eyes looking at me! Down there in the darkness!"

The plank was trembling alarmingly now, and one corner was almost off the rock. Colin tried to steady it, but he was afraid to pull the plank, in case the other end should be jerked off its support.

"Sue, crawl; don't look down. Come on; it's only a few feet."

"I can't. I'll fall."

"No you won't. Here; look at me: don't look at the shaft. Come on, Sue."

"I can't. I'll fall."

The plank shifted a good inch.

"Sue; look up. *Look up*! That's better; now, *keep* looking at me, and crawl."

Susan bit her lip, and started to edge her way towards Colin. Immediately the plank began to tremble more than ever.

"I can't do it. Honestly, I *can't*!"

"All right, Sue. Stay there: I'm coming!"

And, without a moment's hesitation, Colin walked out along the plank to join her.

"There now; give me your hand. Do you think you can stand up?"

He bent down, trying to look no further than his sister's face.

Susan grabbed at the hand, and flung her other arm round his knees: the plank rocked furiously. Colin fought for balance: Susan had completely lost hers. Slowly she pulled herself up, clutching her brother all the time, until she stood, trembling, with her arms on his shoulders.

"Now walk. No, wait: I'll tell you when. With me, now; one . . . two . . ."

Colin moved backwards along the plank, feeling behind him painfully for every step.

CHAPTER 11

Prince of the Huldrafolk

"I don't know what came over me," said Susan. "I wasn't afraid to begin with: something was pulling me on all the time."

The children had withdrawn a good distance from the shaft, and were sitting with their backs propped against the tunnel wall. They were both in need of a rest.

"I was so certain that we were right that I could have cried when the tunnel dropped like that. And again, when you said we'd better go on, and we came to the ledge, I wanted to jump into the water!"

"That *would* have made a mess of things!"

"I know; but it was such a strong urge. Crossing the plank was easy. I just *knew* it would be safe, and I wasn't dizzy. But, when I saw those four pairs of eyes glowing in the shaft, something went wrong in my head. The plank wasn't safe and wide; it was old, and rotten, and narrow, and the shaft was trying to swallow me, and those eyes were waiting."

"But how do you know they were eyes? It could have been the light glinting on broken glass, or that white fungus stuff."

"No it wasn't! They blinked, and moved about. I've never been so frightened before; not

313

even when Grimnir caught us. And when I dropped the lamp it was worse.

"But I'm not frightened now; isn't it strange?
As soon as we were off the plank I felt altogether
different. No, it wasn't because we were safe: it's
as though there was a special *kind* of fear reaching
out of the shaft and trying to make me fall. Do
you think they were svarts down there?"

"I don't know; but whatever they were, I think
we'd better move from here. Are you ready?"

They retraced their steps, and presently came
to a break in the wall, and a stairway, cut in the
rock, leading down into a cave.

"Shall we?"

"Yes, anywhere's better than covering old
ground."

But soon they realized that it was not new
country at all. They were walking at the foot of
a cliff, and on top of this was heaped a shelving
bed of sand that almost touched the roof.

"I wish we'd known there was an easier way
to the tunnel," said Colin. "It's bad enough down
here without doing things the hard way."

They were becoming used to conditions underground, and the atmosphere of the place was no
longer oppressive – while they were on the move.
But the loss of the lamp slowed them considerably. They went hand in hand wherever possible,
and Colin held the light, except when they were
in a tunnel; then Susan would take the lead, while
Colin was left to grope along behind in treacherous semi-darkness. Their rest-periods became

more frequent, and Colin made a rule of switching off the light at such times. The battery was not new, and they had neither matches nor candles, and without light there would be no hope.

The children tried to keep to uphill paths, but the switchback tunnels bemused them at every turn.

"I'd like something to eat next time we stop," said Susan.

"All right; but we must go very carefully with the food and drink. We were fools to swig nearly all the lemonade like that, because I shouldn't think any of the water down here is fit to drink."

"Ugh, no!"

"The next small tunnel we find, we'll rest and share the food out. We'll have one sandwich each, but we mustn't have any drink."

"Oh, Colin, I'm parched! My mouth feels as though it's full of glue, and I'm so hot!"

"Me too. But we must be strict with ourselves, otherwise we may never get out."

Colin was very worried about the light. It was strong, but sooner or later its white beam would turn yellow, flicker, and slowly die. He said nothing of this to his sister, but she was not blind to the danger.

"Ah, here's a likely place," said Colin.

They crawled inside and looked around. Yes, it was very suitable. The tunnel came to a dead end after a few yards, and the entrance was almost filled with sand. Quite a snug little den – until they realized that it was the very same tunnel in which they had first rested. All that distance, and to no purpose.

"And I was beginning to think we were gaining height!" said Colin. "We're like squirrels in a cage! Oh, I could throw something!"

They unwrapped the food.

"Here you are," said Colin; "make the most of it."

"You know, perhaps we *have* climbed a bit," said Susan. "For all we can tell, this tunnel may be near the surface."

"Huh," said Colin out of the darkness. He knew she was only trying to cheer him up.

Susan gave a little cough, and a gasp.

"What's the matter? Got a crumb in your throat? That's what comes of being greedy! I suppose it means you'll have to have a drink now. Why can't you be more careful?"

Colin reached for the lamp and pressed the switch. He was alone.

"*Sue!!*"

He scrambled round in the tunnel: it was empty.

"*Sue!!*"

She had gone, pack and all.

Colin squirmed through the entrance and flashed his lamp up and down: there was nothing to be seen. He ran unthinkingly. Tunnels, caverns, tunnels; an endless desolation of sand and rock.

"*Sue! Sue!!*"

And at once he was past running. The sand dragged his steps, he tripped and fell.

"Sue!" No. That's not the way. Keep quiet. Must think. Put the light out! Must find her. But suppose I find the way out? What then? No. Must find Sue. Rest a minute, though: just a minute.

Slowly strength returned to his limbs. Colin humped himself on to his elbows and turned on the lamp.

Svarts! Two of them. They were creeping over the sand, and were caught full in the beam of light.

Colin sprang to his feet; but he was no longer in danger. To take him in the dark had been their plan; to leap, and grasp him with their sinewy hands, and bear him off in sport. But now they reeled back, their eyes blinded by the lamp. They croaked and hissed, blundering along the cave wall, with their arms before their faces, trying to find refuge from their pain. At length they stumbled upon a tunnel, and fought in haste to enter it. There was a last jostling of leathery backs, and they were gone.

All this happened in half the time it takes to tell, and it was over before Colin could gather his wits; but more was still to come. For a muffled cry sounded along the tunnel, and next the scrabble of feet. A svart burst out of the opening, swerved away from the lamp, and fled across the cave. Hard on his heels was the other svart: he paused, uncertain in the light, looked over his shoulder, and started off after his companion.

Something flashed white in the air. The svart shrieked, and crashed on his face in the sand. A broad, two-handed sword had pierced him through and through. Colin's jaw dropped; then, even as his brain struggled to accept the evidence of his eyes, the svart faded, and crumbled like a withered leaf, and all that was left was a haze of dust which settled gently to the floor. For a moment the sword stood reared on its point, then it fell to the ground with a thud.

"Ho! Dyrnwyn, they like not your bite! By the beard of my father, this is poor sport indeed!"

The deep voice boomed out of the tunnel, and into the cave strode a dwarf – a viking in miniature. Yellow hair rolled down his shoulders, his forked beard reached to his waist. His armour was a winged helmet and a shirt of plated mail. About his shoulders hung a cloak of white eagle feathers.

"Breath of Nidhug!" he bellowed, shielding his eyes against the light. "Have I come to this place of unclean air to be half-blinded?"

"I-I'm sorry!" stammered Colin, switching the lamp from the dwarf's face.

"You would have been sorrier ere long, if I had not found you." He took up the sword. "And now, come quickly. More svart-heads must roll soon, and I would share them with my cousin."

"But – who are you? And how did you find me?"

"Durathror, son of Gondemar, am I; Prince of

the Huldrafolk, and friend of the lios-alfar. We have not time for gossip: come."

The sword clashed in its sheath, and the dwarf entered the tunnel.

"But wait a minute!" cried Colin. "I've got to find my sister: she's vanished, and I think the svarts have taken her."

"She is safe, never fear. Now will you come, or must I needs carry you?"

Colin had the greatest difficulty in keeping up with the dwarf, for he set off at a run, and slackened his pace for neither steep slopes nor floundering sands. But they had not far to go. Rounding a corner, Durathor slowed to a walk, and there, in a cave from which no other tunnels led, seated on a pile of rocks and calmly eating sandwiches, were Susan and Fenodyree.

"Sue! Where have you been? I thought I'd never see you again!"

"Oh, Colin, thank goodness you're safe, too!" cried Susan. "If it hadn't been for Fenodyree and Durathor I don't know what would have happened."

"I do," said Fenodyree. "And I say it is well we came up with you when we did."

"Came up with us?" said Colin. "I don't understand."

Susan burst out laughing.

"It wasn't Grimnir or Selina Place following us at all: it was these two!"

"*What?* Do you mean . . . ? Oh no!"

"Ay," said Fenodyree, "and a fine chase we had of it!

"But I have heard from Susan of how you gained the stone, and I say Cadellin, old wizard though he is, was wrong to think you have no place in this. You have shown yourselves worthy this day, and I would take you with us beyond the end of adventure, if you so wished it and it should come to that."

"Cousin Wineskin," interrupted Durathror, "well it is said of you that your tongue would still wag if it were cut out. This talk is pleasant, and no doubt there is much more to be said, but our errand is not over, and I would fain rid my lungs of the stink of this place."

"But of course!" said Fenodyree, jumping to his feet. "Forgive me, Durathror. Let us go. The way to the light is not long, and we shall tell all our tales in Fundindelve within the hour."

"I hope so," said Durathror. "But you must know that when I found the Young Dog there were svarts with him, and one, alas, still lives. I feel our journey will be merry ere it is done."

"Quickly then!" said Fenodyree. "We should not have lingered. Susan, behind me; then Colin; Durathror will guard the rear. Nay, do not look so amiss, Colin; Durathror meant no insult. Your name, in my own tongue, is as he said, and it is an old name, and bears much honour. Now let us go with speed."

As they hurried along, Colin managed to find out from Susan all that had happened to her.

It appeared that two svarts had seized her from behind, almost stifling her with their hands, and had carried her off. She had heard Colin's shouts die away, and was on the point of despairing altogether, when there was a loud cry, and the svarts dropped her and ran. She felt someone leap over her and follow in pursuit; but she almost died of shock, she said, when the voice of Fenodyree, close beside her, asked if she was unharmed. In the distance there were two shrieks, followed by the sound of returning footsteps; and so she met Durathror.

"But I don't know how it is they managed to do all this in the dark."

"How can an eagle fly? How can a fish swim?" laughed Fenodyree over his shoulder.

"Yes, but how did you find *me* so quickly?" said Colin. "Was it luck?"

"Luck?" shouted Durathror. "I had but to put my ear to the ground, and your bellowing all but split my head! The wonder of it is that I found no more than two of the svart-alfar in your company."

"Shh!" said Fenodyree, holding up his hand. "We must go carefully now."

He listened, ear to the ground, as Durathror had done.

"Svarts are moving, but they are far away. There may be no danger here, yet."

The tunnel opened into a broad gallery; before them rose an outcrop of rock, and it was the shape of a lion's head. Above the head the gallery stretched to a great height, cutting through other levels and caves as it went.

"This is the Cave of the Svartmoot, and no place for us at any time."

The words were barely out of Fenodyree's mouth when a faint sound came to them from far away. Colin and Susan had heard it once before: it was the gong that had brought the svart-alfar out of the Devil's Grave on Stormy Point on the night when the children had been run to earth in the marsh below the Holywell.

"Ha!" cried Durathror, and the sword Dyrnwyn sang aloud as she sprang from her sheath in an arc of light.

"Not now; not now," said Fenodyree. "It would be a good fight, but we should go under, and the stone with us. We must pass unseen."

Durathror lowered his arm unwillingly, an expression of disgust on his face.

"By the cow of Orgelmir!" he growled. "Yours is sour counsel! I shall not forget this day. Never before has one of the house of Gondemar turned from battle – and with such carrion, too. When all is safe in Fundindelve I must needs come here and put right this ill."

"Your arm may yet grow tired ere you see the light," said Fenodyree. "That is the call to svartmoot. We must hurry."

He scrambled lightly on to the lion's shoulders, and the others followed. From the shoulder they climbed up a wall, pocked with smooth footholds, to a narrow ledge that curved round to a gallery, overlooking the head. The sound of many feet could now be heard drawing nearer. Every tunnel murmured.

Fenodyree made for a passage that wound into the roof.

"Quickly, now! They are coming by this way, too, and we must reach hiding before they meet us."

The tunnel wall ended, and they were upon a wide platform: far beneath lay the cave. At the back of the ledge was a recess.

"In here! And show no light."

Colin switched off the lamp, and felt the dwarfs press to him as they crowded as far away from the entrance as they could. Susan, crushed against the rear wall, could hardly breathe.

They were none too soon; for barely had they settled themselves when the svarts were upon them. They swept by the opening like a racing tide. For a full minute Colin and Susan listened to the slap of feet, and the hiss of breath. And then the unseen crowd was past, and the noise of its going blended into the general confusion of rustling, croaking, piping, and pulling, which grew steadily louder as svarts poured into the cave from every direction, and the air grew rank with their presence.

As though at a given signal, the hubbub died, and a tense quiet fell upon the assembled multitude. The svartmoot had begun.

CHAPTER 12

In the Cave of the Svartmoot

"Do not move," Fenodyree whispered. "Durathror and I go to watch the moot. We shall come back as soon as we know what they intend."

The dwarfs went so quietly that even in that silence Colin and Susan heard nothing.

Below them, some minutes later, a voice began to speak in harsh, high tones. The language was unintelligible: it was full of guttural and nasal sounds, and the words hovered and slurred most jarringly. The speaker was working himself into a state of excitement, or anger, and the crowd was carried with him. It began with a muttering, soon building to a howl at every pause in the address.

Colin felt a hand on his arm.

"Come with me," said Fenodyree. "Shortly you will see; but keep low."

Colin groped his way on all fours till he reached Durathror, who was lying at the edge of the platform, and mumbling into his beard. Not long after, Susan joined them. The noise below was now continuous.

"They are cowards," said Fenodyree, "and must be driven to a frenzy to meet our swords. But he does his work well.

"Ha, I guessed it would be so! They are powerless before sudden light, therefore they are to prepare themselves with firedrake blood; and here is the Keeper!"

The hysterical voices diminished to a murmur of intense excitement. Then, for a second, the cave was hushed.

"Down!" whispered Fenodyree. "He is taking off the cover!"

A sheet of fire sprang upwards past the ledge, and boiled against the roof.

"Eeee – agh – hooo!" roared the svarts.

The flames sank to a column twenty feet in height, which lit the cave with a red glare. A similar light had burned in St Mary's Clyffe earlier that day.

"You may look now," said Fenodyree.

Colin and Susan raised their heads, and the memory of what they saw remained with them ever after.

The floor and walls of the cave were covered with svarts. They swarmed like bees. The first two layers of galleries were thick with them, and the children were glad Fenodyree had climbed so high. The lion's head, and a small space beneath its jaws, formed an island in a turbulent sea. On top of the rock stood two svarts, one black, the other white, and they were man-size.

"There you see Arthog and Slinkveal, lords of the svart-alfar. Slinkveal is cunning past the thoughts of men, but Arthog it is who speaks, and carries out his brother's word; and his heart is blacker than his hide. See now the firedrake:

the eyes of svarts can look on it without pain, and it makes them strong to face the purer light of day: henceforth your lamp will be no weapon."

The flame was rising out of a stone cup, full of a seething liquid, that was held by a hideous, wizened svart who sat cross-legged on the sand beneath the lion's jaws. He was obviously very old, and his sagging skin was piebald, white and black.

"It is time we were gone," said Fenodyree. "We have a comfortless road ahead. Crawl to the tunnel, and do not show your light until I give you word."

For a few yards only, the red glow lit their way. Behind them the tumult increased again.

"There is a corner ahead," said Fenodyree, "and once round that you may use your lamp."

He hurried them along at a relentless pace; and he seemed very despondent. Durathror, on the other hand, was in a much improved temper, and began to laugh to himself as he jogged along behind.

"Did I not say the journey would be merry? Ha! By the blood of Lodur, it is better than all I thought! So we are to be tracked down, are we? And we are to be met at the plankshaft, I hear; and if, all else fails, they wait for us at the gate. Let us hurry to the gate, Cousin Squabnose, for I would have these rat-eaters remember the gate in after-time, what few there will be to sing of it when we have passed!"

Fenodyree sighed, and shook his head.

"You forget our charge, old Limbhewer. Fire-frost is more to us than life, or death in glory: we must sink our pride, and run before these goblins. The gate is not for us."

"Not for us? Then how, pray, shall we gain the upper world? There is no other road."

"There is: just one. And, in its fashion, it bears more perils than the gate, though these cannot be mastered by the sword. At least, if we should perish on this road, Firefrost will lie hidden for untold centuries to come; for we are going where no svart will ever tread, nor any living thing, and only I, in all the world, can tell the way."

"But Fenodyree," cried Susan, "what do you mean? There are lots of entrances!"

"Not here. We are in West Mine, and from it there was one exit made. But so deep did men delve that they touched upon the secret places of the earth, known only to a few; and, of those, my father was the last. There were the first mines of our people dug, ages before Fundindelve; little remains now, save the upper paths, and they are places of dread, even for dwarfs. The way is hidden, but my father taught me well. Never have I trod the paths, save in evil dreams, and I had always hoped to be spared the trial; but now it has come to that."

"Nay, speak this no more," growled Dura-thror. "I like it not."

They travelled on without rest, talking little, for Colin and Susan had not the energy, and Durathor was subdued by what he had heard.

"It is not far," said Fenodyree, "to . . . ah!"

Ahead of them a light flickered on the wall: the source of the light was hidden round a bend in the tunnel, but the dwarfs did not have to guess what to expect.

"What say you now, cousin?" whispered Durathror eagerly. "Do we run like shadows before this light, or do we snuff it out?"

Fenodyree's face was grim.

"We are too near; we must not turn back."

"Good! This shall we do: let the men-children stand here. Go you forward to younder opening, and stay hidden, with drawn sword, till I call. I shall wait behind this boulder. Hold your ground, Stonemaiden; be not afraid. No svart will touch you, that I can promise!"

And he melted into the dark.

The light grew stronger, and cast shadows on the wall; spindly shadows, with broad heads and hands; and round the bend came the svarts.

There were ten of them, white svarts, with pug-noses. Each carried a torch of wood that had been dipped in the flame of the firedrake's blood. From a girdle round each of their waists hung a crude axe or hammer. The head was a roughly worked stone, kidney or dumb-bell shaped; there was a groove about the middle, round which was bent a withy lashed tight with rat-skin thongs.

Colin and Susan involuntarily shrank closer together, and the lamp trembled in Colin's hand. The svarts halted; a deep sigh ran through them; and slowly they began to advance.

In spite of the knowledge that Durathror was close at hand, the children had to fight to stop themselves from running.

The svarts came on: the last of them was past Fenodyree. They held the torches high, and the other hand was poised to clutch. Colin flashed the lamp in their eyes, but they did no more than blink, and laugh hungrily. The children retreated a step. The svarts rushed forward. But at that moment Durathror stepped from behind the boulder, his sword Dyrnwyn in his hand, and bowed low before them, and addressed them in their own tongue.

"Hail, O eaters of toadstools! We are well met!"

The svarts fell back, mouths agape, and hissing after the fashion of giant lizards. But those to the rear of the pack had more courage.

"See!" they cried. "It is he whom we must kill! The men-children are of no matter, but our lords have long wanted *his* life, and for him was the moot held."

"No! No!" screamed another. "There is the maid who tricked us, and see! see! *she has the stone once more!!*"

"The stone! The stone! The stone!"

"The morthbrood have played us false!"

"Or she has stolen it!"

"Seize them! We shall take the stone to ourselves!"

Their eyes glowed green and yellow as desire mastered their cowardice.

"Ho!" cried Durathror. "So there is courage in svart-alfar-heim! This is a day of marvels, to be sure! Come, let my sword test the mettle of your new-grown backbones!"

"We come! We come!"

And they hurled themselves upon the dwarf.

"Gondemar!" bellowed Durathror, and he whirled Dyrnwyn above his head with both hands. Two svarts died under that stroke. They buckled at the knees, and crumbled into dust.

"Gondemar!"

Sparks flew as iron rang on stone, but there were now six svarts in the tunnel, and four torches guttering on the sand. Six to one: far too few for battle, whatever the prize. The svarts turned tail, and ran. Durathror rested on his sword.

"Cousin, it would seem Dyrnwyn is too bitter for their taste: let them then savour Widow-maker!"

Fenodyree came from hiding, and the svarts halted in dismay.

"It is the white one's dog!"

"What does *he* here?"

"It is a trick!"

One of the svarts turned, and ran towards Durathror, but, seeing he was alone in this he scuttled back to his comrades, who were by this time in distress. Fenodyree was laying about him in silence. He did not feel Durathror's joy of battle: these creatures stood between him and his purpose, and must be killed: that was all. He was no born fighter.

The uproar grew less and less. Fenodyree's round helmet spun under foot, and his mail shirt rang with the dint of blows: but not for long. Soon the two dwarfs stood gazing at each other across a litter of torches and stone hammers.

"I see Widowmaker is well named!" Durathror chuckled. "She has gained two upon me in this fight; I lead you now by one only. I must find me more svarts!"

"Nay, come away, cousin; we must not turn from the path, nor rest, till we are beyond their reach."

Colin stooped to pick up a hammer. It was heavy, but balanced well.

"Shall we take a couple? They may be useful."

"They would drag you to your death, where we are going," said Fenodyree. "Leave them; we do not need such tainted things."

"Durathror," said Susan, as they journeyed on, "where do the svarts go when they disappear?"

"To dust, my Stonemaiden; to dust. They cannot endure the bite of iron: it has a virtue that dissolves their flesh – and would all creatures of Nastrond were as they!"

"Here is the first of our trials," said Fenodyree, "but it is naught that a cool head will not overcome."

Before them the tunnel ended in a drop: they were in the roof of a cave, and across the emptiness another tunnel lay. A broken ledge, no more than a few inches wide, and sloping outwards, ran to it along the overhanging wall.

"There are handholds," said Fenodyree. "Give me your light, so that you may see, and have both hands free when you come."

It looked so easy as they watched him go crabwise across the wall. He moved smoothly and surely, and in a matter of seconds he was there.

"Susan now, please. If your fingers have need of rest, halfway you will find an iron spike to grip: it is firm. I shall light you."

It was easier than Susan expected, apart from the fact that the lamp could not light hands and feet at the same time, which was occasionally unsettling. Also, she would never have imagined how comforting an iron spike could be. When her hand closed round it, it was as though she had reached an island in a busy street. Susan was loath to leave that spike. She stretched out for the next hold, found it, and was transferring her weight, when something smashed into the wall close by her head, and splinters of rock seared her cheek. She was caught in mid-stride, and for two dreadful seconds she hung by one hand from the spike. The lamp's beam never faltered, and Fenodyree's calm voice checked her panic.

"A foot to the right, Susan. More; more. There. Now draw up your feet; another inch, good. You are safe. Come slowly; do not be afraid."

Across from Fenodyree, Colin had seen the stone axe spin in the lamplight and crash against the rock; and, at the same time, he had heard behind him a sword being drawn.

"Cross as quickly as you may," said Durathror's voice in his ear. "Stay not for me. I go to teach this trollspawn manners."

And, with a ringing cry, Durathror threw himself off the ledge into empty space. As he dropped beyond the light his cloak seemed to fold about him in a curious way.

"Are you ready?" called Fenodyree.

Colin looked across, and saw his sister and Fenodyree together on the other side.

"Yes, I'm ready . . . but Durathror!"

"He knows what he is about. He will not be long."

Nor was he. Colin had just gained the safety of the tunnel mouth when he heard the dwarf's voice right behind him.

"I lead you *now*, cousin! Three skulked below. They heard our coming and hid their torches: they died swiftly."

He was a little breathless, or perhaps indignation had the better of him, for it was the first time he had ever been surprised in ambush.

"But how did you do it?" cried Colin. "I saw you jump off the ledge: weren't you hurt?"

Durathror threw back his head and laughed.

"Woefully!"

He held out his sword hand: the knuckle of his little finger was skinned.

"Do not jest with them," smiled Fenodyree.

"They have not long been among us, and there is still much they do not know."

They started along the tunnel. Fenodyree walked very slowly, and when he spoke his voice was grave.

"Listen to me now. We are about to leave West Mine. Were we to stay, we should certainly die, though we took twice four hundred svarts with us, and the weirdstone of Brisingamen would be lost. We may still die: fear is in me greater than I have ever known. I say this now, so that when I lead you into seeming madness you may know that I do not act rashly – or if I do, there is no other course.

"We are to pass through the upper galleries of the Earldelving to where they touch upon another mine, the like of this, though smaller. The paths were never wide or high, and the earth has stirred many times in her sleep since they were dug: the road may no longer be as I was taught, and we may lose ourselves for ever. But it is our only chance, if chance it be, and we must take it. And here is the threshold; once beyond it, we may rest awhile."

They were at the corner of yet another cave. Two of the three walls that they could see were like any other in the mine, rough-hewn and fluted. But the third, immediately to their right, was awesomely different. Its face was smooth and grey, and it shot almost vertically, like a steel spade, into the ground – or rather, where the ground should have been; for at the dwarf's feet

lay a shaft, a sloping chimney of stone. And it
was into this that Fenodyree was pointing.

CHAPTER 13

"Where No Svart Will Ever Tread"

Durathror grunted, and picked up a lump of stone and tossed it into the hole. It glanced off the smooth cliff and rocketed out of sight past a bend in the shaft. For an age the hollow crashing of its fall was heard, then silence, and, when all but Fenodyree had judged that that was the end, a single, final, thump.

"We must go down *there?*" whispered Susan.

"And before our courage fails. Durathror, will Valham aid us here?"

"Nay, cousin; the magic is mine alone; and I could not take you, for she was made for elves and finds my unburdened weight a trial."

"It is as I thought. Will you stay here, then, lest svarts roll boulders on our heads?"

"That I *can* do, and will."

"Good. Colin, Susan, follow me; step where I step; do not hurry. So we shall come safe to the end."

Fenodyree began to climb down the oblique first pitch of the shaft, jamming himself into the angle between the two rock faces. Loose stones rattled down before him, and only the biggest sounded the end of their fall.

"There is room for you both here," he called from the bend; "come singly, Colin first."

Colin lowered himself over the edge into the gully, and worked his way down to within a yard of Fenodyree.

"That is near enough," said the dwarf. "Susan!"

"Yes."

"Stop when you are as close to your brother as he is to me: we must not crowd each other."

"Right."

It was unpleasant to crowd there helplessly while a river of stones bounced off head, shoulders, and knuckles; but Susan was not long about it.

"This is the problem," said Fenodyree when the clatter of debris had faded away. "The shaft is like a bent knee, and we are in the crook, therefore the slope down which we can climb is on the opposite side from us. It is steeper, too. But I think I see a way. Across there, about five feet down, is a ledge. If we jump from here and grasp the ledge we shall be well on our road."

"We shall be if we miss!" said Susan.

"The deed is nothing. It is the thought that breeds fear; and we achieve little by lingering."

And Fenodyree jumped. His fingers snatched for the rock, caught it, and he lay against the sloping wall of the shaft, and did not speak or move. At first the children thought he was unconscious, but they were soon to find for themselves how easy it was to be winded in such a fall.

"It is a good hold," said Fenodyree. He eased

337

himself a couple of feet from the ledge, and took up a secure position astride a corner of the shaft.

"Throw me your light."

"But what if you drop it?" said Colin.

"I shall not drop it."

Colin let the lamp fall, and the dwarf caught it in both hands.

"Now jump; you cannot miss."

Can't I? thought Colin.

He had a brief impression of blackness stretching under him, and of the ledge hurtling upwards, before the air was squashed from his lungs by vicious impact with the rock. Blue and red stars exploded in his brain, and a vacuum formed where his lungs should have been; but Fenodyree's steadying hand was in the small of his back, and as his senses cleared, Colin realized that his fingers had closed upon the ledge, and were holding him, although he was numb from the elbows down.

When the children and Fenodyree had recovered from the effects of the drop they considered the next stage of their journey. Colin was perched just below Fenodyree, while Susan had pulled herself on to the ledge and was wishing she could spare a hand to massage her aching ribs. It felt as though every bone in her body had been shaken loose by her fall.

"There are no more bends for a distance," said Fenodyree, "but whether there is a safe passage I cannot tell."

The V-shaped gully continued for thirty feet,

and they made good progress. Fenodyree held the lamp, leaving Colin and Susan both hands free; but light was still a problem. For when Fenodyree was above the children, their shadows hid the rock below, causing them to grope blindly for holds; and when he was below, it was difficult for him to shine the light without blinding them. He could, however, direct their feet to holds that he had tested, so they decided on this order of descent.

At the foot of the gully three sides of the shaft opened out like the shoulder of a bottle, leaving the remaining side, the all but sheer rock face, within reach.

"We can't go down there!" said Colin, aghast. "It's as smooth as ice!"

"The eyes of men were ever blind," said Fenodyree. "Can you not see the crevices and the ledges?"

The children peered down the shaft, but still it seemed to them impassable.

"Ah well, you must put your trust in me, that is all. We shall rest here a little, for there will be no haven after this until we near the end."

He called up the shaft, "Is all quiet with you, cousin?"

"Ay, though the chill of this place is beyond belief! It is well I have my cloak! Svarts draw nearer, but they move slowly. I fear they will not come in time."

"Are you ready?" said Fenodyree to the children.

"As ready as we ever shall be, I suppose," said Susan.

"Good. Colin, you are well lodged, so your sister will go first. I shall clear a way for you as far as I can. Have patience, and rest while I am gone, for it will be a hard climb."

Fenodyree let himself down to the full extent of his arms, and scuffed around with his toes until he had found, and cleared, a ledge; then he searched for a lower finger-hold, and in this way slowly began the descent. The wall was not quite as smooth as Colin and Susan had thought, but the accumulated sand of years rendered the many cracks and projections invisible to the children's eyes.

Minutes, or hours, later (for it seemed an eternity in the nothingness of the shaft) the children heard Fenodyree returning. Colin switched on the lamp, and the dwarf's face, lined and grey with effort, came into view.

"All . . . is . . . clear. Or . . . nearly so. We must . . . not . . . delay . . . now."

Colin handed him the lamp, and Fenodyree climbed down to his first station, from which he guided Susan on to the rock face. As soon as she was immediately above him, he descended a little further, and soon Colin was left alone to his thoughts.

Susan and Fenodyree moved quickly, for the holds were precarious, giving no more than finger and toe room, and often barely that. To remain still for more than a few seconds was to be in serious danger of falling. Yet momentum was hard to check, and Susan more than once came near to losing control of her speed; but, with Fenodyree's help, she achieved a balance between these two fatal extremes.

Colin had nothing to do but to avoid cramp and to watch the dwindling oblong of light and his sister's foreshortened silhouette. And as he looked, he gradually became aware of an optical illusion. Being in total darkness himself, he could see nothing of the shaft except the small area lit by the lamp in Fenodyree's hand; and as this drew further away his sense of perspective and distance was lost, so that he seemed to be looking at a picture floating in space, a moving cameo that shrank but did not recede. He was so fascinated by this phenomenon that he barely noticed the cold, or the strain of being wedged in one unalterable position.

The patch of light contracted until it appeared to be no bigger than a match-box, and Colin was wondering how deep the shaft could possibly be, when the light was extinguished. But before he had time to be seriously alarmed, he heard Fenodyree's voice shouting up to him, though what the message was he had no idea, for distance and the shaft reduced it to a foggy booming, out of which not a single intelligible word emerged. Still, the tone of the voice held no urgency, so he presumed that Susan was at the bottom and that Fenodyree was on his way up – which, in fact, was what the dwarf had intended him to understand, and Colin had not long to wait before the lamp flashed on a yard below where he was sitting.

"Oh," said Fenodyree, "I am a sight . . . weary . . . of this shaft! Durathror!"

"Ay?"

"When we are . . . below . . . I shall . . . call. What . . . of the svarts?"

"They went by another road. More follow."

The shelf on which Susan was resting lay at the foot of the wall. At this point there was a kink in the shaft, like the bend of a drainpipe, and Fenodyree had said that the true bottom of the shaft was not far below.

Susan flexed her fingers, and wriggled her toes. The bulk of the descent had not been too bad, once she had developed a rhythm, and her nerves had settled, but the last fifty feet of the wall were perpendicular, and the strain on her fingers had proved too much, and, on three occasions, only Fenodyree's quick reactions had saved her from coming off the rock.

The sound of the dwarf's voice brought Susan out of her thoughts, and she saw that Colin was beginning the final stretch, the crucial fifty feet. He was lowering himself over the sharp ridge that marked the end of the inclined pitch, and it was punishing him no less than it had his sister: he would carry the bruises for days. And how Fenodyree climbed with only one free hand was a marvel. He was nearing the end of his third trip up and down the shaft, and there he was, taking

Colin's weight on his shoulder and guiding him to the next hold.

"Twenty feet more, Colin, and we shall be there! Bring your left hand down to the inside of your right knee. Your other hand will fit there, too. Steady? Now lower yourself as far as your arms will let you. There is room for your left foot. Right hand out at your shoulder's level; not so far! There. Six inches down with your right foot." Fenodyree stepped on to the shelf. "Now your left hand to the side of your hip . . ."

A minute later Colin was standing beside Susan.

"We are not yet at the foot," the dwarf reminded them. "See what awaits."

He guided them down the shelf to the mouth of the lower end of the shaft. The shelf grew rapidly steeper, and very smooth. There were no holds at all.

"What do we do now?" cried Susan.

"We slide! Oh, never fear, it is no great way, and there is sand to break your fall."

The children remained apprehensive, but Fenodyree insisted that there was no danger, and, to prove his word, he sat at the top of the shelf and pushed off with his hands. There was a swish, silence, and a soft bump.

"It is as I said," called Fenodyree, and he shone the light upwards.

"All right," said Susan, "but . . . oh!!"

The chute was far smoother than Susan had anticipated and, caught off her guard, she tobogganed helplessly into the air, and landed at the dwarf's feet with her knees in her stomach, winded for the second time in the space of an hour. It was small consolation that Colin fared no better. Fenodyree had not lied: there *was* sand, but it was wet and, consequently, hard.

While the children lay croaking, Fenodyree cupped his hands to his mouth and shouted:

"Du-rath-ror!"

An answering voice echoed in the shaft.

"We shall rest here," said Fenodyree, "but we must not stay long, for if we do not win clear of the Earldelving by sunset we shall have no choice but to stay there until the dawn, and that would be grim indeed."

"Nay, then," said Durathror, "let us forgo our rest!"

He was standing on the shelf at the foot of the great wall.

"But . . ."

"But how have you . . . ?"

"I fell!" shouted Durathror merrily. "See!"

And he leapt down to join the children and Fenodyree. His cloak whirled about him, and he landed lightly on his feet with as little disturbance as if he had skipped from the bottom treads of a staircase.

The foot of the shaft opened into a small chamber, three or four feet high, and it was flooded except for the pyramid of sand in the middle.

Fenodyree bade the others make themselves as comfortable as possible, but it was not easy to

344

stay dry, and, at the same time, to be out of the path of any svart-sent boulders that might land in their midst.

Colin and Susan divided the remains of the food and drink between the four of them. And as they ate, the dwarfs pieced together the events that had brought them so unexpectedly to hand in time to rescue Susan and to bring havoc among the svarts.

This was their story. Durathror and Fenodyree were walking near Castle Rock when the kestrel Windhover brought news that Grimnir had risen from the lake and had entered St Mary's Clyffe. The dwarfs knew that where Grimnir was, there would be Firefrost, and that this may be their chance. Cadellin was prowling in the hills towards Ragnarok to find out if word of the stone had spread, for he was as anxious as Grimnir to keep its present whereabouts a secret. He could not possibly come; so the dwarfs decided to attack alone, and in no time Fenodyree had gathered his armour, and they were on their way.

They heard of the children's arrival from Windhover, whom they had arranged to meet in the cover of the garden next to St Mary's Clyffe. Grimnir and the Morrigan, said Windhover, were in an upper room: there was unpleasantness behind curtains downstairs. The hounds were loose.

"Do you wait by the entrance wall," said Durathror.

"Windhover shall take me where these morthdoers hide, and I shall disturb them, and, with Dyrnwyn drive all thought of Firefrost from their heads. Wait for a space after you hear me fall upon them, seek the stone in the lower room, for there I think it will be, and so to Fundindelve, where I shall join you if I may."

Then Durathror went with the kestrel to the room under the eaves. It was as Colin and Susan had begun to suspect: he had the power of flight. It lay in his cloak of eagle feathers, a survival from the elder days, and a token of great friendship.

When his moment came, Fenodyree ran for the door; to his surprise it was open, and he entered warily. On finding the curtained room empty he was perplexed, but he had no time to search further, for as he was about to try the kitchen door it was thrown open, and Durathror cannoned into him. There was savage joy stamped on his face as he spun Fenodyree into the cloakroom where the children had lately been hiding, and closed the door. Seconds later Grimnir stumbled out of the kitchen, followed by Shape-shifter. The empty room, the open door.

"The dwarf has taken it!" screamed Shape-shifter, and they both rushed out into the mist.

"Have you the stone?" whispered Fenodyree incredulously.

"Nay, but it is in good hands!"

They came out from the cloakroom: the mist had rolled away; in the distance a hound bayed.

"I could not kill the morthdoers, since their magic is greater than my sword, but they will feel her smarts for many a day." Durathror chuckled. "I came to join you in the end, but, entering yonder room, I saw two things to make me pause. There is a cupboard against the wall, and a hound of the Morrigan made clamour against it; but the door was closed, and I had seen what closed it – a small white hand, cousin, and Firefrost shone upon the wrist! I slew the beast; the rest you know."

Fenodyree ran into the kitchen.

"Come out, children! Susan! Colin!" He seized the cupboard handle. "Oh, you will be remembered when . . ." He stared into the shaft, and saw a square of wood begin to grow rapidly larger as it climbed towards him out of the far depths.

"And it was but luck that brought us to you when we were beyond hope," said Durathror.

"If only we'd known!" cried Susan.

"Ay," said Fenodyree; " 'if only'. We should have been in Fundindelve ere now."

The children told their story, and when they described the crossing of the plank the dwarfs grew excited.

"Hair of the Moondog!" shouted Durathror. "And did you not go on?"

"Oh yes," said Colin, "but the tunnel finished on a platform over a lake."

Durathror put both hands to his head and groaned in mock despair.

"Had you but known it," said Fenodyree sadly, "the water is little more than a foot deep,

347

and the way from there leads to the gate, not half a mile distant."

After such a revelation the children had not the heart to talk. They huddled, wrapped in their thoughts, and their thoughts were the same. Here they sat, at the bottom of a shaft, at the end of the world; they had gained the weirdstone of Brisingamen, but that success promised to be the beginning, and not the end of danger, and where it would lead them they dared not think.

"We must move now," said Fenodyree.

When they switched on the light Colin and Susan examined their surroundings in detail for the first time: and an awful truth dawned on them. There was no obvious way out of the chamber. Two tunnels led off in opposite directions, but they were flooded, and the roofs dropped steadily to meet the green-tinged water.

"Fenodyree! How do we get out of here?"

"Ay, cousin," said Durathror, "all the while since I came I have sought a way to leave, but I see none."

Fenodyree nodded towards the smaller of the tunnels.

"Did I not say that the road was hard? Colin, is the wrapping for your food proof against water?"

"Yes, I think so. But Fen⸰ . . !!"

"Then when we start, cover the light with it. You will have to trust to my eyes alone for a time."

"And may I have your covering for Valham, my cloak?" said Durathror to Susan.

He unbuckled his feathered cloak and rolled it tightly to fit into the sandwich bag, and Susan fastened it in her pack, which if anything, seemed lighter for the load.

"Put out the light," said Fenodyree. "And have courage."

CHAPTER 14

The Earldelving

The water was so cold that it took their breath away. Even Durathror, the hardened warrior, could not stifle the cry that broke from his lips at the first shock.

They waded along the tunnel for a short distance before having to swim, and they had not gone much further when Fenodyree stopped and told the others to wait while he went ahead. He drew a deep breath, there was a flurry and a splash, and he did not answer when Colin spoke.

"Where has he gone?" asked Susan.

"The roof and water meet where he left us," said Durathror.

Two minutes passed before Fenodyree broke the surface again, and it was some time after that before he could speak.

"It is no distance," he said when at length his breathing was under control, "and the air is fresh, but the roof is low for many yards, so we must swim on our backs."

Another swirl, and he was gone.

"I'll wait about a minute," said Susan. She was more frightened than she cared to admit, but she hoped Colin and Durathror would think that her teeth were chattering with the cold alone.

"Right. Here goes."

"She has great courage," said Durathror. "She hides her fear better than any of us."

"Are you scared, too?" said Colin.

"Mortally. I will pit my wits and sword against all odds, and take joy in it. But that is not courage. Courage is fear mastered, and in battle I am not afraid. Here, though, the enemy has no guile to be countered, no substance to be cast down. Victory or defeat mean nothing to it. Whether we win or lose affects us alone. It challenges us by its presence, and the real conflict is fought without ourselves. And so I am afraid, and I know not courage."

"Oh," said Colin. He felt less isolated now, less shut in with his fears. "Well, I'd better be on my way."

"Good luck to you," said Durathror.

Colin held his dive as long as possible, but the icy water constricted his lungs, and he soon was in need of air. He rose to what he implored would be the surface, but his hands and the back of his head scraped against the roof. Flustered, he kicked himself into a shallow dive, his stomach tightening, and his head seeming about to burst. This time. No! Again he struck the roof. What was wrong? Why was there no air? Fenodyree had said . . . ah! He remembered! Swim on your back: the roof is low. That's it! Colin turned frantically on to his back; the knapsack pulled at his shoulders and began to tilt him upside-down. He threshed the water and managed to right himself. And then his lips broke surface. The air

351

rushed out of his lungs, and Colin promptly sank, swallowing a lot of water. He kicked off so violently from the tunnel floor that he nearly stunned himself on the roof, but it quelled the panic, and he lay on his back, breathing air and water by turns.

The roof was certainly low; in order to keep his lips above water he had to squash his nose against the rough stone of the ceiling, which made progress as painful as it was difficult.

After twenty yards, Colin was relieved to find that the distance between surface and roof was increasing, and, before long, he was able to turn on to his face and swim more naturally. But where were the others? He trod water.

"Hallo! Ahoy! Sue!"

"Here!"

It was Susan's voice, and not far ahead, either. Almost at once the water grew shallow, and then he was knee-deep in mud, and Fenodyree's arm was about him.

"Oh, let me sit down!"

Durathror joined them presently, and he was in great distress.

"Squabnose," he gasped, "I have been near death many times, but never has he stretched out his hand so close, or looked more terrible!"

Colin unwrapped the lamp to discover how it had withstood the rough passage. It was none the worse, and by its light the children saw that they were lying on a bank of red mud, soft and very sticky. Ahead of them was a tunnel, but it was far different from any in West Mine. The roof ran square to the walls, and nowhere was more than a yard high. The colours were striking, for the walls were of a deep-red shale, and the roof was a bed of emerald copper ore.

The going was difficult enough without the mud. It was not so bad for the dwarfs, but Colin and Susan developed a severe ache in neck and back very quickly. The tunnels never ran straight, and they would branch five times in as many yards. Caves were few, and seldom bigger than an average room. Water was everywhere; and what few shafts barred the way were flooded, and therefore easily crossed.

After half a mile the relatively open passages were left behind, and now even the dwarfs were forced to crawl all the time. Roof falls became frequent, too, and negotiating them was an arduous business. The children were continually surprised by the way in which it was possible to force their bodies through holes and cracks that looked as though they would have been a squeeze for a kitten, but they found that, no matter how impracticable a gap appeared, if a head and one arm could be pushed through together, then the rest of the body would, eventually, follow.

Now and again they would come upon a stretch of rock over which the water had washed a delicate curtain. This was to be found where a vein of ore lay just above the roof: the water, trickling through the copper, over the years had spread a film of colour down the wall, ranging from the palest turquoise to the deepest sea-green.

The tunnels grew more constricted and involved. Susan particularly disliked having to worm herself round two corners at once. She thought of the picture of Alice in the White Rabbit's house, with an arm out of the window, and one foot up the chimney.

"That's just how it is here," she grumbled; "only this ceiling's lower!"

Fenodyree called a halt in a cave into which they fitted like the segments of an orange. But they could stand partially upright, which was some relief.

"We have put the greatest distance behind us," said Fenodyree, "but it is from here that our chief dangers lie. Between Durathror's feet is the passage that will take us to the light."

"*What?*" cried Susan. "But that's only a rabbit-hole!"

"If it were the eye of a needle, we should still have to pass through it to gain the upper world. But do not despair: we are not the first to come this way, though I think we shall be the last. My father travelled the Earldelving seven times, and he was an ample dwarf by our reckoning.

"Now we must make ready. Take note of what I say, for this is the last chance of speech until we come to safety, and there will be no room for error."

Under Fenodyree's instructions, Colin and Susan took off their knapsacks – a complicated manoeuvre in that space – and fastened them by the strap to one ankle. Susan's pack held Durathror's cloak, and Colin was still carrying the lemonade bottle; this he discarded. Fenodyree advised him to put away his lamp, for, he said, hands would be needed more than eyes.

He bade Durathror take off his sword.

"Keep her ever before you," he said, "and so neither Dyrnwyn nor the son of Gondemar will be lost."

And he unbuckled his own sword and pushed it into the opening.

Durathror stood alone in the silence of the underworld. He took the empty bottle that Colin had thrown down, and set it upright in the middle of the floor. A wry smile touched his lips as he looked at it. And shortly afterwards the cave was empty, save for this one monument to wild endeavour.

Both the children had the greatest difficulty in entering the tunnel. For the first yard or so it sloped downwards, and then turned uphill, not sharply, but enough to cause acute discomfort at the bend. Sand choked the entrance, though even when that was behind them the tunnel was so heavily silted that it was almost beyond the children to move at all. They lay full length, walls, floor, and roof fitting them like a second skin. Their heads were turned to one side, for in any other position the roof pressed their mouths into the sand and they could not breathe. The only way to advance was to pull with the fingertips and to push with the toes, since it was impossible to flex their legs at all, and any bending of the elbows threatened to jam the arms helplessly under the body.

The tunnel was unlike any they had met in the Earldelving, for, although it was not straight, it did not branch. This factor, and the plugging of the tunnel by four bodies, meant that the leader was the only one to be able to breathe at all well.

They became unbearably hot. Sand lodged in every fold of skin, and worked into mouth, nose, and ears.

Colin found that he had to rest more and more frequently. He thought of the hundreds of feet of rock above and of the miles of rock below, and of himself wedged into a nine-inch gap between.

"I'm a living fossil! Suppose I stick here: *that*'ll make archaeologists sit up!"

Ahead, Fenodyree was battling with a fresh difficulty. He had reached a spot where the tunnel bent abruptly under upon itself like a hairpin, and teasing Widowmaker's rigid blade through the angle, at arm's length, was no simple task. Strained nerves and muscles are not an aid to fine judgement. He succeeded, but it was some time before he was in any condition to follow his sword. Fenodyree was coming to the end of his last reserve of strength.

Susan felt the obstacle with dismay. It was not possible! But where was Fenodyree? He must have found a way round, so perhaps, like most hazards underground, it was easier than it looked. Anyway, lying there thinking about it would not do much good, so she tucked in her head, and jack-knifed round into the lower level. It was unpleasant, especially when her heels scraped the roof, but her weight carried her down, and it was soon over.

Colin was an inch taller than his sister, and that was disastrous. His heels jammed against the roof: he could move neither up nor down, and the rock lip dug into his shins until he cried out with pain. But he could not move.

Durathror, coming up behind, took in the situation at once.

"Can you hear?" he shouted at Colin's ankles.

"Yes."

The reply was barely audible.

"Try – to – turn – to – your – side! Then – to your stomach! I – shall – guide – your – feet! Are – you – ready?"

"Yes."

Durathror's sword jutted beside Colin's feet, and although it was in its scabbard, matters would not be improved if it became entangled with Colin's wildly jerking legs.

Colin screwed himself round in the tunnel. It was really not possible, but desperation tipped the scales; and once he was on his stomach, his knees bending with the tunnel, there was just enough play for Durathror to force Colin's legs round the angle, and from then on Colin was better off than any of the others, because they were now lying on their backs, and in that position movement was even more exhausting and unpleasant.

Fenodyree jerked his way along with renewed vigour, for this bend was the last great hazard, according to his lore. Imagine, then, his horror when his sword splashed in water. He twisted his head all ways. He could not see; but his hands brought him bad news. The tunnel dipped, and was flooded to the roof. This had not been so in his father's time; so much for the elder days!

The end of the tunnel was not yet. How far did the water lie? Inches? Yards? He would have to squirm along, holding his breath (and he was panting uncontrollably at the start!), in the hope that he would come to air. Retreat would be impossible, as it was now. And that decided him. Better a quick road to forgetfulness than a lingering one. But it called for nerves of steel to edge forward into the water, and, at the last, under.

This moment was to be endured three times more as Susan, Colin, and Durathror made the choice that was no choice. But once they grappled with the terror it did not last: for the water had collected in a shallow, U-shaped bend, not two yards long, and they all emerged on the other side before their lungs were drained of air. They cried or laughed, each according to his nature, but the sound in all cases was the same.

Not much later the floor began to drop away from the roof, and it was possible to crawl on hands and knees. The children wrestled with the sodden webbing of their packs and talked rapidly and loudly of the perils they had faced, and said how good it was to move freely again.

"Taken all in all," said Fenodyree, "the Earldelving has not used us ill: I had feared it would be more cruel. From here we shall be in little danger, provided that we respect the smaller risks."

They now pressed on with all speed, for there could be scarcely an hour of daylight left, and the prospect of having to spend the night in wet clothes, with mud for a bed, was in no way appealing.

After a time, Susan thought she saw a faint grey blur ahead of them past Fenodyree's shoulder. She switched off the lamp.

"Here, Sue! What are you playing at?"

"Look! Daylight!"

It was: and soon they had reached it. They were at the end of the tunnel, and at the bottom of a shaft. The converging lines of its gleaming, wet sides mounted to a tiny square of blue, a whole world away.

"We've not got to climb up this shaft, have we?" said Colin.

"Nay," laughed Fenodyree, "we shall be in dire straits ere I ask *that* of you! Our way is easier by far."

He raked about with his feet behind the pile of rubbish at the bottom of the shaft.

"It is somewhere . . . ah, I have it!"

He dragged to one side a mass of decaying branches to reveal a hole in the floor.

"Here is the exit from the Earldelving: once through here, we cannot return."

It was a sloping continuation of the shaft, though only half its breadth, and it was cut through stiff clay that glistened without ledge or fissure.

"It is a pleasant ride," said Fenodyree, seating himself on the edge, and grinning at Susan. He peered down between his feet, nodded, and let go. A faint splash marked the end of his glissade, and his voice sounded cheerily a long way below.

Susan lowered herself into the hole with extreme caution, but the edge crumbled beneath her hand, and yet again she disappeared from view like a bullet from a gun. She careered over the greasy surface, faster and faster, and landed waist-deep in a mixture of water and mud that broke her fall, but had little else to recommend it.

"Oh!"

"If you put your hand out to your left," said Fenodyree close behind her. "You will find a corner of rock: pull yourself out with that. Good. Now feel your way round to the tunnel. We shall soon be out of here."

The tunnel was flooded to a depth of three feet, and was sticky with clay, but it was high, and not long. At its end rose a shaft that offered few difficulties, for it was composed of a series of inclined pitches, connected by wide shelves, so that it was more like scrambling up a giant stairway than climbing a shaft. Only the last dozen feet were at all dangerous: here the rock was vertical, but the holds were many, and the top was gained without trouble. From there a short passage led into a circular cave – and daylight; real, accessible daylight. A tree trunk resting against the wall took Fenodyree, with the others packed behind him, up into a gully that overlooked the cave: the gully became a ravine and above was open sky; cold, crisp, dry air filled their lungs.

The side of the ravine was scored with holes and ledges, and children and dwarfs almost fell over each other as they swarmed up the last monotony of stone, out of the eternal, stagnant silences, into light, and life, and wide horizons. Then there was grass beneath them, and a wind upon their cheeks.

CHAPTER 15

A Stromkarl Sings

Beyond the ravine wound the elf-road and the dwarfs lost no time in hustling Colin and Susan on to it, but once there they permitted themselves to relax, for as long as they remained on the road, said Durathror, they would be hidden from searching eyes.

They made a bizarre picture in their all-over coats of red mud, encrusted with yellow sand that spared only their more pliable features, and these were daubed with red, as if they were in war-paint. But none of that mattered now as they stepped out for Fundindelve, and their aching limbs only sweetened the prospect of rest. After all they had undergone in the barren caves, this scene of beauty, the waning light among the scented pines, was almost unreal.

"It's like a dream,' said Susan: "just like a dream. I can even imagine there's music all around us!"

"So can I!" said Colin. "It's like a harp. What can it be?"

"A harp," said Fenodyree, smiling. "See, on Goldenstone, a stromkarl plays."

They had come to a junction in the path, and to their right stood a boulder, with nothing golden about it that the children could see: it was like any outcrop of weathered, grey sandstone, except that it had been crudely worked to an oblong shape by men long dead, and few now can tell its purpose.

On top of the stone sat a young man, plucking the strings of a harp. He was less than three feet high; his skin lustrous as a pearl; his hair rippling to his waist in green sea-waves. And the sad melody ran beneath his fingers like water over pebbles.

When summer in winter shall come
Then shall be danger of war.
A crow shall sit at the top of a headless cross,
And drink of the noble's gentle blood so free.
Between nine and thirteen all sorrow shall be
    done.
A wolf from the east shall right eagerly come
To a hill within the forest height.
Beside a headless cross of stone,
There shall the eagle die.

"Why do you sing the old prophecies?" said Durathror. "Are they now to be fulfilled?"

"Who knows? I do but sing of the summer that has come in winter. Does your road lead to Fundindelve?"

All the while the stromkarl was speaking, his hands plucked the silver strings, and the tone of his bell-like voice against the background of music was a song. He looked at neither the children nor the dwarfs once the whole time, but concentrated on his harp, or gazed out towards the hills.

"It does indeed," said Fenodyree, "and we take with us the weirdstone of Brisingamen!"

"I am glad," said the stromkarl. "But you will not go to Fundindelve."

"What do you say? How shall we not?"

"The hooded one sits by Holywell, and the Shape-shifter watches the gates: and to them are gathering the morthbrood. The svart-alfar will be there at sunset, and with the night are coming others. No birds will fly, save the eyes of the Morrigan. It will be dark within the hour; see to it that you are not under the sky at that time."

"Our swords will be ever at your command for this!" said Durathror. "You have done more than guard our lives."

The stromkarl lowered his head.

"My people will aid you where they may; fare you well!"

And he jumped down on the other side of Goldenstone, and they did not see him again.

"It never crossed my mind that this would be their course," said Fenodyree, "obvious though it was. Oh, I am not wise in judgement as a dwarf should be!"

"Nay," said Durathror, "your wits have served us nobly this day. But what is there for us now?"

"I do not know."

"Can we get to the farm before dark?" said Colin.

"That is a *good* plan!" Fenodyree smote his

hands together. "With luck, the morthbrood will not hear of your part in this until the svart-alfar come, and they may be late if they are still searching for us in West Mine. We should reach the farm, but whether it will be shelter for the night I cannot be certain."

"What of the stone?" said Durathror.

"We must find Cadellin," said Fenodyree. "In his hands it will be secure, and he can wield its might for our safekeeping."

"Why, then, give me the stone! He shall have it ere you can reach the farm!"

"Do you see those?" said Fenodyree, pointing across the fields.

"I see; but what of it? Rooks flock homeward daily at this hour, and in greater numbers than are flying there."

"Did you not hear the stromkarl say that no bird flies this day? Those are not rooks: you would be torn asunder within the minute. They know where Cadellin is as well as I, and that we must find him."

"Then how shall we do this?"

"We must go stealthily, on foot, and seek him in the hills."

Colin looked at the rolling mass of the Pennines, out of which the first shadows of night were creeping.

"But how do we find him up there, and how can we move without being seen? It's nearly all open moorland."

"We move by day, when their eyes are weakest,

and if there is scant cover for us, there is more chance that we shall see the morthbrood from afar. As for Cadellin, I am to meet him on the summit of Shuttlingslow yonder at dawn on the morning of the fourth day from this. There is little hope of finding him sooner. Our greatest task will be to avoid the morthbrood for so long."

They headed for the farm with all speed, keeping under cover wherever possible, though the lanes were almost deserted at that time of day. Only the occasional farm-labourer cycling home disturbed their progress, for the dwarfs insisted on hiding at any sign of life. "The morthbrood travel in many guises," said Durathror.

They came over the Riddings as the first stars were shining, and they saw Gowther's solid figure, Scamp at his heels, going the round of the shippons and stables to fasten up for the night. The individual, isolated sounds of twilight, the clink of a chain, the rattle of a door, the ring of boots on cobbles, carried far on the evening air.

Gowther was crossing to the house as the weary party entered the farmyard.

"Hallo!" he said, eyeing them up and down. "What have we got here? You look as if you've been through every marl-pit between here and Wornish Nook! Hey, and where are your bikes?"

"It is a good story, farmer Mossock," said Fenodyree, "but I would fain have a roof over my head for the telling of it."

"What?" said Gowther. He peered hard at the dwarf. "Here, wait a minute: I know thee! You're the feller as threatened me some months back, anner you? Well, I've got a bone or two to pick with thee; *and* I'd like to know what mischief you've been getting these childer into!"

He loomed over the dwarf, and made to grab hold of him, but Widowmaker came from her scabbard like lightning, and the broad blade's point rested against Gowther's cask of a chest.

"I am he: and much sorrow has come of your words that day, though it is not of my doing.

"I mean you no harm, farmer Mossock, and I crave your help; but every moment we stand here exposed to watching eyes adds to our peril. Let us right our grievances behind locked doors."

"You've *got* to trust him, Gowther!"

"You *must*!" cried Susan. "He's saved our lives more than once today!"

"And it *is* dangerous to be out here!"

"You'll understand when we tell you!"

Gowther looked at the anguished faces of the children, then down at the steady blade.

"All reet," he said slowly. "You can come in. But you dunner move a step towards the door while you've got that thing in your *hond*. And think on, I want an explanation; and it had best be good!"

Fenodyree sheathed his sword, and smiled.

"It will be *interesting*, farmer Mossock."

"Well! This is the rummest do *I've* come across! It is that! What about thee, Bess?"

Bess was ironing Fenodyree's rapidly washed

tunic, and she pointed with her flat-iron at the two dwarfs, who were squatting on either side of the hearth wrapped in blankets.

"Theer's little use in saying pigs conner fly, when you see them catching swallows! But I dunner like the sound of it at all.

"And you say as you've to get our Bridestone to the top of Shuttingslow by Friday morning? Well, that wunner be difficult. You two con stay here, if you've a mind to, and catch a bus from Macclesfield to Wildboarclough, and then all you'll have to do is climb up the hill and meet your wizard."

"We must take no chances," said Fenodyree. "That would be a dangerous course; we shall go on foot."

"Well, I don't see it, myself," sniffed Bess.

"When do we start?" asked Susan.

"At dawn tomorrow. We dare not stay long in any place."

" 'We'?" said Bess. "Oh, no! If you think you're dragging these two childer off on your madcap errands you con think again!"

"Oh, but *Bess* . . . !!"

"Ay, it's all very well saying 'but Bess'! What would your mother do if she knew of these goings on? She's enough to worry about as it is. And look at the state you were in this evening! You conner run risks like that and get away with it every time."

"Mistress Mossock," said Durathror, "the Stonemaiden and her brother are children, but they have warriors' hearts: they deserve well of this quest."

"That's as may be. But what should we say to their parents if they went out of here in the morning, and never came back? We're responsible for them, tha knows."

"If Colin and Susan do not see this through to the end in the company of those best fitted to help them," said Fenodyree, "their chances of ever setting eyes on parents or home again will be less than little. They have thwarted evil this day, and it will be a pledge of honour for witch and svart alike to make good that wrong. It would be madness to leave them unprotected here."

"Ay, I follow your meaning – if all we've heard is true," said Gowther. "Yon's a good point. But we're still responsible, choose how you look at it." He stood up to knock his pipe out against the bars of the grate. "I'll be coming with you in the morning."

As soon as the dwarfs were dressed, they wrapped themselves in their blankets and said they would sleep for a couple of hours, but they were to be woken immediately at the least hint of trouble. They had already seen to it that everybody's bedding had been brought down into the kitchen, for they insisted that they should all stay in the one room that night, with ample supplies of food, light and fuel.

At nine o'clock Durathror awoke and said he was going outside to see how the land lay.

369

He stole across the farmyard and up the hill to the top of the Riddings. The light north-easter that had been blowing for many days had veered to the north, and was much stronger. The full moon was rising in a clear sky; clear, except for the north. There, banks of cloud were piling on the horizon, and Durathror frowned. He sniffed the air, and looked warily all about him.

"Wind's getting up a bit, inner it?" said Gowther when the dwarf returned.

"Ay; it is not a good wind: I have doubts."

Colin and Susan had dropped off to sleep very early, and by eleven o'clock Gowther and Bess were nodding in their chairs.

Shortly before midnight Scamp began to growl. It started as a distant rumble deep in his chest, and grew to a hard-throated snarl. His lips curled and his hackles rose. Durathror and Fenodyree quietly drew their swords and took up stations either side of the door. Scamp barked, but Gowther hushed him and sent him under the table; yet still he whined, and growled, and rolled his eyes. All ears were straining to catch the least sound, but no sound came.

"Happen it's a fox," whispered Gowther.

Fenodyree shook his head.

"Something is coming: I can feel it."

"Mossock!" said a voice just outside the door. "Mossock, are you there?"

"It is the Place woman," whispered Durathror to Gowther.

"Ay, I'm here. What do you want?"

"You know what we want. Hand over to us the children, the dwarfs – and the stone, and you shall go unharmed."

"And supposing I tell thee to go and jump in the Bollin, what then?"

"Do not play the fool with us, Mossock. You have a minute in which to open this door before we break it, and you. Your house will fall, and weeds will grow on this land for a hundred years. Hurry! We are not usually so indulgent. Do not ask for trouble."

"Pay no heed: she is bluffing," said Fenodyree. "They cannot pass over a threshold unasked. It is an old binding spell stronger than any they can weave."

"Oh? Reet! Did you hear that, Mrs Place? Well, to make it quite clear how we stond, here it is straight, and simple. *You conner come in!*"

There was a moment's silence before the Morrigan spoke again, and now her voice was soft, and more menacing than before.

"We did not expect it to be so easy. But do not deceive yourselves by thinking that, because we cannot enter, you are safe. Wherever you are, and whatever you do, there is no escape, for we have called those to whom such spells are meaningless, and tomorrow night they will come to you. Listen, dwarfs! Can you not hear them? The mara are stirring. Soon they will be awake!"

CHAPTER 16

The Wood of Radnor

Along the crest of the Riddings the morthbrood watched Shape-shifter climb laboriously up from the farm. Grimnir sat a little apart from the brood, while over the top of the hill, in an old quarry, were mustered the svart-alfar.

"They are all there," said the Morrigan. "And they will not be drawn, though we think the threat of the mara will bring them out once the night is gone. On the move, we shall have them; but we must raise the fimbulwinter at daybreak.

"Is Slinkveal here? Good. The svart-alfar will remain in the quarry until dawn. You will not be needed, but then again, you may.

"The watchers have been chosen, and know their duties. Grimnir will accompany us to resume our work."

Durathror and Fenodyree kept watch by turns throughout the night, and at six o'clock they woke the others; by seven all were ready to go. Day was near, and there was a hard frost.

Colin, Susan, and Gowther were taking with them a change of clothing, food for the whole party, and groundsheets. Fenodyree had made himself a cloak out of an old blanket.

They were about to shoulder their packs when there came a gentle knock at the door.

"Ay, who is it?" said Gowther.

"It's me, maister Mossock. Is owt up?"

"Oh, wait on a minute, Sam: I'll be reet with thee."

Gowther waited until the dwarfs had hidden in the next room before he drew the bolts and unlocked the door.

"Theer! Come in, lad. I was hoping you'd be here before I went."

"I saw the curtain were pulled to," said Sam Harlbutt, "and the shippons were fast, so I thowt as how happen summat was wrong."

"Oh no, theer's nowt wrong; but – er – I've been called away – er – sudden like, and young Colin and Susan are coming with me. We should be back by Saturday. Con you manage by yourself? I'll get John Carter to give thee a hond, if you like."

"Oh no, maister Mossock, I'll be all reet."

He showed not the least surprise.

"But I'd best get on with the milking pretty sharpish, hadn't I? Dick Thornicroft'll be here with his wagon in half an hour."

"Oh ay! Er – ay, you'd best do that now."

Gowther felt Sam's unspoken criticism, but could think of no explanation to give him. It was their practice to share the milking. Gowther taking the morning, and Sam the evening. The cows ought to have been milked an hour ago, but

Fenodyree would not let Gowther put his foot over the doorstep while it was still dark.

"Er – Sam, if Dick comes before you've finished, ask him to call when he's been to Barber's."

"Right-ho, maister Mossock."

"And Sam!"

"Ay?"

"When you've done milking, I'd like you to take Bess in the cart to her sister's at Big Tidnock: she'll be stopping theer while we come back. The dog'll be going, too."

"Oh, right-ho, maister Mossock."

Sam Harlbutt was an imperturbable as only a Cheshire man can be.

They waited until Sam was well into the milking before they slipped quietly out into the lane.

"Which way?" said Gowther.

"Let us first follow the road to the back of this hill," said Durathror. "From there we may see much to interest us."

The lane ran past the mouth of the quarry behind the Riddings, and Gowther was rather perplexed when Durathror suggested beginning their journey with a scramble about inside.

"It's nobbut an owd sond-hole. We shanner get far running round here!"

"We shall not be long," said the dwarf. "I want . . . ah! As I thought! Svarts were here in the night, but I do not think there was much else with them. Come with me now to the hilltop."

He ran backwards and forwards along the Riddings like a hound beating for a scent.

"Nor was there aught worse than the morthbrood here. That is good. But yonder is what I do not like. Cousin Fenodyree, what make you of those clouds to the north? How is it they have not changed since I saw them under the moon? The wind should have carried them to us long ago."

"Hm," said the dwarf. "Fimbulwinter?"

"Ay. They do not mean to lose. First, they drive us out with the threat of the mara. We dare not bide. Next, they watch us through the day, and when we reach some lonely place, they pen us close under the fimbulwinter till night comes, and they can take us as they wish."

"Wait on," said Gowther; "what's all this 'fimbulwinter' business? And you've not told us yet . . ."

"I know," broke in Fenodyree. "But there are some things better left untold. It will be time enough to fear the mara when we see them; and I hope we shall not do that. Meanwhile you will rest happier for your ignorance."

"That makes me a *lot* easier, I must say!"

Fenodyree smiled, and inclined his head politely.

"You're a supercilious little feller when you want to be, anner you?" said Gowther testily. He was a direct open man, who liked everything to be clearly defined. He could not tolerate haziness or uncertainty; and he had not quite overcome

the countryman's natural distrust of strangers –
such strangers, too!

"I do not mean to give offence," said the dwarf.
"But I must ask you to lean on our judgement in
this venture. You are in our world now, and
without us you will not regain your own, even
though it lies at your feet."

Gowther looked down at Highmost
Redmanhey, then back at the dwarf. There was
a long pause.

"Ay. I spoke out of turn. You're reet, and I'm
wrong. I'm sorry."

"It is of no matter," said Fenodyree.

"Oh, look!" said Colin, anxious to change the
subject. "We're not the only people out early
this morning. There are two hikers down by Mr
Carter's; can you see them?"

In the lane below, a man and a woman, both
rucksacked, and wearing anoraks, ski-trousers,
and heavy boots, were leaning over a field gate,
apparently absorbed in a map.

"There are two more behind us on Clinton
hill," said Susan.

Sure enough, a quarter of a mile away, not
much higher than where they were standing, two
hikers gazed at the wide plain and its rim of hills.

"Happen it's a rally," said Gowther.

"Ha! It is indeed!" laughed Durathror shortly.
"Those are witches and warlocks, or I am not my
father's son!"

"What?" said Colin. "Are *they* the morthbrood?"

"There is the danger," said Fenodyree. "They mingle with others unnoticed, and can be detected only by certain marks, and that not always. For this reason must we shun all contact with men: the lonely places are dangerous, but to be surrounded by a crowd would be a greater risk."

Gowther shook his head, and pointed his ash stick at the "hikers".

"You mean to tell me it's the likes of them as we've to run from? I was thinking more of broomsticks and tall hats!"

The whale-backed Pennines, in their southern reaches, crumble into separate hills which join up with the Staffordshire moors, and from the Cheshire plain two hills stand out above all the rest. One is Bosley Cloud, its north face sheer, and southwards a graceful sweep to the feet of the Old Man of Mow, but, for all that, a brooding, sinister mountain, for ever changing shape when seen from meandering Cheshire lanes.

The other is Shuttlingslow. It is cone in outline, but with the top of the cone sliced off, leaving a flat, narrow, exposed ridge for a summit. And three days hence on, that ridge, eight miles from where they now were, Firefrost would be given into safe hands – if the morthbrood could be kept at bay for so long.

"Ay, and that's another thing," said Gowther. "What are we going to do between now and Friday? It's nobbut half a day's tramp to Shuttlingslow from here."

"Hush!" said Fenodyree. "There are keen ears listening. The where and the when are all they do not know of our plans. If we can shake off these bloodhounds and lie hidden until nearer the time, we may reach the hill. Trees and running water will shield us best; and for a start we must try to lose the morthbrood spies in the wood that fringes Radnor mere. We shall keep to this lane until we come opposite the middle of the wood: there we shall enter and, with luck, come out at the far side alone."

"But we shall need more luck to remain alone," said Durathror, "for I fear that little escapes *those* eyes."

Above their heads wheeled a cloud of ragged-winged birds. Out over the plain other flocks were sweeping in what, from the height of the Riddlings, could be seen to form a very definite pattern, an interwoven net of such efficiency that any one section of the ground of, say, a mile square, was rarely left uncovered by any one flock for more than a minute at a time. And they flew in silence, the only living things in all the sky. The hikers continued to pore over the map, and to admire the view.

Fenodyree led the way back to the crossroads, where the old Macclesfield road, Hocker Lane, ran left to Highmost Redmanhey, and right to Nether Alderley. To Alderley they turned, and walked beneath the round shoulder of Clinton hill. Below, across the fields, was Radnor Wood.

"I'll tell you what," said Gowther. "Tom Henshaw seems to be as mithered with these birds as much as we are: he's getten enough scarecrows, anyroad."

"Ay," said Durathror, "and can you tell me, farmer Mossock, what need he may have of them on pasture land?"

It was as Durathror said. Every field within sight held a tattered figure with outstretched arms – even those under grass, and with cows in them.

"Now I wonder what's up with owd Tom! He did say as how he'd been having queer turns off and on since before Christmas, but this is . . .'

"No time to linger," said Fenodyree. "You will embarrass our companions."

They looked round, and saw that the two hikers who had been leaning over John Carter's gate were now walking casually along some distance behind, to all appearances engaged in nothing more sinister than knocking off the tops of dead fool's-parsley with their sticks. A flock of thirteen birds closed in and began to glide in circles overhead.

"*Are* they scarecrows?" asked Colin as they continued down the lane.

"Mostly," said Fenodyree. "But eyes for the morthbrood, every one."

The road gradually converged on Radnor Wood until the two were running together, with only a low stone wall between them, and at a bend in the road Fenodyree said:

"When the morthdoers round this corner, we must be hidden.

"Now! Over the wall!"

Brambles were waiting for them on the other side, but they tore themselves free, and ran as best they could through the scrub and undergrowth of the matted fringe of the wood after Fenodyree, who was dodging nimbly over the rough ground and heading for the thickest patch of timber in sight.

At once the birds began to raise a great rumpus, but Durathror, bringing up the rear as usual, saw nothing of the hikers before the trees closed around him.

As soon as they were in the shade of the beeches the prickly undergrowth thinned out, and they made good speed, zigzagging through the lessening gaps between the trees and the masses of rhododenron. For a short time the birds screamed overhead and then they dropped through the branches and circled in and out among the trees, calling assuredly, deliberately, as though relaying information.

Fenodyree relaxed the pace to a quick walk.

"There is no need to hurry," he said resignedly. "I hoped to find cover while they pondered. This wood did not favour the morthbrood in the elder days, and I thought the memory of it would hold them long enough for . . ."

His words were drowned by an outbreak of screeching above their heads. Instinctively they drew together, back to back, and the dwarfs' hands flew to their swords. All round them birds were crashing heavily to earth: for ten seconds it might have been raining crows. Then the woods were still.

Gowther bent to pick up a tumbled mass of black feathers that had landed at his feet, but Durathror stopped him.

"Do not touch it!" he said. "They are evil even in death."

He turned the bird over with the point of his sword. Imbedded under the heart was a small, white-feathered arrow; and at the sight of it all colour fled from Durathror's cheeks.

"The lios-alfar," he whispered. "The lios-alfar!"

Trembling, he put away his sword, and looked to the sky.

"Endil! Atlendor! It is I, Durathror! This is well met!"

"Peace!" said Fenodyree. "They are not here."

"Are they not?" cried Durathror. "Ho! I tell you, cousin Wineskin, that our journey will be happier from this hour. If the lios-alfar are come from exile there is little we need fear between now and Friday's dawn, do you not *see?*

"Atlendor, welcome! Airmid! Grannos!"

But for all Durathror's shouting, nothing happened. He ran hither and thither calling, calling, but echoes and the hollow voice of the north wind in the tree-tops were his only reply.

"Thrurin! Skandar!"

Fenodyree shook his head sadly.

"Come away. The lios-alfar have been gone from the Long Wood of Radnor these two hundred years. They do not return. Come! They are not here; none but the morthbrood will answer your call."

Durathror walked slowly back to join the others.

"But it can be only the lios-alfar." There was complete bewilderment in his voice. "Why do they not know me?"

Fenodyree crouched to examine the arrow more closely.

"Well, whoever fired yon conner be much of a size," said Gowther. "If it's eighteen inches long that's all it is, and what sort of a body could use the bow to fit it?"

"The elves of light," said Fenodyree, "the lios-alfar. This is an elven shaft. Yet still I do not think they are with us. It is more like to be the work of stromkarls."

"*Stromkarls?*" cried Durathror. "Have you ever known the river-folk to take up arms? It is the lios-alfar!"

"Eh up! What's yon?" said Gowther, and pointed into the trees.

Something white moved among the branches, though not even Gowther could say where it first appeared. It fell gently towards them, swinging backwards and forwards with a graceful, swooping, dipping motion, and landed at Durathror's feet. A white eagle-feather.

The dwarf grabbed it, and flourished it under his cousin's nose.

"*See!* A token! And from an elven cloak! What say you now?"

Fenodyree looked hard at the feather, and then at Durathror.

"It is the lios-alfar," he said.

Fenodyree urged them on with all speed after the delay. No other sign from the elves, if they *were* elves, was forthcoming, and Durathror was prevailed upon to curb his excitement, and to turn his thoughts to their immediate problems.

"But it is hard," he said to Colin later in the day, when they were sharing the same cloak in an effort to stay alive, "it is hard to lose the companionships of elves. And if one has been dearer to you than your own kin, a more than brother right from earliest memory, the loss is nigh unbearable. When Atlendor took his people northwards I thought to renounce my heritage, and go with him, but he would not have me come. 'You have a duty to discharge,' he said, 'one of great weight.' The eyes of the lios-alfar see not only the present. By Goldenstone we said our farewells, and he gave to me Valham, and I parted with Tarnhelm, the greatest treasure of the huldrafolk." Durathror smiled ruefully. "I exchanged the power of going unseen for the power of flight, and Gondemar, my father, cast me out in his anger. So have I wandered all these years, barred from my people and from the elves. Had not Cadellin pitied me, and opened to me the gates of Fundindelve, mine would have been a desolate lot."

But all this came much later in the day, and for the present the children and Gowther were left to make what sense they could of the dead birds and Durathor's ravings.

Not that there was time for thought. They were forcing their way down an almost extinct track of frozen, rutted leaf-mould, between rhododendrons of such size that the branches met over their heads as well as across their path, when Fenodyree held up his hand. They stopped; listened.

"Footsteps! Into the bushes!"

They forced their way through the glossy hide of leaves into the tangled, bare branches that comprised the main bulk of the growth.

"Stay wherever you are, and do not move!" whispered Durathror fiercely. "He is close."

It was difficult to see through the bushes in the dappled light. They heard someone approach, but caught only a glimpse of dark clothing. Whoever it was, he was breathing heavily. Then, as he came level with where they were hiding, he stopped. Colin, Susan, and Gowther prayed that the beating of their hearts was not as loud as it sounded. Durathror and Fenodyree exchanged glances.

"Phew! Be hanged to old Place!" muttered a deep voice, and the owner of it sat himself down on the trunk of a fallen beech that lay across the path; and in that position his face could be seen. It was Mr Hodgkins, a local businessman.

Every morning during the week, between the

hours of eight and nine, he was to be found, with dozens like him, on the platform of Alderley Edge station, carrying his briefcase and tightly folded newspaper, and tightly rolled umbrella. But now, in place of the stiff white collar and formal, city clothes, James Henry Hodgkins's frame was clad in thick ski-trousers, and a hooded anorak, above which protruded the neck of a sweater. A beret hid his thinning hair, round his lean neck were snow goggles, leather gauntlets hung by tapes from his wrist, nailed boots encumbered his feet, and down his lined, sallow, businessman's face ran rivulets. He put his back against the roots of the tree, took out his handkerchief, and began to mop.

Five pairs of eyes watched him in agony. Neither the children, Gowther, nor the dwarfs had had time to make themselves comfortable among the branches, even if that were possible, but were standing frozen in the most awkward attitudes, cramped, precariously balanced. Any movement would have set the leaves dancing at the end of their snake-like branches. It was as though they were dangling in a snarl of burglar alarms. However, James Henry was not one to waste time unduly, and as soon as he was restored to a more even temperature he pulled himself up and went on his way, cursing the unwieldy rucksack that chafed his shoulders and was always becoming entangled with the bushes.

"Well!" said Gowther. "Owd Hodgkins! Ten

years he's been a customer of mine. It just shows, you con never tell."

"I didn't breathe once the whole time!" said Susan.

"I *couldn't*!" said Colin. "There was a branch twisting my collar, and it nearly strangled me! It's not much better now. Is it safe to move yet, Fenodyree?"

"Ay, if we can," said the dwarf.

He was wrestling to free his leg, which was hooked round the knees by a branch. But the branch swung higher at every jerk, and Fenodyree was being tipped gradually backwards off his feet. He looked so ridiculous, his knee level with his ear, that the others would have been tempted to laugh at his plight, had not they found themselves in difficulties as soon as they tried to move.

These were old bushes, and behind the green outer cover lay the growth and litter of a hundred years: tough, crooked boughs, inches across, stemming to long, pliant, wire-like shoots; skeins of dead branches which snapped at a touch, forming lancets of wood to goad and score the flesh; and everywhere the fine, black, bark dust with the bitter taste that burnt throat and nostrils and was like fine sand in the eyes.

"It's as . . . bad . . . as walking . . . on an old . . . spring mattress!" said Colin.

They had to step on to the thicker branches to clear the snare at ground level, and once off the ground they were helpless. The bushes dictated the direction in which they could move, and movement was not easy. Branches would give beneath their feet, and spring back awkwardly, catching limbs, and making even Gowther, for all his weight, lurch drunkenly, and grab in desperation the nearest support, which was invariably a change for the worse. And always they seemed to be forced to climb, with the result that they were soon two or three feet from the ground. Sense of direction left them: they just took the line of least resistance. But they noticed, with growing concern, that the earth, or what they could see of it, was becoming less like earth and more like water. Ice-covered puddles were frequent; very frequent; broader; deeper; they joined each other; and then there was water tinkling the pendants of ice at the bush roots, and no earth at all. Ahead, the curtain was not so dense, and Fenodyree, with renewed enthusiasm, plunged, bounced, rolled, and squirmed, and his head broke free of the chaos. Before, on either side, beneath, lay Radnor. The rhododendrons spread for many yards out over the mere, their roots gripping deep in the mud; and at the point where they stretched farthest into the water, five faces bobbed among the leaves like exotic flowering buds.

"Happen I'm nesh," said Gowther, "but I dunner foncy a dip today. I'm fair sick of this here cake-walk, though; so what do we do, maister?"

"Nay, do not ask me, my friend. I am past thought," said Durathror.

"We must go back," said Fenodyree. "Cousin, we may have space to draw our swords here. If we can do that, we shall cut an easier road to the path."

Dyrnwyn and Widowmaker, after much effort, were drawn from their scabbards, and by leaning backwards over the water, the dwarfs gained room for the first, most difficult strokes. After that, in comparison with what had gone before, the progress was much easier. The dead growth, and the leaf-bearing tentacles fell to the keen temper of the swords, which left only the thicker limbs to be negotiated, and they were not the obstacles they had been when the all-smothering lesser branches were there to aid them. The real danger, and it was a risk that had to be taken, was that the dwarfs were carving a track that could not fail to be visible from the air.

"Now we must run," said Fenodyree as, hot, weary, smarting from a hundred pricks and scratches, they tumbled on to the path. "For the morthbrood know where we are."

Only when they had put much dense woodland behind them did Fenodyree allow a few minutes for rest.

"Are we making for anywhere in particular?" asked Colin.

"Not for the moment," said Fenodyree. "I have a place in mind that may be the saving of us – if we can reach it. But I shall not speak of that while there is danger of hidden ears."

"Cousin," said Durathror, "do you hear?"

They fell silent, tensely listening.

"Ay; it is an axe."

They could all hear it now – the clear, rhythmical ring of steel in timber.

Gowther relaxed.

"I know who yon is," he said. "It'll be Harry Wardle from the Parkhouse. He's all reet. I've known him since we were lads. If theer's been onybody in this end of the wood today, it's as like as not he'll have seen 'em. Let's ask him."

"Hm," said Durathror. "I would rather not meet with men at this time; trust no one."

"But Harry and I were at school together: he's a good lad."

"He may be all you think," said Fenodyree. "If he is, he may be able to help us. Speak with him; Durathror and I shall watch. If he is of the morthbrood he will not raise the alarm."

They halted at the edge of a clearing. A lean, bony, middle-aged man, with close-cropped, iron-grey hair, was standing with his back to them, and wielding a long-handled felling axe.

"How do, Harry," said Gowther.

Harry Wardle turned, and smiled.

"Hallo, Gowther! What's brought thee down here?"

"Oh, I'm just out for the day with young Colin and Susan here."

"Eh, you farmers! I wish I could take time off when I wanted! How is the farm these days?"

"Middling, for the time of the year, tha knows. Could be worse."

"And Bess?"

"She's champion, thanks. Busy morning, Harry?"

"Fair. Couple more trees to drop after this before dinner: but I'll be having baggin after this one's down. Care for some?"

He nodded towards the flask and sandwiches that were lying on a tree stump.

"No; thanks, Harry, all the same, but we mun be getting on."

"Just as you please. Going far?"

"I dunner know: as far as we've a mind to, I expect. Mony folks about today, Harry?"

"Not a soul, till you come along."

"Well, if onbody does show up, you hanner seen us, reet?"

A slow grin spread over Harry Wardle's face.

"I've never clapped eyes on thee, Gowther. What's up? Are you fancing a cock pheasant or two? Because if you are, take a look round Painter's Eye; but dunner say to onybody as I told thee."

Gowther winked slyly.

"Be good, Harry."

"Be good, lad."

They waved, and left him, and a moment later the sound of his axe rang out behind them through the trees.

"Well?" said Gowther. "What did I say?"

"He is no warlock," said Fenodyree, "but there is that about him I do not trust; it would have been wiser to pass him by."

"Hush!" said Durathror. "Listen!"

"I can't hear anything," said Colin.

"Nor me," said Gowther.

"But you *should* hear something!" cried Fenodyree. "Why has your friend's axe been stilled?"

"Eh? What?" said Gowther, suddenly flustered. "Here! Howd on a minute!"

But Durathror and Fenodyree were speeding back towards the clearing, drawing their swords as they ran.

The clearing was empty. Harry Wardle, axe, flask, and food, were gone.

"But . . ." stammered Gowther, his face purple, "but . . . it's not . . . no, not *Harry*. No! He'll have nipped back to the Parkhouse for summat, that's what!"

"If that were so," said Fenodyree, "he would have come up with us, for we were heading for the Parkhouse, were we not?"

"Ay, I suppose we were," Gowther looked stunned.

Durathror, who had taken the path on the other side of the clearing, returned, shaking his head.

"As you say, farmer Mossock," said Fenodyree, "you can never tell."

CHAPTER 17

Mara

"We must not act rashly," said Fenodyree. "Fear is our enemies' greatest ally."

"Ay," said Gowther, "but let's be moving, shall we? I dunner mind admitting I've had a shock; and standing here talking while who knows what may be creeping up on us inner improving things."

"But which way shall we go now in least danger?" said Fenodyree. "That is what we must decide. I put no trust in blind flight, and though time is precious, a little may be well spent in counsel. Remember, your Harry may have to travel some distance to give his warning."

"Well, they know what direction we're following now, don't they?" said Colin. "And I don't suppose Harry Wardle realizes we're on to him, so why not double back on our tracks?"

"That is good," said Durathror. "The hares will dart north while the hounds run south."

"I think . . . not," said Fenodyree. "It is a good plan in many ways, but we have too great a charge to take the risk. Consider: it is probably that the body of the morthbrood is to our rear. They will come southwards through this wood, and along its flanks. If we lie in the thicket, and they pass by, ours will be the advantage. But if we should be found, far from help, unable to wield a sword for the dense growth, what need then of fimbulwinter or the mara? And if we should win through their line unnoticed, our way would grow more perilous. North of here lie villages: too many men. South, the land is open for ten miles and more. We are not far from the southern boundary of this wood: let us hurry southwards. If we are clear of Radnor before the alarm has spread, the morthbrood may waste time in sitting round to mark where we run clear."

So it was agreed; they walked swiftly and carefully, close together, and the swords were naked.

Durathror kept glancing upwards at the patches of blue sky. He was troubled. Then he began to sniff the air.

"Is it near, cousin?" asked Fenodyree.

"It is. An hour, two hours; not more."

"Yon warlock, with his snow-garments, removed any doubts," said Fenodyree to Gowther and the children. "The morthbrood have called Rimthur to their aid, and the ice-giant's breath, the fimbulwinter, is upon us. We must bear it if we can."

The curtness of his speech told them more than the words. He was pale beneath his nut-brown skin, and even Gowther felt in no need of further explanation.

After they had skirted the Parkhouse and its outbuildings the wood declined into timbered parkland, which thinned to open fields, and under the last cluster of trees, the dwarfs halted to consider the next move. To their right was the Congleton road, bordered by a stone wall. On their side of the wall a belt of woodland followed the road, and the open ground between where they were crouching and this thicker cover was sparsely dotted with trees. A flock of birds wheeled overhead. No human figures were to be seen; the intermittent buzz of traffic on the road was the only noise beyond the wind.

"Where may our way lead now?" said Durathror.

"It's a deal too exposed for me," said Gowther. "And if we carry on we come to Monks' Heath, which is a sight worse. But hold on a minute: let's have a look round. It's a while since I was round here. I wish them birds would give it a rest!" He scanned the country before them. "It'd be better if we could reach them trees by the wall; ay, yon's the best road. Sithee: they go reet down the wall, and bend across to Dumville's plantation, and that'll take us round the edge of Monks' Heath to Bag brook. From there we may – we *may* – be able to nip across to the game coverts by Marlheath at Capesthorne. It's these next two hundred yards as is going to be the biggest snag. But happen if we keep an eye open for birds we con pick our time and dodge about a bit till we're theer."

And that is what they did. Choosing a moment when the sky was clear, they darted towards the road like frantic ants, weaving from tree to tree in bursts of speed that amazed Gowther: he had not run like this for thirty years. But they reached the strip of woodland before the next patrol flew by.

The trees left the road almost at right angles and continued across the fields as what Gowther called Dumville's plantation. For most of its length it was very narrow, only a matter of feet in places, but it gave splendid cover from the air. After half a mile the wood swung right and headed south once more; it curved over the brow of a low hill, and from there a good view of the surrounding country was obtained.

"It's well-wooded, at any rate," said Susan.

"But it will appear bare to you for most of our journey," laughed Fenodyree. "Things are not as they were: in the elder days ours would have been an easier task. There were true forests then."

"I wonder who yon is on Sodger's Hump," said Gowther.

They all looked. A mile away, above the crossroads on Monks' Heath, a grassy hill stood out above the land. It was like a smaller Shuttlingslow – or a tumulus. It had the tumulus's air of mystery; it was subtly different from the surrounding country; it *knew* more than the fields in which it had its roots. And this uneasy mood was heightened by a group of Scots pines that crowned the summit. They leaned towards each other, as though sharing secrets. And outlined among the trees was a man on horseback. Little detail would be seen at that distance, but the children thought that he was probably wearing a cloak, and possibly a hat. He sat completely motionless.

"I . . . cannot tell who he is," said Durathror, after much peering. "There is that about him that strikes a chord of memory. What think you, cousin?"

Fenodyree shook his head.

"It could, and could not, be one I know. It would be strange to find *him* here. It is almost certain to be a warlock guarding the crossroad."

But, for some time after, the dwarfs were withdrawn, and pensive.

The trees dropped to the Macclesfield road in the hollow where it crossed Bag brook, and, dividing his attention between birds and traffic, Fenodyree was kept busy for a good ten minutes while he shepherded the others to the opposite side of the road and under the bridge arch. This accomplished, the dwarfs, for the first time since the disappearance of Harry Wardle, put away their swords.

"I begin to have hope of this quest," said Fenodyree. "We are well clear of Radnor, and I think the morthbrood have lost the trail."

"Ay, but I hope we dunner have to stay under this bridge all day, patting ourselves on the back," said Gowther. "I wouldner say as this mud is over fresh, would you?"

"We shall move at once!" said Fenodyree.

"Here is what we shall attempt. North of Shuttlingslow lies Macclesfield forest, as wild a region as any on the hills; but men have covered much of it with spruce and fir. Do you know it?"

"Ay," said Gowther. "It starts above Langley reservoirs. I dunner reckon much to it, though – mile after mile of trees on parade; it inner natural."

"That is the place: a dungeon of trees. But their sad ranks grow thickly, and there is little chance of finding aught that hides within. The forest will keep us till Friday's dawn, when we shall climb over the last mile of moorland to Shuttlingslow."

"As easy as that?" said Gowther.

"*If* we can gain the forest," said Durathror.

Fenodyree's plan was to head south for a few miles before turning east, and to travel, wherever possible, through woods. The intervening stretches of country, he hoped, would be crossed by following the lines of streams. Ignoring discomfort, the advantages of this plan were many. Along the streams, alder and willow were certain to be found, linked by lesser growths, reeds, rushes, and straggling elder. Moving lower than the adjacent fields would make for greater stealth, since there would be no danger of being outlined against the sky. And, in the last resort, it would be possible to lie close under the bank if caught in the open by the approach of birds. Also, running water kills scent, which might be important, for there were still two of the hounds of the Morrigan left alive.

All this Fenodyree explained; his plan was

accepted without dissent, and they now began the most arduous part of their journey, falling into a pattern of movement that was to govern them for slow, exhausting miles. They had to keep together as a body, yet move and act as individuals, each responsible for finding, and gaining, cover before birds were overhead, and pushing on as soon as the sky was clear. Desperate scrambles, long periods of inactivity, mud, sand, water, ice, malicious brambles; one mile an hour was good progress.

The brook led them south-west, towards the left of Sodger's Hump, and inevitably crossing under the Congleton road, which was not at all to anybody's liking. However, a few yards short of the bridge, though still dangerously close, a tributary joined Bag brook. It flowed in an acute angle from the left, from the direction of the Capesthorne game covert. This meant that they were almost doubling back on their tracks, but it promised to be such an accommodating route that no one regretted the lost ground or wasted energies: it was worth all that to be travelling in exactly the right line – an experience that was to prove all too rare. Not long after turning up this smaller brook they saw the first hikers on the fringe of Dumville's plantation.

The brook came from a valley of birch scrub and dead bracken; this was an improvement on bare fields, but ahead towered a sanctuary of larches, and the crawl seemed endless.

"By the ribbons of Frimla!" said Durathror

when they were beneath the laced branches. "It is good to drop that coward's gait and walk on two legs."

"I only hope the birds are deaf," said Susan.

The ground was covered inches deep with dead larch twigs and small branches. It was impossible not to tread on them, and with five pairs of feet on the move, dwarfs and humans passed through that wood with a sound like a distant forest fire.

From the larches they crossed a small area of scrub to a plantation of firs – specimens of Gowther's despised "trees on parade". But these trees were well grown, and there were few low branches. The floor was mute; no sun cut through the green roof: here twilight lay hidden at noon. Everybody was more at ease than at any time since leaving Highmost Redmanhey.

"It's a treat not to think eyes are boring into your shoulder blades, inner it?" said Gowther.

"And to be out of the sun," said Colin. "It was trained on us like a spotlight."

"Well, the light's certainly dim enough in here," said Susan. "It's taken till now for my eyes to get used to the change."

"I mun be still a bit mazed, then," said Gowther, "for to my way of thinking it's coming on darker instead of lighter."

"It is," said Fenodyree.

The wood broke on the foot of a small hillock, and there all was plain to see.

The blue sky and brilliant sun had vanished.

From horizon to horizon the air was black and yellow with unbroken clouds.

"These are but the outriders," said Durathror. "Do we stay here beneath shelter, or move on?"

"On," said Fenodyree. "While we may."

A path took them through the covert, past many green pools; and, at a plank that spanned a boundary ditch, all shelter ended. Before them was parkland, the nearest wood a quarter of a mile away across open country that offered no scrap of cover.

"Well, that's that, inner it?" said Gowther. "What do we do now? Wait while night?"

Fenodyree shook his head.

"We must not travel in the dark; not when we are so far from help. We shall move soon. The storm is at hand, and at its height it will pluck even the morthbrood from the sky. Then shall we cross."

They did not have to wait. The first snow whipped by as Fenodyree finished speaking, and the next moment the world had shrunk to a five-yard circle, shot through with powdered ice, and bounded by a wall and ceiling of leaping grey.

"Naught can find us in this!" shouted Fenodyree against the skirl of the wind. "Now is our chance!"

Once they were out of the shelter of the wood the full weight of the storm flung itself upon them. Susan, Colin, and the dwarfs were picked up and thrown to the ground, while Gowther lurched as though he had been stunned. They groped their way together, and linked arms, Gowther in the middle as anchor, and the wind frogmarched them at a giant-striding run directly to their goal.

It was the shallowest of valleys. They bounced over the edge, and were dropped by the storm as it leapt across the gap. Close to where they landed a fallen tree threw up soil-clogged roots, a natural shield against the wind.

"We shall fare no better than this," said Fenodyree, "and we cannot battle with such a storm, so let us make the most of what we have."

At first it was enough to be out of the storm's reach: the snow hissed past, and little settled. But the air was cruel; and behind the roots there was not much space for five people to move, so they crouched and stood by turns, and the breath froze on their lips, and their eyelashes were brittle with ice.

The children pulled on all their spare clothing, and huddled to share the dwarfs' cloaks. Gowther came off worst. He had to make do with sticking his feet into the rucksack, and wrapping himself about with the clammy, cold, rubber-scented groundsheets. It was then that Durathror spoke of the lios-alfar, and of his friendship with Atlendor.

"But why should the elves leave here in the first place, and where did they go?" asked Colin when the tale was ended.

"The lios-alfar," said Durathror, "are the elves of light, creatures of air, the dew drinkers. To them beauty is food and life, and dirt and ugliness, death. When men turned from the sun and the earth, and corrupted the air with the smoke of furnaces, it was poison to the lios-alfar; the scab of brick and tile that spread over this land withered their hearts. They had to go, or die. Wherever men now were, there were noise and grime; only in the empty places was there peace. Some of the lios-alfar fled to the mountains of Sinadon, some to the Isle of Iwerdon across the Westwater, and others past the Depths of Dinsel in the south. But most went north with Atlendor to far Prydein, even beyond Minith Bannawg, and there they dwell upon the high hills. Now some, at least, have come south, but to what end I cannot tell, nor why they are hidden from me. But there can be no evil in it, that much is certain."

During the afternoon the wind dropped, and the roots were now no shelter from the snow. It fell steadily, monotonously, so that it seemed to the half-frozen figures behind the tree as though they were on a platform that moved upwards through a white, beaded curtain. Reality, space, and time dissolved in the blank, soaring, motionless world. Only an occasional squall drew back the curtain for a second or two, and destroyed the hypnotic illusion.

Towards nightfall Fenodyree made up his mind. Ever since the wind had ceased to clamp them behind the tree roots he had been weighing the advantages, and disadvantages, of moving on.

As things stood, they were more than likely to lose their way, and they were dangerously close to Alderley, and to the Edge. No, that was a risk he did not want to take. But, on the other hand, it was becoming obvious that they could not survive the night in the open. Already they were experiencing the fatal, warm drowsiness of exposure, and the mesmerism of the snow was undermining their resistance to the peril. Both Gowther and Colin had had to be roused more than once.

"We must move," said Fenodyree. "If we do not find a roof for our heads we shall not have need of one by morning, I shall see if there is better cover downstream. The fewer tracks we make in this snow the safer we shall rest, but it would not be wise to go alone. Farmer Mossock, will you come with me?"

"I will that!" said Gowther. "I've about had enough of this place!"

Fenodyree and Gowther disappeared through the curtain.

They followed the valley for a quarter of a mile, and came to a cart track near to where it joined the Congleton road on their right.

"Hey!" said Gowther. "I know wheer we are! Straight on'll be Redesmere, and theer's some pretty thick woods just ahead: it's mainly rhododendron again, but happen we con make ourselves summat out of it. It's the best we'll find round these parts."

"It may be better than you think, my friend!"

said the dwarf, his eyes gleaming. "I had given no thought to Redesmere."

They retraced their steps. All the time, Gowther had been at pains to put his feet exactly in Fenodyree's tracks, and his boots had blotted out the dwarf's smaller prints. Going back, they trod the same tracks as on the outward journey, and the result would give any hunter much to think about.

The snow was now a foot deep all over, and considerably more where it had drifted.

"We shall cut branches here and there to make a thatch, if nothing better comes of Redesmere," said Fenodyree. "But we must not waste a moment, since it is past sunset already, and that is danger even before the coming of night. If we are to . . . ah!!"

"What . . . ?"

"Sh! *Look!*"

In the time that had elapsed since they passed that spot on the way to Redesmere *something* had crossed their path, leaving tracks like nothing Gowther had ever seen in all his days. A shallow furrow, two yards wide, had been swept through the snow, and along the centre of the furrow ran the print of bare feet. Each foot was composed of a pointed big toe, divided by a cleft from the single wedge that filled the place where the other four toes would normally have been. The prints were evenly spaced – three yards apart.

"Hurry!" gasped Fenodyree. "And may we come in time!"

He did not draw his sword.

"I've a real snow-thirst," said Susan. "More than anything else at this moment I'd like a gallon of milk."

"Oh don't," groaned Colin. "A gallon would only wet my lips!"

The stream-water was too cold to drink: it numbed their throats, and made their teeth ache. And their mouths were dry and sweet with fatigue.

They spoke little, for conversation had died long ago: it took too much effort. They moved only when cramp demanded.

After Gowther and Fenodyree had been gone about twenty minutes, Susan, developing pins and needles in all her limbs, got up to stamp around and flap her arms. She was on the point of crouching down again when she heard a faint swishing sound, as of somebody wading through the snow. Thinking the others were returning, she stood on tiptoe to peer out of the valley. This brought her eyes just above ground-level; and at that moment a flurry of wind pulled aside the veil of snow. A second later the wind had gone by, and the veil fell back into place, but in that instant, Susan's eyes had registered every detail of the thing that was passing within ten yards of where she stood.

It bore some resemblance to a woman, an ill-proportioned woman, twenty feet high, and green. The long, thick-set trunk rested on massive legs with curving, bloated thighs. The arms were too short, muscular at the shoulders, but tapering to puny, indeterminate hands. The head was very small, elliptical, and scarcely broader than the neck on which it sat. There was no hair; the mouth was a shadowed line; the nose cut sharply down from the brow, between the eyes that were no more than dark smears. It wore a single garment, a loose tunic that reached to the ground, and clung to the body in folds like wet linen. The flesh gleamed dully, and the tunic, of the same colour and texture, might have been of the same substance. A statue of polished malachite; but a statue that moved.

Susan began to scream, but before the sound reached her lips, a rough hand was clapped over her mouth, and Durathror pushed her down into the snow.

"Lie still!"

For a time, above the beating of her heart, she felt the earth shake beneath a ponderous tread that died away.

"Did you see it?" she whispered.

"I saw it. We must find my cousin: next time our luck may not hold."

"What is it? What's wrong?" said Colin from the bottom of the slope. But as he spoke Fenody-ree, with Gowther on his heels, staggered out of the gloom and caught Durathror by the arm.

"Mara!"

"It has this instant gone by," said Durathror. "It did not see us: there is still too much light."

406

"So did it miss our tracks. Come: we have found shelter."

"Then why do we delay?"

They slipped down the valley as quickly as they dared.

"Is curiosity satisfied now, farmer Mossock?" said Fenodyree when Susan had given a breathless description of what she had seen.

"Ay, it is that! But what in creation *are* they?"

"Troll-women: from rock are they spawned, and to rock they return if the sun should find them above ground. But by night they are indestructible, all-powerful. Only our wits can save us now, and be thankful we have more than they, for the mara's brain is as meagre as its strength is great."

The words were barely out of his mouth when a thin cry, like the plaintive voice of a night bird, yet cold and pitiless as the fangs of mountains, came from behind them.

"Run! It has found our trail!"

They had crossed the path where Fenodyree had turned back, and were forcing a way between the bushes when the mara called a second time, and now it was near.

"Steady!" cried Gowther. "We munner get separated in here!"

The thicket was not impenetrable, but it was close enough to make it difficult for five people to move quickly through it together. The snow was no longer falling: it was almost night.

Again the voice.

"Stay!" cried Durathror.

They had all heard: it was not an echo. It was an answering call – from in front!

Immediately there came another from the right, and the sound of snapping branches and rustling undergrowth. Hemmed in on three sides, they were, for the moment, spared the anguish of decision. They swung left. The voices were continuous now.

Durathror ran ahead of the rest. Susan was nearest to him, trying to keep in his wake, and as they came to a thick screen of brush, Durathror put up his arms to shield his eyes, and forced his way through. Susan's dive after him was halted by a stifled cry from Durathror, followed by a splash.

"What's happened?"

"Where are we?"

"What is it?"

"Are you all right?"

Susan put her head through the gap – and looked out across an apparently limitless sheet of water. In the gathering darkness she could not see any land. Beneath her, to his waist in the water, Durathror struggled to climb back through the weeds and dead vegetation to the land. By this time the others had all reached the spot.

"*Redesmere!*" said Gowther savagely. "I should have thowt of that one!"

"Back!" spluttered Durathror.

"But we conner!"

"We have no choice," said Fenodyree, "and

very little time. We may pass through the net: we may."

Without a word Colin turned, and the rest hurried after.

"Colin, wait! Let me lead you!" Fenodyree called softly.

"All right . . . oh!"

"*Colin!!*"

"Stop, everybody!" cried Colin. "There's water here, too!"

"*What?* Theer conner be! Here, wait on a minute!"

Gowther turned off left, and plunged into the bushes: ten seconds later he was back, only to vanish in the opposite direction without speaking. When he reappeared he was walking very slowly.

"I dunner ask onybody to believe this," he said, "but we're on an island."

CHAPTER 18

Angharad Goldenhand

"And it inner very big, either," said Gowther.

"But . . . but . . . it *can't* be an island!" said Susan.

"I know it conner: but it is."

"It's not *possible!*" said Colin.

"That's reet."

"But . . ."

Laughter broke in on their bewilderment, and they were aware of the dwarfs sitting in the snow, each with his back against a tree, at ease, and openly amused.

"It is in truth an island," said Durathror. "And, by the blade of Osla! I did not look to such a fair ending to this day's work."

"Hush!" said Fenodyree. "And lie low awhile."

On the nearer shore, fifty yards away, three mara were casting about to pick up the vanished scent. They wailed, and whooped, and peered at the ground, uprooting bushes and bending trees.

Gowther pressed himself further into the snow: he was exposed, and obvious: it would not be long before the mara would put two and two together, and wade out to the island, and then . . .

Having flattened everything for yards around,

the three shapes stood on the lake side, facing out across the water.

This is it, thought Susan. How far can I swim in these clothes? But the mara did not move: their bodies merged into the shadows. All was quiet. And then they turned, and disappeared into the wood: the whooping broke out again, and continued until all sounds were lost in the distance.

Gowther stood up, and shook the snow out of his clothes.

"They must be pretty dim!" said Colin. "Why didn't they find us? Anyone with half an eye could have guessed where we were: our footprints must have ended at the water."

"But the mara have not half a *mind*," said Fenodyree. "Our tracks were all they had to follow, and when they ended the trail was lost. Nothing was moved on the lake, there were no tracks, therefore there was nothing to find: so their minds work. They will wander now until dawn, and let us hope there are few men abroad this night."

"Yes, but they knew we were somewhere close," said Susan. "Why didn't they try this island?"

"Ah, but they did not *know*: they have never seen us. All they have seen are tracks that end in water. For the mara that is no puzzle; their minds look no further than their eyes, and I think that to their eyes this island is hidden."

"Is it now?" said Gowther heavily. "You dunner surprise me in the least! Happen you con also tell us how we come to be here without

411

wetting our feet, *and* how we're going to get back to land again!"

"I do not doubt that we shall walk from here at sunrise," said Fenodyree, "and, meanwhile, sleep safely and well.

"This is the Isle of Angharad Goldenhand, the Lady of the Lake, and it is one of the Two Floating Islands of Logris. It was lodged against the shore when Angharad guided our feet hither. Here no evil will threaten us. For one night we may lie at peace, and the Lady will watch over us."

"Very comforting!" said Gowther. Melting snow was sliding down the inside of his collar, and he was tired. "But wheer is this 'lady' of thine? I conner see owt but snow and trees, and I doubt *they* wunner make a warm bed!"

"She is there, though we do not see her, and we are under her protection. Now we must eat a little, and sleep."

A hunk of dry bread, and a mouthful of cheese, washed down with snow, made their supper. Hungry, damp, cold, and thirsty beyond measure, Susan curled up between the roots of a tree. Her ground-sheet was more of an affliction than a comfort. A long night of misery stretched ahead: sleep would never come. But come it did, and surprisingly quickly. A warm languor crept through her limbs: her brain told her to resist, but she could not. "This is how you freeze to death." "Well, there's nothing to be done about it now. And it's the . . . first . . . time I've

been . . . warm . . . for years . . . years . . ."
The snow against her cheek was a pillow of swan's
down. The scufflings of Gowther and Colin in
their exhaustion and discomfort were carried far
away beyond her reach. Susan slept.

It was a curious dream. Much of it seemed to be
no more than a mixture of all her waking thoughts
and wishes, timeless, disjointed, as difficult to
hold as an image in rippling water. And then, for
long periods, the people, and voices, and episodes
of her dancing brain would fall into place, and
become so vivid, so concrete, that there was
nothing of dreaming about them. But always,
after a while, the pattern would break. It was
a painting in which the brush strokes became
detached from the canvas, and drifted away as
isolated scraps of colour, only to regroup themselves to show the scene advanced a little in time.
But this was the main thread of Susan's dream.
  She was sitting cross-legged with Colin, Gowther, and the dwarfs under the trees of the island.
Before them were golden dishes piled high with
meats, and spices, fruits, and cool, green cresses.
Redesmere flashed blue in the light of high
summer. Stromkarls were laughing and playing
in the water, others listened to the music of the
voice of Angharad Goldenhand. She sat between
the children, dressed in a robe of white linen. She
was tall, and slender, and fair; her long, plaited
hair like red gold; and on her brow a band of
gold.

It seemed that nothing of their adventures was unknown to her, and she had much to tell. The lios-alfar of the west, said Angharad, grew fewer every year. Only beyond Minith Bannawg did they hold court in great numbers; and then they had heard rumour of the capture of Firefrost by Grimnir and the Morrigan, the elf-lord Atlendor son of Naf had come south to find what truth there was in the tale. He was ill of the smoke sickness when he reached the island, and Angharad nursed him to health. Then, when the stromkarl came from Goldenstone the previous evening, Atlendor decided to go back to his people, since news of Firefrost was good and there was need of him in Prydein. He had set out that morning, in haste to be clear of the sullied air, and he dared not stay for words when he put an end to the spies in Radnor Wood.

The dream ran on in a world of sunlit laughter, and stromkarls brought Fenodyree and the children cloaks of red muspel hair, woven from the beards of giants, and lined with white satyrs' wool; and there were four cloaks sewn together to cover Gowther's broad shoulders.

"And for you," said Angharad Goldenhand, "for whom the danger is most real, take this bracelet of mine. It will guard you on your journey, and when the other is with Cadellin Silverbrow, think of this as fair exchange: it has many virtues."

She took from her arm a band of white metal, and fastened it about Susan's left wrist.

"May the Sleepers lie safe in Fundindelve."

"Thank . . . thank you."

Susan was overwhelmed a little by such generosity; normally it would have embarrassed her, but she could not be embarrassed in the warmth of Angharad's smile.

The picture dissolved once more, but those golden eyes, full of sunlight, remained steadfast through the wheeling colours of her dream.

"Thank you," said Susan.

The golden eyes faded.

"Thank you. Thank you!"

Her voice sounded loudly in her head; the kaleidoscope receded into a blank screen of consciousness, against which her words fell with a peculiar lack of resonance. Susan knew she was almost awake: awake to a world of snow, and hunger, and weariness, and great peril. Desperately she tried to force her way back into sleep, to make *that* reality, but the wall was too strong. One by one her senses returned. She felt air cutting into her lungs like blades of ice, and when a drifting snowflake landed gently on her cheek she groaned, and thrust her head into the crook of her elbow. Instantly Susan forced her eyes open, and strained to bring them into focus; but the remains of sleep were heavy upon her, and it was a full quarter of a minute before she knew beyond doubt that her cheek had not lied.

Susan was wrapped in a cloak of bronze-red hair, lined with a fleece of curls.

There was something enclosing her wrist,

something that had not been there earlier. She worked her arm free of the cloak to see what it was. A silver bracelet.

The others were awake now. Colin and Gowther fingered their cloaks as though in a stupor. A waning moon shone in a clear sky of frost.

"But it was a *dream* . . . !!"

". . . and the stromkarls . . ."

"It conner have happened . . ."

"Did you see . . . ?"

"So did I!"

"It was summer, too!"

". . . and all that food."

"Are you hungry?"

"No!"

"Theer's only our footprints in the snow, and all."

"But these cloaks . . ."

"And what about this?" said Susan.

"Ay, that is a precious gift," said Durathror.

They had forgotten the dwarfs, in their astonishment.

"Oh, *hallo!*" said Gowther. "I'm glad as somebody here knows what they're about! Witches, boggarts, and green freetings I've had to take in one day, and after that I conner feel inclined to argue with owt you say, but now that we're getting to the stage wheer I dunner know whether I'm sleeping or waking, I begin to wonder if I'm dreaming the whole lot!"

"Dreams, glamour, they are not easy to tell apart," said Fenodyree, "and men have ever thought dreams are not reality. The Lady of the Lake is a skilled weaver of enchantment. She knew that without help we could not have survived the night. Now, with muspel cloaks upon our backs, we need not fear the cold of fimbulwinter, even though the ice-giants themselves came south. And *that* gift may be more than all."

He pointed to the bracelet. It had an air of great age. Along the outer face it was lightly incised, and inlaid with black enamel, much of which was missing. One half was a plain, coiling, leaf design, flanked by two oblongs of a diamond lattice pattern, with four spots within each diamond. On the other half, between two more oblongs, was an inscription in heavy, square lettering that was unknown to Susan.

"Yes, but in what way is it valuable?"

"I cannot tell you. But Angharad would not wear it for ornament alone."

"She might have told me what it was for, though."

"Perhaps it would not do for you to learn all its secrets at a time: sudden power is an evil, dangerous thing for any hands. Wear this always, guard it as you would the stone, and I know it will not fail you in need. And, above all, let it remind you of one who gave shelter and aid to those whose downfall would lift a weight of sorrow from her heart."

"What do you mean?" said Colin. "I don't understand. She's on our side, isn't she?"

"Ay, but you must know this: Angharad Goldenhand is wife to one who sleeps in Fundindelve; a great captain. A week had they been married when the king summoned his knights to go under the earth. Seven days of happiness to last her down the years. Do you see now how generous she has been? We are rescued, fed, and clothed, and are going on our way the better equipped for our task, yet if we succeed, Angharad Goldenhand may not greet her lord for many a hundred years to come."

CHAPTER 19

Gaberlunzie

The sun had risen, but the mara were far beyond its reach as they reclined upon the floor under the lion's head in the Cave of the Svartmoot. Arthog and Slinkveal and other svarts were present, too, and there must have been fifty of the morthbrood ranged along its walls. In one corner what looked like a mound of rags, parchment-covered sticks, and old boots writhed and twitched. On top of the head stood Shape-shifter and Grimnir, and the cave was lit by the red glow of the firedrake held in the lap of the aged, piebald svart, in his seat below the lion's jaws. Selina Place was speaking in the Common Tongue.

". . . and a coven of our sisters killed by elves, and yet you saw nothing! Mossock and the children reach the far end of Radnor, yet *you* saw nothing! They *must* have passed you! Such incompetence, brother Galleytrot, could see us all in Ragnarok ere midnight."

"But they didn't pass me!" blustered James Henry Hodgkins. "I'd have seen them!"

"But they did, and you did not. One more error, dear brother, and you will be svart-meat.

"And while Ragnorak is on our lips, let us speak plainly to you all. Nastrond has no word of us, but he *will* hear, and when that time comes

419

all your lives will be forfeit if we cannot wield the stone. Lest any of you have not our faith in success, you must know that the boundary is sealed. Any who try to cross will be slain: so let no one think to find favour with Nastrond through betrayal.

"Now to our plans. We do not believe the humans have survived the night. All dwellings and outhouses were watched, so they must have stayed in the open. Dwarfs are hardier, but we doubt if they can endure such cold, therefore we expect to hear news quickly. The search is to continue until the stone is found, for if it has passed to the elves all your efforts will be needed.

"Today the skies will be clear. This cannot be helped, since it will take till sunset to bring more cloud. By night we shall have enough to give unbroken cover for as long as we wish, though, so that you may follow tracks more easily, there will be no further snow. Thus the mara and the svart-alfar will be able to hunt throughout the day, if needs be.

"The lyblacs and the morthbrood will now go to relieve their fellows, and will pass on our instructions. Remember, the sky is full of eyes; cowards and traitors will not run far. That is all."

The heap of rags spilled over, and broke into a number of tattered forms, which rose jerkily to their feet like scarecrow marionettes, and slunk, spindly and stooping, out of the cave.

"It is not what you say Nastrond has learnt from

his spies that we fear, so much as his own mind," said Shape-shifter to Grimnir, closing the door of the broom cupboard after her. "We have felt it probing our thoughts often within the last month. There is no telling when he will act. And the svarts are not to be trusted if they fear us less: an example must be made of one or two without delay – that has always been the best encouragement. We shall have to 'unmask' a 'traitor' at the next moot."

With the first light, the island had grounded close to a stream on the opposite side of Redesmere from where the mara had lost the trail.

Clothed in the featureless snow, the countryside seemed vast; limitless as a desert, and as silent as a mine, the land offered no cover. Any movement against that background would be seen for miles, a line of footprints could not be missed, and in the brittle air any sound would carry undiminished to distant ears.

Durathror suggested, and the others reluctantly agreed, that their best course was to walk along the actual bed of the stream, but as close to the bank as possible. And so it was that, with the extra hardship of legs frozen from the knee down, they took up the pattern of the previous day's travel. Happily, the muspel cloaks had the property of sliding round obstacles without catching or tearing, and, worn with the lining on the outside, and the hood up, were good camouflage.

Ten minutes after sunrise, the first birds swept overhead.

The morning wore on, monotonously, though not uneventfully. Half a dozen scarcrows were by-passed, and two pairs of hikers came near to achieving their purpose, and a swift death. But these moments, and an occasional set of footprints, were all that distracted attention from the task of wading upstream.

By noon they had advanced a little over a mile; then Gowther stopped.

"I've been thinking," he said. "If we follow this brook much longer we'll be turning north, and pushing up into Henbury, and we shanner be so very far from wheer we started. Now just over yonder is Pyethorne wood, and that borders on Thornycroft pools, and, if I remember, we'll find a stream as will take us in the reet direction from theer. Shall we have a look?"

Unfortunately, though, to gain the wood they had to skirt the edges of a field, cross a lane near to the lodge of Thorneycroft hall, and make their way over two hundred and fifty yards of exposed parkland.

They managed to reach the lane undetected, but as they lay under the hedge, the remaining stages looked to be by far the worst check they had yet encountered.

"I see no way," said Durathror, creasing his eyes against the glare of the sunlit snow. "And to await night here would be madness."

"But do we have to go through there?" said Colin. "Can't we work round to somewhere else?"

"Ay, I've been thinking about yon, too," said Gowther, "but I doubt we shanner do better elsewheer. Sithee: if we go north we'll be moving back on Alderley, and we'll have put Macclesfield between us and wheer we want to get to. If we take our road by the south, we'll have to pass through Gawsworth, unless we go quite a step out of our way; and if you'll be guided by me, we'll steer clear of Gawsworth, matters being as they are. Some mighty queer things happen theer at the best of times, without all this. No, Pyethorne wood's the place: it's our nearest water, and we should go no closer to Gawsworth than Dark Lane and Sugarwell, which is all to the good."

"I think we must choose your way," said Fenodyree after some argument. "But how are we to gain the wood?"

"We'll have to chance it," said Gowther. "And if we meet onybody, let's hope they know nowt about us. No, I hanner forgotten the birds, neither. But theer's been enough folks gone along this lane, and down the drive, for our tracks not to stond out a mile – especially if we watch wheer we tread. Now, if we flop down in a heap at the side of the drive every time the birds come over, and make sure as we've no bits and pieces sticking out from under our cloaks, we should be all reet. Now listen: you follow the drive till it binds reet almost at the hall. I'll go first, so as I con come back and tell you if theer's ony snags. Then you'll see two paths, one going left, and the other pretty near straight on to the wood. I just hope as how we shanner be the first to have used it today. Give me twenty minutes, and I'll meet you theer."

"Farmer Mossock," said Fenodyree. "I see we have a new leader! You shrewdness will take us to Shuttlingslow better than my slow wits!"

"No," said Gowther, "it's just that I like to be doing: so long!"

The sky was clear; he stepped into the road, and walked through the drive gateway, and past the lodge.

Twenty minutes later Susan and Durathror followed, and ten minutes after, Colin and Fenodyree.

"The lodge was bad," said Susan, "but after the strain of that drive I nearly collapsed when we had to walk out in full view of the big house and all those staring windows."

"*We* had to drop flat twice in front of the house!" said Colin. "If anyone was watching, they must have thought we were mad."

"Ay, it was a bit strenuous," said Gowther. "How do you think we fared?"

"The birds missed us, I think," said Fenodyree, "and I saw no one in the rooms. How was it with you, cousin?"

"I saw no one, and heard naught: we have done well."

But garrulous old Jim Trafford was a small man, and it was his afternoon off. By half past two he was in his accustomed corner in the Harrington Arms, and monopolizing the conversation of four of his acquaintances.

"I reckon it's twice as cowd as it were eleven year back," he said. "I've see nowt like it; it's enough fer t'send you mazed. Eh, and I think it's takken one or two like that round 'ere this morning. No, listen! It were nobbut a couple of hours since, nawther. I were up at th'all, going round seeing as they were orreet fer coal afore I come away, and one o' th'fires were low, like, so I gets down fer t'give it a poke. Well, I'm straightening up again, and I 'appens fer t'look out o' th'winder, and what does I see? I'll tell yer. Theer was two little fellers, about so 'igh, gooing past th' 'ouse towards Pyethorne. No, listen! They wore white caps wi' 'oods as come over their faces, and they kept peering round, and up, and down, and walking 'alf back'ards. I'll swear as one 'em 'ad a beard – a yeller un it were. It's th' gospel truth!

"Well, I shakes me 'ead, and carries me bucket into th' next room. Fire's orreet theer, but scuttle wants a lump or two. On me way out I looks through th' winder, and theer they are again! And this time I sees a good bit o' beard, but now it's black!

"Round and round they scowls, then they drops flat on their faces, and pull their 'eads and legs in like tortoises. It's a fact! You conner 'ardly see 'em agen th' snow. Well, after a minute two, they gets up, and off they trots, back to back now, if you please! Then smack on their faces

425

again! I tell yer, I couldner 'ardly credit it. I watches them while they're near to th' wood, then they puts down their 'eads, and runs! It's this 'ere frost what's be'ind it, and no error. Theer'll be a few like them, I'll tell thee, if we 'ave much more o' this . . . Eh, Fred! What's to do? Art feeling ill? What's th' 'urry?"

The door slammed.

"Eh, what's up wi' 'im? Eh, you lot, come over 'ere! See at Fred! 'E's gooing up th' avenue as though 'is breeches was on fire!

"I tell yer, it's the weather!"

Pyethorne wood is not large. Much of it is little more than a neck of land dividing the two lakes of Thorneycroft hall, and it was in this part of the wood that Gowther waited for the others to join him. Together again, they decided to rest for an hour or so before exploring the far end of the lake to the east of the hall.

"We must keep guard by turns," said Fenodyree. "Durathror and I shall divide night between us, and, until we reach the forest, one of you will watch over the midday halt. Is it agreed?"

They curled up in their muspel cloaks, and forgot the snow. Even their ice-bound feet grew warm, and after such a morning, sleep was not long in coming.

Colin had offered to take the first turn. He sat upon a tree stump, and looked about him, seeing the beauty of the day for the first time. The air was still; and although the sun shone in a cloudless sky, there was not enough warmth in its rays to melt the thin blades of snow that stood inches high even to the tips of the slenderest twigs on every tree. Pyethorne was a wood of lace that day. There had been floes on Redesmere at dawn, but now the ice here was unbroken, thick, and blue as steel.

Out across the ice was an island, so overgrown with trees that it was as though they sprouted straight out of the lake; and at first that was all Colin could see; but as the minutes went by something began to take shape within the trees. The impression was strongest when he did not look directly at the island, but, even so, for long enough he could not be certain that there *was* anything there. And then, like a hidden figure in a picture puzzle it came unexpectedly into focus, and Colin gasped. It was a square tower, old, ruinous, so hemmed in by trees that if Colin had had anything other to do than sit and look about him for an hour and a half, he would never have noticed it.

I must see how long it takes the others to find that, he thought, laughing at his own blindness, and he continued his watch.

Then, oddly, the tower began to grow on Colin's nerves. He felt that it was staring at him with its expressionless eyes. He sat with his back to it, but that made matters worse, and he had to turn round. Imagination, he told himself. A tower could not help but look sinister in that condition; obviously no one lived there. But Colin could not settle unless he was facing the tower.

He began to range his eyes from left to right, across the lake and back again, but never once did he look directly at the island. And, of course, the urge to do so grew stronger. Worse, he thought how unpleasant it would be if he turned his head, and saw – something. Then in his imagination he pictured these "somethings", and from that it was a simple step to believing they really were there. Colin drew a deep breath. Having allowed himself to be worked into such a state, there was only one thing to do. He looked full at the tower.

His yelp of fright brought the dwarfs bounding to their feet. There, not forty yards away, among the outer trees of the island, was a man dressed all in black, and seated on a black horse, and his eyes were fixed on Colin.

"What is wrong?" whispered Fenodyree, but Colin could only point. At this the rider began to walk his horse towards them across the ice. In silence they watched him come.

He was tall, and sparely built, though little of him could be seen under his full cloak. Black riding-boots, silver spurred, came to his knees; on his head was a wide-brimmed hat. His hair, green as a raven's wing, curled on his shoulders, framing a lean, brown face. Small gold rings pierced his ears; and his eyes were blue – a fierce blue, burning with an intensity to rival the heart of Firefrost.

When he was still some yards away he reined in his horse.

"I have been looking for you," he said in a deep voice. Yet it was not only deep, but soft also, with a lilt in it that was not Scots, or Irish, or Welsh, but could have been all three. Some of the apprehension that had been gripping Gowther and the children left them.

"Welcome, Gaberlunzie," said Fenodyree. "Yesterday we saw you from afar, but could not be sure. Will you not come among the trees? The Morrigan and her brood harry us, and the spies are out."

The stranger looked at the sky.

"I thought there were no birds," he said.

He dismounted, and brought his horse under the trees.

Fenodyree quickly told their story, and the man called Gaberlunzie heard him in silence.

"And therefore we must be on Shuttlingslow at Friday's dawn to meet Cadellin Silverbrow, or the world we know may not endure. Will you stay with us, and help us?"

The blue eyes stared into space; then Gaberlunzie gave his answer.

"I shall not bide. Listen to my say. Beyond Minith Bannawg there is trouble breeding greater than this – or so we fear. The lios-alfar of the north are not enough to act alone. So I have come to gather to their aid kinsmen and allies. I have wandered through Dyfed's plundered land, along the shores of Talebolion, many a weary month to

Sinadon. And I am needed in Prydein within the week.

"I stopped by Fundindelve to ask for help, but there was no answer, only the morthbrood. The storm caught me before I could reach Angharad Goldenhand, and when darkness came I heard the mara and sought this island without delay. It was a cold swim, and the sun rose before I dared to sleep.

"I must turn northwards this day: my duty lies there. But what help there is in me you shall have before I go. If I leave you at the forest by nightfall, will that serve you well?"

"That would almost end our labours," said Fenodyree. "But alas, we dare not move openly: by day the skies are watchful, and by night the mara walk. We crawl on our bellies to our noble end!"

"But now you will ride!" laughed Gaberlunzie. "No, I do not trifle with you."

"*Look!*" cried Susan, her voice hoarse with alarm.

So intent had they been that they had not noticed the wall of mist come creeping over the snow. Like a white smoke it curled among the trees, and eclipsed the far end of the lake even as Susan spoke.

"Grimnir!" said Durathror.

"Whist now!" said Gaberlunzie, who was the only one undisturbed. "Sit you all down again. It is nothing of the sort. It is what I have been expecting. Cloudless skies, snow, such frost as this, and darkness not two hours away – what more natural than a good, white mist to blind the morthbrood and speed us on our road? Now on to my horse, and away!"

The fog was about them, absolute.

"You hold on a minute!" said Gowther. "Before we try to fit six on one horse, I'd like to know how you think we're going to find our way in this lot. It's about as much as I can do to see my feet."

"Do not worry, friend: my eyes are not your eyes, and my horse is not of earthly stock: we shall not stumble. But come! Are we to argue here until the day of doom? Mount!"

And they did mount. Durathror and Fenodyree bunched together in front of Gaberlunzie; behind him sat the children, and behind them Gowther, his arms on either side of Colin and Susan, holding Gaberlunzie's cloak in his fists.

Gowther expected to come off within a minute of starting – that is, if the horse *could* start. But a flick of the rein, and they were away like the wind; no horse ever sped so smoothly. Fields, hedges, ditches, flowed under its hoofs. The snow muffled all noise of their passage as they plunged full tilt through the mist. The air whipped about them, and their hands grew black, and cold grasped their heads as if with pincers.

After a while they left hedges behind, the land became broken and uneven, but they did not falter. Wide trenches opened under them, one after another, dangerously deep; and ghostly, broken walls, gaping like the ruins of an ancient citadel, lowered on either side. It was as though they were riding out of their own time back to a barbaric age, yet they were running only by the peat stacks of Danes Moss, a great tract of bogland that lay at the foot of the hills.

Trench after trench they crossed, and each a check to the morthbrood, should they follow after; for Gaberlunzie was of a cunning race. And so they came into the hills, and down to a lonely road in a valley.

"We are in the forest now," said Gaberlunzie.

He swung his horse off the road, and in one sailing leap they were among the trees. A broad path cut upwards through the close-set ranks, and here Gaberlunzie slowed to a walk.

"I shall not stop; you must leave as best you may, so that my trail will be unbroken. Do not stop to cover your own, but look for a place of shelter. Later you will see foxes: do not harm them."

"But what of yourself?" said Fenodyree. "It will not do to be abroad after sunset."

"The morthbrood are welcome to the chase! For I shall go by Shining Tor, and Cat's Tor, and the Windgather Rocks, and the sun will rise for me out of the three peaks of Eildon. I do not think the morthbrood will be then so keen."

Five minutes later they said their goodbyes, and tumbled into the snow.

"Do as I have said," called Gaberlunzie, "and

you will come to no harm here; and when you meet Cadellin, say I wish him well."

Durathror was the last to leave, and as he picked himself up, the form of Gaberlunzie, one hand raised in farewell, blended into the mist, and passed out of his sight for ever.

"I don't like the idea of leaving all these tracks," said Colin.

"There is little else we can do," said Fenodyree. "And I feel that Gaberlunzie knows what he is about. Our task is to hide, and this is the place. Take care lest you shake the snow from the branches!"

The trees grew only a few feet apart, and the sweeping branches came close to the ground, so close that even the dwarfs had to crawl, while Gowther had to pull himself along on his stomach.

They went downhill from the path a good way before Fenodyree stopped.

"Here will be as safe as anywhere. Even without the mist you can see no more than a few yards. Let us make ourselves as comfortable as we can, for we shall not stir again until we go to greet Cadellin."

Down the path through the forest two slim shadows moved. Coming to the trampled snow, and the trail leading under the branches, they stopped, and sniffed. And then they began to roll and frolic all around: two foxes sporting on a winter hillside. When every trace of human feet

433

was obliterated, they set off down the trail, throwing the snow into confusion as they fought.

The sound of their approach reached the dwarfs' ears, and they waited, sword in hand, for whatever was drawing near. Then the foxes tumbled into sight, and landed on their haunches, side by side, flecked with snow, their red tongues lolling, and their sharp eyes narrowing, in a wicked, panting grin.

For a while they sat there, and Durathror was about to speak, but they flung up their tails, and streaked away downhill.

"Thank you," said Fenodyree.

"Why?" said Colin. "What were they doing?"

"Covering our tracks rather well, I reckon," said Gowther. "Now yon's what I *call* clever."

"And the scent of a fox is stronger than that of either men or dwarfs," said Durathror, smiling.

He smiled again, alone to himself in the night while the others slept, when he heard the baying of hounds pass over the hill, and fade into the far distance.

CHAPTER 20

Shuttingslow

No one slept much all through the second, and last, night in the forest. It had been a strain on the nerves to lie inactive, yet constantly alert, for a whole day. The cold was no longer a problem, and the food of Angharad was safeguard against hunger and thirst for many days, so there had been nothing to do but wait, and think.

It was as though the night would never end; yet they could find little to talk about, wrapped in their cloaks, five dim shapes against the lighter background of the snow.

And, because of the snow, it was never quite dark, even in the forest: and although they could not approach the dwarfs' powers of sight the children found that, as the night wore on, they could see well enough to distinguish between individual trees and the hillside.

Tension mounted with every hour. But at last Fenodyree said:

"Dawn is not far off. Are we ready?"

They climbed up the path. The marks of hoofs were still there for the dwarfs to see, but they were overlaid with many tracks: hound, svart, and others.

After a long drag uphill they came above the

forest on to a bleak shelf of moorland; and out of the far side of the plateau, half a mile distant, the last two hundred feet of Shuttingslow reared black against the paling night.

They halted, and stared, prey to their emotions at the sudden appearance of the long-sought goal. It was so very near.

"Yonder it is," said Durathror, "but shall we ever reach it?"

They looked cautiously around. The snow lay two feet deep upon the moor. Not a tree could be seen in the gloom; only a dark line of wall, the dry stone walling of the hills, cut across the landscape. Once committed to this waste, once they had made their mark, there could be no drawing back. And after all those miles of stealth it seemed madness to walk out across such naked land. More, an actual fear of the open spaces came over them, even the dwarfs; they felt light-headed, and weak-kneed, and longed for the security of a close horizon.

Then Gowther squared his shoulders. "Come on," he said, "let's be doing." And he strode off towards Shuttlingslow.

It was a hard trek, and a stiff climb at the end of it, but both were achieved without sight of the morthbrood or any of their kind. Up they toiled, hands and feet working together on the near-perpendicular slope; up and up, till their lungs felt torn and their hearts were bursting. Thirty feet more! They had done it! In spite of all the forces ranged against them, they had done it!

They lay panting on the flat summit ridge. All about them was nothing but the air. When exultation had died, they crawled round until they were lying in a rough horseshoe, facing outwards. In this way, while keeping together, they could watch all the surrounding land except for the southern approach, which was hidden by the far end of the ridge. The crest of Shuttingslow is only a few yards wide, and they were able to talk without raising their voices.

Fenodyree reckoned that dawn was less than half an hour away. All eyes strained to pick out Cadellin as soon as he should appear. Once Durathror thought he saw him, but it was a trollwoman striding across a hillside miles away. It grew lighter. North, south, and east, the hills rolled away, and to the west, the plain, a lake of shadow into which the night was sinking.

"Isn't it time we were seeing him?" Colin asked. He could now see the straight track they had drawn across the plateau. The others, too, were glancing in that direction.

"The sun has not yet risen," said Fenodyree. "He will come."

But he did not come. And soon they could no longer pretend that it was night. There was no break in the ceiling of cloud, but the day would not be denied.

"It looks as if we've shot our bolt, dunner it?" said Gowther. "Do we just lie here and wait to be picked like ripe apples?"

"We must wait until the last moment," said

Fenodyree. "And wherever we go now we shall not escape the eyes of the morthbrood."

"It looks like being a grand day, then: Friday the thirteenth and all!"

"Ay," said Durathror. " 'Between nine and thirteen all sorrow shall be done.' "

Their spirits drained from them: their trail stood out as clearly as if it had been painted black. And there was no Cadellin.

Occasional specks moved singly or in groups across the white backcloth of hills, and, out on the plain, from the smudge that was Alderley Edge, drifted what might have been a plume of smoke, but was not.

"Now that *they* are astir," said Durathror, "Cadellin must needs come quickly, or he will come too late."

As it gained height the column of birds split into patrolling flocks, two of which headed towards Shuttingslow. When they were a mile away it became obvious that one flock would pass to the south of the hill, and the other to the north. The northerly flock raced over the plateau, and the watchers on the hilltop wanted to close their eyes. Suspense did not last. The leader swung round in a tight circle over the line of footprints, and brought the flock slowly along the trail, close to the ground.

"*Do not move!*" whispered Fenodyree. "It is our only chance."

But the muspel cloaks were not proof against keen eyes at close range. The whole flock shot skywards on the instant, and broke north, south, east, and west to din the alarm. One or two remained, at a safe height, and they cruised in beady silence. The specks in the distance slowed, changed course, and began to move in towards a common centre – Shuttlingslow. More appeared, and more still, and distant, thin voices were raised in answer to the summons, and mingled with them the whine of the mara, and a baying note, that the children had heard once before at St Mary's Clyffe, and Fenodyree more recently in the forest. From all over the plain clouds of birds were rushing eastwards. Durathror stood up.

"Is this the end of things, cousin?"

"It may be."

"Where is Cadellin Silverbrow?"

"I cannot think! Unless it be that he is dead, or prisoner, and either way *we* are lost."

"But if he's coming from *that* direction," cried Colin, pointing south, "we shouldn't see him until he was right at the top!"

"Fool that I am! Quick! We may throw away all hope by standing here!"

Halfway along the ridge the birds attacked. In a cloud they fell, clawing and pecking, and buffeting with their wings. And their attentions were directed against Susan above all. In the first seconds of advantage they fastened upon her like leeches, and tangled thickly in her hair. And their strength was human. But before they could drag her from the hill Drynwyn and Widowmaker were among them.

Backwards and forwards along the crest the conflict raged, until the ground was red and black, and still they came. Not before fully a quarter of their number had been hewn from the air did they abandon the fight.

Durathror and Fenodyree leaned on their swords, heads hanging. All were torn and bleeding; but the wounds were not deep.

"It is well they broke," panted Fenodyree, "for I was near spent."

"Ay," said Durathror, "it will go hard with us if they come again."

Gowther reversed his grip on his ash stick, which he had been wielding with terrible effect, and pointed.

"And yon have not been idle, sithee. We'll have to be thinking quick!"

The morthbrood were pouring in from all sides; only to the south-west was the land not thickly dotted with running figures. The near groups were not heading for the top of Shuttingslow, but were moving to encircle it; and out of the valley of Wildboarclough, seven hundred feet below at the foot of the hill's eastern slope, came a band of svarts, five hundred strong. There was no Cadellin.

"Can we stem this flood, cousin?" said Fenodyree.

Durathror shook his head.

"By weight of numbers they will conquer. But since it has come to this we must draw what teeth

440

we may before we go down to rest. And it is how I would wish to die, for so have I lived."

"Well, *I'm* not going to let them have the stone as easily as that!" cried Susan. "You stay if you like, but I'm off!"

And she started down the hill at a mad speed towards where the numbers of the morthbrood were thinnest.

"Come back, Sue!" shouted Colin.

"No!" said Gowther. "She's the only one round here as is talking sense. Well, come on! Are you fain to let her go by herself?"

They sprang after Susan; floundering in the snow, leaping, bounding, falling, rolling, they hurtled after her, unmindful of bruises, caring nothing for safety, while the air clamoured with the shriek of birds.

Once off the escarpment their gait slackened, yet they were making every effort to hurry. The snow was knee-deep, and clogged the feet like a nightmare. Rocks, reed clumps, hummocks of grass sent them stumbling at every stride. The birds flew low but did not attack.

Over Piggford moor Susan ran, flanked by dwarfs with gleaming swords. A few stray svarts, and the loose-limbed scarecrow creatures barred the way from time to time, but they fell back at the sight of the hard blades. They preferred to join the crowd that was now sweeping round the sides of Shuttlingslow.

The moor curved down three hundred feet to a stream that Susan did not discover in time, and they all slithered into the water, and lost precious seconds there. Choking, they scrambled up the opposite hill. And that climb exhausted the last of their strength. It beat them mentally as well as physically, for it was a convex slope, and the skyline, the apparent top of the hill, was always receding. It was never far away, but they could never reach it. Soon it was nearly beyond them to climb the stone walls that blocked their path, and when they did totter to the crest, and saw that it was only a wide shelf, and that a further incline awaited them, all but Durathror collapsed as though their legs had been cut from under them.

Durathror looked behind him. Except for one or two stragglers, Piggford moor was bare. Yet the noise of the chase was loud: he heard it clearly, even through the bedlam of the milling birds. The morthbrood must have crossed the stream.

"*Up!*" he cried. But they were not at the top of the final rise when the pursuit came into sight. The svarts, with their snow-skimming feet, and the tireless, bobbing lyblacs had outstripped the morthbrood, and they had at their head one that was worse than all – a mara, grey and terrible. And before the mara ran the two hounds of the Morrigan, their blind heads low to the scent, and their mouths hanging red.

"Stay not for me!" shouted Durathror, facing about.

For a second Fenodyree wavered, then he

nodded, and pushed the others on towards the crest of the hill.

The hounds were well ahead of the mara, and the first, drawing near, slowed to a walk, ears pricked forward.

"Ha!" cried Durathror.

The hound paused.

"Ha!"

And as it leapt he ducked, and thrust upwards with both hands to his sword, and the beast was dead before it hit the ground. But it wrenched Dyrnwyn from Durathror's grasp in its fall, and then the other sprang. But Durathror was lightning itself in battle, and the teeth closed not on his throat, but on his forearm which he rammed between the wet jaws, and over he went, hurled on to his back by the weight of the monster. And while they wrestled the mara strode by unheedingly.

Durathror fumbled for the dagger at his waist: he found it, and the end was quick.

But he could do nothing to save the others. Already the mara towered over them. Bravely, rashly, Fenodyree launched himself upon it, but Widowmaker flew from his hands in a shower of sparks at the first blow, and, leaning down from its twenty feet of grim might, the troll grasped Susan by the wrist, and plucked her from the ground.

The scream that cut the air then stopped svarts and lyblacs in their tracks, and even the birds were hushed. Durathror hid his face, and groaned; tears flooded his cheeks. Again the piteous cry, but weaker now. Durathror knew his heart must break. Again. And again. Shouting wildly, mad with grief, he rose, and snatched for his sword. But the sight that met him brought him straight to his knees. For, limp, in the snow, just as she had fallen, was Susan. Beside her was the mara, and *it was shrinking*! Like a statue of butter in a furnace heat it writhed and wasted. Its contours melted into formlessness as it dwindled. No sound did it utter again, save a drawn-out moan as movement finally ceased. And there on the moor-top stood a rough lump of rock.

Half-unconscious, Susan knew little of the mara's fate. As the spiral-patterned clouds and flashing lights withdrew from before her eyes she could only stare at Angharad's bracelet, dented and misshapen from the grip of the stone-cold hand that had fastened upon her wrist.

"Are you all reet, lass?"

"What did you *do*?"

"I'm not hurt. It was the bracelet, I think. What's happened?"

The svarts and lyblacs were in confusion, and, for the moment, lacked the united courage to advance. Durathror was quick to seize the chance. He faced the crowd, and spoke in a voice for all to hear.

"See how the invincible perish! If such is the fate of the mara, how shall *you* endure our wrath? Let him who loves not life seek to follow further!"

The mob slunk back. But now the morthbrood

444

were at hand, and they were not to be so promptly awed. He knew he had won only a breathing space – just long enough to prevent their being overrun while Susan gathered her strength.

And then Durathror saw what he had lost all hope of seeing: a lone man on the top of Shuttlingslow, two miles away. And as he looked he saw the tall figure leave the crest, and begin to descend.

Durathror joined the others; they, too, had seen.

"But I dunner think yon bunch have," said Gowther. "Now, how are we going to hold out while he gets here?"

"It is an hour's journey over this ground," said Fenodyree.

The morthbrood were conferring with the svarts: there was much shouting, and waving of hands. The svarts were not keen to risk the mara's end, while the morthbrood did not want to take the brunt of the dwarfs' swordsmanship themselves. The Morrigan, in her black robes, was screaming furiously.

"Cowards! Liars! They are but *five*! Take them! Take them *now*!"

Fenodyree did not wait for more.

"Come," he said. "We cannot hold them if *she* is here. We must seek where we may make a stand against them."

A hundred yards was all they had, and as soon as they moved, the morthbrood surged after them. From the beginning there was little promise of escape, but when they crossed over the top of the hill, and came to a deeply sunk, walled lane, and saw warlocks streaming along it from both sides, they realized finally that this was the end of all pursuits, and, though it may seem strange, they were glad. The long struggle was nearly over, either way: a load of responsibility was lifted from their hearts.

"We shall run while we can!" cried Fenodyree; and he jumped down into the lane and pulled himself over the wall on the other side. "Look for a place for swords!"

But they had no choice. Lyblacs, armed with staves, thronged the side of the valley below them.

"A circle!" shouted Gowther. "Colin! Susan! Into th' middle!"

And so they took their stand: and all evil closed upon them.

"They are not to die, yet!" cried the Morrigan. "Who takes a life shall answer with his own!"

Back to back the dwarfs and Gowther fought, silently, and desperately. And in between crouched the children. The bestial shouts, the grunts and squeals of dying svarts, echoed from valley to valley. Fenodyree and Durathror wove a net of light with their swords as they slashed, and parried, and thrust. And when Gowther swung his stick skulls split and bones cracked. Their one hope was to survive until the wizard came; but where an enemy fell there was always another to take his place; and another, and another, and another, and another.

They fought themselves to a standstill. Gowther's stick was knocked from his hands, but he bent and took up a svart-hammer in either hand, and from that moment the slaughter increased. Following his example, the weaponless children snatched themselves weapons, and entered into the fight.

And thus for a while the battle ran their way. But it was the last flare of a guttering candle before the night swamps all. The end came suddenly. A svart-hammer crashed home above Fenodyree's elbow, and the bone snapped with the noise of a whiplash. His sword-arm hanging useless, Fenodyree was a broken wall, and soon the enemy would pour through the breach. Durathror acted. He pushed out his free hand behind him while keeping his eyes fixed on his work.

"The stone! Give me the stone!"

Without questioning, Susan ducked behind Gowther, took off the chain bracelet, and locked it about Durathror's wrist. As she did so, a dozen pairs of hands clutched her, and dragged her backwards: but too late. Durathror sprang into the air. Valham enfolded him, and he turned towards Shuttlingslow in a last attempt to save the stone.

And the birds fell upon him like black hail. He disappeared from sight as though into a thunder cloud. The lightning of his sword flashed through the smoke of birds, and the earth grew dark with their bodies; but there were also white eagle feathers, with blood upon them, and their number grew.

The battle on the ground was done: all eyes were upon that in the air. Nothing of Durathror could be seen as the cloud moved slowly away, but few birds were dropping now.

Lower down the hillside a round knoll stood out from the slope, topped by a thin beech wood; and on its crown a tall pillar of gritstone jutted to the sky like a pointing finger. Clulow was its name.

Over this mound the last blow was struck. A white object fluttered out of the base of the mass, hovered for a moment, pitched forward, and crashed through the trees, and lay still.

Down rushed the lyblacs and svarts, howling. At the noise, the figure stirred. Durathror raised his head. Then he hauled himself upright against a grey trunk, steadied himself, and began to walk up the hill. He lurched and stumbled from tree to tree. His mail shirt was ripped half from his back, and Valham hung in ribbons. Often he would stand, swaying on his feet, and it seemed that he must fall backwards, but always he would stagger on, bent almost double, more wound than dwarf, and, at the last, leaning his full weight upon his sword.

So Durathror came to the pillar of stone. He put his back against it, and unclasped his belt. Loosening it, he threw it round the column, and buckled it tightly under his arms so that he should not fall. When this was done, he grasped Dyrnwyn in both hands, and waited.

For ten yards around, the hilltop was bare of trees, and at the edge of the circle the svarts halted, none wanting to be the first to cross the open ground and meet that sword. But it was only for a moment.

"There is the stone!" cried Shape-shifter from behind. "*Take it!*"

"Gondemar!" thundered Durathror.

Where he found the strength is a mystery and a great wonder. But such was his fury that none could withstand him, not even Arthog, lord of the svart-alfar, that was as big as a man. In the thick of the press he came against Durathror, and Durathror brought his sword round in an arc. The svart parried with his hammer, but Drynwyn clove through the stone, and Arthog's head leaped from his shoulders. But no sword can shear through stone unpunished, and at the next stroke the blade snapped halfway to the hilt. Yet still Durathror fought, and none who faced him drew breath again; and the time came when the svarts and lyblacs fell back to the trees to regain their strength and to prepare a last assault.

Durathror sagged in his harness, and the stump of Dyrnwyn hung by his side. His head dropped forward on to his chest, and a silence lay upon the hill.

CHAPTER 21

The Headless Cross

Grimnir ran. Fear, excitement, greed drove him.

From the top of Shuttlingslow he had watched the chase right to the fall of the mara; and from that high vantage point he had seen something else, something approaching rapidly, away to the north, and although he had been on his guard against danger from that quarter for months, the form it had taken, and the time it had chosen to appear, could not have disturbed him more.

He came unnoticed over the hill above Clulow soon after Arthog died, when every eye was upon Durathror as the svarts withdrew from that still figure with the splintered sword. His gaze rested on the prisoners, each held by two warlocks of the morthbrood, standing between the main body and the wood; and Grimnir checked his stride, hope and distrust conflicting within him.

For above the clearing in the wood circled a carrion crow. It spiralled down, barely moving its wings, and came to rest on top of the standing-stone. A long time it perched there, watching, motionless. The silence was overpowering. And then the crow launched itself into the air, and resumed its measured glide. Closer to the drooping warrior it came, closer . . . closer, *and settled on his shoulder*. But Durathror did not move. His trial was over.

A sigh rose through the trees, and the crow hopped from the dwarf's shoulder to the ground. Straight to his wrist it went: and from there back to the pillar, with Firefrost dangling at its beak. The bird threw up its head, neck feathers blown into a ruff, and, with wings outstretched, began to dance a clumsy jig. It rolled grotesquely from side to side, its head bobbing up and down, and a yell of triumph burst forth on every side.

Grimnir cast a quick glance over his shoulder. Yes, he must act at once. If the crow should drop its eyes and look above the throng it could not fail to notice . . . Swiftly he strode down the hill and pushed through the morthbrood. And as he went a new cry moved with him; for in turning to see who was coming so impetuously from behind, the crowd looked beyond him . . . and panicked.

Colin, Susan, Gowther, and Fenodyree had watched Durathror's battle in an agony of helplessness. Fury and despair had done their worst; their minds were numb with shock. So it was with little interest or emotion that they turned their heads when the note of fear ran through the morthbrood. Then Grimnir came upon them. He faltered, but only for a second. "Kill them," he said to the guards.

Susan opened her mouth, but no sound would come. For the first time in memory or legend

451

Grimnir had spoken. And the voice was the voice of Cadellin.

The morthbrood were scattering in all directions. The guards were more intent on saving their own lives than on taking life away from others. For this is what they saw. Racing out of the north was a cloud, lower than any that hid the sun, and black. Monstrous it was, and in shape a ravening wolf. Its loins fell below the horizon, and its lean body arched across the sky to pouncing shoulders, and a head with jaw agape that even now was over the far end of the valley. Eyes glowed yellow with lightning, and the first snarls of thunder were heard above the cries of the morthbrood. There seemed to be one thought in all their minds – escape. But when Managarm of Ragnarok is about his master's bidding, such thoughts are less than dreams.

The svarts and lyblacs were beginning to break when Grimnir entered the wood. He kicked and trampled through them towards the pillar. The crow was still there, squatting low, its head deep in its shoulders, glaring at the oncoming cloud. It saw Grimnir on the edge of the clearing, read his purpose in a flash, and sprang. But Grimnir was too agile. He jumped, snatched high, and his fingers closed about the bird's scaly shins, and swept it out of the air. The other thin, gloved hand wrenched Firefrost from its beak. Grimnir cast the heap of feathers viciously against the pillar, and fled.

"Eh up!" said Gowther. "Here he comes again!"

The children and Fenodyree were still groping at the implications of what had just happened and it was not until Gowther cried, "And he's getten thy bracelet!" that they came back to life.

They might not have been there for the notice the morthbrood and all the rest took of them. Even Grimnir ignored them as he sped up towards the lane.

"After him!" shouted Fenodyree. "He must not escape!"

The hillside was thick with pell-mell bodies, but Grimnir could not be easily lost, and they set off blindly, without thinking what they could do if they caught him. Grimnir leapt on to the wall and stood poised, as though staring at something in the lane. Then he turned, and ran back down the hill, moving faster than ever. But Grimnir had barely left the wall when he staggered, and a sharp cry broke from him, and he toppled on to his hands. A double-edged sword stood out from his back. Along the blade coiled two serpents of gold, and so bright were they that it pained the eyes to look on them.

Slowly Grimnir rose, until he was on his feet. The sword dropped to the ground. He took three steps, swayed, and fell backwards. The deep cowl slid from his face, and the madness was complete. It was the face of Cadellin twisted with pain, but nevertheless Cadellin; kind, noble, wise, his silver beard tucked inside the rank, green, marsh-smelling, monk-like habit of Grimnir the hooded one.

Susan thought she was out of her mind. Colin could not think or speak. Fenodyree wept. Then there was a crunching of rock above them, and they looked up: someone was climbing over the wall. It was Cadellin.

He came towards them over the snow, and his eyes, too, were full of tears. No words were spoken in greeting, for it was a moment beyond words. Cadellin dropped on one knee beside Grimnir, and the tears spilled on to his cheeks.

"Oh, Govannon!" he whispered. "Govannon!"

Grimnir opened his eyes.

"Oh, my brother! This is the peak of the sorrow of all my years. That it should come to this! And at my hand!"

Grimnir raised himself on one elbow, and, ignoring Cadellin, twisted his head towards the wood. An eager light gleamed in his eyes. Among all the haphazard scuttling, one figure moved with a set purpose, and that was Selina Place, who was running towards the little group as fast as she could, her robes streaming behind her.

Grimnir brought his head round and stared at his brother, but he did not speak. Their eyes spoke through the barrier of years, and across the gulf of their lives.

Again Grimnir turned to Selina Place. She was close. He looked up into the smoking jaws of Managarm, then at Cadellin. A bleak smile touched the corners of his mouth, and he lifted his fist, and dropped the stone into Cadellin's hand, and fell back, dead.

Cadellin took up the sword, and sheathed it. He strove to keep his voice level.

"I am sorry we could not meet at dawn," he said. "I did not expect to come upon the mara." He looked at Firefrost resting in his palm. "Nor did I expect this. There will be much to tell in Fundindelve. But first . . ."

He turned to the Morrigan. She stood a dozen yards away, glowering uncertainly. She was not sure what had happened. Then Cadellin held up Firefrost for her to see.

"Get you to Ragnarok!"

Selina Place, fury in every line of her, shrieked and ran. And as she ran a change came over her. She seemed to bend low over the ground, and she grew smaller; her robes billowed out at her side; her thin legs were thinner, her squat body heavier; and then there was no Selina Place, only a carrion crow rising into a sky of jet.

"Make haste," said Cadellin, "or we ourselves shall be lost. Gowther Mossock, will you stand here in front of me? I shall put my hand on your shoulder. Colin, Susan, stand on either side; take hold of my robe; do not let go. Fenodyree, sit by our feet; cling fast to my hem. Is Durathror not with you?"

"He is here," said Fenodyree. "But he will not come again."

"What is it you say?"

Fenodyree pointed.

"*Durathror!* Quick! We must guard him!"

"Stay!" cried Fenodyree as Cadellin made towards the wood. "There is not time, and it would be of no use. See! Managarm is on us!"

All the sky to the north and east was wolf head. The mouth yawned wider, till there was nothing to be seen but the black, cavernous maw, rushing down to swallow hill and valley hole. Witches, warlocks, svarts, lyblacs, stampeded southwards, crushing underfoot any that blocked the way. The birds outdistanced them all, but they were not swift enough.

One bird alone did not go south. It flew towards the advancing shadow, climbing ever higher, until it was a black dot against a blacker vault, and even a dwarf's eyes could not tell if it did clear the ragged fangs that sought to tear it from the sky.

As the hill slid down the boundless throat Cadellin lifted his right hand, and held Firefrost on high. Gowther stood firm. Colin and Susan clasped their arms about Cadellin's waist, and Fenodyree grappled to him with his one good arm as much of the wizard's robes as he could hold.

"Drochs, Moroch, Esenaroth!"

A cone of light poured down from the stone, enclosing them in a blue haze. A starving wind, howling like wolves, was about them, yet the air they breathed was still. Slanting yellow eyes were seen dimly through the veil; hungry eyes. And there were other noises and other shapes that were better left unknown.

The fury raged and beat against the subtle armour, but it was as nothing to the power of Cadellin Silverbrow with Firefrost in his hand.

And at last, at once, the darkness passed, and the blue light faded. Blinking in the sunlight of a brilliant sky, the survivors of the wrath of Nastrond looked out over fields of white; wind-smoothed, and as empty of life as a polar shore. No svart or lyblac stained the snow; no gaunt figure lay close by; the pillar of Clulow was bare. Away to the south a black cloud rolled. There was joy, and many tears.

And this tale is called the Weirdstone of Brisingamen. And here is an end of it.

THE MOON
OF GOMRATH

Alan Garner

For Ellen,
Adam and Katharine

CONTENTS

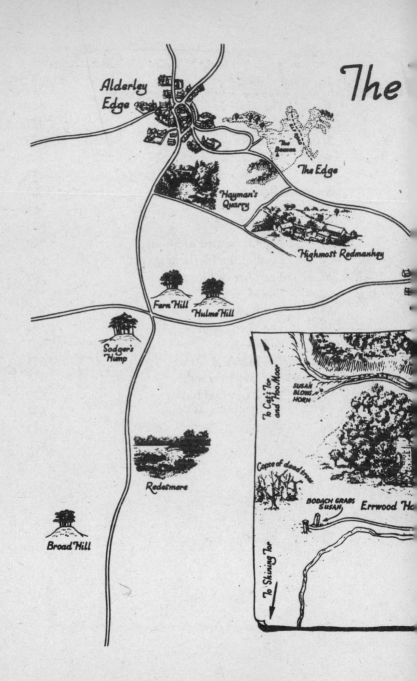

Alderley
Edge

The

The Beacon

The Edge

Hayman's
Quarry

Highmost Redmanhey

Fern Hill

Hulme Hill

Sodger's
Hump

To Cat's Tor
and Foo Moor

SUSAN
BLOWS
HORN

Copse of dead trees

Redesmere

BODACH GRABS
SUSAN

Errwood H

To Shining Tor

Broad Hill

Hunters' Land

Cat's Tor

Hoo Moor

Errwood Hall

Shining Tor

To Buxton

Macclesfield

Errwood Hall

River Goyt

"And for to passe the tyme thys book shal be plesaunte to rede in, but for to gyve fayth and byleve that al is trewe that is conteyned herein, ye be at your lyberté."

William Caxton
31 July 1485

CHAPTER 1

The Elves of Sinadon

It was bleak on Mottram road under the Edge, the wooded hill of Alderley. Trees roared high in the darkness. If any people had cause to be out in the night, they kept their heads deep in their collars, and their faces screwed blindly against the Pennine wind. And it was as well they did, for among the trees something was happening that was not meant for human eyes.

From a rib of the Edge a shaft of blue light cut the darkness. It came from a narrow opening in a high, tooth-shaped rock, and within the opening was a pair of iron gates thrown wide, and beyond them a tunnel. Shadows moved on the trees as a strange procession entered through the gates and down into the hill.

They were a small people, not more than four feet high, deep-chested, with narrow waists, and long, slender arms and legs. They wore short tunics, belted and sleeveless, and their feet were bare. Some had cloaks of white eagle feathers, though these were marks of rank rather than a protection. They carried deeply curved bows, and from their belts hung on one side quivers of white arrows, and on the other broad stabbing swords. Each rode a small white horse, and some sat proudly erect, though most drooped over the pommels of their saddles, and a few lay irrevocably still across their horses' necks, and the reins were held by others. All together they numbered close on five hundred.

Beside the iron gates stood an old man. He was very tall, and thin as a young birch tree. His white robes, and long white hair and beard flew with the gale, and he held a white staff in his hand.

Slowly the horsemen filed through the gates into the glimmering tunnel, and when they were all inside, the old man turned, and followed them. The iron gates swung shut behind him, and there was just a bare rock in the wind.

In this way the elves of Sinadon came unnoticed to Fundindelve, last stronghold of the High Magic in our days, and were met by Cadellin Silverbrow, a great wizard, and guardian of the secret places of the Edge.

CHAPTER 2

The Well

"Eh up,"said Gowther Mossack, "what's this?"

"What's what?" said Colin.

"This here in the *Advertiser*."

Colin and Susan leant forward to look where Gowther's finger pointed to a headline near the middle of the page.

PLUMBING THE DEPTHS

Speculation has been aroused by the discovery of what appears to be a thirty-foot well, during excavations in front of the Trafford Arms Hotel, Alderley Edge.

While workmen employed by Isaac Massey and Sons were digging to trace a surface water drain they moved a stone flag and discovered a cavity. The lowering of a weighted string showed that the depth was thirty feet, with fifteen feet of water. The well was in no way connected with the drain, and although the whole of the covering was not removed it was estimated that the cavity was about six feet square with stone walls covered with slabs of stone.

It has been suggested that at one time there was a pump in front of the hotel and that excavations have revealed the well from which water was pumped.

Another theory is that it may probably be an air shaft connected with the ancient mines, which extend for a considerable distance in the direction of the village.

"The funny thing is," said Gowther when the children had finished reading, "as long as I con remember it's always been said there's a tunnel from the copper mines comes out in the cellars of the Trafford. And now there's this. I wonder what the answer is."

"I dunner see as it matters," said Bess Mossock. "Yon's nobbut a wet hole, choose how you look at it. And it can stay theer, for me."

Gowther laughed. "Nay, lass, wheer's your curiosity?"

"When you're my age," said Bess, "and getting as fat as Pig Ellen, theer's other things to bother your head with, besides holes with water in them.

"Now come on, let's be having you. I've my shopping to do, and you've not finished yet, either."

"Could we have a look at the hole before we start?" said Susan.

"That's what I was going to suggest," said Gowther. "It's only round the corner. It wunner take but a couple of minutes."

"Well, I'll leave you to it," said Bess. "I hope you enjoy yourselves. But dunner take all day, will you?"

They went out from the chip shop into the village street. Among all the parked cars, the Mossocks' green cart, with their white horse, Prince, between the shafts, stood thirty years behind its surroundings. And the Mossocks were the same. Bess, in her full coat, and round, brimmed hat held with a pin, and Gowther, in his waistcoat and breeches – they had seen no reason to change the way of life that suited them. Once a week they rode down from Highmost Redmanhey, their farm on the southern slope of the Edge, to deliver eggs, poultry, and vegetables to customers in Alderley village. When Colin and Susan had first come to stay at Highmost Redmanhey everything had seemed very strange, but they had quickly settled into the Mossocks' pattern.

Gowther and the children walked at Prince's head for the short distance up the street to the De Trafford Arms, a public house built to Victorian ideas of beauty in half-timbered gothic.

A trench about three feet deep had been dug along the front of the building, close against the wall. Gowther mounted the pile of earth and clay that stood beside it, and looked down into the trench.

"Ay, this is it."

Colin and Susan stepped up to join him.

The corner of a stone slab was sticking out of the trench wall a little way above the floor. A piece of the slab had broken off, making a hole three inches wide; that was all. Susan took a pebble, and dropped it through the gap. A second later there was a resonant "plunk" as it hit water.

"It dunner tell you much, does it?" said Gowther. "Con you see owt?"

Susan had jumped into the trench, and was squinting through the hole.

"It's – a round – shaft. There seems to be something like a pipe sticking into it. I can't see any more."

"Happen it's nobbut a well," said Gowther. "Pity: I've always liked to think theer's summat in the owd tale."

They went back to the cart, and when Bess had done her shopping they continued on their round of deliveries. It was late afternoon before all was finished.

"I suppose you'll be wanting to walk home through the wood again," said Gowther.

"Yes, please," said Colin.

"Ay, well, I think you'd do best to leave it alone, myself," said Gowther. "But if you're set on going, you mun go – though I doubt you'll find much. And think on you come straight home; it'll be dark in an hour, and them woods are treacherous at neet. You could be down a mine hole as soon as wink."

Colin and Susan walked along the foot of the Edge. Every week they did this, while Bess and Gowther rode home in the cart, and any free time they had was also spent wandering on this hill, searching –

For a quarter of a mile, safe suburban gardens bounded the road, then fields began to show, and soon they were clear of the village. On their right the vertical north face of the Edge rose over them straight from the footpath, beeches poised above the road, and the crest harsh with pine and rock.

They left the road, and for a long time they climbed in silence, deep into the wood. Then Susan spoke:

"But what *do* you think's the matter? Why can't we find Cadellin now?"

"Oh, don't start that again," said Colin. "We never did know how to open the iron gates, or the Holywell entrance, so we're not likely to be able to find him."

"Yes, but why shouldn't he want to see us? I could understand it before, when he knew it wasn't safe to come here, but not now. What is there to be scared of now that the Morrigan's out of the way?"

"That's it," said Colin. "Is she?"

"But she must be," said Susan. "Gowther says her house is empty, and it's the talk of the village."

"But whether she's alive or not, she still wouldn't be at the house," said Colin. "I've been thinking about it: the only other time Cadellin did this to us was when he thought she was around. He's either got tired of us, or there's trouble. Why else would it always be like this?"

They had reached the Holywell. It lay at the foot of a cliff in one of the many valleys of the

475

Edge. It was a shallow, oblong, stone trough, into which water dripped from the rock. Beside it was a smaller, fan-shaped basin, and above it a crack in the rock face, and that, the children knew, was the second gate of Fundindelve. But now, as for weeks past, their calling was not answered.

How Colin and Susan were first drawn into the world of Magic that lies as near and unknown to us as the back of a shadow is not part of this story. But having once experienced the friendship of Cadellin Silverbrow, they were deeply hurt now that he seemed to have abandoned them without reason or warning. Almost they wished that they had never discovered enchantment: they found it unbearable that the woods for them should be empty of anything but loveliness, that the boulder that hid the iron gates should remain a boulder, that the cliff above the Holywell should be just a cliff.

"Come on," said Colin. "Staring won't open it. And if we don't hurry, we shan't be home before dark, and you know how Bess likes to fuss."

They climbed out of the valley on to the top of the Edge. It was dusk: branches stood against the sky, and twilight ran in the grass, and gathered black in the chasms and tunnel eyes of the old mines which scarred the woodland with their spoil of sand and rock. There was the sound of wind, though the trees did not move.

"But Cadellin would have told us if we couldn't—"

"Wait a minute!" said Colin. "What's down there? Can you see?"

They were walking along the side of a quarry. It had not been worked for many years, and its floor was covered with grass, so that only its bare walls made it different from the other valleys of the Edge. But their sheerness gave the place a primitive atmosphere, a seclusion that was both brooding and peaceful. Here night was gathering very quickly.

"Where?" said Susan.

"At the other end of the quarry: a bit to the left of that tree."

"No—"

"There it goes! Sue! *What is it?*"

The hollows of the valley were in darkness, and a patch of the darkness was moving, blacker than the rest. It flowed across the grass, shapeless, flat, changing in size, and up the cliff face. Somewhere near the middle, if there was a middle, were two red points of light. It slipped over the edge of the quarry, and was absorbed into the bracken.

"Did you see it?" said Colin.

"Yes: if there was anything there. It may just have – been the light."

"Do you think it was?"

"No."

CHAPTER 3

Atlendor

They hurried now. Whether the change was in themselves or in the wood, Colin and Susan felt it. The Edge had suddenly become, not quite malevolent, but alien, unsafe. And they longed to be clear of the trees: for either the light, or nerves, or both, seemed to be playing still further tricks on them. They kept imagining that there was white movement among the tree tops – nothing clear, but suggested, and elusive.

"Do you think there was anything in the quarry?" said Susan.

"I don't know. And, anyway, *what*? I think it must have been the light – don't you?"

But before Susan could answer, there was a hissing in the air, and the children leapt aside as sand spurted between them at their feet: then they saw that there was an arrow, small and white, imbedded in the path, and as they stared, an impassive voice spoke out of the dusk above their heads.

"Move not a sinew of your sinews, nor a vein of your veins, nor a hair of your heads, or I shall send down of slender oaken darts enough to sew you to the earth."

Instinctively Colin and Susan looked up. Before them a very old silver birch threw its trunk

478

in an arch across the path, and among the branches stood a slight figure, man-like, yet not four feet high. He wore a white tunic, and his skin was wind-brown. The locks of his hair lay close to his head like tongues of silver fire: and his eyes – were the eyes of a goat. They held a light that was mirrored from nothing in the wood, and in his hand was a deeply-curved bow.

At first, Colin and Susan stood, unable to speak, then the tension of the last few minutes broke in Colin.

"What do you think you're doing?" he shouted. "You nearly hit us with that thing!"

"Oh, the Donas! Oh, the holy Mothan! It is himself that can speak to elves!"

Colin and Susan started at the sound of this rich voice that welled with laughter. They turned, and saw another small, but stockier, figure standing on the path behind them, his red hair glowing darkly in the last light. They had rarely seen such an ugly face. It was big-lipped, gap-toothed, warted, potato-nosed, shaggily thatched and bearded, the skin tanned like brambles at New Year. The left eye was covered with a black patch, but the right eye had the life of two in it. He was unmistakably a dwarf. He came forward and clapped Colin on the shoulder, and Colin rocked under the blow.

"And it is I, Uthecar Hornskin, that love you for it! Hey now! Will his mightiness come down out of yon tree and speak with his friends?" The white figure in the tree did not move: he seemed not to hear what was said. "I am thinking there is more need of elf-shot in other parts of the wood this night than here! I see Albanac coming, and he in no quiet mood!"

The dwarf looked down the path beyond Colin and Susan. They could not see far in the dark, but they heard the faint sound of hooves pounding towards them. Nearer and louder they grew, and then out of the night came a black horse, wild-eyed and sweating, and halted in a spray of sand. Its rider, a tall man, himself clothed in black, called up into the tree. "My lord Atlendor! We have found it, but it is free of the wood to the south, and moving too fast for me. Ermid son of Erbin, Riogan son of Moren, and Anwas the Winged, with half their cantrefs, have it in sight, but they are not enough. Hurry!" His straight hair hung black upon his shoulders, gold glinted at his ear, and his eyes were like burning ice. A deep-crowned, wide-brimmed hat was on his head, and about his shoulders was a cloak fastened with a silver buckle.

"I go. Albanac shall teach my will to these folk." The elf ran lightly along the birch trunk and disappeared into the crown. There was a rush of white in the surrounding trees, like swirling snow, and a noise like wind in the branches.

For some time nobody spoke. The dwarf gave the impression that he was enjoying the situation and was happy to let others make the next move; the man called Albanac looked at the children; and Colin and Susan were recovering from their surprise, and taking in the fact that they were back in the world of Magic – by accident, it seemed; and now that they were back, they remembered that this was a world of deep shadows as well as of enchantment.

They had been walking into it ever since they reached the quarry. If they could have recognized this atmosphere for what it was, the successive shocks of elf, dwarf, and rider would not have been so breathless.

"I think now," said Albanac, "that the matter is out of Cadellin's hands."

"What do you mean?" said Colin. "And what's all this about?"

"As for what I mean, that will take some telling, and what it is about is the same thing. And the place for it all is Fundindelve, so let us go together."

"Is there not more urgent business in the wood this night?" said Uthecar.

"Nothing that we can do," said Albanac. "The speed and the eyes of elves are the only hope, and I fear they will not be enough."

He dismounted from his horse, and walked with the children and the dwarf back along the path. But after a little while, Susan noticed that they were not making for the Holywell.

"Wouldn't it be quicker that way?" she said, pointing to their left.

"It would be," said Albanac, "but this way the path is broader, which is a good thing this night."

They came to a wide expanse of stone and sand

which spilled down the face of the Edge. This was Stormy Point, a place of fine views in daylight, but now it was friendless. From here they crossed over the rocks to Saddlebole, which was a spur of the hill jutting into the plain, and halfway along this stood a tall boulder.

"Will you open the gates, Susan?" said Albanac.

"But I can't," said Susan. "I've tried often enough."

"Colin," said Albanac, "will you put your right hand to the rock, and say the word 'Emalagra'?"

"What, like this?"

"Yes."

"Emalagra?"

"Again."

"Emalagra! *Emalagra!*"

Nothing happened. Colin stood back, looking foolish.

"Now Susan," said Albanac.

Susan stepped up to the boulder, and put her right hand against it.

"Emalagra. See? It's no good. I've tried every—"

A crack appeared in the rock; it grew wider, revealing a pair of iron gates, and beyond these a tunnel lit by a blue light.

CHAPTER 4

The Brollachan

"Will you open the gates?" said Albanac.

Susan stretched out her hand, and touched the iron gates. They swung open.

"Quickly now," said Uthecar. "It is a healthier night within than without."

He hurried the children through the gates, and the rock closed after them the moment they were all inside.

"Why did they open? They wouldn't before," said Susan.

"Because you spoke the word, and for another reason that we shall talk about," said Albanac.

They went with Albanac down the paths of Fundindelve. Tunnel entered cave, and cave gave way to tunnel: caves, and tunnels, each different and the same: there seemed to be no end.

As they went deeper the blue light grew pale and strong, and by this the children knew that they were nearing the Cave of the Sleepers, for whose sake the old dwarf-mine of Fundindelve had been charged with the greatest magic of an age, and its guardian was Cadellin Silverbrow. Here in this cave, waiting through the centuries for the day when Cadellin should rouse him from his enchanted sleep to fight the last battle of the world, lay a king, surrounded by his knights, each with his milk-white mare.

The children looked about them, at the cold flames, now white in the core of the magic, flickering over the silver armour, at the horses, and the men, and listened to the muted, echoing murmur of their breathing, the beating of the heart of Fundindelve.

From the Cave of the Sleepers the way led uphill, by more tunnels, by stark, high-arching bridges over unknown depths, along narrow paths in the roofs of caves, across vaulted plains of sand, to the furthest caverns of the mine. And finally they came to a small cave close behind the Holywell that the wizard used for his quarters. In it were a few chairs, a long table, and a bed of skins.

"Where's Cadellin?" said Susan.

"He will be with the lios-alfar, the elves," said Albanac. "Many of them are ill of the smoke-sickness: but until he comes, rest you here. There is doubtless much you would know."

"There certainly is!" said Colin. "Who was that shooting arrows at us?"

"The elf-lord, Atlendor son of Naf: he needs your help."

"*Needs our help?*" said Colin. "He went a funny way about getting it!"

"But I never thought elves would be like *that*!" said Susan.

"No," said Albanac. "You are both too hasty. Remember, he is under fear at this time. Danger

484

besets him; he is tired, alone – and he is a king. Remember, too, that no elf has a natural love of men; for it is the dirt and ugliness and unclean air that men have worshipped these two hundred years that have driven the lios-alfar to the trackless places and the broken lands. You should see the smoke-sickness in the elves of Talebolion and Sinadon. You should hear it in their lungs. That is what men have done."

"But how *can* we help?" said Susan.

"I will show you," said Albanac. "Cadellin has spoken against this for many days, and he has good reason, but now you are here, and I think we must tell you what is wrong.

"In brief, it is this. There is something hiding in the dead wastes of the Northland, in far Prydein where the last kingdom of the elves has been made. For a long while now the numbers of the lios-alfar have been growing less – not through the smoke-sickness, as is happening in the west, but for some cause that we have not found. Elves vanish. They go without a sign. At first it was by ones and twos, but not long since a whole cantref, the cantref of Grannos, was lost, horses and weapons; not an arrow was seen. Some great wrong is at work, and to find it, and destroy it, Atlendor is bringing his people to him from the south and the west, gathering what magic he can. Susan, will you let him take the Mark of Fohla?"

"What's that?" said Susan.

"It is the bracelet that Angharad Goldenhand gave to you."

"*This?*" said Susan. "I didn't know it had a name. What good is it to Atlendor?"

"I do not know," said Albanac. "But any magic may help him – and you have magic there. Did you not open the gates?"

Susan looked at the band of ancient silver that she wore on her wrist. It was all she had brought with her out of the wreckage of their last encounter with this world, and it had been given to her, on a night of danger and enchantment, by Angharad Goldenhand, the Lady of the Lake. Susan did not know the meaning of the heavy letters that were traced in black, in a forgotten script, upon the silver, yet she knew that it was no ordinary bracelet, and she did not wear it lightly.

"Why is it called that?" said Susan.

"There are tales," said Albanac, "that I have only dimly heard about these things, yet I know that the Marks of Fohla are from the early magic of the world, and this is the first that I have ever seen, and I cannot tell its use. But will you give it to Atlendor?"

"I can't," said Susan.

"But the elves may be destroyed for lack of the Mark!" said Albanac. "Will you fail them when they most need help?"

"Of course I'll help," said Susan. "It's just that Angharad told me I must always look after my bracelet, though she didn't say why: but if Atlendor needs it, I'll go back with him."

At this, Uthecar laughed, but Albanac's face was troubled.

"You have me there," he said. "Atlendor will not like this. But wait: is he to know? I do not want to burden him with fresh troubles if they can be avoided. Perhaps this would be of no use to Atlendor, but let me take it to him, Susan, so that he can try its powers. If they are deaf to him he will accept your provision more easily."

"And why should himself not be away beyond Bannawg sooner than the fox to the wood, and the Mark with him?" said Uthecar.

"You do not know the lios-alfar, Hornskin," said Albanac. "I give you my word that there will be no deceit."

"Then another word shall go into Cadellin's ear," said Uthecar, "lest Atlendor should think black danger merits black deed. None of the lios-alfar will leave Fundindelve if Cadellin bids them stay."

"No," said Susan. "I trust you. And I think I trust Atlendor. Here you are: let him see what he can do with it. But please don't keep it any longer than you need."

"Thank you," said Albanac. "You will not be sorry."

"Let us hope so," said Uthecar. He did not look at all happy. "But from what I have heard of you, I am thinking you are not wise to put off your armour. The Morrigan does not forget, and she does not forgive."

"The Morrigan?" said Colin. "Where? Is she after us again?"

Although the children had first crossed this woman in her human shape, they had soon learnt that there was more to her than her ungraciousness. She was the Morrigan, leader of the witch covens called the morthbrood, and above that, she could wake the evil in stones and brew hate from the air, and she was terrible in her strength. But mainly through Colin and Susan her power had been broken by Cadellin Silverbrow, and they had not been certain that she herself had survived the destruction that had overwhelmed her followers.

"The morthbrood is scattered," said Albanac, "but she has been seen. You had best ask him who brought word of her." He nodded towards Uthecar. "This honey-natured dwarf from beyond Minith Bannawg in the Northland."

"Why? Have you seen her?" said Colin.

"Have I not!" said the dwarf. "Are you all wanting to know? Well then, here is the tale.

"On my way south I came to the hill of the Black Fernbrake in Prydein, and a storm followed me. So I was looking for rocks and heather to make a shelter for the night. I saw a round, brown stone, as if it were set apart from other stones, and I put my arms about it to lift it up – and oh, king of the sun and of the moon, and of the bright and fragrant stars! the stone put arms about my neck, and was throttling the life of me!

"Ask not how, for I cannot say, but I plucked

myself free; and then the stone was the Morrigan! I sprang at her with my sword, and though she took out my eye, I took off her head, and the Black Fernbrake's sides called to her screech.

"But the head leapt a hard, round leap to the neck again, and she came at me loathingly, and I was much in fear of her. Three times we fought, and three times I lifted her head, and three times she was whole again, and I was near death with pain and faintness.

"So once more I set iron to her shoulders, but when the head was making for the trunk I put my sword on the neck, and the head played 'gliong' on the blade, and sprang up to the skies. Then it began to fall, and I saw that it was aiming at me, so I stepped aside, and it went six feet into the ground with the force it had. Was that not the head! Then I heard stones crunching, and a chewing, and a gnawing, and a gnashing, so I thought it was time for me to take my legs along with me, and I went on through the night and the winnowing and the snow in it."

They were waiting now for the wizard to come. And while they waited, Uthecar saw to it that talk never flagged.

He told how Albanac had met him one day, and had spoken of a rumour that something had come out of the ground near Fundindelve and was being hunted by Cadellin Silverbrow. Having himself been idle too long, Uthecar had decided to make the journey south from Minith Bannawg, in the hope that Cadellin would be glad of his help. He was not disappointed. The matter was greater than he thought –

Long ago, one of the old mischiefs of the world had brought fear to the plain, but it had been caught, and imprisoned in a pit at the foot of the Edge. Centuries later, through the foolishness of men, it had escaped, and was taken at heavy cost. Albanac's news was that man had loosed the evil a second time.

"And there was no knowing in the nard, shrivelling world," said Uthecar, "where we might find the Brollachan again."

The Brollachan. "Now the Brollachan," said Uthecar, "has eyes and a mouth, and it has no speech, and alas no shape." It was beyond comprehension. Yet the shadow that rose in Susan's mind as the dwarf spoke seemed to her to darken the cave.

Shortly after this, Cadellin arrived. His shoulders were bowed, his weight leaning on the staff in his hand. When he saw the children a frown grew in the lines about his eyes.

"Colin? Susan? I am glad to see you; but why are you here? Albanac, why have you gone behind me to do this?"

"It is not quite so, Cadellin," said Albanac. "But first, what of the lios-alfar?"

"The elves of Dinsel and Talebolion will be slow to heal," said Cadellin. "These that have come from Sinadon are stronger, but the smoke-sickness is on them, and some I fear are beyond my hand.

"Now tell me what has brought you here."

He spoke to the children.

"We were – stopped by Atlendor – the elf – and then Uthecar and Albanac came," said Susan, "and we've just heard about the elves."

"Do you think badly of Atlendor," said Albanac. "He is hard-pressed. But Susan has given us hope: I have the Mark of Fohla here."

Cadellin looked at Susan. "I – am glad," he said. "It is noble, Susan. But is it wise? Oh, you must think I have the destruction of elves at heart! But the Morrigan—"

"We have spoken of her," said Albanac quickly. "The bracelet will not be with me for long, and I do not think that witch-queen will come south yet awhile. She will have to be much stronger before she dare move openly, and she does not feel safe even beyond Minith Bannawg, if Hornskin's tale speaks true. Why else the shape-shifting among rocks unless she fears pursuit?"

"That is so," agreed Cadellin. "I know I am too cautious. Yet still I do not like to see these children brought even to the threshold of danger – no, Susan, do not be angry. It is not your age but your humanity that gives me unrest. It is against my wishes that you are here now."

"But *why?*" cried Susan.

"Why do you think men know us only in legend?" said Cadellin. "We do not have to avoid you for our safety, as elves must, but rather for your own. It has not always been so. Once we were close; but some little time before the elves were driven away, a change came over you. You found the world easier to master by hands alone: things became more than thoughts with you, and you called it an Age of Reason.

"Now with us the opposite holds true, so that in our affairs you are weakest where you should be strong, and there is danger for you not only from evil, but from other matters we touch upon. These may not be evil, but they are wild forces, which could destroy one not well acquainted with such things.

"For these reasons we withdrew from mankind, and became a memory, and, with the years, a superstition, ghosts and terrors for a winter's night, and later a mockery and a disbelief.

"That is why I must appear so hard: do you understand?"

"I – think so," said Susan. "Most of it, anyway."

"But if you cut yourself off all that while ago," said Colin, "how is it that you talk as we do?"

"But we do not," said the wizard. "We use the Common Tongue now because you are here. Among ourselves there are many languages. And have you not noticed that there are some of us stranger to the Tongue than others? The elves have avoided men most completely. They speak the Tongue much as they last heard it, and that not well. The rest – I, the dwarfs, and a few more

– heard it through the years, and know it better than do the elves, though we cannot master your later speed and shortness. Albanac sees most of men, and *he* is often lost, but since they think him mad it is of no account."

Colin and Susan did not stay long in the cave: the mood of the evening remained uneasy and it was obvious that Cadellin had more on his mind than had been said. A little after seven o'clock they walked up the short tunnel that led from the cave to the Holywell. The wizard touched the rock with his staff, and the cliff opened.

Uthecar went with the children all the way to the farm, turning back only at the gate. Colin and Susan were aware of his eyes ranging continually backwards and forwards, around and about.

"What's the matter?" said Susan. "What are you looking for?"

"Something I hope I shall not be finding," said Uthecar. "you may have noticed that the woods were not empty this night. We were close on the Brollachan, and it is far from here that I hope it is just now."

"But how could you see it, whatever it is?" said Colin. "It's pitch dark tonight."

"You must know the eyes of a dwarf are born to darkness," said Uthecar. "But even you would see the Brollachan, though the night were as black as a wolf's throat; for no matter how black the night, the Brollachan is blacker than that."

This stopped conversation for the rest of the journey. But when they reached Highmost

Redmanhey, Susan said, "Uthecar, what's wrong with the elves? I – don't mean to be rude, but I've always imagined them to be the – well, the 'best' of your people."

"Ha!" said Uthecar. "They would agree with you! And few would gainsay them. You must judge for yourselves. But I will say this of the lios-alfar; they are merciless without kindliness, and there are things incomprehensible about them."

CHAPTER 5

"To a Woman yt was Dumpe"

About half a mile from Highmost Redmanhey, round the shoulder of Clinton Hill, there is a disused and flooded quarry. Where the sides are not cliffs, wooded slopes drop steeply. A broken wind pump creaks, and a forgotten path runs nowhere into the brambles. In sunlight it is a forlorn place, forlorn as nothing but deserted machinery can be; but when the sun goes in, the air is charged with a different feeling. The water is sombre under its brows of cliff, and the trees crowd down to drink, the pump sneers; lonely, green-hued, dark.

But peaceful, thought Susan, and that's something.

There had been no peace at the farm since their return. Two days of talk from Colin, and the silences made heavy by the Mossocks' uneasiness. For Bess and Gowther knew of the children's past involvement with magic, and they were as troubled by this mixing of the two worlds as Cadellin had been.

The weather did not help. The air was still, moist, too warm for the beginning of winter.

Susan had felt that she must go away to relax; so that afternoon she had left Colin and had come to the quarry. She stood on the edge of a slab of rock that stretched into the water, and lost herself in the grey shadows of fish. She was there a long time, slowly unwinding the tensions of the days: and then a noise made her look up.

"Hallo. Who are you?"

A small black pony was standing at the edge of the water on the other side of the quarry.

"What are you doing here?"

The pony tossed its mane, and snorted.

"Come on, then! Here, boy!"

The pony looked hard at Susan, flicked its tail, then turned and disappeared among the trees.

"Oh, well – I wonder what the time is." Susan climbed up the slope out of the quarry and into the field. She walked round the wood on the far side, and whistled, but nothing happened. "Here, boy! Here, boy! Oh don't, then; I'm – oh!"

The pony was standing right behind her.

"You made me jump! Where've you been?"

Susan fondled the pony's ears. It seemed to like that, for it thrust its head into her shoulder, and closed its velvet-black eyes.

"Steady! You'll knock me over."

For several minutes she stroked its neck, then reluctantly she pushed it away. "I must go now. I'll come and see you tomorrow." The pony trotted after her. "No, go back. You can't come." But the pony followed Susan all the way across the field, butting her gently with its head and nibbling at her ears. And when she came to climb through the fence into the next field, it put itself between her and the fence, and pushed sideways with its sleek belly.

"What do you want?"

Push.

"I've nothing for you."

Push.

"What *is* it?"

Push.

"Do you want me to ride? That's it, isn't it? Stand still, then. There. Good boy. You *have* got a long back, haven't you? There. Now – whoa! Steady!"

The moment Susan was astride, the pony wheeled round and set off at full gallop towards the quarry. Susan grabbed the mane with both hands.

"Hey! Stop!"

They were heading straight for the barbed wire at the top of the cliff above the deepest part of the quarry.

"No! Stop!"

The pony turned its head and looked at Susan. Its foaming lips curled back in a grin, and the velvet was gone from the eye: in the heart of the black pupil was a red flame.

"*No!*" Susan screamed.

Faster and faster they went. The edge of the cliff cut a hard line against the sky. Susan tried to throw herself from the pony's back, but her fingers seemed to be entangled in the mane, and her legs clung to the ribs.

"*No! No! No! No!*"

The pony soared over the fence, and plunged

past smooth sandstone down to the water. The splash echoed between the walls, waves slapped the rock, there were some bubbles: the quarry was silent under the heavy sky.

"I'm not waiting any longer," said Bess. "Susan mun get her own tea when she comes in."

"Ay, let's be doing," said Gowther. "Theer's one or two things to be seen to before it rains, and it conner be far off now: summat's got to bust soon."

"I'll be glad when it does," said Bess. "I conner get my breath today. Did Susan say she'd be late?"

"No," said Colin, "but you know what she is. And she hadn't a watch with her."

They sat down at the table, and ate without talking. The only sounds were the breathing of Bess and Gowther, the ticking of the clock, the idiot buzz of two winter-drugged flies that circled endlessly under the beams. The sky bore down on the farm-house, squeezing the people in it like apples in a press.

"We're for it, reet enough," said Gowther. "And Susan had best hurry if she dunner want a soaking. She ought to be here by now. Wheer was she for, Colin? Eh up! What's getten into him?" Scamp, the Mossocks' lurcher, had begun to bark wildly somewhere close. Gowther put his head out of the window. "That'll do! Hey!"

"Now then, what was I saying? Oh ay; Susan. Do you know wheer she's gone?"

"She said she was going to the quarry for some peace and quiet – I've been getting on her nerves, she said."

"What? Hayman's quarry? You should have said earlier, Colin. It's dangerous – oh, drat the dog! Hey! Scamp! That's enough! Do you hear?"

"Oh!" said Bess. "Whatever's to do with you? Wheer've you been?"

Susan was standing in the doorway, looking pale and dazed. Her hair was thick with mud, and a pool of water was gathering at her feet.

"The quarry!" said Gowther. "She mun have fallen in! What were you thinking of, Susan, to go and do that?"

"Bath and bed," said Bess, "and then we'll see what's what. Eh dear!"

She took Susan by the arm, and bustled her out of sight.

"Goodness knows what happened," said Bess when she came downstairs half an hour later. "Her hair was full of sand and weed. But I couldner get a word out of her: she seems mazed, or summat. Happen she'll be better for a sleep: I've put a couple of hot-water bottles in her bed, and she looked as though she'd drop off any minute when I left her."

The storm battered the house, and filled the rooms with currents of air, making the lamps roar. It had come soon after nightfall, and with it a release of tension. The house was now a refuge, and not a prison. Colin, once the immediate anxiety for Susan had been allayed, settled down to spend the evening with his favourite book.

This was a musty old ledger, covered with brown suede. Over a hundred years ago, one of the rectors of Alderley had copied into it a varied series of documents relating to the parish. The book had been in Gowther's family longer than he could say, and although he had never found the patience to decipher the crabbed handwriting, he treasured the book as a link with a time that had passed. But Colin was fascinated by the anecdotes, details of court leets, surveys of the parish, manorial grants, and family histories that filled the book. There was always something absurd to be found, if you had Colin's sense of humour.

The page that held him now was headed:

EXTRACTS: CH: WARDENS' ACCS. 1617

A true and perfect account of all such Sumes of Money as I, John Henshaw of ye Butts, Churchwarden of Neither Alderley and for ye parish of Alderley have received and likewise disburst since my first entrance into Office until this present day being ye 28 May Anno Di. 1618.

	£	s.	d.
Imprimis Payed for Ale for ye Ringers and oure Selves	0	3	2
Item to John Wych his bill for a new Sally Poll	0	2	0
Item to a man yt had his tongue cut out by ye Turks	0	0	2

Item to Philip Lea half his bill for walking	0	1	6
Item to a pretended Irish gentleman	0	1	3
Item spent for cluckin to make nets	0	1	8
Item to a woman yt was dumpe	0	0	6
Item spent when I did goe throw ye town to warne those to bring in ye wrishes yt had neglected on ye wrish burying day	0	0	4
Item given to a Majer yt had been taken by ye French and was runeated by them	0	1	0
Item payed to Mr. Hollinshead for warrants to punish ye boys' Immoralities	0	0	8

But the next entry took all the laughter from Colin's face. He read it through twice.

"Gowther!"

"Ay?"

"Listen to this: it's part of the churchwardens' accounts for 1617.

'Item spent at Street Lane Ends when Mr Hollinshead and Mr Wright were at Paynes to confine ye devil yt was fownde at ye Ale house when ye new pipe was being put down and it did break into ye Pitt.'

"Do you think it's the hole at the Trafford?"

Gowther frowned. "Ay, I'd say it is, what with the pipe, and all. That side of Alderley near the Trafford used to be called Street Lane Ends, and I've heard tell of a pub theer before the Trafford was built. Sixteen-seventeen, is it? It conner be part of the mines, then. They didner come that

501

way until about two hundred years back, when West Mine was started. So it looks as though it was the well of the owd pub, dunner it?"

"But it couldn't be," said Colin. "It was called 'ye Pitt', and by the sound of it, they didn't know it was there. So what is it?"

"Nay, dunner ask me," said Gowther. "And who are yon Hollinshead and Wright?"

"They're often mentioned in here," said Colin. "I think they were the priests at Alderley and Wilmslow. I'd like to know more about this 'devil'."

"I dunner reckon much on that," said Gowther. "They were a superstitious lot in them days. As a matter of fact, I was talking to Jack Wrigley yesterday – he's the feller as put his pickaxe through the slab – and he said that when he was looking to see what he'd got, he heard a rum kind of bubbling sound that put the wind up him a bit, but he thinks it was summat to do with air pressure. Happen yon's what the parsons took for Owd Nick."

"I dunner like it," said Bess from the doorway. She had just come downstairs. "Susan's not spoken yet, and she's as cold as a frog. And I conner think wheer all the sand's coming from – her hair's still full of it – and everything's wringing wet. Still, that's not surprising with two hot-water bottles, I suppose. But theer's summat wrong; she's lying theer staring at nowt, and her eyes are a bit queer."

"Mun I go for the doctor, do you think?" said Gowther.

"What? In this rain? And it's nearly ten o'clock. Nay, lad, she inner that bad. But if things are no different in the morning, we'll have the doctor in sharpish."

"But what if she's getten concussion, or summat like that?" said Gowther.

"It's more like shock, I reckon," said Bess. "Theer's no bruises or lumps as I con see, and either way, she's in the best place for her. You'd not get much thanks from the doctor for dragging him up here in this. We'll see how she is for a good neet's rest."

Bess, like many country-women of her age, could not shake off her unreasoned fear of medical men.

Colin never knew what woke him. He lay on his back and stared at the moonlight. He had woken suddenly and completely, with no buffer of drowsiness to take the shock. His senses were needle-pointed, he was aware of every detail of the room, the pools of light and darkness shouted at him.

He got out of bed, and went to the window. It was a clear night, the air cold and sweet after the storm: the moon cast hard shadows over the farmyard. Scamp lay by the barn door, his head between his paws. Then Colin saw something move. He saw it only out of the corner of his eye, and it was gone in a moment, but he was never

503

in any doubt: a shadow had slipped across the patch of moonlight that lay between the end of the house and the gate that led to the Riddings, the steep hill-field behind the farm.

"Hey! Scamp!" whispered Colin. The dog did not move. "Hey! Wake up!" Scamp whined softly, and gave a muted yelp. "Come on! Fetch him!" Scamp whined again, then crawled, barely raising his belly from the floor, into the barn. "What on earth? Hey!" But Scamp would not come.

Colin pulled on his shirt and trousers over his pyjamas, and jammed his feet into a pair of shoes, before going to wake Gowther. But when he came to Susan's door he paused, and, for no reason that he could explain, opened the door. The bed was empty, the window open.

Colin tiptoed downstairs and groped his way to the door. It was still bolted. Had Susan dropped nine feet to the cobbles? He eased the bolts, and stepped outside, and as he looked he saw a thin silhouette pass over the skyline of the Riddings.

He struggled up the hill as fast as he could, but it was some time before he spotted the figure again, now moving across Clinton hill, a quarter of a mile away.

Colin ran: and by the time he stood up at the top of Clinton hill he had halved the lead that Susan had gained. For it was undoubtedly Susan. She was wearing her pyjamas, and she seemed to glide smoothly over the ground, giving a strange impression that she was running, though her movements were those of walking. Straight ahead of her were the dark tops of the trees in the quarry.

"Sue!" No, wait. That's dangerous. She's sleep-walking. But she's heading for the quarry.

Colin ran as hard as he had ever run. Once he was off the hill-top the uneven ground hid Susan, but he knew the general direction. He came to the fence that stood on the edge of the highest cliff and looked around while he recovered his breath.

The moon showed all the hill-side and much of the quarry: the pump-tower gleamed, and the vanes turned. But Susan was nowhere to be seen. Colin leant against a fence-stump. She ought to be in sight: he could not have overtaken her: she must have reached here. Colin searched the sides of the quarry with his eyes, and looked at the smooth black mirror of the water. He was frightened. Where was she?

Then he cried out his fear as something slithered over his shoe and plucked at his ankle. He started back, and looked down. It was a hand. A ledge of earth, inches wide, ran along the other side of the fence and crumbled away to the rock face a few feet below: then the drop was sheer to the tarn-like water. The hand now clutched the ledge.

"Sue!"

He stretched over the barbed wire. She was right below him, spreadeagled between the ledge and the cliff proper, her pale face turned up to his.

"Hang on! Oh, hang on!"

Colin threw himself flat on the ground, wrapped one arm round the stump, thrust the other under the wire, and grabbed at the hand. But though it looked like a hand, it felt like a hoof.

The wire tore Colin's sleeve as he shouted and snatched his arm away. Then, as Susan's face rose above the ledge, a foot from his own, and he saw the light that glowed in her eyes, Colin abandoned reason, thought. He shot backwards from the ledge, crouched, stumbled, fled. He looked back only once, and it seemed that out of the quarry a formless shadow was rising into the sky. Behind him the stars went out, but in their place were two red stars, unwinking, and close together.

Colin sped along the hill, vaulting fences, throwing himself over hedges, and plunging down the Riddings to the farm-house. As he fumbled with the door, the moon was hidden, and darkness slid over the white walls. Colin turned. *"Esenaroth! Esenaroth!"* he cried. The words came to him and were torn from his lips independent of his will, and he heard them from a distance, as though they were from another's mouth. They burned like silver fire in his brain, sanctuary in the blackness that filled the world.

CHAPTER 6

Old Evil

"I think we mun have the doctor," said Bess. "She's wet through again – it conner be healthy. And that blessed sand! Her hair's still full of it."

"Reet," said Gowther. "I'll get Prince ready, and then I'll go and ring him up."

Colin ate his breakfast mechanically. Bess and Gowther's voices passed over him. He had to do something, but he did not know what he could do.

He had been woken by Scamp's warm tongue on his face. It must have been about six o'clock in the morning: he was huddled on the doorstep, stiff with cold. He heard Gowther clump downstairs into the kitchen. Colin wondered if he should tell him what had happened, but it was not clear in his own head: he had to have time to think. So he tucked his pyjamas out of sight, and went to light the lamps for milking.

After breakfast Colin still had reached no decision. He went upstairs and changed his clothes. Susan's door was ajar. He made himself go into the room. She lay in bed, her eyes half-closed, and when she saw Colin she smiled.

He went down to the kitchen, and found it empty. Bess was feeding the hens, and Gowther was in the stable with Prince. Colin was alone in the house with – what? He needed help, and Fundindelve was his only hope. He went into the yard, frightened, desperate, and then almost sobbing with relief, for Albanac was striding down the Riddings, the sun sparkling on his silver buckles and sword, his cloak swelling behind him in the wind.

Colin ran towards him and they met at the foot of the hill.

"Albanac! Albanac!"

"Why, what is it? Colin, are you well?"

"It's Sue!"

"*What?*" Albanac took Colin by the shoulders and looked hard into his eyes. "Where is she?"

"I don't know – she's in bed – no – I mean – you must listen!"

"I am listening, but I do not follow you. Now tell me what is wrong.'

"I'm sorry," said Colin. He paused, and then began. As he spoke, Albanac's face grew lined and tense, his eyes were like blue diamonds. When Colin started to describe how he had followed Susan to the quarry Albanac interrupted him.

"Can we be seen from her window?"

"No – well, just about. It's that end window at the front."

"Then I would not be here."

They moved round until the gable end of the house hid them from any windows.

"Now go on."

When the story was finished Albanac laughed

bitterly. "Ha! This is matter indeed. So near, after all. But come, we must act before the chance is lost."

"Why? What—?"

"Listen. Can we enter the house without being seen from the window?"

"Ye-es."

"Good. I think I have not the power to do what should be done, but we must think first of Susan. Now mark what I say: we must not speak when we are nearer the house.

"Lead me to the room. I shall make little sound, but you must walk as though you had no guile. Go to the window and open it: then we shall see."

Colin paused with his hands on the latch and looked over his shoulder. Albanac stood at the top of the stairs; he nodded. Colin opened the door.

Susan lay there, staring. Colin crossed to the window and unlatched it. At the sound, Albanac stepped into the room: he held the Mark of Fohla, open, in his hand. Susan snarled, her eyes flashing wide, and tore the blankets from her, but Albanac threw himself across the room and on to the bed, striking Susan under her chin with his shoulder and pinning her arm beneath him while he locked the bracelet about her wrist. Then, as quickly, he sprang back to the door and drew his sword.

"Colin! Outside!"

"What have you done?" cried Colin. "What's happening?"

Albanac's hand bit into his shoulder and flung him out of the room. Albanac jumped after him and slammed the door shut.

"Alb—"

"Quiet!" said Albanac, and his voice was iron. "When she is free, then must we beware. Let us hope the bracelet causes such pain that escape means more then vengeance."

They stood motionless, rigid; the only sound was the creaking of Susan's bed; then that stopped. Silence.

"Albanac! *Look!*"

A black coil of smoke was sliding under the door. It rolled forward on to the floor, where it gathered in an unstable pyramid, which grew.

"If you would live," whispered Albanac, "stay by me!"

The pyramid was now some three feet high. Near the top glowed two red eyes: near the base was what could have been a shadowy mouth, or a shallow beak. Then the thing began to grow. It grew in many directions, like a balloon, and it grew in spasms, with moments of rest in between.

Albanac raised his sword, and spoke in a hard, clear voice.

"Power of wind have I over thee.

"Power of wrath have I over thee.

"Power of fire have I over thee.

"Power of thunder have I over thee.

"Power of lightning have I over thee."

The pyramid now filled the house: it was no longer a pyramid: it was everything – a universal darkness in which there were two flat discs, the colour of blood, and a ribbon of blue fire that was Albanac's sword.

"Power of storms have I over thee.

"Power of moon have I over thee.

"Power of sun have I over thee.

"Power of stars have I over thee."

The blank eyes swam closer, now as big as plates, and the darkness began to pulse, and Colin gripped Albanac's cloak like a drowning man; for the pulse was the rhythm of his heartbeats, and he could not tell where he ended and the darkness began.

"Power of the – heavens – and – of the worlds – have I – over – thee.

"Power – power – *I cannot hold it!*"

Albanac lifted his sword above his head with both hands, and drove it down into the blackness between the eyes.

"*Eson! Eson! Emaris!*"

There was a glare of light, and a tearing crash. The house quivered, the door burst inwards, a wind shrieked through the room, and all was quiet. Albanac and Colin slowly raised their heads from the floor, and pulled themselves upright against the doorposts.

The room was smashed and the furniture scattered, the window frame had splintered from the wall. Albanac's sword was in pieces. Only Susan was undisturbed: she lay quietly, breathing deeply, fast asleep. Colin went to the bed and looked down at her.

"Sue. It *is* – Sue?"

Albanac nodded.

There were voices outside in the yard, then heavy footsteps on the stairs, and Gowther stood in the doorway.

"What—?"

Bess appeared behind him.

"Who—? Oh dear! Oh dear! Oh! Oh! Oh! Oh!"

"Howd thy noise, lass," said Gowther. He looked at Albanac. "Now, maister, what's all this about?"

"That, farmer Mossock, was the Brollachan."

"The *what*?"

"Ay, and there is work to be done, and swiftly – though I doubt if we shall pick up the trail. I must go to Fundindelve, but I shall be back. Let Susan sleep, and see to it that the bracelet stays on her wrist, then she will be safe."

"I was just on my way for the doctor," said Gowther.

"No!" Albanac turned to Gowther. "You must not do that. Let Cadellin see her first."

"But—"

"Believe me! You may do harm. This is no business for men."

"No? Happen you're reet – and happen you're not. She's looking better, I'll grant you. All reet: we'll wait on a bit: but you'd best be sharp."

"Thank you, farmer Mossock."

512

Albanac ran from the house, and they watched him till he crossed over the Riddings, and not a word was spoken.

Words were spoken later. Bess and Gowther listened to Colin's story, and they accepted it. They had to. The wrecked bedroom was too compelling a witness.

They had spent several hours repairing what they could and patching up the rest. Through it all Susan had slept without a break: for Bess it was the one consolation of the day. It was a restful sleep, not the dead, withdrawn, near-coma that had troubled Bess more than she would admit. Susan was still pale, but it was a healthy paleness compared with what had gone before.

The tap at the door was so light that if they had not been sitting quietly at the table over a late tea they would not have heard it.

"Was that someone knocking?" said Gowther.

"I think it was," said Bess. "But I might be wrong?"

"Hallo," said Gowther. "Who is it?"

"Albanac."

"Oh!" Gowther crossed to the door. "Er – ay, come in."

Albanac entered the kitchen, followed by Uthecar and Cadellin. The wizard stooped under the beams: when he stood upright his head could not be seen.

"Er – take a seat, will you?" said Gowther.

"Thank you," said Cadellin. "How is Susan?"

"Oh, she's still asleep; and we've not tried to wake her, seeing how Albanac here said we should leave her be, but she's looking much better – else we'd have had the doctor to help her by now, I'll tell thee."

"*Still* sleeping?" said Cadellin.

"You have not taken the bracelet from her wrist?" said Albanac sharply.

"No."

"I think we must see her," said Cadellin.

"What's wrong?" said Colin. "Why are you all looking so grim?"

"I hope there is nothing wrong," said the wizard. "Albanac came in time, and it is well he did. The Brollachan does not willingly leave a body until it is beyond repair. Susan has escaped – I hope without injury – but it would be wise for us to see her."

"Look," said Bess, who had been sitting agape since the moment she saw the wizard, "I dunner pretend to follow this here, but if Susan needs attention, the doctor's the mon to do it. I've said so all along."

"Ay," said Gowther; "you con go and have a look at her, if you wish, but that's all. After what she seems to have been through, the less mumbo-jumbo theer is about her the better. We're having the doctor in tomorrow to give her a good over-hauling, and then we'll see."

"Hm," said Cadellin.

They went upstairs. Susan was still asleep. Cadellin looked at her.

"It is safe to wake her, farmer Mossock. Her body is not hurt, and she is rested."

Bess leant over the bed and shook Susan gently. "Susan. Come on, love: it's time to wake up." Susan did not move. Bess shook her harder. "Come on, lass. Wake up." But Susan gave no signs of waking, no matter how Bess tried.

"Mistress Mossock," said Cadellin softly, "let me try."

Bess stepped back, and the wizard took hold of Susan's wrist and felt her pulse, then he lifted her eyelid. "Hm." He put his left hand on her brow, and closed his eyes. The room was silent. A minute, two minutes passed.

"Is she all right?" said Colin. The wizard did not reply. He seemed to be scarcely breathing. "Cadellin!"

"Here! What's going on?" said Gowther, and made to grab Cadellin's arm. But Albanac stepped in front of him.

"No, farmer Mossock: do not interfere."

As he spoke, Cadellin opened his eyes. "She is not here. She is lost to us."

"*What?*" cried Colin. "What do you mean? She's not dead. She can't be! Look! She's only asleep!"

"Her body sleeps," said Cadellin. "Let us leave her now: there is something you must know."

CHAPTER 7

Old Magic

"The Brollachan," said Albanac, "has no shape. It must take that of others. But no mortal frame can bear it for long: it is too fierce a tenant. Soon the body stretches, warps, becomes the *wrong* shape, then it dwindles, crumbles, is a husk, and the Brollachan sloughs it as a snake its skin and takes another. We came in time with Susan: had we not, she would have withered like the white lily in the black frost. Now she is safe: if we can find her."

"But are you sure it's Sue upstairs?" said Colin. "When I touched her hand last night it felt – different – not a hand at all."

"Do not worry," said Cadellin. "That would be a memory from an earlier shape: such things linger with the Brollachan: its mind is slow to change. Do not men who have lost a limb often feel pain in hand or foot that is not there?"

"But wheer's all this getting us?" said Gowther. "Susan's lying up theer, and we conner wake her. Summat'll have to be done."

The wizard sighed. "I do not know the answer, farmer Mossock. The Brollachan drove her from her body, and where she is now I cannot see. She is beyond my magic: we shall call on other powers to find her, and until she is found she must lie here, and the bracelet of Angharad Goldenhand must never leave her wrist."

"I wish it never had," said Albanac. "I brought it to her the moment Atlendor gave it back to me, but that was not soon enough."

"Now see here," said Gowther, "how long is this caper to go on for?"

"It will not be a short business," said the wizard. "Weeks – months – let us hope not years. She is far away."

"Then it's the doctor for her, reet here and now," said Gowther. "I've had enough messing about."

"Farmer Mossock, you would pour water on burning oil!" cried the wizard. "Is it not clear to you yet? This is no matter for mortal skills. What would happen? She would be taken from us. Our task would grow five-fold."

"Ay, but hospital's the place for her if she's going to stay like this: she'll need special feeding, for one thing."

"No. We shall take care of her. She will be safe with us. Farmer Mossock, the worst you could do is what you plan to do. Susan's danger, *our* danger, will increase if you do not go our way in this."

Gowther looked searchingly at the wizard. "Well – I dunner like this at all – but I've seen enough of you to tell that you know what's what in these goings on. So we'll compromise. I may as well be hung for a sheep as a lamb. Unless

Susan takes a turn for the worse, I'll do nowt about it for the next three days."

"Three days!" said Cadellin. "There is little can be done in three days."

"Ay, well, I wouldner know," said Gowther. "But that's the way it is."

"Then we must accept it, and hope for second thoughts." The wizard rose from his chair. "Colin, will you be at Goldenstone at noon tomorrow? There is something that Susan will need."

Colin turned off the road on to the track that ran along the wood side. On his left were pine and oak, on his right the fields and hills.

He came to the grey block of sandstone that stood at the border of the path and was called the Goldenstone. It was so crudely shaped that few people would notice that it carried the mark of tools, and was not one of the many outcrops on the Edge, but had been placed there at some time of the world for a forgotten purpose. Uthecar and Albanac were sitting with their backs against it.

"Sit you here, Colin," said Albanac. "It is as dry as anywhere. How is Susan?"

"She's no different. Have you found anything that'll help?"

"We have not," said Uthecar. "Though rest has been far from our heads and sleep from our eyes since we left you."

"Cadellin uses all his power," said Albanac, "but not even he can see where she is. But take good heart to you: we shall not give up, and others help us. We have come now from Redesmere: the Lady of the Lake sends you this – there will be no need of other food." He handed Colin a leather bottle. "Wine from the table of Angharad Goldenhand has many virtues."

"Thank you," said Colin. "But you are going to find Sue, aren't you? It is just a question of time? And in what sort of a place is she? How can she be somewhere else when she's lying in bed?"

"I will not lie to you," said Albanac. "The Susan that sleeps is Length and Breadth and Height: but the real Susan is none of this. The two you have always known as one, but the Brollachan split them like a new-whetted blade in kindling."

"I am thinking," said Uthecar. "I am thinking that Cadellin will not find her."

"He must, and will," said Albanac. "I had not thought to see you so quickly cowed."

"Nay, you take me wrong. I am thinking that the High Magic is too keen for the task."

"I do not understand."

"You try too hard. Be not so nimble-witted!" said Uthecar. "Consider: it is said that the sword that lies by the Sleeper in Fundindelve would cleave a hair on water, draw blood from the wind. But would you use its temper to fell this oak? So here: the Brollachan is of the Old Evil – it does not move on such airy places as Cadellin knows. For the Old Evil the Old Magic is best. Against an army a thousand strong give me the king's sword, but for this oak I would be having the cottar's axe."

"I had not thought that way," said Albanac. "You may be right. And we must leave no hope untried. But what Old Magic is there now? It sleeps, and should not be woken."

"Alas, I have no head for such things," said Uthecar. "I was asking the lios-alfar, but they would never look so low."

"But what shall we do?" cried Albanac. Uthecar's words seemed to have put new life into him. Even Colin, though bewildered, caught some of the fire.

"If I were thinking, not knowing much of lore, of what would be the strongest charm for all ill times," said Uthecar, "I should say the Mothan. But where it may grow in this flat southern land, I could not be telling."

"The Mothan!" said Albanac. "I have heard of it! But it is a magic plant, not easy to be found, and we have three days."

"Tell me about it," said Colin. "I'll find it."

Uthecar looked at him. "Ay. It would take such purpose as I see in you.

"It is a fickle plant: it grows only on the heights of the old, straight track, and flowers only in the full of the moon."

"It's full moon tomorrow night!" cried Colin. "Where is this track?"

Both he and Albanac were on their feet, but Uthecar stayed where he was.

"There are many tracks. All are lost. I know

of two beyond Minith Bannawg, but not even an elf could be there in time. There may be others here. If you stand on the old, straight track when the full moon will rise along it, then you will see it: it is hidden at all other times."

"Are there any here?" said Colin wildly, turning to Albanac.

"I do not know. Again, I have heard of them: but they were made at a time before dwarfs, and before wizards. And they are part of the Old Magic, though we do not know their purpose, and dead things stir when *it* moves."

"Look! I've *got* to find this track! There must be a way. Why did you tell me about it if you knew it was no use?"

"I was wondering if the track is known here," said Uthecar. "Alas, it is not. But catch courage! It is the Old Magic, simple, warm. Faith and resolution can touch its heart. If the Mothan is to be found, you will find it, though I know not where it may be."

"But how shall I start to look for it?" said Colin.

"Believe that help will come: search: try: think of Susan: never lose heart. Be here tomorrow at this time, and we may have better news."

Colin walked back to Highmost Redmanhey unaware of his surroundings. The old, straight track: the old, straight track. It was all so vague. The old, straight track. Yet he knew that somewhere he had heard of it before Uthecar had mentioned it, which was ridiculous, since how

521

could he know about something magical that was little more than hearsay to those who lived with magic? But the harder he tried, the further memory receded, and the more certain he became that he could answer the question if he could remember.

Back at the farm Colin ate a dismal meal. He had given up the search for the old, straight track, and was preoccupied with thoughts of Susan. The Mossocks ate in silence, their faces drawn with worry.

Then, as often happens when the mind has left a problem, the picture that had been eluding him rose through Colin's thoughts.

"Got it!"

He leapt from his chair and raced upstairs to his room. He dived across the bed, and hauled Gowther's suede-covered ledger from its shelf. Somewhere in these four hundred and fifty pages was a reference to the old, straight track: he knew he had seen it: now the entry stood out in his mind: it was opposite a page of heraldic notes: there was a drawing of a coat of arms – a chevron between three boars' heads. But even so, Colin was in such a state that he had to thumb through the book twice before he found it, and then, as he read, the dry scholarship of the rector's notes seemed so removed from the excitement of magic that he began to doubt.

"Today I walked the line of an old, straight trackway, made by our rude forebears, I am forced to believe, prior to the coming of the antique Roman to these shores.

I have followed this road from Mobberley to the Edge. It was engineered, if that be the term, at so remote an era that all record of it is lost, save the frequent mounds and stones erected to indicate the way. Of these, the Beacon and the Goldenstone are the most remarkable on the Edge, and from the latter, where I terminated my excursion, it seemed that the trackway was aligned with the peak of Shining Tor, which stands distant nine miles towards Buxton.

One cannot cease to marvel at the felicity of these unknown architects, who, ignorant of all the arts of science—"

Colin shut the book. The elation had gone. But what else was there to hang on to except this? He had to try.

"Are you all reet, lad?" said Bess when he went downstairs. "You look as if you've lost a shilling and found sixpence."

"No: it's all right," said Colin. "I'm sorry about that. It was something I'd remembered in the old book. Do you know where the Beacon is on the Edge?"

"Ay," said Gowther. "It's the highest part of the Edge. You know when you go along the top path from Castle Rock to Stormy Point? Well, just before you bear left, it's the round hill above you on your right. You conner miss it: theer used to be a stone hut on the top, and you con still see the foundations."

"Do you mind if I go and look at it this afternoon?" said Colin.

"Nay, of course not," said Bess. "It'll give you summat to do, and theer's nowt like being active to take your mind off things."

"Thanks; I shan't be long."

Gowther was right. There was no mistaking the Beacon. It was a smooth-skinned mound, obviously artificial, and it stood clear of the trees on the highest point of the Edge. It looked like a tumulus.

Colin walked all over and about the mound, but the only track was modern, and anything but straight.

From the Beacon, Colin set off through the trees to the Goldenstone, which was a quarter of a mile away, along no track that he could see. On reaching it, Colin continued in a straight line past the stone, over a slight rise of ground, until he came to the edge of the wood, a few yards further on. From here, across the fields, was the high ridge of the Pennines, and at one point, directly ahead of Colin, the line of hills rose to a shallow but definite peak. Again, nowhere was there any hint of a track.

Shining Tor, presumably, thought Colin. Well, the notes were right, at least. I suppose I'd better tell Albanac. It's all there is to go on, unless *he's* turned something up.

CHAPTER 8

Shining Tor

"It could be," said Albanac. "It could be. Though we think of Goldenstone as elvish, I remember it is said the elves found it here when the road was made."

" 'Could be'!" shouted Uthecar. "You would doubt the wolf has teeth unless they were tearing the throat of you! 'Could be'! It *is*! It *is*! The Old Magic has quickened to our need: it has shown you the way to its heart, the old, straight track from the Beacon hill. There you must stand this night, Colin, and take what chance may come."

"That is what I do not like," said Albanac. "Strange memories linger on the Beacon."

"What of that? I shall be there, Colin, and my sword shall keep you."

For Colin the rest of the day dragged heavily. He checked in his diary and in the newspapers the time when the moon should rise: then he was struck by an agony of thought. What if it should be a cloudy night? Would that make a difference? So he read the weather forecasts and climbed the Riddings three times to look at the sky. But he need not have feared. It was a clear night when at last he crept from the farm-house and made his way to the wood.

He met Uthecar at the Goldenstone, and they walked together through the quiet darkness.

"Will the moon rise along the track?" said Colin.

"That is our greatest chance," said Uthecar. "But I think it will. If it does not, then there is little we can do."

"And how shall I know the Mothan when I see it?"

"It grows alone among the rocks: there are five points to its leaves, its roots are red, and it mirrors the moon. You will know it when you see it."

They climbed up the mound on which the Beacon had stood. At the top was a little sandy space, and a few blocks of sandstone. They settled themselves upon the blocks, and waited. The dwarf's sword lay across his knees.

"What am I to do with the Mothan when I find it?" said Colin.

"Take the flower, and a few of the leaves," said Uthecar, "and give them to Susan: but see to it that you harm not the root, nor take all the leaves."

They sat quietly. Colin did not want to speak. He could not keep his voice from trembling, and all the time he was short of breath. Then, after repeatedly looking at his watch, Colin stood up and began to pace backwards and forwards across the top of the mound. He peered at the darkness. Nothing moved or showed. At last he sank down upon a stone and put his head between his hands.

"It's no good," he said flatly. "The moon should have risen five minutes ago."

"Do not grieve yet," said Uthecar. "The moon will have to climb from behind the hills. Stand up, Colin: be ready."

The dwarf moved down a little way from Colin, leaving him alone at the top of the mound. There was a moment of silence, then Colin said:

"Listen. Can you hear that?"

"I hear a night-sound: that is all."

"Listen! It's music – like voices calling, and bells of ice! *And look! There's the track!*"

Suddenly through the trees and over the Beacon hill a shimmering line had flowed, a mesh of silver threads, each glistening, alive. Colin had seen something like it once before, on a rare morning when the sun had cut a path through the dewed, invisible carpet of spider's webs that covered the fields. That had been nothing to the beauty he saw now. The track quivered under his feet, and he gazed at it as though spellbound.

"Run!" called Uthecar. "Do not waste your time!"

"But which way?" cried Colin. "It stretches left and right as far as I can see!"

"To the east! To the hills! Quickly! The track will be lost when the moon passes from it! Run! Run! And fortune follow you!"

Colin leaped down the hill, and his feet were winged with silver. Trees blurred around him, once he felt Goldenstone hard beneath him, then he burst from the wood, and there was the old, straight track, dipping and flowing over the rounded fields and rising, a silver thread like a distant mountain stream, up the face of the hills to the peak of Shining Tor, and behind it the broad disc of the moon, white as an elvan shield.

On, on, on, on, faster, faster the track drew him, flowed through him, filled his lungs and his heart and his mind with fire, sparked from his eyes, streamed from his hair, and the bells and the music and the voices were all of him, and the Old Magic sang to him from the depths of the earth and the caverns of the night-blue sky.

Then the track rose before him, and he was in the hills. The moon was clear above Shining Tor. And as he sprang up the wall of the high cliff peak the path faded like a veil of smoke. Weight took his body and pulled him from the hill, but Colin cried one great cry and snatched for the cliff top: the bells were lost in the sobbing of his breath, the drumming of his blood.

He opened his eyes: rough gritstone lay against his cheek, grey in the moon. From between his fingers, clutching the rock, curled leaves, five-pointed, and beneath the hollow of his hand was a faint gleam of moonlight.

Over Wildboarclough the cone of Shuttlingslow stood apart from the long ridges, watchtower to the plain which lay like a sea from Rivington Pike to the surge of Moel Fammaw. But Colin saw none of it, for his eyes and his being were fixed on the delicate Mothan which he held cupped in his hands.

He had taken the flower and two of the leaves. The petals flickered with a cold, glow-worm light, and the fine hairs on the leaves were silver. Minutes passed: then Colin folded the Mothan gently into a leather bag that Uthecar had given him for the purpose, and looked about him.

The old, straight track had vanished, but below Shining Tor the road from Buxton began its winding drop into Macclesfield. Colin walked along the ridge to the end of the cliff, and picked his way over the rough moorland down to the road.

It was midnight. The road was strange, cold, smooth under his feet after the reed-clumps and boulders of Shining Tor. Once the flush of excitement had passed, and it had passed quickly with the climb from the hill, he felt tired – and increasingly ill at ease. The night was so still, and the road so lonely in the moonlight. But then Colin thought of Susan lying in bed at Highmost Redmanhey, and the Mothan in his pocket, and of the wonder of the evening, and his steps grew lighter.

Light steps. That was what he could hear: behind him. He stopped and listened. Nothing. Looked. The road was empty. It must be an echo, thought Colin, and he set off again. But now he was listening consciously, and soon he began to sweat.

He heard his footsteps hard on the road, and

after them an echo from the drystone wall and the hill, and through footstep and echo a pad, pad of feet, and, by the sound, the feet were bare.

He stopped. Nothing. Looked. The road was empty. But the moon threw shadows.

Colin set his teeth, and walked faster. Footstep. Echo. Footstep. Echo. Footstep. Echo. *Footstep. Echo.* He breathed again. Nerves! Nothing but – pad, pad, pad. Colin spun round. Did any shadow move?

"Who's there?" he shouted.

"Air! Air! Air!" said the hill.

"I – I can see you, you know!"

"Ho! Ho! Ho!"

It says much for Colin that he did not run. The panic was close, but he thrust it down and forced his brain to reason. How far to Macclesfield? Four miles? No point in running, then. He slowly turned, and began to walk. And although he could not go ten paces without looking back, he drew steadily away from Shining Tor. He saw nothing. But the footsteps that were never quite echoes stayed with him.

After half an hour Colin was beginning to think that he would perhaps reach the town, for whatever was following him seemed content to follow: it never shortened the distance between them. Then, approaching a sharp corner, Colin heard something that stopped him dead. It was a new sound, and it came from in front: hoofs – the sound of a horse walking slowly.

He looked behind him. Still nothing. But he

could not go back. And away from the road there was too much unknown. Yet why should he be afraid of this new sound? Colin was at such a pitch that he was afraid of his own voice. He could make no decision: he was caught.

His eyes were fixed on the road where it licked out of sight like a black tongue. The gentle clop of the hoofs seemed to go on for ever. The road would always be empty—

It was a black horse, and its rider was cloaked and wore a wide-brimmed hat.

"Albanac!"

Colin staggered forward, laughing. A touch of reality – even such reality – and the scene had changed. Colin saw himself in perspective. It was a fine night of full moon among peaceful hills, and Susan was waiting for him to bring the Mothan. From the time he had left the Beacon till now he had been on another plane of existence: it had been too much for his imagination.

"Albanac!"

"Colin! I thought you would be somewhere on the road. Have you the Mothan?"

"Yes!"

"Come, then. We'll be away to Susan."

Albanac reached down and lifted Colin into the saddle before him, and turned the horse towards Macclesfield.

"Why, Colin, you are wet and trembling. Is anything amiss?"

"No. It's just that it's all been a bit unsettling. I've had quite a time!"

"Ay, so I see."

As he said this, the horse turned its head and looked back along the road. It snorted, and its ears flattened to its skull.

Albanac twisted in the saddle. Colin, half enfolded in the cloak, could not see the road behind, but he felt Albanac's body stiffen, and heard the breath hiss through his teeth. Then the reins slapped the high neck, and the horse leapt away with all the tempest of its fairy blood, and the speed of its going drove questions back into Colin's throat, and the night filled his ears, and the cloak cracked in the wind.

Nor did Albanac stop until they came to the Riddings, and they looked down upon Highmost Redmanhey, timber and plaster magpied by the moon, and a lamp in the window of the room where Susan lay.

"Why is there a light?" said Colin.

"All is well," said Albanac. "Cadellin waits for us."

The little room was crowded. When Colin opened the door Bess cried, "Oh, wheer have you been? You shouldner have—"

"That'll do, lass," said Gowther gently. "Did you get what you went for, Colin?"

"Yes."

"And are you all reet?"

"Yes."

"Well, that's all as matters. Let's see what's to be done, then."

Colin took the flower and leaves from his pouch.

"You have run well," said Uthecar. "It is the Mothan. Give it to your sister."

"Here you are," said Colin, and handed the Mothan to Cadellin. But the wizard shook his head.

"No, Colin. This is the Old Magic: it will not bend to my mind. Let Uthecar take it: he is better skilled in this lore."

"Nay, Cadellin Silverbrow," said the dwarf. "It will not hear me. Mine is not the need. It is through Colin that it moves. Do you fold the flower within the leaves and put them in her mouth."

Colin went to the bed. He folded the Mothan tightly and opened Susan's jaws with his finger just enough to work the pellet past her teeth. Then he stood back, and for everyone the silence was like a band of steel about the head. Three minutes went by: nothing happened.

"This is daft," said Bess.

"Quiet!" said Uthecar hoarsely.

Another long silence. Colin thought he was going to collapse. His legs were trembling with the effort of concentration.

"Listen!" said Albanac.

Far away, and, if anywhere, above them, they heard a faint baying, and the deep winding of a horn. The baying grew nearer, and now there was the jingling of harness. The horn sounded again:

it was just outside the window. And Susan opened her eyes.

She stared wildly about her, as though she had been woken in the middle of a dream. Then she sat up, and pulled a face, and put her hand to her mouth. But Uthecar sprang across the room and hit Susan hard between the shoulder blades with the flat of his hand.

"Swallow it!"

Susan could not help herself. She hiccupped under the blow, and the Mothan was gone. Then Susan leapt out of bed. She ran to the window and threw it open so recklessly that the lamp was knocked into the yard below and exploded in a glare of paraffin. Susan leant out of the window, and Colin blundered across the darkened room and grabbed her by the shoulders, for she seemed intent on something that made her forget danger.

"Celemon!" she cried. "Celemon! Stay for me!"

Colin pulled her back over the sill – then clutched the frame to save himself from falling, for the shock of what he saw in the sky above the farm took his legs from under him.

He could not say if they were stars, or what they were. The sky was a haze of moonlight, and in the haze it seemed as though the stars had formed new constellations, constellations that moved, had life, and took the shape and spangled outline of nine young women on horseback, gigantic, filling the heavens. They milled around above the farm, hawks on hand, and among them pranced hounds with glittering eyes and jewelled collars. The riders wore short tunics, and their hair gleamed along the sky. Then the horn sounded again, the horses reared and flared over the plain, and the night poured shooting-stars into the western sea.

Only Colin had seen this. As he turned back to the room Bess appeared in the doorway with a lamp. Susan stood facing the window, tears on her cheek. But when light filled the room she relaxed, and sighed.

"How is it with you, Susan?" said Cadellin.

She looked at him. "Cadellin. Bess. Gowther. Uthecar. Colin. Albanac. Oh! Then what was that? I'd forgotten you."

"Sit on the bed," said Cadellin. "Tell us what you know of these past days. But first, Mistress Mossock, will you bring Susan food and drink? It is all she needs to secure her now."

This was soon done, and while she ate, Susan told her story. She spoke hesitantly, as though trying to describe something to herself as much as to anyone else.

"I remember falling into water," she said, "and everything went black: I held my breath until the pain made me let go, but just then the water rushed away from me in the dark, and – well – although the darkness was the same, I was somewhere else, floating – nowhere in particular, just backwards and forwards, and round in nothing. You know how when you're in bed at night you can imagine the bed's tilted sideways, or the room's sliding about? It was like that.

"That wasn't too bad, but I didn't like the noises. There were squeakings and gratings going on all round me – voices – no, not quite voices; they were just confused sounds; but they came from throats. Some were near and others far away. This went on for a long time, and I didn't like it. But I wasn't frightened or worried about what was going to happen to me – though I'm frightened now when I think of it! I didn't like being where I was, but at the same time I couldn't think of anywhere else that I wanted to be. And then all at once I felt a hand catch hold of my wrist and pull me upwards. There was a light, and I heard someone shouting – I think now it was Albanac – and I started to move faster than ever; so fast that I was dizzy, and the light got brighter and brighter, and it made no difference when I shut my eyes. Then I began to slow down, and the glare didn't hurt so much, and I could see the outline of the hand that was holding me. And then I seemed to break through a skin of light, and I was lying in shallow water at the edge of a sea, and standing over me was a woman, dressed in red and white, and we were holding each other's wrist and our bracelets were linked together – and Cadellin! I've just realized! Hers was the same as mine – the one Angharad gave me!"

"Ay, it would be," said the wizard quickly. "No matter: go on."

"Well, she undid her bracelet and slipped it out of mine, and we walked along the beach, and she said her name was Celemon and we were going to Caer Rigor. I didn't feel there was any need to ask questions: I accepted everything as it came, like you do in a dream.

"We joined the others who were waiting for us on a rocky headland, and we rode out above the sea towards Caer Rigor, and everyone was excited and talked of home. Then suddenly there was this bitter taste in my mouth and all the others had it, too, and no matter how hard we rode, we couldn't move forward. Celemon said we must turn back, so we did, and then I felt dizzy again, and the taste in my mouth got worse until I thought I was going to be sick, and I couldn't keep my balance, and I fell from the horse, over and over into the sea, or fog, or whatever it was. I was falling for hours, and then I hit something hard. I'd closed my eyes to stop myself from being sick, and when I opened them I was here.

"But where is Celemon? Shan't I see her again?"

"I do not doubt it," said the wizard. "Some day you will meet, and ride over the sea to Caer Rigor, and there will be no bitterness to draw you back. But everything in its time. And now you must rest."

They left Susan with Bess and went downstairs to the kitchen.

Colin was light-headed with exhaustion and bewilderment, and on the way downstairs his attempt to describe what he had seen when he had pulled Susan from the window was lost on all but Cadellin, who seemed to take it all as confirmation of his own thoughts.

"Caer Rigor," said the wizard. "Caer Rigor. Oh, we are in deep water now. Caer Rigor. It is well you found the Mothan when you did, Colin, for once there, neither the High nor the Old Magic would have brought her back.

Three times the fulness of Prydwen we went into it:
Except seven, none returned from Caer Rigor.

"That is how it is remembered in song. Ay, it is not often the Old Magic does so much good."

"What do you mean?" said Colin. "It's not Black Magic, is it? Please explain! And what happened to Sue?"

"It is difficult," said the wizard. "I would rather leave it till we have rested. But if you are bent on this, then I must tell you – though at the end you may understand less than you do now.

"No, Colin, the Old Magic is not evil: but it has a will of its own. It may work to your need, but not to your command. And again, there are memories about the Old Magic that wake when it moves. They, too, are not evil of themselves, but they are fickle, and wrong for these times."

"It is indeed so," said Albanac. "The Hunter was on the road."

"You saw him?" said Cadellin sharply.

"I saw him. He came down with Colin from

his bed on Shining Tor. He would want to know who had roused him."

"What?" said Colin. "Who's this? On the road? I heard someone following me, or I thought I did, but when I met you it all seemed so silly."

"Ay, well, perhaps it was."

"Yes, but what are you talking about?"

"An old memory," said the wizard. "No harm came of it, so no more need be said now. Let me try to explain what Susan has just told us. That is what may affect us all."

"Surely to goodness you dunner reckon much on that!" said Gowther. "It was nobbut a dream! She said so herself."

"She said it was *like* a dream," said Cadellin. "I wish I could dismiss it so: but it is truth, and I suspect there is even more than she remembers.

"The Brollachan thrust her from the one level of the world that men are born to, down into the darkness and unformed life that is called Abred by wizards. From there she was lifted to the Threshold of the Summer Stars, as far beyond this world of yours as Abred is below: and few have ever gone so far, fewer still returned, and none at all unchanged.

"She has ridden with the Shining Ones, the Daughters of the Moon, and they came with her from behind the north wind. Now she is here. But the Shining Ones did not leave Susan of choice, for through her they may wake their power in the world – the Old Magic, which has long been gone from here. It is a magic beyond our guidance: it is a magic of the heart, not of the head: it can be felt, but not known: and in that I see no good.

"And Susan was not prey of the Brollachan by chance. Vengeance was there, too.

"She was saved, and is protected, only by the Mark of Fohla – her blessing and her curse. For it guards her against the evil that would crush her, and it leads her ever further from the ways of human life. The more she wears it, the more need there is to do so. And it is too late now to take it off.

"Is that not enough, without calling the Old Magic from its sleep? I should be lighter in my heart if I knew that what you have quickened this night could as easily be laid to rest."

Colin lay awake, the day and night racing through his head, long after the wizard had gone. So much was unanswered, so much not understood, so much had been achieved – in spite of himself, he felt: he had been only a tool. But Susan was safe, Susan was – Colin sat up in bed. Beneath the open window he had heard a soft, familiar sound. Pad, pad, pad, pad, pad. He jumped out of bed and crept to the window.

The farm-house hid the yard in shadow. Colin listened, but there was now no sound. He peered – and could not choke the cry that leapt in his throat. The roof's shadow was a straight line along the bottom of the shippon wall across the yard, and above this line was the shadow of a pair of antlers, the curved, proud antlers of a stag.

At the noise the shadow moved and was lost. Pad, pad, pad. The night was silent once the footsteps had died away.

CHAPTER 9

The Horsemen of Donn

The next morning Susan appeared to be in no way the worse for all that had happened to her. She looked well and felt well. But Bess insisted on her staying in bed, and the doctor was called. She was quite put out when the doctor said he could find nothing wrong with Susan.

Days passed. The children spent most of the time discussing what each of them had seen and done. Susan found that she was rapidly forgetting what had happened to her between the fall into the quarry and her swallowing of the Mothan. It *was* like a dream; clear and more real than anything else at first, but soon lost under the more tangible flood of waking impressions. She could add little to the brief tale she had told within minutes of her return.

She was more concerned over Colin's experiences with the Brollachan, and though he gave her only an outline of what had happened, his story broke her sleep for several nights.

Colin went into more detail when trying to describe what he had seen in the sky after he had pulled Susan from the window, but he found it beyond him. The clearest picture he could give was to liken the riders and their hounds to the figures in the star-maps in an old encyclopedia at home, where the stars of the constellations formed part of the outline drawn by an artist to show that the kite of Orion was really three-quarters of a giant, and the W of Cassiopeia was a woman sitting in a chair. But none of this matched Susan's knowledge of the riders. To her, Celemon had been a normal person, as solid in her state of existence then as Colin was to her now. She could not grasp the rest.

And neither of them could make anything of the footsteps Colin had heard, nor did Gowther help when they asked him if there were any deer on the Edge.

"Why, no," he said. "Theer used to be some at Alderley Park in Lord Stanley's time, but they went years ago."

Yet what excited Susan more than anything else was Colin's finding of the old, straight track, and his journey along it to the Mothan. And when they climbed up from the Holywell late one day, and saw the Beacon mound dark in starlight above them, Susan could not pass it by.

They had been to Fundindelve at the request of Albanac to find out what Atlendor had been able to do with Susan's bracelet. It was a short answer: he had done nothing: the power was not his. Their visit had dragged into a prolonged argument about whether Susan should go north with Atlendor, and always the talk had kept swinging round from the elves to the Brollachan, both being at the front of Albanac's worries.

"For," he had said, "I do not like to leave, and

the Brollachan still loose. It is well away, but we must find it, and just now there is no finger of a road to its hiding place. Yet soon the lios-alfar must ride, and I am pledged to ride with him. That is not a choice I am wanting to make."

It had been a tiring and inconclusive discussion. But now there was the Beacon.

"Let's go up," said Susan.

"All right," said Colin. "There's not much to look at, though."

"I know. But I'd like to watch the moon rise – I suppose there's no chance of seeing the track, but I want to be there, so that I'll know how you felt; if that doesn't sound silly."

"Wait a minute," said Colin. "What about Bess and Gowther? It's late already, and it'll be another half-hour, I'd say, before the moon rises."

"They know where we are," said Susan over her shoulder. "And I don't think Gowther'll be bothered. Come on!"

Colin followed Susan up the bare slope of the Beacon, and they sat on the stone blocks at the top. He pointed out the line of the track as accurately as he could remember it. Then it was a matter of waiting for the moon, and before long the children were both bored and cold.

"Have you got a match with you?" said Susan.

"No, I don't think so."

"Well, have a look."

Colin turned out his pockets, and at the bottom of the fluff, crumbs, and balls of silver paper he found one grubby matchstick.

"Do you think it's safe to light a fire?" said Colin.

"It should be. There aren't any trees here, and this sand will stop it from spreading."

The children gathered kindling of rowan twigs, and among the trees at the bottom of the hill they found a naked, long-fallen pine, as smooth as bone.

"Don't build it too dense," said Susan, "or it won't start."

From match to twig to branch the light grew, until the pine wood spurted fire. The flames leapt high, and within seconds the whole pile roared. Colin and Susan threw the wood they had gathered on to the flames, but the more they threw, the faster the wood burnt.

"Steady," said Colin. "It'll get out of control if we don't watch it. There's too much resin in the wood."

But Susan was carried away by the urgency of the fire. She ran down to the pine tree, and began to pull on a heavier branch.

"Here, come and give me a hand, Colin! This'll make it really go."

"No!" Colin's voice was suddenly tense. "Don't put any more on. There's something wrong. I'm cold."

"It's only the wind," said Susan. "Oh, do hurry! There'll be nothing left!"

She swung all her weight on the branch, and stumbled as it broke from the trunk. Then she started to drag the branch backwards up the hill. Colin ran to her, and caught hold of her arm.

"Sue! Can't you feel it? It's not giving out any heat!"

"Who now brings fire to the mound at the Eve of Gomrath?" said a cold, thin voice behind them.

Colin and Susan turned.

The flames were a scarlet curtain between hill and sky, and within them, and part of them, were three men. At first their tall shapes and haggard faces danced and merged with the blazing pine branches, and were as unstable as any picture that the mind sees in the shadows of a fire: but even while the children looked, they became more solid, rounded, and independent of the flames through which they stared. Then they were real, and terrible.

They were dressed all in red: red were their tunics, and red their cloaks; red their eyes, and red their long manes of hair bound back with circlets of red gold; three red shields on their backs, and three red spears in their hands; three red horses under them, and red was the harness. Red were they all, weapons and clothing and hair, both horses and men.

"Who – who are you?" whispered Colin. "What do you want?"

The middle horseman stood in his saddle, and raised a glowing spear above his head.

"Lo, my son, great the news! Wakeful are the steeds we ride, the steeds from the ancient mound. Wakeful are we, the Horsemen of Donn, Einheriar of the Herlathing. Lo, my son!"

And he threw his spear high in the air. It flashed four times, and he caught it and brandished it in front of him. Then the three horsemen rose slowly out of the fire, and the flames splashed from them to the ground like red mercury. They loomed black against the glare of the hill top, but ragged beards of light still played along the heads of their spears.

"Run," said Colin to Susan.

But they were not halfway to the trees before there was a drumming of hoofs, a flutter of cloaks, and Colin and Susan were hooked off their feet by steel-sinewed arms and thrown across the necks of horses that hurled themselves through the night as though world's ruin were at their heels.

When the silver bracelet had been given to Susan by Angharad Goldenhand, she had been told that, even though she did not know the secret of its power, it would not fail her in great need. So now, when through the hammering of blood in her head and the thunder of hoofs close by her ears she gradually pulled her wits together and saw the glint of the metal in the rising moon, Susan began to flog both horse and rider with the arm that held the bracelet. But it had no effect. The rider grasped her wrist, and looked at the bracelet dispassionately: then he lifted her with one hand and set her in front of him astride the horse. He did not fear to lose her, for such was their speed that Susan clung to the mane with both hands, and gave thought neither to escape nor to further blows.

Southward from the Beacon they went, by Windmill wood and Bent's wood, past Higher House and Jenkins Hey, two miles through the night down the long back of the Edge. Then they came out upon wide parkland, and before them stood a mound, and on its top was a close group of pines.

The horsemen drew rein, and the two holding Colin and Susan came abreast of the leader. The night was suddenly still. Sheets and pennons of mist lay in the air, and the mound rose darkly through them.

The leader moved forward to the foot of the mound, raised his spear, and cast it up into the trees. As it sped it kindled from the flames that ran along the edges of the blade, and it glanced off the trunk of the nearest pine and swooped back into the red hand that had sent it.

The flames on the shaft died. But the trees were now ablaze. The fire roared and towered as it had done at the Beacon, and again there was no heat, nor did it appear to consume the trees. The voice of the rider was a sword through the deep cadence of the flames.

"Wakeful are the sons of Argatron! Wakeful Ulmrig, Ulmor, Ulmbeg! Ride, Einheriar of the Herlathing!"

A breeze stirred the mist into dancing ribbons, and the flames trembled and it seemed that there was movement within them, and voices. "We ride! We ride!" And out of the fire came three men.

Their cloaks were white, fastened with clasps of gold, and a whip was in the hand of each. Their hair was yellow, tight curled as a ram's head, and their horses white as the first snow of winter on the black mountain of the lean north wind.

As soon as they appeared, the red riders turned about and away again into the night. Colin, pinned across the neck of the last horse, glimpsed white cloaks falling into line behind.

It was a short ride, not half a mile through park and wood to Fernhill, five stark pines on its crest. Again the spear flew, again the trees blazed, and the voice called.

"Wakeful the son of Dunarth, north-king, mound-king! Wakeful is Fiorn in his hill! Ride, Einheriar of the Herlathing!"

"I ride! I ride!"

A lone figure came from the trees. His face was stern, heavy-browed, his beard plaited, two-forked, his mane black, awful, majestic. He wore a tunic of coarse hair without any cloak, and a round shield with five gold circles on it, and rivets of white bronze, hung from his neck. In his hand was an iron flail, having seven chains, triple-twisted, three-edged, with seven spiked knobs at the end of every chain. His horse was black, and golden-maned.

Now down they rode, the red and the white

549

and the wild king, over Monks' Heath, a mile to the loneliness of Sodger's Hump – the Soldier's Hump – with its ring of pines, where strange, pale lights are said to move among the trees on certain nights of winter. But now the light was one and red.

"Wakeful is Fallowman son of Melimbor! Wakeful is Bagda son of Toll! Ride, Einheriar of the Herlathing!"

"We ride! We ride!"

Round heads of black hair they had, the same length at neck and brow, and their eyes gleamed darkness. They wore long-hooded, black cowls, and carried black, wide-grooved swords, well balanced for the stroke. The horses were black, even to the tongues.

Wood and valley and stream swept by, field and hedge and lane, by Capesthorne and Whisterfield, three miles and more, Windyharbour, Withington, Welltrough, and there stood Broad hill, the Tunsted of old, and its pines flared red under the spear.

"Wakeful are the sons of Ormar! Wakeful Maedoc, Midhir, Mathramil! Ride, Einheriar of the Herlathing!"

"We ride! We ride!"

Their cloaks were blue as rain-washed sky, their yellow manes spread wide upon their shoulders: five-barbed javelins in their hands, and their silver shields with fifty knobs of burnt gold on each, and the bosses of precious stones. They shone in the night as if they were the sun's rays.

The horses' hoofs were polished brass and their hides like cloth of gold.

Now the Einheriar were complete. They turned towards Alderley and the Beacon hill, and for a long time after the tracks of the horses endured in the turf and on the rocks with the fury of the riding, and the air behind them was all aglow with little sparks.

CHAPTER 10

Lord of the Herlathing

Colin thought he was going to die. Cool waves rolled over him, shutting him off from the singing pain in his head and the one bruise of body. He could no longer cry out against the pain, for his nerves and muscles seemed to have been shaken out of all co-ordination, and he gasped as silently as a fish.

For Susan this ride to the Beacon was less hard, but her mind was dazed by the pace and shock, until the finger of the burning shone through the trees.

The riders approached the Beacon without any slackening of speed, and when they reached it they swung in a circle about the mound, and pulled their horses to a skidding halt. The leader rose slowly to the top of the mound and into the fire. He stretched his spear downwards and touched the ground with its point, and Susan had her wish. The old, straight track flowed from the spear like a band of molten steel from a furnace. But now it was not moon-silvered, as Colin had seen it, but a tumbling river of red flame-curls which darted through the wood and beyond sight.

The horseman lifted both his arms and threw back his head:

Wakeful is He in the Hill of the Dawn!
Wakeful is He to the flame of the Goloring!
From heat of the sun, and cold of the moon,
Come, Garanhir! Gorlassar! Lord of the
Herlathing!

All was quiet. No one moved. Then faintly, from a distance, there came a voice, clear, like a blend of trees and wind, rivers and starlight; nearer, nearer, chanting, wild:

And am I not he that is called Gorlassar?
Am I not a prince in darkness?
Garanhir, the torment of battle!

Where are my Reapers that sing of war
And a lance-darting trembling of slaughter;
Of the booming of shields in the cry of the sword,
The bite of the blue-headed spear in the flesh,
The thirst of the deep-drinking arrows of wrath,
And ravens red with the warring?

And away among the trees appeared the figure of a man. He came loping to the Beacon along the old, straight track, and the light played on the muscles of his body in rippling patterns of black and red. He was huge and powerful, yet with the grace of an animal; at least seven feet tall, and he ran effortlessly. His face was long and thin, his nose pointed, and nostrils flared; his eyes night-browed, up-sweeping, dark as rubies; his hair red curls; and among the curls grew the antlers of a stag.

The horseman answered him:

Swift the hoof, and free the wind!
Wakeful are we to the flame of the Goloring!
From heat of the sun, and cold of the moon,
Hail, Garanhir! Gorlassar! Lord of the
Herlathing!

Then he backed slowly from the fire, and when the runner came to the circle and sprang in a stride to the top of the mound, all the horses knelt, and the riders lifted their arms in silence.

Susan looked at him and was not afraid. Her mind could not accept him, but something deeper could. She knew what made the horses kneel. Here was the heart of all wild things. Here were thunder, lightning, storm; the slow beat of tides and seasons, birth and death, the need to kill and the need to make. His eyes were on her, yet she could not be afraid.

He stood alone and still in the cold flames, and they flowed round him and took his shape, so that he was outlined in blood, and scarlet tongues streamed upwards from the points of his antlers. He seemed to draw the light of the fire to himself; it dwindled, and the flames sank as though they were being pulled down through his flesh, and he grew, not in size, but in power, until the only light was that of the moon, and he stood black against it.

Then he spoke. "It is long since wendfire kindled the Goloring. What men had remembered the Eve of Gomrath?"

The two riders carrying the children moved forward.

Colin felt deep eyes sweep through him, and exhilaration, breathless as fear, lifted the pain from his body.

"It is good to wake when the moon stands on the hill."

Something close to laughter stirred in his voice, and he bent down and set Colin upright astride the horse's neck. Then he turned to Susan, and was about to speak, when the rider lifted Susan's arm and showed the Mark of Fohla white on her wrist. It glowed with more than reflected silver, and the black characters engraved on it trembled as though they had life.

Lightly and briefly and without a word, the dark majesty dropped on one knee and Susan's hand was taken and laid upon a cold brow. Then he rose and lifted Colin and Susan from the horses, and put them down at the top of the mound, and turned away.

"Ride, Einheriar of the Herlathing!"

"We ride! We ride!"

Turf spattered the children, and for an instant the night was a tumult of rushing darkness, and then the children were alone.

They sank down on the stones, and looked at each other. "That's – that's what I saw in the farmyard," said Colin. "That's what followed me."

"They didn't care what happened to us," said Susan blankly. "They weren't interested in us at all."

"He followed me right back to the farm."

"But perhaps it's just as well," said Susan: "I wouldn't hope for much if they thought we were in the way."

"Now was that bravely done?"

Colin and Susan jumped as the voice broke in on them. They peered in the direction from which it had come, and saw a dwarf standing under the trees.

"Uthecar!" shouted Colin, and they ran down the hill to meet him. "Uthecar?"

"Who are you?" said Susan.

The dwarf looked at them. "How shall we undo all this?" he said.

He was dressed in black, and there was a gold-hilted sword at his waist. His hair and beard were cleanly cut, and he carried himself proudly, and his voice was firm, so that the authority of his bearing removed all ill-nature from his words.

"I'm – sorry," said Colin. "What have we done wrong? Was all that our fault?"

"How was it not? None but fools would bring fire to the mound at any time; but to do so on this night of all nights of the year, and to burn wendwood! What is Cadellin thinking to let you from his sight? But come, we must see what your friends will do: it may not be too late to put them back in the mounds."

"But we'll never find them!" cried Susan. "They galloped off like the wind."

"I think they have not gone far," said the dwarf. "Let us see."

He stole away, and the children ran to keep up with him.

"But what's it all about?" said Colin. "Who were they? And who was – he?"

"The Wild Hunt. The Herlathing. That is what you have sent out on us. It was enough to rouse the Hunter; he alone would have taken some laying. But now that the Einheriar ride after him we shall have to act quickly, or wide numbers will go to sleep with light in their eyes, and only the raven will find profit! But quiet now: I think we are on them."

They had come to a cliff-top over a valley. The dwarf crawled to the edge and looked down. Colin and Susan joined him, but although they could hear movement at the foot of the cliff they could see nothing, for the rock overhung the ground below. They crawled along to where the cliff fell away to a sloping bank, and from this bank they could see clearly.

They were at the Holywell, and the second gate of Fundindelve. Along the path that ran past the well the Einheriar were drawn in line, and at the well, his antlers nearly level with the children's faces, was Garanhir, the Hunter. He held a cup of some white metal, and the riders took it one after the other and drank deeply, then lifted it and poured the last drops over their heads, and moved on.

For each rider Garanhir stooped and filled the cup from the well, and the water gleamed as the old, straight track had done at the touch of the spear, and all the marsh below shone red.

The dwarf worked back from the edge, and beckoned the children to follow him. He took them round the head of the valley and along the opposite ridge to where they could watch the silhouettes of the Einheriar against the dim glow.

"We are too late," said the dwarf. "Now that they have drunk at the well this is wizard's work. Beard of the Dagda! Are we to talk until all that ever slept is woken? Which may happen yet, for once the Old Magic moves, it moves deeply – even without the help of wendfires!

"Listen: do you see where we are now? Over the ridge behind us are the iron gates; have you the opening of them?"

"Yes – I think so," said Susan.

"Then go to Cadellin: tell him that the Einheriar ride. We shall keep watch here."

"All right."

Susan disappeared, and a few minutes later the ground quivered under their feet, and the skyline of the ridge was tinged with blue. Colin turned back to look at the Holywell. Although the light was not good, he could tell that the riders were milling together, and he could hear hoofs stamping restlessly.

"I think they're going," said Colin. "What shall we do?"

A dry scrape of metal answered him. He glanced over his shoulder, and saw the moon pale on the gold-hilted sword as it came from its sheath, and pale in the eyes behind the sword.

"We shall walk," said the dwarf.

As she entered the tunnel, Susan thought she heard Colin shout, but the noise of the rock and clang of the gates drowned his voice, if it was his voice, and when the echoes had died there was only silence thudding in her ears. Susan hesitated: her hand reached out to the gates; then she told herself that if anything had begun to happen there was even more need to find Cadellin quickly, so she turned and ran down the tunnel.

This was the long approach to the wizard's cave: the whole labyrinth of Fundindelve lay between, and soon she realized that she did not know the way. In the tunnels her footsteps and breathing enclosed her in waves, but unnerving as this was, the blue-hazed infinity of the caverns was worse.

At last she was forced to rest, and while she leant, trembling, against a cave wall, her reason overcame her urgency, and from that moment she started to use her eyes. Even so, an hour had passed since she had left Colin before Susan found a tunnel that she knew, and it was another ten minutes before she reached the cave.

Uthecar and Albanac were with the wizard.

"What is it, Susan?" said Albanac, jumping to his feet.

"Einheriar! – Einheriar! – the Hunter!"

"The Einheriar?" said Cadellin. "How do you know—?" He whirled round, and began to run up the short tunnel that led to the Holywell.

"Wait!" called Susan. "They're just outside!"

The wizard took no notice of her, and after him raced Albanac, a stride ahead of Uthecar. By the time Susan reached the well they were all standing on the path, the dwarf studying the ground, and Cadellin looking out over the plain. The light had gone from the water, and the woods were silent. But then Uthecar said:

"They were here, and it was so."

"And they have drunk of the well," said Albanac.

"We must find them," said Cadellin, "though I doubt if they will be compelled to the mounds. It is bad."

"It is worse," said Uthecar. "I am thinking that this is the Eve of Gomrath – and I smell wendfire."

"It cannot be!" cried the wizard.

"I – I'm afraid we did it," said Susan. "We lit a fire on top of the Beacon. That's what started it all. They came out of the fire."

"Why should you light a fire there?" said Cadellin in a voice that made Susan want to run.

"We were waiting for the moon to rise – and – we were – cold."

The wizard shook his head. "It is my fault,"

560

he said to Albanac. "I should have been stronger in my purpose. Come: we lose time. We must find their track."

"Colin will know which way they went," said Susan. "They were keeping watch on here from across the valley."

" 'They'?" said the wizard.

"Yes," said Susan. "He and the dwarf: they're just this side of the iron gates."

"What dwarf?" said Uthecar. "There are no others here."

"Yes there is," said Susan. "He's dressed in black, and – "

"Take us," broke in Uthecar. "And waste no breath."

Susan felt a coldness in her heart. She set off along the path, and did not speak until she reached the spot where she had left Colin.

"Where are they?" She knew it was a useless question. "What's happened?"

"Dressed in black, was he?" said Uthecar. "And was there a golden hilt to his sword?"

"Yes: and his belt, and the straps below his knee were gold, too."

"Do you know him?" said Cadellin.

"Know him? Ha! Know yon viper? I know him! But what has brought him south from Bannawg I will not guess, save that it is no good thing. For I tell you this: though you looked, you would not find from sea to sea a worse dwarf than Pelis the False."

CHAPTER 11

The Dale of Goyt

"There is a mind at work against these children," said Cadellin. "So much is certain."

They had returned to the wizard's cave, and were sitting at the long table. Atlendor had joined them.

"But what can we do?" said Susan.

"Think, and hope," said Cadellin.

"I would rather seek and find," said Uthecar. "Work your magic, Cadellin Silverbrow, but there may be more use of eyes and blades. Pelis is not here, and where he is, there I would be; for I am thinking the death of him is in my sword."

"Then go," said Cadellin. "But take care in the night."

The dwarf rose from the table, and was about to enter the tunnel when Atlendor spoke. "Uthecar Hornskin, you will not go alone. It is on me to go with you."

"As you wish," said Uthecar shortly, and dwarf and elf left the cave together.

"Their swords will be about their own ears," said Cadellin, "if danger does not unite them.

"Now, Susan, rest here. I must leave you for a while: but Albanac will stay."

"But I couldn't!" said Susan. "I must do something to find Colin."

"If Atlendor and Uthecar cannot find him," said the wizard, "then you will not, and all that is left is magic."

"I can't stay here and do nothing!"

"Susan! There is danger for you outside Fundindelve. You *must* stay here."

"But Bess'll be nearly out of her mind!"

"I am glad you think of her," said Cadellin. "Do you see the pain you cause by meddling in our world? I must speak to farmer Mossock now and tell him that you will not go home until this matter is settled. I cannot hope that he will be persuaded, but you have left me no other choice."

And though Susan argued, Cadellin remained firm, and both were angry when the wizard left the cave.

"I can't stay cooped up here!" said Susan. "I've got to get out and find Colin!"

Albanac passed his hand over his face. He looked exhausted.

"There is nothing we can do now, Susan. We may need all our strength later, so try to sleep. I know that I am spent."

"But I've got to get out!"

"And how long is it since you were eating your heart away to get in?" said Albanac. "If you cannot sleep, then sit here, and talk."

Susan flung herself on to the bed of skins, and for some minutes was too choked with frustration to talk. But there were so many questions in her mind that this could not last.

"Albanac, who is the Hunter? And what did we do?"

"He is part of the Old Magic," said Albanac. "And though Cadellin may not agree, I think that what you did was not brought about by chance. The Old Magic has been woken, and it has moved in you, and I think it led you to the Beacon.

"In the time before the Old Magic was made to sleep, it was strongest on this night, the Eve of Gomrath, one of the four nights of the year when Time and Forever mingle. And wendfire was lit at the Goloring, which is now the Beacon, to bring the Einheriar from the mounds and the Hunter from Shining Tor. For the Old Magic is moon magic and sun magic, and it is blood magic, also, and there lie the Hunter's power and his need. He is from a cruel day of the world. Men have changed since they honoured him."

"You keep saying the Old Magic has been woken," said Susan, "but if it's as strong as this, how did it ever come to die out?"

"That is the work of Cadellin," said Albanac. "To wizards, and their High Magic of thoughts and spells, the Old Magic was a hindrance, a power without shape or order: so they tried to destroy it. But it would not be destroyed: it would only sleep. And at this season called Gomrath, which lasts for seven nights, it sleeps but lightly."

"So there's nothing bad about it at all," said Susan. "It just got in the way."

"Yes. You may even say the wizards acted without right. But then, as ages pass, the world changes; so it is true that the Old Magic is wrong for these times. It does not fit the present scale of good and ill."

"But it's more natural than all these spells," said Susan. "I think I understand it better than anything here."

Albanac looked up. "You would say that. For it is woman's magic, too, and the more I see, the more I know that the Mark of Fohla is part of it."

"What does the Hunter do? What's he for?"

"Do? He *is*, Susan: that is enough. There you see the difference between the Old and the High. The High Magic was made with a reason; the Old Magic is a part of things. It is not *for* any purpose."

Susan could feel the truth of what Albanac had said, although she could not understand it. She thought again of Colin. If only she had stopped when she heard him shout. Pelis the False.

"Albanac?"

"Mm?"

She rolled over to look. Albanac was sitting with his head resting on his arms.

"Nothing; it's all right."

Susan listened as Albanac's breathing grew deeper. He was asleep.

And there's nobody else here, she thought. That tunnel goes straight to the Holywell. What was it? Emalagra?

She moved quietly round the table, and tested every step until she reached the wall behind the well. She laid her hand on the long crack in the rock, and spoke the word of power.

The grinding of the rock echoed down the tunnel, and Susan forced herself through the opening as soon as it was wide enough to take her shoulder. Then she ran.

Uthecar and Atlendor sat in the moonlight on the wooden bench on Castle Rock, an outcrop that stood from the trees high above the plain.

"He is not in the wood," said Uthecar. "And from here the world is wide."

"If he is not in the wood," said Atlendor, "think you he may be under it?"

"Is it that the lios-alfar have cunning?" said Uthecar. "For that is just what Pelis the False would be about! He knows we shall search, and far. Where better to hide than where he was last seen? There are places close on Saddlebole beyond the iron gates; quickly!"

They sped through the woods, past the Holywell, past the spot where Colin and the dwarf had vanished, past the iron gates, to a hollow above a dark slope of beeches. Here there were many recesses, and caves, and cramped tunnels into the rock. Atlendor drew his sword, and approached one of the tunnels. It was so blocked at the entrance that even he would have to worm his way in.

"Nay," said Uthecar, "you have not the eyes for it! If he is there, cold death is your destiny."

"But I have the nose for it," said Atlendor. "The cave that holds a dwarf is not to be mistaken."

"To it, then," said Uthecar.

He stood back, his eye glinting savagely, and watched the elf's hips slide into the opening.

"It goes some way into the hill," called Atlendor, "and there is not space to wield a sword. The air is foul, certain, but I doubt that he is here."

Uthecar swore an oath, and turned away in rage. And as he did so, he had a glimpse of a snarling, fanged, red mouth, and eyes of green fire set in a broad head, with short ears bristling sideways from the flat top of the skull, and of white claws hooked at him, and all hurtling towards him through the air. Without thought his arms flew to protect his face, and then he was knocked spinning by a glancing blow. As he staggered to gain his balance, Uthecar saw that he was not the immediate object of the attack, for the furred shape was already halfway into the opening through which Atlendor had passed. There was not time to draw sword. Uthecar sprang forward, and just managed to get both hands to the short, bushy tail as the flanks disappeared.

It felt as though he was holding a half-released spring of irresistible power. Uthecar planted his legs on either side of the hole, and threw himself

567

backwards. The hind feet lashed at him, but he avoided them, and by swinging from side to side he managed to keep them from winning fresh purchase in the ground. This just about made the struggle equal, but he knew that he could not hold out for long. And Atlendor's muffled, but critical, voice did not help. He was obviously unaware of what was happening.

"One-eyed Hornskin! Who blocks the hole?"

"If the rump-tail – should – break," shouted Uthecar, "your throat – will know that!"

Uthecar's shoulders felt as though they were being torn from his back, and the power to grip was leaving his wrists. There had been no reply from Atlendor.

Then the body kicked under him, and went limp, and before he could prepare himself, all resistance went, and he fell backwards, pulling a dead weight on top of him.

Uthecar picked himself up, and looked at the body at his feet. It was a wild-cat, well over three feet long, and it had been stabbed through the throat. Atlendor stood by the tunnel, wiping his sword on a handful of grass.

"A palug," said Uthecar. "I am thinking that there is too much in these woods that has come from beyond Bannawg."

Every time Colin stumbled, the sword jabbed in his ribs. The pace that the dwarf demanded was not easy to keep over such ground at night. Nor would the dwarf allow him to speak; an extra

568

jab was the answer as soon as Colin opened his mouth.

They came to Stormy Point, and here the dwarf stopped, and whistled softly. A voice replied from across the rocks, and the sound of it made Colin's skin crawl; for it was cold, and deeply pitched, and hard to place, whether animal or not. Then at the edge of the trees something moved, and began to come towards Colin and the dwarf. It was a wild-cat, and behind it were others. More and more they came from the trees, until the ground was so thick with them that it seemed to be covered with a rippling coat of hair.

The cats milled round Colin and stared at him. He was surrounded by pale green stones of light. The dwarf sheathed his sword. A number of the cats grouped about Colin as an escort: they pressed close, but did not touch him. The remainder broke, and disappeared into the trees, spreading widely to kill pursuit.

From Stormy Point Colin ran until they were clear of the wood. He had no choice: or rather, he had, but the hissing that threatened behind him, and the eyes that were turned on him, every time his pace slackened, made him choose quickly. But once they were in the fields the dwarf relaxed to a walk, and the loping jog of the wild-cats became a smooth carpet of movement.

All through the night they travelled eastwards under the waning moon. They went by Adders' Moss, past Withenlee and Harehill, to Tytherington, and then into the hills above Swanscoe, up and down across ridges that swelled like waves: by Kerridge and Lamaload, Nab End and Old-gate Nick, and down Hoo Moor above the Dale of Goyt: mile after mile of killing ground, bare of all trees and broken only by gritstone walls. And then, deep at the bottom of the moor, they came to a small, round hill on which rhodo-dendron bushes grew thickly; and about the hill curved a track.

They followed the track into the rhododen-drons; far below on their right a stream sounded. Above the track were what looked like the remains of terracing, overgrown, forgotten. Colin, whose angry fear had long been smothered by exhaustion, grew increasingly more uneasy: there was something here, in this rank garden set in the hills, that was not good.

The track divided, and the cats drove Colin to the left-hand fork. It ran level for a few yards, and then made a sharp bend, and as he rounded this, Colin stopped, in spite of the cats.

Before him, on a terraced lawn, was a house, big, ugly, heavy, built of stone. The moon shone palely on it, yet the light that came from the round-arched windows and the open door seemed to be moonlight, also.

"We are home," said the dwarf. It was the first time that he had spoken for several hours.

The cats moved forward, and at that instant a cloud slid over the moon. "Stay!" cried the dwarf.

But Colin had pulled up short of his own

accord. For as the moon disappeared, the light inside the house faded. Now the house lay barely visible against the hill behind it, yet what was to be seen made Colin stare. It could have been a trick of the darkness, but somehow the building had lost its form, had slumped. Surely that was the sky through one of the windows: he could see a star. And then the cloud passed, and the moon shone on the house, and the windows threw light on to the grass.

The dwarf drew his sword. "Now run," he said, and he pushed Colin towards the house. The cats surged forward, bearing him with them through the door.

Colin found himself in an entrance hall, cold in the shadowless light. In front of him was a wide stone staircase, and from the top of the staircase a harsh voice spoke.

"Welcome. Our teeth have long rusted seeking *your* flesh!"

Colin recognized the voice. He did not have to look at the woman who was coming down the stairs to know that she was the Morrigan.

She was heavily built, her head was broad, and it squatted on her shoulders, and her mouth was wide, and as cruel as her eyes. She wore a robe so deeply blue that it was black, and it was tied with a scarlet cord. The cats made way for her, and fawned after her as she moved across the floor towards Colin.

"No. We are so far in your debt that nothing of you shall escape from the place into which you have come, save what birds will take away in their claws."

She put out a hand to fondle one of the cats, and Colin saw that she wore a bracelet. In design it was identical with Susan's, but its colours were reversed: the characters here were a pallid silver, and the bracelet itself was black.

CHAPTER 12

The Mere

Uthecar and Atlendor sat in the wizard's cave and cleaned their wounds. "It is not I that will be going out again this night," said the dwarf. "If Susan has stepped through the gates then if we found anything of her it would not be worth the finding. There is a palug in every tree! We had to kill a score to win from Saddlebole to the gates."

Both he and the elf were gashed with deep wounds, and their clothes were in strips.

"She has the Mark: that may keep her," said Albanac. "I must go to look for her."

"But *you* have not the Mark," said Uthecar. "If Susan has lived until now, she will have shown herself unneedful of us. If you must seek, then wait until day. Ride now, and palug teeth will meet in your neck."

The noise of the opening rock had made Susan lose her nerve. She thought Albanac would be only seconds behind her, and with no idea of where she should look for Colin, she ran blindly, taking no notice of way or distance. Somewhere in the wood she stopped for breath. All the while, urgency had pounced on her back, and every step had seemed to be made a fraction of a second and an inch ahead of a seizing hand. Now she stopped, and the air quietened round her and lost its pursuit: she could almost hear it rustling to a halt about her. But this was not imagination: there *had* been a quick dying of movement into silence, and now Susan felt that the night was bearing down on one point, and that point was herself.

She tried to reason, but that was useless, since all reasoning could tell her was that she had no chance of finding Colin. And the concentration in the air throbbed like plucked strings. Susan stared so hard all around her that the blackness seemed to be spotted with light – pale flecks of green; and then she noticed that, instead of swimming in rainbow patterns, as such lights do when the eyes strain against darkness, these lights did not change colour, but were grouped close to the ground, motionless, *in pairs*. They were eyes. She was surrounded by a field of green, unwinking, hard eyes – every one fixed on her.

The cats closed in. Now Susan could see them as individuals: there were two or three dozen of them, and they walked stifflegged and bristling. Susan was too frightened to move, even as they approached, until one of the cats hissed, and lunged at her with its claws. Before she had time to realize that the blow would not have touched her, Susan jumped in the opposite direction, and here the cats gave way and made a green passage for her, and their intention was plain. She found that she could move freely where they wished her to go, but if she veered from that line or tried to stop, claws were unsheathed.

She knew that whatever the danger was that Cadellin had feared, these cats were part of it: there was too much intelligence in their movements for them to be ordinary cats, and that was the least strange aspect of them.

So for a while, just as had happened earlier with Colin, Susan was herded through the wood. The cats did not touch her, but they walked close, and urged her to run: and this eagerness showed Susan her weapon against them.

She had been stumbling at nearly every step in the flat and broken moonlight, but it was a particularly violent twist of her ankle that threw her sideways, right off balance. She flung out a hand to break her fall – and the cats leapt away from the hand as though from a burning coal. Susan crouched on her knees and looked at the circle of cats: it took some time for her to absorb this new fact consciously: she stretched out her wrist, and they fell back, spitting. They were afraid of the Mark. She stood up, and took the bracelet off her wrist, and gripped it so that it formed a band across her knuckles, then she stepped forward, swinging her hand in front of her in a slow arc. The cats gave way, though they snarled, and twisted their heads from side to side, and their eyes flashed hate.

Susan had no idea of where she was, but the best direction seemed to be back the way they had come. So slowly she turned about, and began to walk; and the cats let her pass, though they flanked her as closely as before. The difference was that the choice belonged to Susan.

Now it was a matter of fighting every step, because the cats did not give an inch willingly, and if Susan could have found the strength to hold out mentally against all that was concentrated on her, she would no doubt have been able to reach Fundindelve unharmed. But although the physical compulsion had gone, the malice ate into her will: and she was very frightened, and alone. The first swell of triumph had soon collapsed. Cadellin seemed much less unreasonable than she had judged him to be a short time ago.

Susan held out for perhaps half an hour, and in that time she had gained less than a mile – not long or far, but it was as much as she could stand. The strain was too great. Thrusting the Mark in front of her, she plunged forward, with no other aim beyond immediate escape from the pressure of those eyes. And, of course, she did not escape. The cats bounded after her, no longer milling round her, but streaming close, almost driving her, anywhere, it did not matter, as long as it was faster, and faster, blindly through the wood, waiting for their moment, and it came.

Susan was running so wildly that only luck kept her upright, but that could not save her when she came to the top of a rise and the ground ended under her feet. She fell little more than her own height on to a wide path, but she fell awkwardly and with the force of her running, and sprawled headlong. The Mark flew from her grip, and bowled across the sand towards the far edge of the path.

Susan scrambled after it, but she was too late. Below the path the hill fell steeply to the plain in a scree of pebbled sand and boulders, and already the bracelet was gathering speed down the slope. Susan looked over her shoulder, and did not pause. The cats were ten yards away, and there was something in them that told her that they had forgotten their original purpose, and wanted only revenge. She leapt down the scree after her bracelet, so intent upon it that she ignored the pitch of the slope: and after a few steps her weight began to run away with her. Her legs scissored into strides, each one raking longer than the last, her feet as heavy as pendulums. She tried to lean backwards, but she could not control her body at all. And the Mark of Fohla drew away from her, travelling faster than she was, and increasing its speed, dancing over the stones: and then it hit a boulder, and sprang into the air, and at the peak of the bound it stopped, and hung, spinning, but did not fall.

At first the bracelet was a clean band of silver, catching the moon, but then it began to thicken raggedly into white fire like a Catherine-wheel. The fire grew broader, and there was now no bracelet, but a disc of light with a round black centre that had been the space enclosed by the bracelet, and the disc grew until it filled all Susan's vision, and as the last rim of night disappeared it seemed that the edges of the fire came towards her and the black middle receded, though it did not diminish in size, so that instead of a disc it was now a whirling tunnel, and Susan was rushing helplessly into it.

The ground vanished from under her feet, and she ran, still out of control, but the swinging weight had gone from her legs. The tunnel spun about her, so that she felt she was running on the roof and on the walls as often as on the floor. She ran timelessly, but the black circle in front of her, which gathered the perspective to itself, and so appeared to mark the end of the tunnel, slowly began to increase in size, and the blackness was no longer even, but speckled with grey. The contrast grew with the circle, and colours started to emerge, and Susan was looking at trees, and water, and sunlight. Then the circle was bigger than the fire, and soon it was a complete picture fogged with silver at the edges, and that thinned like dawn mist, and Susan ran out of the tunnel on to grass. She stopped, breathless, and looked about her.

She realized at once where she was: she was standing on an island, thick with trees, in the middle of Redesmere, a stretch of water that lay four miles to the south of Alderley. But it was now day, and by the warmth of the air, and the glint of light on the water, the song of birds, and the green on the trees across the lake, it was summer, too.

Something nearly as strange had brought her

to this island once before, and it was then that she had first put on the bracelet. Her heart lightened as she looked round for the person she knew she would find – Angharad Goldenhand, the Lady of the Lake. And there was Angharad, standing among the trees, tall, slender, dressed in long robes, her hair the colour of gold, her skin white as the snow of one night, her cheeks smooth and even and red as foxgloves: and in her hand was Susan's bracelet.

CHAPTER 13

The Bodach

Angharad smiled. "It is time for you to know more of your place in these things," she said, and she fastened the bracelet on Susan's wrist. "Come with me."

She took Susan by the hand, and they went through the trees to a clearing, and there they sat down. Susan felt the burden of loneliness slip from her as Angharad spoke, for Angharad knew all that had happened; there was no need for Susan to explain.

"Little of this is chance," she said, "for good or evil, and on your shoulders it may all lie."

"Mine?" said Susan. "But why me?"

"Firstly, all your danger rests with the Morrigan."

"The Morrigan?"

"Yes: she is here, and revenge fills her heart. It will be long before she is restored to her old power, but even now she is a threat to the world, and all her will is turned against you. She has Colin at this moment, and will use him to destroy you, if she can. For the Mark of Fohla is a protection against her, though it will not always be so."

"But why *me*? Why do *I* matter?" said Susan. "I don't know anything about magic. Why can't you or Cadellin deal with her?"

"When you put on the Mark you put on a destiny," said Angharad. "That is what Cadellin feared. And at this time through you alone can we work most surely. For, you see, this is moon magic, and we wear a part of it." She held out her wrist, and Susan saw a white bracelet there. "Our power waxes, and wanes: mine is of the full moon, the Morrigan's is of the old. And the moon is old now, so she is strong."

"Then how do I fit in?" said Susan.

"You are young, and your bracelet is the young moon's. Then you can be more than the Morrigan, if you have courage. I am able to put you on the road now, and help you guard against the Morrigan while the moon is old, but that is all. What do you say? Will you help?"

"Of course I will. I've no choice, really, have I?" said Susan. "*She*'ll still be after me, whatever happens, and Colin won't stand a chance."

"That is so," said Angharad. "Revenge was great in her, but now, if not before, she will know that you wear the Mark. The new moon is always her fear, and at this time above all, for it will be the moon of Gomrath, when our magic was strongest in the world, and may be yet again.

"The Morrigan will try to destroy you before you take on the power. You must carry war to her now, and hold her. If you succeed, she may never be a threat to us. If you fail, she may grow beyond confining.

"Now take this." Angharad gave Susan a leather belt. From it hung a small, curved horn, white as ivory, and the mouthpiece and the rim were of chased gold.

"She in her art will call on other power, and you will have little. So take this horn: it is the third best thing of price that was ever won, and is called Anghalac. Moriath gave it to Finn, and Finn to Camha, and Camha to me. Blow it if all else is lost, but only then. For once Anghalac sounds you may not know peace again, not in the sun's circle nor in the darkling of the world.

"Remember: only – if – all – else – is – lost – "

"I – shall – " said Susan.

The magic was ending. The island swung away from her into sleep. Angharad's last words came out of a distance, and echoed in her head: she could not stay awake: her mind sank into darkness beyond the reach of dreams. . .

Susan listened to the water for a long time before she opened her eyes. Its sound brought her gently awake, and then she turned on to her back, and looked at the stars. She was on the bank of a river, which ran along the bottom of a valley among high and barren hills. Yet close by her was a stone gateway, and beyond it a drive led into a coomb of trees.

There was a road by the water, but Susan was drawn to the coomb. Road, valley, and sky were lifeless, but the gate was odd beyond the fact of its being there at all. She examined it closely: it was of iron, chained, and padlocked, and all were sharp with rust.

Susan climbed over the gate, and began to walk

up the drive. On her left a stream went down to the river, and after a few yards rhododendron bushes closed in. The drive was straight, and had once been broad, but the rhododendrons had run wild in neglect, and the drive was now a thread of sand that picked up faintly the yellow of the lop-sided moon.

The water gurgled behind the bushes, and was the only sound, and that deepened as the pathway rose above the trench that the stream had cut through the rock; and everywhere the rhododendrons suffocated the valley. Their mass hung over Susan like a threat: she felt that all those millions of leaves, each acrid, leathery, breathing, alive, were piled into one green-celled body, that together they had an awareness that was animal. This may have been only imagination, but the effect on her was that every sense became sharpened, and she moved as delicately as a wild creature, avoiding twigs and loose stones almost unconsciously, never doubting that she was near to Colin.

Twice the path crossed the stream, and here there were stone bridges with crumbling parapets. The second of these bridges was almost half a mile up the drive from the gate, and by this time Susan had reached a fine pitch of awareness. Her eyes used every mote of light, and she could see all that was on the path, and as much of the borders as the rhododendrons allowed. The second bridge stood at a fork in the valley: in the fork was a bush-covered hill, and the stream and

583

a tributary flowed on either side of it, becoming one at the bridge. The path continued up the left-hand arm of the valley, and standing close to the bridge, in the shadow of the rhododendrons, unmoving, was what looked like a man.

He held a spear and a small, round shield. The light caught the dome of his head, and touched his chest and shoulders, but the rest of him was in shadow: and he was so still that Susan could not be sure that he was not a piece of eccentric statuary.

Susan watched him, or it, for several minutes, and not once was there a tremor of life to help her make up her mind. There was no question of turning back: she knew that she must go on at all costs, and that the risk was too great to chance walking past the figure at the bridge.

There was no point in trying to force a way through the bushes: the only alternative was the stream, which at this spot was not far below the path. Susan moved back until she was out of sight of the bridge, and then she lowered herself down the bank and into the water.

The stream was quite shallow, but very rocky, and sometimes there were pools into which Susan fell waist-deep. She could not walk silently, but the rattle of the water over the boulders covered any noise Susan made, and she kept close against the bank, where the shadows were thick. The bridge itself was the worst part. It was low, and the air stank of slime, and Susan fell against things that moved away from her in the darkness.

Once clear of the bridge, she found that the banks grew higher and steeper, but she continued for another hundred yards or so before daring to leave the water. The bank here was nearly vertical, and consisted of wet leaf-mould and earth. Eight or nine times Susan clawed her way up to within feet of the broken terrace-work that supported the path, only to fall back in the wake of a land-slide. But at last she got her shoulders on to the path, and managed to pull herself up.

The drive was now its original width, and a few yards further on, a branch curled away to the right. Susan paused, wondering whether to continue uphill, but she decided to explore the branch at least as far as the bend.

She moved as quietly as ever, but all her wariness could not stop the gasp that came from her when she saw what was beyond the turn of the bend.

The path bordered a terraced lawn, approached by steps, and on the lawn was a mansion of stone, built in the heavy Italian style of the last century. All the windows glowed with a light that was stronger than the moon, but of the same quality, and lifeless.

Susan knew that this was what she was meant to find. This was the heart of the evil. The Morrigan was here – and so was Colin. Susan started towards the house, and then halted. No, she thought. I don't know where to look, or what to do. She'll probably have us both. I've got to let

Cadellin know she's here: he'll be able to deal with her.

Above the door of the house was a square tower, and as if to confirm Susan's thoughts, a figure appeared in one of the arched windows of the tower. It was the Morrigan. She stared down at the lawn, and although Susan was in shadow she felt as if a strong light was on her, and it took all her control to stand quite still while the Morrigan looked out at the night. When she moved away from the window, Susan crept back along the drive.

The house had frightened her. Why me? she thought. Why couldn't Angharad tell Cadellin? She must have known. "On your shoulders it may all lie," that's what she said. Well, she might have told me more about it. *I* don't know any magic, and those that do are scared of the Morrigan, so I'd not be much use in there by myself. I've got to find Cadellin.

Susan had reached the junction of the paths. She could turn left, down the valley, or continue climbing to the right. She did not want to negotiate the bridge again, for now she was certain that whatever was guarding it was not ornamental sculpture. But then where was she? And in which direction was Alderley? She found her bearings with the help of the Plough: the uphill path ran nearly due west. Which is the right way if I'm in the Pennines, she thought, but not much good if this is Wales. But if it *is* Wales, I'm forty miles from Alderley, so it'd better be the Pennines. She set off up the hill.

The path continued as before, but not for long. The rhododendron tangle ended, and in front of Susan was an empty gateway in a stone wall, and beyond this, open ground fell gently for a distance, and then reared to a whale-backed ridge of mountain that dwarfed the world. It made Susan's knees weak and her head spin to look at it. But, beyond the ridge, she hoped, was the plain, and Alderley: and at least there were no rhododendrons.

Susan stepped through the gateway, and as she did, someone rose out of the shadow of the wall. In the open light she could see him clearly now, whether he was the same that had guarded the bridge or another guarding the wall. He was not quite as tall as Susan. His head was bald and smooth, and his ears were pointed, the eyes almond-shaped, glowing, and the nose was hooked and thin. His spear was like a leaf, and his body was covered with flat locks of hair, dense as scales.

Susan stood rooted with shock, and could not move even when the man reached out and gripped her by the arm. But the cry that broke from the wide mouth then released her muscles. For as he touched her, the Mark had shone fire, and a white flame had streaked up her arm and cut at the hand like a whiplash. The man dropped against the wall, and did not move again.

Susan ran from the gate down to the open

moor, but she was hardly at the foot of the mountain when there was a shout, and, looking round, she saw another armed man leap over the wall in pursuit.

But was he a man? There was something wrong in the way of his running. He was quick and lizard-dry over the grass: his legs raked forward in pecking strides, and the knee joint seemed to be reversed, while below the knee the leg was thin, and the feet were taloned.

Susan had a fifty-yard lead, but she was climbing while the other was still on the downward slope. She scrambled upwards, trying to keep some energy in reserve, but she was driven by the need for escape.

A spear sighed over her shoulder, and stood out of the ground. This pursuer was not going to risk closer contact. Susan thought to pluck up the spear and use it against its owner, but she could not bring herself to face him, nor to use it, nor even to touch it. So again and again she ran on, renewing her lead while the spear was retrieved, and watching for the next throw.

She came to a group of dead trees that stood gnarled on the hillside, and she lurched through them from trunk to trunk, grateful for their slight protection. But she was so spent that when she stumbled she could not get up. She twisted herself round, her back against a tree, instinctively facing the danger.

The creature was on the fringe of the trees, running with the spear held high. He wavered a moment, searching in the poorer light, then came on. And as he passed the first tree, part of the crooked bole seemed to detach itself and rise up before him, and there was a long gleam of light that shortened and disappeared under his ribs. He screamed, and fell.

"So it is bodachs we have now!" said a disgusted voice. "Is there no end to the garbage of Bannawg?"

CHAPTER 14

The Wild Hunt

Uthecar turned to Susan. "Before this night, Cadellin thought you dead; I am doubting if you would prove him wrong."

"Uthecar!" cried Susan. "How have you got here?"

"Is it not enough that I am here?" said the dwarf. He pulled Susan to her feet. "For the bodach loves steep ground more than a hare of the mountain. The irondeath would have been yours by now – and that may be yet: a bodach dead, and not quietly. It would have been wiser to take his head, but your bodach is swift in thrusting the spear, and it is a long sweep that must open his throat, for it is hard as a bull's hide."

Uthecar and Susan began to climb the hill together. They walked, since Uthecar knew that there was nearly a thousand feet of moor above them, and if they were going to be followed, running would not save them.

They could not see the house from the moor, and as they climbed, the valley of rhododendrons shrank to a dark line, and then fell below the curve of the hill.

Uthecar made Susan tell him what she had

seen before he would give any explanation of his presence among the dead trees.

"But how did *you* find out where the Morrigan is?" said Susan. "You've been very quick."

"Not as quick as you are thinking," said Uthecar. "It was last night that Colin was taken."

"But it can't have been!" said Susan. "Everything's happened so fast! It was only about four or five hours ago!"

"It was not," said Uthecar. "You have been under enchantment on the island of Angharad Goldenhand. Earth-time is not there: years could have passed: it is the magic of the Lady that made it but a day and a night.

"As for me, that is simple. After moonrise Pelis the False came to Fundindelve, and spoke before the gates, saying that if you were not ready to go with him tomorrow, and your bracelet in his care, he would send Colin back to us, a little at a time.

"At first I thought to spill his pride in dark waves upon the ground, but that will come: first let us hurt his advantage. So Albanac kept him in talk, and I went out by the Holywell, and when he left I followed him here. But that valley is thick with dread, and much of it will not be answered with the sword. So we shall bring Cadellin, and while he traffics with the Morrigan I shall test the nature of Pelis the False, though I tread through a sea of bodachs to his heart."

They were high on the mountain: the world was empty. Susan and Uthecar moved over the heather, specks in the tarnished light.

"What are these – bodachs?" said Susan.

"The sweepings of Bannawg," said Uthecar. "They are kin to goblins, but they have more heart – I will not say courage. The scream of blades is their only love, and if they are thick about the Morrigan we shall not win Colin easily. Will you be climbing faster?"

An edge came into his voice at this question.

"Why? What's wrong?" said Susan.

"Look behind you," said the dwarf.

But Susan saw nothing except the hill's back, and the opposite moorland across the Dale of Goyt, like the belly of a weir, monstrously still.

"No. Where?"

"There, and there, and there, and there, in the heather."

She saw them – tongues of movement darting over the ground, backwards and forwards, in and out, lower down the hill, green-eyed.

"Scouts," said Uthecar. "It is not the palug-cat we have to fear, but the bodach that follows. I would be putting a deal of wind between us and them."

Susan and Uthecar increased their pace, not yet running, and the cats poured over them openly, now that they had been seen, and they began to call to each other in relays down the mountain with voices that were like an ache and a desolation of the soul.

Their numbers frightened Uthecar. He had not reckoned on so many. They would swamp him in a minute, and might even smother the bracelet long enough for Susan to be killed – if that was the purpose.

But the palugs did not attack, and Susan and Uthecar came to the top of the ridge. A stone wall ran along its spine, which sloped gently upwards to their left, and fell on their right to a saddle, rising to a peak beyond. In front was a valley, and more hills, but on the other side of these was the plain. They were nine miles from Alderley.

They climbed over the wall, and were about to start down the valley, when they saw a line of bodachs cross the bottom of the saddle into the valley to cut them off. The only way now was uphill to the left. They kept by the wall, where the ground was smoother with sheep tracks, and the palugs drove them on, those beyond the wall moving a little ahead.

The slope was too gentle for Susan and Uthecar not to run, but every stride was weighted. So they staggered into the trap. For they were soon on top of the hill, and the relief at the level ground was cut short by the cliff that dropped under them. And as they turned back they saw that the palugs that had been running ahead were over the wall and had made a half-circle with those that followed. The cliff was not an impossible height, but the ground at its foot was only a little less steep, and it was thick with boulders. Far below a road wound through the hills.

"Do not think to jump," said Uthecar. "You would smash your bones. Here at least neither palug nor bodach will be on our necks. Though I fear it will help us little: see."

Twenty or more bodachs were now in sight; and a group of three were at the top, almost a quarter of a mile ahead of the others. They stopped at the edge of the half-circle of palugs and leant on their spears, gloating, and deciding which should have the pleasure of the kill, since there was little to fear in a girl, and a one-eyed dwarf armed with a sword.

"Behind me, and crouch low," whispered Uthecar. "I have a thought for these three. If it should fail, then jump quickly, and trust in the Lady."

"I've got this horn," said Susan. "Shall I blow it?"

"It was meant for worse than this, I fear," said Uthecar.

But before he could say more, one of the bodachs came through the palugs' ranks in two thudding strides, his shield high, and spear poised. And as he landed between Uthecar and the palugs, Uthecar threw his sword in an underhand arc. It caught the bodach in the stomach, and sent him writhing to the ground. With the impetus of his throw, Uthecar went after the sword, and he reached the bodach before he hit the turf. In the same movement he tore the shield from the bodach's arm, and went down on one knee behind it as the spears of the other two bodachs slashed towards him. They bit through the shield, and stood out on the other side, but they did no harm.

Uthecar grabbed his sword and the spear of the dying bodach, and flung himself backwards to the cliff before the palugs had time to gather themselves to spring. Then it was too late for their courage. Each palug saw its own death in that sword, and their minds were not quick enough to catch the dwarf's strategy.

Uthecar pushed the bristling shield and the spear into Susan's arms, and sprang back through the cats on the rebound. He was over them, untouched, in four strides, and on top of the defenceless bodachs. The sword flashed twice, and Uthecar was among the cats with two shields on his arm. But the cats were more ready for him this time. He seemed to be wading through black glue that draped him to the waist: bodies rattled against the shields about his head, and his sword was a spark of lightning round his feet. But he plodded clear, and joined Susan at the cliff's edge.

When the main force of the bodachs reached the top of the hill, they found a girl and a dwarf, armed, and standing on a projecting tongue of rock, so that they could be attacked only from the front, and singly.

It was no fight. For a while the bodachs strutted about the hill-top trying to find a point of vantage, then, frustrated, they began to throw their spears, but when they saw that these were more likely to be used later against themselves, or lost over the cliff, than to hit a mark, they tried to rush the dwarf. However, five quick deaths halted them, and they stood back, shaking their heads in rage.

The palugs were unhelpful. Their way was to hunt as a pack: individual contests were not looked for, and there were several skirmishes involving blood when an attempt was made to drive them against Uthecar's sword.

So, after the first minutes, a stalemate appeared to have been reached.

"If we could last till dawn, we should win clear," Uthecar said. "Since neither the bodach nor the palug loves the sun. But what word has reached the Morrigan by now? If she should come, well then, good night indeed."

Uthecar had seen palugs head back towards the Dale of Goyt: he knew what that meant. And all the time both cats and goblins were coming out of the valley, and were thick on the hill-top.

"We shall not see the sun rise if we stay here," he said. "Yet what else is there for us?"

"Do you know where we are?" said Susan. "There's a road below us."

"Ay, that much I can tell. This is Shining Tor. Between your feet the Mothan grew, and here the Hunter slept."

"What? Here? Do you mean *here*?" She was so surprised that she took her eyes off the bodachs, and looked round at the jagged tor, her thoughts full of the light that had stared at her in the dying flames of the Beacon. And then a pain, cold as a razor, struck across her arm deep into the bone. *"Oh! I've been hit!"* Susan grabbed her wrist;

yet when she looked there was neither blood nor wound, but the Mark of Fohla shone with white fire, and the black characters engraved on it appeared to hover above the face of the metal, and now she could see the word of power.

"Uthecar! I can read what's on my bracelet!"

"Speak it, then!"

He had stepped across to cover Susan when she dropped her spear, and his eye could not leave the bodachs, who were edging closer, waiting for the first chance.

"It says 'TROMADOR'."

The hill shook at the word. The air pulsed as at a note below the range of hearing, and the web of heaven trembled, making the stars dance, and their glittering echoed, "tromador, tromador", down the night, and out of the sound came a wind.

It was a wind that was never imagined: it leapt on Susan's back, and crushed her to the rock: her fingers grew into every crack, and she pressed her body so close that the rock spun. For it was a wind that would take hair from a horse, and moorgrass from the ground: it would take heather from the hill, and willow from the root: it would take the limpet from the crag, and the eagle from its young: and it came over the gritstone peaks, howling and raging, in blazing sparks of fire.

The bodachs and palugs were rolled in a heap against the wall, and held there by the wind. The grass moved like a scalp on the hill.

Then, as it came, the wind died. Susan and

Uthecar lifted their faces, and groped for their spears: the shields had gone faster than leaves in autumn. But they never touched their weapons, for twelve horsemen were close to where they lay. They sat as still as death, and in front of them was a man with seven-branched antlers sweeping from his head, cruel against the sky.

The foremost rider was red, and carried a spear. He lifted it, and his voice cut like a blade.

There is a cry in the valley;
Is it not He that pierces?
There is a cry on the mountain;
Is it not He that is wounding?
There is a cry in the woodland;
Is it not He that conquers?
A cry of a journey over the plain!
A cry in every wandering vale!

The three red riders, the Horsemen of Donn, levelled their spears; the white cloaks of the sons of Argatron parted, and three curled whips were seen; dark Fiorn, north-king, mound-king, poised his iron flail behind his shoulder, and the seven chains rang together, softly, baleful; Fallowman son of Melimbor drew his black sword; it hissed in its sheath like an adder; the sword of Bagda was drawn; the sons of Ormar couched their javelins behind their silver shields, and the hoofs of their horses were brazen moons.

Garanhir, the Hunter, tossed his head; his voice belled, wild as a stag.

"Ride, Einheriar of the Herlathing!"

"We ride! We ride!"

The palugs had started to slink backwards, ears flat, eyes narrow with fear, when the horseman spoke, but when the voice of Garanhir blared over them they were driven mad, as though the note of his voice had spoken to them and loosed their reason. They bounded over the heather, fleeing. But the bodachs scrambled from the pile the wind had made of them, and knelt closely together behind their shields, holding their spear butts to the ground, the blades pointing for the horses' chests. Yet javelin and flail, whip, sword, and spear were among them before they could strike, as the Einheriar swept them like a wave, rolling their heads as shingle.

Garanhir strode through the bodachs' ranks: he took them by the necks, and drove their heads together.

"Ride, Einheriar of the Herlathing!"

"We ride! We ride!"

The broken ranks scattered, and the Herlathing charged across the hill, cutting, flaying, harrying the goblins and cats back to the valley.

Susan stood in wonder, appalled at the vigour of bloodshed that the riders showed: Garanhir was dark to the waist, and strips hung from his antlers. But Uthecar pulled her off the rock, and started towards the end of the cliff.

"Let us not stay," he said. "The Wild Hunt has saved us – will you now await the Morrigan?"

599

"But look," said Susan. "They're *enjoying* what they're doing."

"Enjoy? You have called the Wild Hunt, Susan. This is no toy-magic! Be thankful that *your* head is not rolling in the dale."

They worked clear of the rocks, and down to the road, but Uthecar would not take it. He made a direct line for Alderley, avoiding open ground as much as possible, and he kept the pace unbroken through the night. The noise of slaughter soon died.

When day came, Uthecar and Susan were in a field at the top of the Edge, on the border of a tongue of the woodland. The moon was low in the sky. Susan was breathless, very tired, but Uthecar looked more relaxed than he had been all night.

"We are there," he said. "Close in the wood, by the Goldenstone, an old elf-road goes to Fundindelve. It will be some shield to us, for even the Morrigan cannot walk an elf-road without pain, and lesser troubles cannot walk it at all."

"Come on, then," said Susan. "Let's run."

She was suddenly apprehensive: a shadow passed over her mind from the east. But before they could take another stride, they heard a voice call behind them.

"*Imorad! Imorad! Surater!*"

And at the voice, it was as though ice locked their muscles. Uthecar cried out, and after that stood still, but Susan, though there seemed to be crystals in every joint, could force her limbs to move. She turned her head, and saw the Morrigan on the fringe of some trees across the field. She held a long sword, and her right hand was stretched towards Susan and Uthecar, the fist clenched, and the little finger and forefinger extended.

"Must – run," whispered Susan.

She was able to walk, but each stride was a heavy wade; her body was dead as lead; it was like trying to run in a nightmare. But all that Uthecar could move was his eye.

"Try – run," said Susan.

Her throat was numb with cold. She pushed her hand out to the dwarf, and closed her fingers jerkily on his wrist to pull him along. But the moment she touched him, Uthecar felt the life flicker in his bones, and by turning all his heart to the effort, he could swing his legs, hips pushed forward, arms circling wide of the body, as though in water. So together Susan and Uthecar moved into the wood, which here was only a few yards deep, and the Morrigan came after them, her sword ready.

"Road – road – there," said Uthecar. He put his head to the left, and Susan saw a track, bordered with earth walls, running straight along the other side of the wood. They willed themselves on, for the Morrigan was so close that they could hear her breathing, and tumbled over the bank on to the elf-road, and the deadness fell from them.

"Loose my arm, and give me your hand," said

Uthecar. "The power against her is in you, but I would have my sword free. She will not be held long."

They ran along the track, the Morrigan keeping pace with them on the other side of the bank. For all her bulk, she could move quickly. But they noticed that she was looking at the sky, and seemed to be anxious. They were close to the Goldenstone when she faltered, and stopped.

"Stay," said Uthecar. "She is not at ease: beware!"

The Morrigan stood, panting, twenty yards away.

"The wish of my heart to you, dwarf!" she screamed.

Uthecar threw himself to the ground, dragging Susan with him, and shouted at the top of his voice:

"The wish of your heart, carlin, be on yonder grey stone!"

There was a swirl in the air over Susan's head like the beat of a bird's wing, and the Goldenstone rent from top to base. Flying chips of rock stung Susan's skin, and when she looked again the Morrigan was not there.

CHAPTER 15

Errwood

"If I had found them before they drank at the well," said Cadellin, "they could have been forced to the mounds. But the water has confirmed them here, and this will last for seven nights, and in that time who can tell what they will not do?"

"I would be taking less care for the Herlathing than for the Morrigan," said Uthecar. "For the one I was glad to see, and the other can never be too far from my life. Ask the Goldenstone if I speak true!"

"I can't understand that," said Susan. "She was right on top of us, and then she looked at the sky, broke the Goldenstone and disappeared."

"Where was the moon?" said Cadellin.

"I didn't notice."

"It was about to set," said Uthecar. "Think you she was fearful of that?"

"It may be," said Cadellin. "Her power lies there. But she is not helpless when the moon is down. What special charge was there on her that she could not stay?"

"Look," said Susan. "If she was going back to the house, Albanac could follow her on his horse – she can't be halfway there yet – and we might see what's wrong."

"Shape-shifting will take her, if she has need, faster than my horse," said Albanac. "But I will go if Uthecar will ride with me to point the way."

"Nay!" said Uthecar. "Give me the head that stays hewn, or none at all! Two swords are no guard. Take Susan with you: then sword, hoof, and Mark may keep you in daylight."

"Surely you wouldn't have gone without me?" said Susan, looking at Cadellin.

"I think Angharad Goldenhand is wrong," said the wizard, "but you are so far from your own world that I should do no more harm to meddle now. Go with Albanac. But I beg you to take no risk."

Susan and Albanac went down to one of the lower caves, where Albanac's horse was stabled with the horses of the lios-alfar. Then they left Fundindelve by the iron gates and rode away towards the Goldenstone. They were wary of every tree, but they saw no cats at all, and as soon as they were in the fields the horse leapt forward and they sped towards Shining Tor. Farm dogs barked, men stared, but Albanac had no time for caution, and the land grew empty as they climbed into the hills.

Carrion birds were fighting among the heather along the top of Shining Tor, and they rose as clouds when Susan and Albanac passed through them. The horse walked now, and Albanac was on his guard, searching both sky and moor, one hand easing his sword in its sheath.

They rode beside the wall nearly as far as the

saddle of the hill, then they turned right and went down towards the valley. The day was still. Nothing moved.

They halted in the copse of dead trees, but there was no trace of the bodach, and the rhododendrons made the valley inscrutable.

"You couldn't see the house from here, anyway," said Susan. "It's on the other side of that round hill in the mouth of the valley."

"We must go close, then," said Albanac. "But I do not like what I see, even at this distance."

When they came to the gateway, Albanac's horse flattened its ears, but went on without hesitation, treading softly.

In daylight the place was still forbidding. Bushes and decayed stonework, dank, green, and weeds on the path, the stream killing small noises so that the skin crept in fear of unheard approaches, and the valley narrowing in overhead.

Susan pointed to the left-hand fork of the drive.

"It's just round that bend," she whispered.

Albanac nodded. They edged forward. The horse seemed to know the risk. Albanac drew his sword as they reached the corner – and Susan gave a shout that sent birds crashing through the trees in fright.

For the terrace that held the lawn was strewn across the path; where Susan had seen an ornamental pond was now a little mound of rushes; the towered, glowing house was a pile of masonry and shattered walls, bracken and nettle showing through the rubble, gaunt with window arches.

"This is long dead," said Albanac.

"But it was a house last night!" cried Susan. "The Morrigan was here. I *saw* her!"

"I do not doubt you," said Albanac. "There is witch-magic here. Come."

He spun the horse round, and set off back along the path at a gallop. There was an urgent need to be clear of the valley: it was as though the danger had yawned at their feet and they were jumping back by instinct while their minds raced to enclose it. But when they reached the open hillside again much of the dread slipped from their backs, and Albanac slowed the horse to a canter.

"What made the house fall?" said Susan. Her voice broke.

"No, Susan: what you saw last night was the work of the Morrigan," said Albanac. "We must find Cadellin, for I think I see light in this, and we may have the advantage of her."

"How?"

"Let us ask Cadellin first: he is a truer judge of these things. But I think that Colin is safer now than he was before, and that, wherever he is, the Morrigan can reach him no sooner than you or I."

"Are you *sure*?"

"No: but let us ask Cadellin."

He urged the horse to the hill, and it went over the flank of Shining Tor like a banner of the wind. For this was Melynlas, the foal of Caswallawn, and one of the Three High-mettled Horses of Prydein.

They were across the hill, and going down towards Thursbitch below Cat's Tor, when they saw a shepherd and his dog walking along a sheep track. The dog ran forward, barking, but a single whistle took him back to the man's heel, and Albanac turned Melynlas aside, and halted.

"There is a house in a valley beyond the hill," he said. "It is fallen and overgrown. Can you say what it is?"

The shepherd looked at Susan and Albanac with only a little curiosity.

"Ay," he said. "Yon'll be Errwood Hall."

"How long is it since anybody lived there?" said Susan.

"I couldn't tell you; but the Hall was pulled down when I was a lad."

"That is what I thought it would be," said Albanac. "Our thanks to you."

"You're welcome," said the shepherd. "Funny time of year for a procession, isn't it? Where's it at?"

"Procession?" said Susan. "What procession?"

"Good day to you," said Albanac, and wheeled Melynlas round.

"Well, it isn't every week you see two folks in fancy dress up this way: I just thought there must be summat doing."

"But I'm not—" said Susan.

"*Two?*" said Albanac, drawing rein sharply. "who else is it you have seen?"

"There was a woman passed me about half an hour since by Thursbitch yonder," said the shepherd, "making for Errwood. I've never seen anybody shift so fast! She was all dressed up in long skirts and that, but she was too far away to speak to."

"Half an hour?" said Albanac. "Can you be certain?"

"Ay, well, say twenty minutes."

"Our thanks to you once more!" cried Albanac, and Melynlas sprang away towards Alderley, and the turf flew about their heads like swallows before rain.

"I think we have her!" Albanac shouted through the noise of their running. "She was there not long before us, and that was too late for her, yet it was close enough for her to see us, but she did not attack – and that means she dared not. I think we have her!"

The ride back to Alderley was faster than any Susan had known, faster even than that of the Herlathing from Broad hill to the Beacon, and the night red with wendfire. Nor did they pause to stable Melynlas, but they entered Fundindelve by the Holywell, straight to the wizard's cave.

"You must act now," said Cadellin when they had told their story. "It seems that she is not yet strong enough of herself to attack you without preparation, unless she can draw upon the moon. All this is moon magic. She has used it to build the memory of the house into stones of hardness, and it is there, I will say, only when the old moon looks on it. If she did not gain the house before moonset, then she is barred from it until the night, and if Colin is there he is safe for a while. You must put yourselves between her and the house while there is light, and at moonrise keep her from the house until Colin is freed."

"We shall need help, then," said Albanac. "three or four cannot guard that house. I think we must talk with Atlendor."

They all went together, in spite of Uthecar's objections to relying on the elves in any way, to the deepest cave of Fundindelve, where the lios-alfar sat grouped in their cantrefs, orderly and silent. The only noise was a spasm of coughing that would break out from time to time in different parts of the cave. Susan could not help being frightened a little by the stillness.

They came to Atlendor, alone at the far end of the cave, and they told him what they were going to do.

"Will the lios-alfar lend their aid in this?" said Albanac. "It is for the one night, and among hills; the smoke-sickness cannot take hold in so short a time."

Atlendor stood up. His eyes shone.

"Can it not?" he said. "But that is no matter.. The lios-alfar ride three nights from this. We have given aid to hunt the Brollachan. This moon magic concerns us not at all. And you are pledged to ride with us, though I see word-breaking in your heart."

"My lord Atlendor," said Albanac, "is it to be said of the lios-alfar that they will not fight black trouble where they find it?"

"Ay. When it deals with men. Too often they are the death of my people. We ride three nights from this, Albanac, and you with us."

He was turning away, as though the subject had been closed, when Susan's voice halted him.

"If you won't help us get Colin out of that house," she said, "we'll see how much moon magic doesn't concern you. What about my bracelet? Have you thought of that?"

Alarm slid across Atlendor's poise like a blink of an eyelid.

"You, too, have pledged yourself to our need," he said coldly.

"And do you think I'm going to help you if Colin's not safe?"

"A promise not fulfilled is none at all," said Atlendor.

"All right, then, it isn't. But what are you going to do about it?"

"You shall have fifty horse and myself to lead them, but not until the sun is down," said Atlendor. "If all is not settled by the third night, the fifty and Albanac shall stay, and I shall take the rest of my people beyond Bannawg."

Albanac spoke quickly: "That is noble, and will serve our need."

"It is foolish, and the vote of force," said Atlendor.

CHAPTER 16

The Howl of Ossar

Susan and Uthecar chose horses from among those of the lios-alfar, and Susan also took a sword and a shield. She had no other armour, since none of the linked mail the elves carried with them fitted her.

They led their horses up to the wizard's cave.

"Isn't there a horse for you?" said Susan.

"I shall not go with you," said Cadellin.

"*Not go?*" cried Susan. "But you *must!*"

"I have thought of this," said Cadellin. "My duty is here, guarding the Sleepers. Only I can wake them. If I were killed, I should have betrayed my trust, and only in Fundindelve can I be certain of life. And, Susan, though the Morrigan thrives, and Colin is in her power, the Sleepers wait for one whose shadow will quench the world, and I must not fail them."

"That is true," said Albanac. "We were too close to the threat to see it fairly. It is better that the Morrigan triumph now than that the Sleepers never wake."

"But what about her magic?" said Susan. "We don't know any."

"That is a chance you must take," said Cadellin. "You are not helpless there. And if you were, Susan, you should not complain. Of your own

611

will you sought this end. I have done what is in me to keep you from it."

"I see no good in further talk," said Uthecar. "There is little of the day left to us for doing what is to be done, unless we are to be a gift to the Morrigan."

"Yes, come on," said Susan.

It was an awkward leave-taking. Susan and Uthecar, while admitting the logic of Cadellin's words, had too much emotion in their own natures to have made such a decision themselves. As they went from Fundindelve, Albanac took Cadellin's hand, and so only he felt the wizard's grief, and saw the light that stood beyond his eyes.

They rode quickly but easily.

"The sword and shield are for palugs," said Uthecar. "Do not be thinking to match them with a bodach's spear. That will be our work."

"But didn't the Wild Hunt see to them?" said Susan.

"I dare not hope for that," said Uthecar. "Some will have escaped, but how many? Let the sun go down, and we shall know."

It was midday when they reached Errwood. They approached less cautiously than before, and Uthecar went about and through the ruins on his horse to decide how they could best prepare for the night.

"It will not be simple to guard the house," he said when he returned. "These three sides are level and open, but at the back there is danger. The space between the walls and the hill is small, and the hill has been quarried sheer in parts, and bushes grow thickly. The Morrigan can be very close and we not know it. This is where we must start."

He went to the back of the house, and began to cut the rhododendrons away from the rock face. Albanac started further along from him, and they worked towards each other, clearing the hill in a strip ten yards wide.

Susan pulled the fallen bushes into close piles along the edge of the shelf on which the house stood, between and above the two arms of the stream.

All this took four hours, and the remaining daylight was spent in hacking as much of the growth as possible on the steep banks below the shelf. The wood from here was made into one heap on the lawn.

Nothing happened at any time to make them think they were in danger. Once or twice Susan thought she heard a dog howling, far away, and Albanac seemed to hear it, too; he would stop his work, and listen, and then go back to felling the bushes, his whole body swinging to the strokes as though he was fighting for his life.

"I would be clear of the valley until the lios-alfar come," said Uthecar at sunset. "Now what bodachs and palugs there may be here will creep from under their rocks and out of their holes, and we should have little time for breath. In open ground they will not be so deadly."

"What about the Morrigan?" said Susan. "I thought we were here to keep her out."

"The moon will not rise yet; until then we shall see little of her," said Uthecar. "But let us make fire quickly now before we go. There is enough wood to burn through the night, and neither bodach nor palug seeks fire."

From under his cloak Albanac produced flint and tinder, and eventually they managed to spark some twists of dry grass into flames, and these by nursing were transferred to twigs and leaves, and so to the bush piles themselves. There were more than a dozen of them, and when they were all ablaze twilight had come.

They mounted their horses, and galloped along the drive to the moor, where they halted, clear of sudden attack.

"How long will it be before the elves get here?" said Susan.

"Not long," said Albanac. "They will have left Fundindelve as soon as the light grew poor, and their horses are fleet as Melynlas when there is need."

They crossed the stream to a flat meadowland, where the horses would have better grazing. The sky was yellow, the black clouds of night drifting in, giving a stark quietness to the valley. But this was broken with a shock that made the horses rear, as a dog howled close by.

"Where is that?" cried Albanac.

"Yonder!" said Uthecar. "High on the hill!"

And there by the dead trees where Uthecar had

killed the bodach loped the shape of a black dog. It was as big as a calf, and so indistinct against the trees, and in that light, as to appear to be made of smoke. It put back its head, and the loneliness bayed again, and then the dog slipped through the wood, and they did not see it.

Albanac sat with his head bowed, unspeaking, for a long time after the voice had died. Uthecar looked at him, but did not move, and the weight that lay on both of them was felt by Susan.

Albanac drew a deep breath. "The Howl of Ossar," he said. But even as he spoke they heard a drumming in the air, growing louder, and the skyline was broken with movement as though an army was rising out of the heather, and down from Shining Tor rode the lios-alfar, with naked swords in their hands, and the blades like flame.

They halted in a swirling crowd after the momentum of the hill, but they did not speak, even among themselves.

"We are come," said Atlendor to Albanac. "Where is the Morrigan?"

"We have not seen her, but she will be close," said Albanac. "We did this minute leave the house: it is ringed with fires, and the ground is clear, though on one side there is much against us. Neither bodach nor palug has been found."

"I smell them," said Atlendor. "They will come. But let us go to the house, and there make ready for what we must; for I smell blood, too."

They rode along the drive, three abreast. The

horses walked, and shields were held at the ready, since by now the last light had gone.

It was impossible for so many to approach the house in silence, but no one talked or made any noise that could be prevented. The light of the elves' swords in the damp air made a nimbus which was reflected coldly in the leather of the rhododendron leaves.

When they came to the fork in the path, Albanac held up his hand to stop the column. Something was wrong; they could all sense it. Then the elves swept forward to take the bend at a gallop. The house was in darkness. The fires they had left a few minutes ago had been snuffed out: the mounds of wood stood black around the house, and the air was bitter with a charred and acrid smell.

CHAPTER 17

The Witch-brand

The elves did not falter. They rode into line, and in a moment they had put a cordon round the house, facing inwards and outwards alternately.

"Quick now!" shouted Uthecar to Albanac. "We must have fire!"

He jumped from his horse, and snatched a handful of dead grass, but the air was so laden with moisture that the grass would not light easily, and the more they hurried, the more they fumbled, and the more the sense of danger crept over them. But when they did start a flame the wood was soon rekindled, for it was still warm.

"Wind would have fed, not killed," said Albanac. "And water would have smoked. This wood is dry. The Morrigan does what she is able before the moon rises."

"And that is enough," said Uthecar. "We must have light, since not all here have the eyes of dwarfs, yet it leaves us no guard but our hands."

"We gain more than we lose," said Albanac. "Why else has the Morrigan starved the fire? Until the moon rises she has not the means to put more than fear and fright into us, and from the shepherd's tale I would guess that shape-shifting is beyond her skill now. She sits out there, and waits for the moon."

"Ay, and what then?" said Atlendor, who had ridden over to join them. "We must show our strength: thus we may not be called to match it with hers. Come with me," he said to Susan, and they rode to the middle of the lawn, where he stopped, and lifted Susan's wrist above her head.

This was the first time Susan had been conscious of her bracelet since the appearance of the Einheriar on Shining Tor, and she was puzzled to find that she could no longer read the word of power. The script which had stood out so clearly from the metal then was now as unintelligible as it had ever been.

One by one the elves came to Susan. They touched the bracelet with their arrows and with their swords, and then went back to the ring of fire. By the time the last elf had taken up his post Susan ached to the bone, but Atlendor still held her arm high, and when the circle was complete he spoke in a voice that went far beyond the light.

"Here is bale for you! Here is a plague to flesh! Come; we are ready!"

He clashed his own sword against the bracelet, and let Susan's arm fall. But as Atlendor did so, there was a gasp from one of the elves below the quarried wall, and he slid round his horse's neck to the ground, a spear between his shoulders.

"One life to save a man," said Atlendor quietly, but before anyone could move, a voice spoke from the hill behind the ruins.

"We come. Have patience. We come."

"That's the Morrigan!" said Susan.

618

"Where is she, Hornskin?" said Atlendor.

"Behind the bushes," said Uthecar. "I cannot see her."

"Hadn't we better get inside the walls?" said Susan. "We're sitting targets here."

"And where should we be but under crushing stones, if the moon rose; and we not knowing?" said Albanac. "If we go to the front of the house we shall be safe from spears, since only on the hill above can they come close."

The lios-alfar had all turned to face outwards. Those who, like the dead elf, had not already put on their shirts of mail hurriedly unrolled their packs.

Susan, Uthecar, and Albanac crouched below the lawn near to what had been the main door of the house.

"It is good to know where she is," said Uthecar. "Think you if we put our swords to the bracelet it will be proof against her magic?"

"It would not kill," said Albanac, "but its virtue may corrupt and gall the wound a sword makes, and I think the arrows will stop her from trying to gain the house by shape-shifting."

"If the house should come with the moon," said Uthecar, "Susan and I shall find Colin within. Do you keep the door here, Albanac."

They waited through the hours to moonrise. Atlendor guarded the fires. There was no move to extinguish them – just the reverse; they seemed to burn faster than holly, and Atlendor was put to it to keep the fires high, and the pile of wood on the lawn began to dwindle. At this rate it would not last long. Atlendor stopped in the act of throwing a branch into the flames. The Morrigan had nearly won. He hurried round, raking the fires together, sacrificing every other one for the sake of the hours left to the night. But after this the Morrigan seemed content to wait. The fire was normal, no bodach sent spears.

The moon rose a long time before it was seen, and it shot high from a cloud, an ugly slip of yellow, taking the watchers by surprise. And though the light it gave was small, and could not even dim the fires, the moment it touched the ruins they shimmered as in a heat haze, and dissolved upwards to a house. The windows poured their dead lustre on the grass, making pools of white in the flames.

"Now!" cried Uthecar, and Susan and he threw themselves up the bank and put all their weight to the door. It swung easily, and they fell over the threshold, and as she stumbled, a spear passed over Susan's head and skidded along the hall. Uthecar kicked the door shut, and the wood rattled under an impact that was made of many separate blows delivered at the same time; points of bronze stood out like teeth. But the door was closed, and even while the echo was still loud, Uthecar and Susan were running up the stairs.

"He will not be near to the ground," said Uthecar, "and we must hurry, since he will not be unguarded, either, and the fire and our coming will be plain to any."

They went from room to room, throwing open the doors, but all were empty. The house rang with their search.

They reached the end of a landing, and Susan was about to charge the door, when Uthecar stopped her.

"Wait! I am not liking this."

He pointed to the upper panel of the door. A design had been painted on it in black, and there were strange characters grouped around the design.

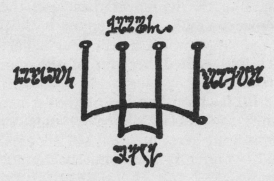

"It is a witch-brand," said Uthecar. "Come away."

"No," said Susan. "It's the first thing we've found. I'm going to look."

She tried the handle carefully: the door opened, and Susan stepped into an enormous room. It was as bare of furniture as any other she had seen, but on the floor a circle had been drawn, about eighteen feet across. It had a double rim, round which were more characters similar to those on the panelling, and in the circle was a lozenge, and a six-pointed star was near each of its four corners. In the centre of the lozenge stood a squat, long-necked bottle which held a black substance that writhed as though it was boiling, though the cork was heavily sealed with wax, and two points of red light swam inside the bottle, always the same distance apart.

Susan approached the circle, and the red sparks stopped their drifting, and hung against the glass. Susan felt compelled to pick the bottle up, but as she reached the circle, the room was filled with a buzzing, like the whine of flies, and the circle rims began to smoke. She stepped back quickly, and at the same time Uthecar caught her by the shoulder and pulled her out of the room. He slammed the door.

"The Brollachan! She has penned it here!"

"*That?*" said Susan "Then we must stop her from getting in here, or she'll set it loose!"

"Small wonder it could not be found," said Uthecar.

"*Listen!*" whispered Susan. "*Somebody's coming!*"

There was one door they had not yet opened at the end of the landing. It was smaller than the others, and from behind it they heard footsteps drawing near.

"Back," said Uthecar. "Give room for swords."

He braced his legs apart, balanced for flight or attack. The running footsteps checked, the door opened, and Uthecar gave a shout of gladness, for in the doorway was Pelis the False, sword in hand, frozen by surprise.

Uthecar sprang, but Pelis was as quick, and the sword bit into the door as it was snatched shut in Uthecar's face. He pulled it open, and ran along the short passage beyond. At the other end Pelis was disappearing up a staircase in great bounds.

"Do not follow," shouted Uthecar to Susan. "Guard here."

The stairs were not long, and at the top was a single door. Pelis was fitting a key into the lock, but he did not have time to open it before Uthecar reached him.

He was no coward. Without a shield he stood, his sword in both hands, his back to the door, and there was not a stroke or a thrust that Uthecar made that was not parried and answered. But the advantage of the shield began to tell, and Uthecar worked Pelis away from the door and to the stairs, and once there, Pelis had to give ground.

Susan listened to the clash of iron, and the heavy breathing which was magnified by the stair-well, and tried to believe that she could make herself use her sword.

When Uthecar and Pelis came into sight she flattened herself against the wall, and watched the glittering play of blades as they swooped, leapt, and sparked about the dwarfs with cruel beauty that had the precision of dancing in it.

"To the room above," Uthecar gasped as he reached the bottom step.

Susan nodded, and began to edge past the fight. Uthecar increased his attack, but even so, Pelis was able to make one vicious cut at Susan as she darted for the stairs. She threw up her shield, and the blow glanced off the rim, and dragged a long groove in the stonework of the wall, but it did not touch her, and she was through.

Susan looked at the key in the lock. Did Uthecar want her to open it? She examined the wood, but there were no marks or lettering visible, so she turned the key, and kicked open the door.

It was a cell of a room; windowless, empty of comfort as the rest of the house; and standing against the opposite wall was Colin.

CHAPTER 18

The Dolorous Blow

Pelis the False hewed at Uthecar's shield. It was riven in two places, and if he could make it useless he would have more chance of halting the slow retreat down the corridor. As a swordsman he was Uthecar's match, but his disadvantage made attack nearly impossible, and though he had got past Uthecar's guard once, the wound was slight, and he himself was losing strength through a gash on the shoulder. The girl alone would be no obstacle as far as weapons were concerned, although he was still suspicious of her bracelet, but he had to finish the dwarf quickly, or the fighting would lose its purpose.

Therefore when he saw Susan appear behind Uthecar, supporting Colin with her arm, Pelis did not hesitate, but backed towards the stairs that led down to the hall. He knew that he would not go far if he turned and ran.

He arrived at the top of the stairs, and cunningly parried Uthecar in such a way that he seemed to be weakening rapidly, and so when he faltered in his guard, Uthecar thought the moment was there, and he brought his arm down in a swing that had all his weight behind it, but Pelis threw himself sideways, rolled over the banisters, and dropped into the hall, while Uthecar pitched off balance helplessly down the stairs.

Pelis ran, not to the outer door, but to another that led off the hall. He was through, and the door closed again, before Uthecar recovered himself. Susan was the first to reach the door, and when she opened it she saw Pelis for an instant against a window that stretched from the ceiling to the floor, and through which the fires on the lawn could be plainly seen, then the dwarf hurled himself at the frame, and disappeared in a splintered cascade of glass.

"Come back," said Uthecar from the hall. "If the lios-alfar do not have him now his life is charmed. Let us go by the door.

"Colin, are you fit to run?"

"Yes," said Colin. "I'm all right. I've not had anything to eat or drink since I got here, that's all, and I was a a bit dizzy to start with, but it's passed off."

"Were you hurt?"

"No: they just stuck me in there, and left me. I suppose you know it's the Morrigan."

"Ay, we have crossed her. But you shall hear of that later. Susan, take Colin by the hand, and when I open the door run close by the wall to Albanac. He will be somewhere near. Beware of empty ground. Are you ready?" He pulled open the door, and then clutched Susan's arm. "*Wait!*"

"What's the matter?" said Colin.

Uthecar did not answer, but ran across the hall to the room from which Pelis had escaped, and when the children joined him they found him standing at the broken window, looking out into the night, which was as silent and impenetrable as the caverns of a mine.

"The moon is hidden," said Uthecar.

"But the house isn't here unless the moon's shining on it," said Susan, "and it still *is* here."

"Ay, but where is 'here'?" said Uthecar. "To the valley this house is 'here' when the old moon is on it, and not at other times; but to the house the valley is 'there' only in the moon. So I am asking what is out 'there' now, and I am not wanting to know the answer. Let us watch for the moon to come, and then through this window as fast as we may."

While they waited, Uthecar questioned Colin, but there was not much to be told. The Morrigan had done nothing with him; he had been taken straight to the room, and locked in.

"Your time would have come," said Uthecar. "Susan was the chief intent, and through you they would bring her here – and so they have brought her, though not as they would wish!"

"But why didn't Pelis take me instead of Colin?" said Susan.

"He did not know how little of the power that is within you had been revealed: he could not presume to bring you by the sword."

"Why's he doing all this?" said Colin. "We didn't think twice about trusting him, with him being a dwarf."

"Ho! There is reason for you!" said Uthecar.

"Why am I here if not for mischief? It is the nature of dwarfs to seek trouble, and with him it is the cause and not the cure that delights."

But before he could say more there was a vibration in the darkness, and blurred lights appeared, which condensed into fires and with the light came noise – hoofbeats, and the clash of weapons.

Uthecar put his shield in front of him, and jumped through the window, the children following at his back, and all three landed together on a path that was between the house and the lawn. Uthecar knelt behind his shield to take in the situation.

The elves were holding their circle against both cats and goblins. If any breached the circle they were not pursued, but were brought down with arrows, and, from the bodies on the ground, the fighting was not new.

The elves were outnumbered by at least two to one, and the cats were everywhere, a torment to the horses, and death to any elf that was unseated.

Despite her opinion of the lios-alfar, Susan had to admire their courage and skill. They were quick as hawks, yet they were calm in their speed, and they did not shout or cry. They must have eyes at the back of their heads, thought Susan.

"I do not see Albanac," said Uthecar. "Let us find him."

They ran to the corner of the house, and came upon Albanac guarding the door.

"How is it?" said Uthecar.

"They attacked with the moon," said Albanac, "but we hold them. And you?"

"Colin is here, unhurt," said Uthecar, "and the Brollachan is within, so we must hold them still."

"*The Brollachan?*"

"Ay: shut in a room of foul magic."

"Tell me more when there is time for thought," said Albanac. "Just now it is labour enough to stay alive."

But although Albanac did not overstate their danger, the fight was slackening. The palugs had little stamina, and the bodachs were realizing that they had lost the impetus of the attack, and were now wasting lives. They withdrew, hoping to tempt the lios-alfar to follow them, but none went.

"This quiet will not last," said Albanac. "Colin, you must have weapons, and I fear they will be ready to your hand."

He crossed the lawn, and moved about among the fires, and when he came back he brought with him a sword and a shield identical to those that Susan carried.

Colin fitted the shield on his arm, and tested the weight of the sword.

"Remember," said Uthecar, "these are for the palug-cat. Do not be picking quarrels with a bodach."

"We'd be a lot better off with guns," said Colin.

"Would you?" said Uthecar. "That is where

we part from men. Oh, you may look here, and find us at the slaughter, but we know the cost of each death, since we see the eyes of those we send to darkness, and the blood on our hands, and each killing is the first for us. I tell you, life is true then, and its worth is clear. But to kill at a distance is not to know, and that is man's destruction. You will find in the bows of the lios-alfar much to explain their nature, which was not always as now."

The last part of Uthecar's outspokenness was mingled with the commotion that started at the bend in the drive and spread to the whole company. Instead of charging from all directions at once, the bodachs and palugs had formed up on the drive and had come in a body. They were through the circle and halfway to the house before anyone knew what was happening, but the elves were swift in their reactions, and they closed in right to the walls.

Now the fighting was desperate, since the elves could not manoeuvre, but stood their ground, using swords alone. The horses reared and slashed with wicked aim.

Uthecar and Albanac held the doorway, the children by their side. The dwarf's instructions to fight only the palugs were impossible to carry out, for cats and goblins seethed in front of them, and it would have been fatal to have tried to discriminate.

The worst moment for Colin and Susan had come when the attack was seconds away, when they knew that they had to lift their swords and bring them down on living things. Colin remembered the games of years ago. The blade he held now was like lime, and the edge like dew. But when he saw the teeth and claws that were rising towards him and no one else, he struck instinctively, and after that the will to live was in control.

The bodachs stabbed with their spears, and leapt high to rake with their clawed feet, and the palugs added their viciousness to the struggle.

But again cold patience wore down rage, and the bodachs fell back, the elves advancing in step with the retreat, until the original circle was formed again.

Albanac kept the children by the house, and they sank to the ground, exhausted; but Uthecar was still in the heat of the fight, and he moved past the elves to the very limit of the fire, throwing down his shield whenever it grew too heavy with the weight of the spears imbedded in it, and snatching another from the mounds that littered the grass.

He looked as though he had cooled to the point of turning back when he gave a shout, and peered along the drive.

"So it is still living you are, and well out of the fight! But I see you! My sword is waking to its hilt for you!"

"Come back!" cried Albanac. "Your reason has gone with the ghosts of the mountains if you think you will live to take a step further!"

But Uthecar was spinning his sword about his head, gathering himself to charge.

"Run, bodachs! Make way! For when I chance to come upon you, as many as hailstones, and grass on a green, the stars of heaven will be your cloven heads and skulls, and your bones, crushed by me and scattered throughout the ridges!"

And he shot forward past the light, into a din of cries and a crash of blades.

"He is mad!" said Albanac. "When his blood is less hot he will wish himself far from this, but it will be too late."

The noise seemed greater than when the house was under siege – bellowing, spitting pandemonium, out of which no one sound emerged. Albanac mounted Melynlas, and rode to the edge of the circle.

"Uthecar!"

"Ay!"

The voice was indistinct.

"How is it?"

"There – is breaking – of spears about the place – where I am. I will not say – but that I may retreat!"

"I am with you!" shouted Albanac.

"Fool!" answered the dwarf.

But Albanac cantered back to the house, turned Melynlas, and broke into full gallop along the drive. A line of bodachs knelt on the fringe of the dark, but Melynlas swept down on them and, as they couched their spears in the gravel, soared high and safe over their heads into the moonlight which the fires made blind to the children and the elves. All the children knew of what followed was told by the sounds that came to them.

And then Melynlas grew out of the night, foaming and red-hoofed. Uthecar rode behind Albanac, still cutting the air, but Albanac was low over the horse's neck, and a gold-handled sword trailed from his side.

CHAPTER 19

The Children of Danu

Melynlas halted, and Uthecar jumped to the ground and eased Albanac from the saddle. He slumped into the dwarf's arms, dragging him off his feet, but Atlendor came to his other side, and between them they half carried him to the shelter of the terrace below the lawn. Gently Uthecar drew the sword out of the wound.

Albanac opened his eyes: they were blue and clear.

"I had hoped it would not be so soon in the night," he whispered.

"Rest you until the battle dies," said Uthecar. "Then you will be safe."

"I am safe," said Albanac. "Here – anywhere. The Howl of Ossar: there is nothing to be done when that one calls."

A group of elves dismounted, and made a cradle of their swords, and lifted Albanac on to it.

"We shall tend him," said Atlendor, and they carried him to a sheltered place between two walls of the house. Colin and Susan went to follow him, but Uthecar shook his head.

"He is better with them," he said. "They are skilled in these things, and we shall be needed here."

For while he was talking, a snigger of laughter had run through the bushes outside the circle, backed by hoots and jeers, and when Uthecar showed that he had heard them, the laughter changed to taunting words.

"Was that not the foray! Well is it said that no iron is as true to its lord as is the spur! Hornskin, will you be bringing me my sword?"

The hate that broke in Uthecar at the touch of this voice was frightening to see. He rushed out to the middle of the lawn, and drove the golden sword into the turf.

"Come now without your bodachs, Pelis son of Argad, and claim your sword!" he cried. "I give you safe passage. But if you leave, and I yet alive, the bows of the lios-alfar shall sing to you. And if I am dead, then none shall stay your going. Here is your sword! Take it!"

There was a minute of silence. But then there were footsteps on the drive, and a black and gold figure came into the light, passing between two of the lios-alfar, who looked at him, but did not lift their weapons against him. He carried a shield, and his stride was firm across the grass.

Pelis the False took hold of the sword, and wrenched it from the ground, and he faced Uthecar without a word for him, nor did Uthecar speak, and they came together like stags. The air shivered at their meeting.

Uthecar was frenzied in attack, since the guilt for Albanac's wound ached in him, and he tried to deaden it with anger. At first he had the advantage, but he was fighting more with his heart than with his head, while Pelis countered, and wasted no strength.

And before long the passion left Uthecar, and weariness seeped into its place. His arms grew heavy, his muscles shot through with cramp, and Pelis the False continued to match him stroke for stroke. And he did not merely check Uthecar: now he was driving the blade aside, and it was Uthecar's shield that rang. He retreated across the lawn, feeling his life wane from him, and then Pelis was through his guard, and the blade sank into his shoulder above the ribs.

The pain cleansed Uthecar's mind of all weariness: he saw that if he did not use this moment there would be no other. He threw his shield from him, and leapt a twisting salmon-leap into the air, high above Pelis, and came down over his arm. The sword went through Pelis to the hilt, and the two dwarfs crashed together, the one fainting, the other dead.

Colin and Susan had watched from the edge of the lawn, and they ran forward and lifted Uthecar, and carried him back to the wall. Colin ripped lengths of Uthecar's tunic into bandages, while Susan cleaned the wound as best she could.

"Did I kill?" said Uthecar.

"Yes," said Colin.

"The wonder is that I am not lying there, black in the light," said Uthecar. "Such rashness merits it. Are you hurt?"

"Only scratches," said Susan.

"And Albanac?"

"I don't know."

"See how it is with him. But go with care," said Uthecar.

Colin and Susan went along to the side of the house towards the corner where the elves had taken Albanac, but they had not gone far when they heard a sound that rooted their feet – the howling of a dog, very near to the house, and in front of them. The notes rose and fell in a sadness that swept the children's minds with dreams of high landscapes of rock, and red mountains standing from them, and hollows filled with water and fading light, and rain drifting as veils over the peaks, and beyond, in the empty distances, a cold gleam on the sea. And into that distance the voice faded like an echo, and Atlendor came towards the children from the shadows of the house.

"Albanac is not here," he said.

"Not here?" said Colin. "But he was badly hurt. Where is he?"

"He has gone to heal his wound: he will come again."

"Why didn't he tell us?" said Susan.

"There was not time: he was called: it is always so with the Children of Danu, since it is their destiny never to be at the end of what they undertake. They help, but may not save."

"When will he come back?" said Colin.

"The Children of Danu are seldom long away," said Atlendor.

"And we shall go. I have kept my word: let us ride now."

"We can't go yet!" said Susan. "What about the Morrigan? And the Brollachan's still in there – if she lets it out you don't know what will happen."

"I know that it has been a dear promise," said Atlendor. He looked at Colin. "One life has cost thirty: it shall not take more. We ride. Make you ready."

Atlendor turned away, and walked back to the corner, where the elves who had carried Albanac were still huddled.

"How *can* he leave everything like this?" cried Susan. "It's not safe, and we mustn't let the Morrigan get back into the house. Doesn't he realize?"

"But he's right," said Colin. "You can't ask him to lose any more for something that isn't important to him."

"Isn't it?" said Susan.

When they reached Uthecar they found Melynlas standing guard over him. The horse pricked up its ears at the sight of the children, and thrust his muzzle into Colin's shoulder.

"How is he?" said Uthecar.

"We didn't see him," said Colin. "They say he's gone. And the elves are going too."

"He knew it was to be this night," said Uthecar. "It was not in us to keep him."

"But how can he go?" said Colin. "Why has he left his horse?"

"He has no need of it," said Uthecar. "You may have thought him a strange man, but Albanac was more than that: he was of the Children of Danu, who came to this land when all was green. They were the best of men."

"Is he dead?" said Colin.

"Not as you would have it," said Uthecar. "Say rather that in this world he has changed his life.

"The Children of Danu are never far from us, and all their days are spent in our cause, but there is a doom on them that they shall not see their work fulfilled, since the gold of their nature might then be dulled, its power turn to selfish ends. When their leaving is close, the Hound of Conaire appears to them, as you have heard and seen. Ossar's howl shadows their lives."

"I can't believe it," said Colin. "It makes everything so pointless."

"He expected no less," said Uthecar, "and there was no place for sadness in him. He will come again.

"But the elves, you say? Is it that they are going too?"

"They're running away," said Susan.

"Then I think the better of them," said Uthecar.

"*You*?" said Susan. "What's the matter with everybody? You mustn't let the Morrigan win!"

"Can I stop her?" said Uthecar. "Listen to me. We have Colin, and there is nothing more to do, since magic holds the Brollachan in its circle. We have killed many bodachs and routed the palugs.

When I was fighting out there I saw but a dozen in all, and when they are spent the Morrigan must needs come herself, and that is no stopping time for me. I fear her, without shame. But also, wounded as I am, the bodach is not dear to me, and for death and its fearful afflictions, and the pang of the blue blades, I will not be clamorous, either."

"I'll stay by myself, then," said Susan.

"You will not," said Uthecar, and began to pick his way over the lawn to where Pelis had fallen. He came back with his sword.

The lios-alfar were backing from the circle to make a column, the wounded in the middle, lashed to their saddles.

"How did they know they were going?" said Colin. "I've never heard any of them speak, except Atlendor."

"It is part of their strangeness," said Uthecar. "They speak to each other through their minds, and from the looks I have seen, they hear what does not pass my lips!"

Susan reluctantly mounted. Colin rode Melynlas, who appeared to have adopted him, and with Uthecar they joined the column of the elves.

The fires were dying for want of attention; the ground was broken with bodies and splintered weapons; the house stood waiting. Susan looked round her at the scene of her failure: and that is how she saw it now. To begin with, Colin had been her only motive; she had faced impossible things for his sake; but now she felt that he had been the first step to her duty, which she was now being made to leave unfinished.

The lios-alfar galloped away along the drive, and, but for their swords and Uthecar's dwarf-sight, they could not have kept their pace, and the spears that came at them would have taken more. As it was, three of the horses lacked riders when they reached open ground.

CHAPTER 20

The Last Ride

The speed of the lios-alfar to Shining Tor was like a March gale, since the moon shone freely, and they were accustomed to the light. But when they were only a little way up the slope, the feeling of wrong became too much for Susan.

"Wait!" she called.

The elves halted, and their eyes were turned on her.

"We must go back. We'll not be safe this way. The Morrigan has got to be kept out of the house."

"We are not bound," said Atlendor. "Come."

"Uthecar, will you go with me?"

"My only craft is the sword," said Uthecar, "and that is denied me now, and I fear the Morrigan more than dishonour. Come away."

"Colin?"

"What's the matter, Sue? You know we can't do any more."

"All right," said Susan, and she drove in her heels, and charged down towards Errwood.

"*Susan!*" cried Uthecar.

"She'll turn back when she sees we're not following," said Colin.

But Susan did not even look. She came to the round hill at the top of the valley, and instead of riding along the drive, on the right-hand side of the hill, she approached the house by a narrow footpath on the left.

"She's going in!" shouted Colin, and he spurred Melynlas after her. But Melynlas would not move. The harder Colin tried, the more he ignored him. It was not the usual stubbornness of a horse: he was quiet and docile: but he would not go.

Colin dropped from Melynlas into the heather, and started to run. Cursing, Uthecar tried to follow him, but Melynlas kicked out at the horse, and bared his teeth, so that it dared not stir, and Uthecar knew that he was too weak to trust his own legs. The lios-alfar sat still.

The path was overgrown and slippery, and the stream ran over rocks far below. Branches whipped Susan's face, but that was little to the cold that seared her wrist.

The path ended. She was at the front of the house, and there on the drive, shapeless in her robes, and surrounded by bodachs and palugs, was the Morrigan.

Susan hauled on the reins, and at the sight of her the bodachs and palugs screamed, for to them she was transformed; their hearts shook, and they fled. But the glamour of the bracelet was not on the Morrigan. She raised her hand.

Now Susan felt the true weight of her danger, when she looked into the eyes that were as luminous as an owl's, and blackness swirling in their depths. The moon charged the Morrigan with such power that when she lifted her hand even the noise of the stream died, and the air was sweet with fear.

"*Vermias! Eslevor! Frangam! Beldor!*"

Something like black lightning came from the Morrigan's hand, and darted towards Susan, who threw up her arm to protect herself: and in doing so, she saw the word of power stand out above the Mark, and though it was not the word she had seen on Shining Tor, she spoke it with all her will.

"HURANDOS!"

And from the Mark sprang a lance of flame, which met the black of the Morrigan halfway to its target, and the two forces grappled each other, crackling, and writhing like snakes.

"*Salibat! Reterrem!*" cried the Morrigan.

The black rippled, grew in thickness, and slowly pushed the white back to the wrist.

Susan rose in the stirrups, and, without her looking at the bracelet, the words poured from her lips, words that she had never known or heard.

"*– per sedem Baldery et per gratiam tuam habuisti –*"

The light grew again, but the Morrigan answered her, and Susan felt herself weaken: the blackness was groping for her like a tentacle. "It shouldn't be me. Why me?" And then the Morrigan's power reached her. Susan arched from the horse into nothingness.

When Susan opened her eyes the Morrigan was

standing with her back to her, facing the house. The Morrigan had been too sure of her art, too scornful of Susan's bracelet, and what should have destroyed had only stunned. But Susan felt that she could do no more; she had tried, and failed. Her duty lay in warning Cadellin or Angharad Goldenhand. Let them deal with this.

"*Besticitium consolatio veni ad me vertat Creon, Creon, Creon, cantor laudem omnipotentis et non commentur –* " The Morrigan chanted tonelessly, her arms outstretched. "*– principiem da montem et inimicos o prostantis vobis –* " Susan crept towards the horse, which was standing as though mesmerized, and she reached it as the Morrigan's voice rose to its climax. "*– passium sincisibus. Fiat! Fiat! Fiat!*"

There was a noise of thunder in the house, and smoke began to pour from an upstairs window, then the whole front wall burst outwards, and a cloud spilled from the house, and in the cloud were two red pools.

Susan did not wait. She scrambled on to the horse, and it came to life under her, and as they sped away she heard the Morrigan cry out, then she was round the corner and on the path above the stream.

The Brollachan grew high above Errwood, strong in itself, and in the moon, and in the power of its keeper. It saw the rider in the valley, and the elves upon the hill, and it stooped to take toll of the long centuries of prison at their hands.

Susan felt the sky go black above her: she

glanced up, and all she saw was night. She lifted
the Mark of Fohla but its silver was dimmed, and
the words would not come. The hill disappeared;
she could see nothing; the air beat with the
rhythm of her blood, and the night swam into
her brain; the world drifted away. And then
Susan heard a voice, urgent, the voice of Angharad Goldenhand, crying, "The horn with the
wreath of gold about its rim! All else is lost!"

Susan tore at her waist with fingers that resisted
her will, and put the horn to her lips.

Its note was music, like wind in the caves of
ice, and out of the wind and far away came hoofs,
and voices calling, "We ride! We ride!" and the
darkness melted. At her stirrup was a man with
tall, proud antlers growing from his brow, and
he ran with his hand upon the horse's neck; and
all about her were booming cloaks, red, blue,
white, and black, and flying manes. She was
swept up and along with them like chaff.

And in the distance, as over a field, she saw
nine women with hawk on wrist, and hounds at
leash, coming to meet her, the gladness carried
Susan past all thoughts but one, the memory of
Celemon daughter of Cei, which the Mothan's
bitterness had driven from her.

She spurred her horse faster to the welcome
that sang through the night and lifted the riders
from their bondage in the dark mounds, but the
voice of Angharad spoke again.

"Leave her! She is but green in her power! It
is not yet!"

And the Hunter took his hand from Susan, and
slowly drew away, no matter how she rode. It
was as though she was waking from a dream of a
long yearning fulfilled to the cold morning of a
world too empty to bear. More than life, she
wanted to share the triumph that was all around
her.

The Einheriar paled, their forms thinning to
air and light, and they rose from her into the sky.

"Celemon!"

But Susan was left as dross upon the hill, and
a voice came to her from the gathering outlines
of the stars, "It is not yet! It will be! But not
yet!" And the fire died in Susan, and she was
alone on the moor, the night wind in her face,
joy and anguish in her heart.

Colin was nearly at the hill when he saw the
Brollachan grow over the trees at the same
moment that Susan appeared from the valley, and
he watched, helpless.

The Brollachan dwarfed the hill, overtaking
Susan so quickly that she looked as if she was
galloping backwards. The cloud lifted, and
formed a lash like the root of a whirlwind, which
swung low over Susan's head, and then struck.
The whole mass of the Brollachan flowed into that
one point, and Colin's ears were stunned by a
blast that knocked him to the ground, and a section of the hill where Susan had been slipped into
the water, and the Brollachan hovered over it.

But as his head cleared, Colin heard another

sound, so beautiful that he never found rest again; the sound of a horn, like the moon on snow, and another answered it from the limits of the sky; and through the Brollachan ran silver lightnings, and he heard hoofs, and voices calling. "We ride! We ride!" and the whole cloud was silver, so that he could not look.

The hoof-beats drew near, and the earth throbbed. Colin opened his eyes. Now the cloud raced over the ground, breaking into separate glories that whispered and sharpened to skeins of starlight, and were horsemen, and at their head was majesty, crowned with antlers, like the sun.

But as they crossed the valley, one of the riders dropped behind, and Colin saw that it was Susan. She lost ground, though her speed was no less, and the light that formed her died, and in its place was a smaller, solid figure that halted, forlorn, in the white wake of the riding.

The horsemen climbed from the hillside to the air, growing vast in the sky, and to meet them came nine women, their hair like wind. And away they rode together across the night, over the waves, and beyond the isles, and the Old Magic was free for ever, and the moon was new.

Note

These remaining pages have little to do with the story, and apart from a wish to acknowledge many debts, nothing would please me more than that they should stay unread. But so many people have shown an interest in the background of the book that some kind of appendix may be justified.

Firstly, every thing and place mentioned, with the exception of Fundindelve, does exist, although I have juggled with one or two local names.

The ingredients of the story are true, or as true as I can make them. The spells are genuine (though incomplete: just in case), and the names are real, even where the characters are invented. A made-up name feels wrong, but in Celtic literature there are frequent catalogues of people who may have been the subject of lost stories, and here it is possible to find names that are authentic, yet free from other associations.

Most of the elements and entities in the book are to be seen, in one shape or another, in traditional folk-lore. All I have done is to adapt them to my own view.

For example: *The Einheriar* were the bodyguard of the gods in Scandanavian mythology; *The Herlathing* was the English form of the Wild

Hunt, and *Garanhir*, "the Stalking Person", one of the many names of its leader. (Herne, King Herla, Wild Edric, Gabriel, and even Sir Francis Drake, are others.) But the nature of the Wild Hunt seemed to be close to the Ulster Cycle of myth, so I have made the Herlathing Irish in manner and bloodiness.

That is how most of the book has been written. The more I learn, the more I am convinced that there are no original stories. On several occasions I have "invented" an incident, and then come across it in an obscure fragment of Hebridean lore, orally collected, and privately printed, a hundred years ago.

Originality now means the personal colouring of existing themes, and some of the richest ever expressed are in the folk-lore of Britain. But this very richness makes the finding of a way to any understanding of the imagery and incident impossible without the help of scholarship, and in this respect the following sources have been invaluable to my own grasshopper research:

The Destruction of Da Derga's Hostel: trans. Whitley Stokes. Paris. 1902 .

Popular Tales of the West Highlands: J. F. Campbell. Alexander Gardner. 1890.

Carmina Gadelica: A. Carmichael. Oliver and Boyd. 1929.

Silva Gadelica: S. H. O'Grady. Williams and Norgate. 1892.

The Black Book of Caermarthen, The Red Book of

Hergest, *The Book of Aneurin*, and *The Book of Taliessin*: trans. W. F. Skene. Edmonston and Douglas. 1868.

The Mabinogion: trans. Gwyn Jones and Thomas Jones. Everyman's Library, No. 97. 1949.

The God of the Witches: M. Murray. Faber and Faber, 1952.

The White Goddess: Robert Graves. Faber and Faber. 3rd ed. 1952.

The Old Straight Track: A. Watkins. Methuen. 1925.

This last book, which argues that pre-historic man used a system of long-distance, straight tracks, marked by stones, cairns, and beacons, is full of the most romantic elements of archaeology and folk-lore.

The spells, and many others, are in magical manuscripts at:

British Museum: Sloane 213, 3826, 3853, 2731, 3648, 3884, 3850.

Bodleian: Bod. MS. Rawl. D.253; MS. Bod. e. Mus. 243; MS. Bod. Rawl. D252; Bod. MS. Ashmole 1406.

The old names have been used for the places inhabited in the story by the dwarfs and elves. *Talebolion* is Anglesey; *Sinadon*, Snowdonia; *Dinsel*, Cornwall; *Prydein*, Northern Scotland. *Minith Bannawg* I have taken to be the Grampians, although there is a possibility that it was a district that is now a suburb of Glasgow.

Fohla is the name of the wife of macCecht, one of the mythical kings of Ireland. She is an aspect of the Triple Moon Goddess.

Finally, long strings of names are poor gratitude to helpers, and meaningless to readers, so there will be none here, but I do want to thank the *Stockport Advertiser* for permission to quote the article on page 11, and Joshua Rowbotham Birtles, of Over Alderley, for being unruffled, in spite of the way I have put him into the book as Gowther Mossock, straight and undiluted.

Lions

THE OWL SERVICE

Alan Garner

In a secluded Welsh valley ringed by wild mountains, the characters and quarrels of three young people unfold as the tragic legend recurs - of two men who once loved the same girl and killed each other, leaving successive generations to play out the terror of that ancient triangle.

A relentless inevitability of events and the brooding power of the supernatural make this an unforgettable book.

'Remarkable ... a rare, imaginative feat, and the taste it leaves is haunting.'
Observer

'In his earlier novels, The Weirdstone of Brisingamen, The Moon of Gomrath and Elidor, Garner used the successful formula of the spilling over of the twilight world of ancient legend into the present day. Here he uses the formula again, with an added depth, and even more compulsive, terror-haunted beauty.'
Financial Times

Lions

RED SHIFT

Alan Garner

Red Shift is a daring exploration of a contemporary love story cut into by two violent fragments from the past. The result is one of the most profoundly imaginative, strange, controversial, and rewardingly demanding novels to have been published in recent years.

'A magnificently multi-layered novel ... and a superbly exciting piece of literature.'
The Times

"*Before I write anything, I always know the last paragraph of the book. I see it quite clearly and after that it is a bit like trying to synchronise lips on a Steenbeck editing machine. I suspend all critical judgement and write maybe 200 words at a time until it comes in a frenzy and I'm writing all the time. When it's finished, I become my own savage editor, going through every word of long-hand before I type anything.*

A friend once said that some writers write to live and others live to write. I'm in the second category."

Alan Garner lives with his wife and two children near Alderley Edge in Cheshire.